WHEN I FIRST SAW YOU

"Hello?"

"Hi Chante. This is Antonio Marks."

She took in a gasp of air at the sound of his low, husky voice. "Hello, Antonio." She managed to say. Closing her eyes, she allowed herself a few seconds to indulge in a fantasy of a man that looked every bit as sexy as the voice sounded on the other end of the phone.

Yeah, right.

"It feels really weird to finally hear your voice after communicating over the Internet for so long."

She gave a short nervous laugh. Antonio didn't know the half of it. Until he had called, all she had known was his nickname. "Yes, it does feel quite strange," she replied as she took a seat on the couch.

"Well, I want you to feel completely comfortable around me. How about we meet in the café downstairs in a half hour?"

She tightened her hold on the phone and took a slow breath. "Sounds good." *Might as well get this over with.* She could then spend the rest of the evening watching a pay-per-view movie. "How will I know it's you?"

Antonio gave a deep seductive laugh. "You'll know, just as I'll know. See you in a few minutes."

When I First Saw You

Angie Daniels

Dafina
Books

Kensington Publishing Corp.
http://www.kensingtonbooks.com

DAFINA BOOKS are published by

Kensington Publishing Corp.
850 Third Avenue
New York, NY 10022

All Kensington Titles, Imprints, and Distributed Lines are available at special quantity discounts for bulk purchases for sales promotions, premiums, fund-raising, and educational or institutional use. Special book excerpts or customized printings can also be created to fit specific needs. For details, write or phone the office of the Kensington special sales manager: Kensington Publishing Corp., 850 Third Avenue, New York, NY 10022, attn: Special Sales Department, Phone: 1-800-221-2647.

Dafina and the Dafina logo Reg. U.S. Pat. & TM Off.

First Dafina mass market Printing: September 2006
10 9 8 7 6 5 4 3 2

Printed in the United States of America

*This book is dedicated to the best fans in the world:
the romance readers!*

Acknowledgments

To contest winner Maria Harris of Tomball, Texas for coming up with a fabulous working title for this story. I truly appreciated your continued support.

To my fantastic family and friends who never tire of supporting me.

To authors Jacqueline Thomas and Toni Staton Harris for giving me some valuable advice. You ladies are awesome!

Chapter One

Will you marry me?

Pops stared at the message on his computer then raised an arthritic hand to the keyboard. After typing a three-letter response, he paused as feelings of doubt washed over him. Shaking his head, he brushed the emotion aside then pointed the mouse and clicked SEND.

"Does he really want to marry my mommy?" Devon asked.

The seventy-eight-year-old man relaxed his thin frame against the black leather chair. A smile touched his lips as he gazed down at his great-grandson's puzzled expression. "Of course he does. Who wouldn't want to marry your mother?" he replied convincingly.

Devon's face relaxed into a wide, snaggle-toothed grin. "My mom is *sooo* pretty. She looks like a movie star."

Pops nodded as his granddaughter's beautiful café au lait face came to mind. "Yes she does."

"I would marry her," Devon announced proudly.

Pops chuckled as he ruffled the little boy's curls. "So would I, son. So would I." Turning his head, he glanced over at the clock at his bedside table to discover it was already eight o'clock. "Come on young man. Time for bed."

With a single click of the mouse, he logged off the

computer then slowly rose and followed the six-year-old down the oatmeal-colored carpeted hallway to the last room on the left. Within minutes, Devon had brushed his teeth and had climbed beneath the covers. Pops took a seat at the end of his bed and together they recited the Lord's Prayer. He had been working with Devon for over a year and his great-grandson practically knew the entire prayer by heart. Pops was so proud of him. However, what he said at the end of the recitation wiped the smile from his face.

". . . and God bless Mr. Tony for wanting to be my new daddy."

Devon's prayers usually made his heart swell. Unfortunately, this was one time Pops walked away feeling uncomfortable.

He shuffled his stiff limbs to the living room where he took a seat on an overstuffed terra-cotta-colored couch. Typically, Pops would have turned on the evening news, but tonight he was too wrapped up in his own thoughts to listen. Instead, he closed his eyelids and prayed that his fascination with the Internet hadn't gotten him in way over his head.

After twenty-five years as a school bus driver, and the loss of his wife Delores to kidney failure, Benny Redmond, known to everyone as Pops, had no reason to remain in Florida and decided to return to his place of birth, Delaware. Three years ago, he had moved in with his granddaughter Chante Campbell, following her bitter divorce.

With Chante at work and Devon now in kindergarten, Pops found he had a lot of idle time on his hand. His granddaughter had suggested he take part in the recreational activities offered at the senior citizen's center. Since he'd had always had a fascination with machines, Pops decided to take a computer class. It wasn't long before he discovered the Internet and became hooked on exploring the World Wide Web. Somehow he had stumbled across the Lonely Hearts Web site. He searched through several ads in hope of finding a companion for himself. Even though he had his granddaughter and

Devon's company, Pops missed female companionship. He was leery of several of the ads he found—women looking for sugar daddies. Then six months ago, he spotted an ad from Mildred Johnson. After several weeks of corresponding, the two finally met at a neighborhood coffee shop. It was love at first sight. The two had been inseparable ever since.

Pops opened his eyes and stared out at the dark sky studded with thousands of brilliant stars. He had gotten the notion to start looking for someone for his granddaughter several months ago, when Devon mentioned he wanted to find his mama a new husband. After giving it some thought, he had gone to his bedroom where he logged on to the computer. With Devon looking on, Pops returned to the Lonely Hearts Web site, and after hours of searching and reading aloud ad after ad, he found a thirty-nine-year-old widower who sounded perfect for Chante.

In Chante's behalf, and with the help of Mildred's feminine touch, Pops replied to the ad, and within two days, he received a response from Antonio Marks. Before he knew it, the on-line relationship had escalated and the two had been e-mailing back and forth for over three months. When Antonio confessed he had fallen in love with Chante's words, Pops replied she had done the same. Then this morning, to his surprise, Antonio had asked Chante to be his wife. Pops spent the entire day weighing the pros and cons and even went as far as sharing the marriage proposal with Devon and Mildred before he had happily accepted.

Pops sighed as he sagged back against the couch. All he wanted was for Chante to be happy again. It had been three years since her divorce, and as far as he was concerned, it was time for her to move on. Not only for her but for Devon as well. He needed a father in his life. And as far as Pops and Devon were concerned, Dr. Antonio Marks was just the man for the job.

As he sat and listened to the soft hum of the dishwasher, his confidence slowly returned. Pops was convinced he had made the right choice. Now all he had to do was find a way to tell Chante she was engaged.

Chapter Two

Chante Campbell rose earlier than usual for a Sunday morning. She wasn't sure if it was because of the sun beaming down on her face or the sound of soft laughter. Turning away from the bright natural light, she lifted one heavy eyelid to find her six-year-old son lying on the bed beside her. A smile curled her lips. "Good morning, sweetheart. What are you doing in my bed?"

Devon laughed and moved to sit up straight. "I wanted to see if you were awake."

She looked at her pride and joy through half-opened lids. Large topaz eyes, a wide dimpled smile, and mocha skin, he was the spitting image of his father. "Of course I'm going to be awake if you come into my room and disturb my sleep," she grumbled, although she couldn't help from grinning. "Could you at least close my blinds back?"

Her son shook his head. "I can't. Pops and I got a surprise." Devon scooted off the bed, dashed to the bedroom door, then yelled, "Pops, you can come in now!"

Chante yawned and stretched luxuriously. Suddenly feeling wide awake, she propped another pillow behind her head. "What are you two up to?" she asked with rising curiosity.

"You'll see," Devon said, half dancing with excitement as he waited for his great-grandfather to appear.

Chante giggled softly. Her son had never been any good at keeping secrets. Whatever the two had cooked up was killing him.

Soon Pops' slow footsteps could be heard coming down the hall. Seconds later, he stepped into the room.

"Surprise! Happy Mother's Day!" Devon shouted as he bounced up and down.

Chante looked at her grandfather who had carried in a breakfast tray loaded down with a meal fit for a queen. Although smiling, she raised a quizzical brow. "Mother's Day isn't until next weekend."

Pops gave her a knowing grin as he lowered the meal before her. "I know, but since you won't be here, we decided to celebrate early. Besides, as far as I'm concerned, every day is Mother's Day in this house." Leaning forward, he planted a warm kiss on her cheek.

"Thanks Pops. Everything looks wonderful." Chante scooted back against the headboard and pulled the tray onto her lap.

"I made the toast," Devon announced as he moved to stand beside Pops, beaming with pride.

"I can tell," Chante murmured as she glanced down at the cold burnt bread. When she looked up again, she gave her son a silly grin. "Sweetheart, you've outdone yourself." Her stomach growled at the smell of country sausage, scrambled eggs with cheese, grits, and hash browns. There was also fresh ground coffee and a glass of orange juice. Nothing came close to her grandfather's down-home cooking. She shifted her gaze and asked him with a smile, "How do you expect me to eat all this food?"

"I'll help you," Devon offered eagerly. He scrambled back onto the bed and took a seat beside her tray.

Pops grabbed his wrist just as he reached for her fork. "Not so fast, young man. That food is for your mother. Yours is on the table." When Devon dropped his head with disappointment, Pops quickly added, "You better hurry down before your pancakes get cold."

Happiness lit up the little boy's face. "Oh, boy! Pancakes!" He dashed out of the room.

"And make sure you wash your hands first," Pops called after him.

Chante giggled as she reached for a sausage. "That boy is a handful."

"Yes, he is," Pops agreed as he took a seat at the end of her bed and watched her eat.

She glanced at her grandfather, eyes narrowed with suspicion. "What did you mean I won't be here next weekend? Where am I going?" she asked between chews.

Pops smiled, his coal-black eyes sparkling with amusement. He had known it was just a matter of time before his words had registered. Reaching into his shirt pocket, he removed a small pink envelope and gave it to her. "I'm sending you on an all-expense paid weekend to downtown Philadelphia. I figure you could use a couple of days to unwind."

Chante shook her head after she glanced quickly over the certificate that granted her a weekend of luxury. "Oh, Pops! This is so sweet of you, but you didn't have to do that. I can unwind right here at home."

He gave her a stern frown. "No, you can't. You'll spend the weekend doing housework. The only way to ensure that you spend the time relaxing is if you leave here Friday afternoon."

"Friday! This Friday?" she asked as her delicate jaw dropped. When he nodded, she shook her head. "I can't arrange coverage that quickly." She was part owner of a small, but successful, literary agency, The Dynamic Duo. While her partner Andrea Harris handled publicity, Chante represented over two dozen authors in a variety of genres.

Pops turned in his seat so that he was facing her. "Why not? You're the boss. I don't see—"

Chante interrupted with a loud groan. "Pops," she whined, "that's beside the point. I am in the middle of negotiations with a major publisher. I haven't even finished reviewing the contract."

His brow quirked at her lame excuse. Being an agent gave Chante the freedom to keep her own hours and the flexibility to work out of her own home. "You have a very competent assistant." Chante opened her mouth for further rebuttal, but he held up a hand. "I insist that you take some time for yourself. Mother's Day is supposed to be a day of relaxation." His voice was soft and firm at the same time.

Chante reached for her coffee mug and sighed inwardly. "I don't know." She had so much work to do. If she took three days off she would never catch up.

"If you don't go, all my money will go down the drain."

Seeing a look of disappointment in his gentle eyes, she finally caved in. "All right."

His frown vanished and a slow smile took its place. "Good," Pops agreed swiftly, and Chante knew the matter was settled.

His eyes twinkled. "You'll have a good time. I promise. I even have you scheduled for a massage and facial on Saturday."

Chante tried not to grin. He was playing dirty. She had always wanted a massage and Pops knew it.

"Now that that's settled, try to relax and enjoy your breakfast." Pops reached for the remote control and turned to her favorite Sunday morning television channel—*Lifetime*.

He left her room and headed toward the kitchen, grinning all the way. As soon as he cleaned the breakfast dishes, he would send Antonio an e-mail, accepting the invitation to meet in Philadelphia on Friday. His devious plot brought on another moment of doubt, but again he brushed it off. Why should he feel guilty if he had his granddaughter's best interest at heart?

he asked himself as he entered the room and found Devon's pancakes drowning in syrup. However, just to play it safe, Pops had decided to wait until it was too late to cancel, to break the news to Chante of her recent engagement. By then she would have no other choice but to meet Antonio. The rest would be totally up to the two of them.

Later that afternoon, Chante pulled into a new subdivision in Smyrna, Delaware that offered large two-story homes, and a taste of luxury. Glancing down briefly at the directions in her hands, she made a left onto Nita Drive. As promised, three houses down, she spotted her sister's black Honda Accord in the driveway. She pulled in behind her, then, after slipping off her sunglasses and leaving them on the dash, she climbed out and gazed up in awe at the brand-new structure.

The traditional Colonial sat back away from the street with half an acre of newly grown grass. Dark red shutters enhanced its brick front. The most unique feature was the elegant front terrace edged in black wrought iron on the second floor.

"Late as usual."

Chante followed the low musical voice to the front porch where her pregnant sister, Chenoa Sinclair, was standing. "Hey Noa," she began as she moved up the driveway. "Pops fixed me such a large breakfast I needed a couple hours to sleep it off." Chuckling, she shifted her gaze back to the house. "Look at this place! It's gorgeous."

"You haven't seen anything yet. Come on in so I can show you around." Chenoa signaled for her older sister to follow her into the house that she and her husband Zearl Sinclair had just closed on, on Friday.

As Chante stepped through the door, her eyes darted quickly around the entryway as she released a series of *oohs*. The rich, polished hardwood floor in the foyer had a southern flair with an oak staircase accented with white spokes.

"I love it," she complimented as she stepped into the living room, admiring the cathedral ceiling and red brick fireplace encased in elegant molding. A formal dining room was directly behind it. Both had numerous large windows allowing in plenty of sunlight. She followed her sister upstairs where there were four spacious bedrooms, including a master suite with a small sitting room and private bath.

After descending the stairs, they moved through a spacious kitchen. French doors lead to a large honey-finished deck, which looked out on to a private backyard dotted with dogwood and pine trees. One thing Chante had always hated about newly constructed homes was the lack of trees, however, this subdivision had preserved the woods surrounding the development.

Leaning against the wooden rail, Chante let out a slow breath, nodding. "This place is fabulous."

"Oh, I'm so glad you think so."

Chante swung around and smiled up at her sister's face. At five-feet-seven inches, she was an inch shorter than Chenoa. "You never told me how you found out about this development?"

Her brandy-colored eyes sparkled with pride. "It was luck. Our realtor called last month to tell us one of her clients had lost the financing for a home they had just built. As much as she hated to see them lose their dream home, she said it was everything that we were looking for, and we had better hurry and come see it before it was put on the real estate listing. Five minutes after we arrived, Zearl and I had her draw up a contract."

Chante shook her head. "I don't blame you. I'm so proud of my little sister." She curved an arm around her thick waist and gave her a big squeeze. When they parted, Chenoa giggled as she rubbed her round belly.

"And just in time, too. As soon as we get settled in we're going to start on the nursery."

She smiled. The couple was having their first child in August. "When are you moving your stuff in?" Chante asked.

"Next week if we get everything packed in time." Chenoa signaled for her sister to follow her into the kitchen.

Chante stepped through the sliding glass door and glanced around the kitchen again. This time she carefully noted the stainless steel appliances, the ceramic backdrop, and the large spacious island at the center of the room that had a pot rack hanging overhead. "This room is a culinary dream."

Chenoa scowled. "Yeah, too bad I'm not much of a cook. However, with the baby coming, I think it's time I learned how to bake cookies and the other things that PTA mothers do."

With her lips quirked in amusement, Chante looked across at her little sister and suppressed a chuckle. With her short tapered hairstyle and blue maternity top with matching knit pants, she looked like a wife anticipating motherhood. As fickle as her sister was growing up, Chante never thought she would see this day.

Chenoa removed two bottles of water from a practically bare stainless steel refrigerator and handed her one. Since there weren't any chairs, Chante leaned over the island in the center of the room.

Chante twisted off the cap. "As soon as you get settled in I'm giving you a housewarming party."

"Sounds exciting," Chenoa retorted dryly.

"Just think of all of the great gifts you're going to get," she said with enthusiasm.

Chenoa narrowed her eyes with a serious glare. "I'm not worried about that. What I'm worried about is Mama trying to take over. You know she is dying to get over here with her decorating ideas. She called this morning and suggested I decorate the downstairs in burgundy and gold. I told her I didn't want something that bold. So she called back thirty minutes later and suggested that we make a trip to the furniture store and look for dark green."

Chante nodded knowingly. Betty Campbell did have a way of trying to take over. Some of her ideas were fabulous, while others took a while to grow on you.

Their mother was a retired English teacher, and ever since she stopped teaching middle school, she had started taking home decorating classes, and had since remodeled their childhood home twice. Her mother could be found every weekend at surrounding flea markets, searching for hidden treasures.

Chante shifted an arched eyebrow, her gaze locked with Chenoa's. "Just tell her you and Zearl are looking forward to decorating your new home together. She'll understand."

Her sister sipped her water while looking unconvinced.

"If you register at Boscov's or tell people to buy you things from Pier One Imports, you won't have to worry about getting a bunch of stuff you don't want. By doing so, Mama will have some idea of how you want to decorate your house."

"I guess." She took another drink then said, "We want to do something soft and warm. Although . . ." she began as she rested her hip against the counter, "I'm still trying to get Zearl to part with that big ugly chair. That chair is older than I am." Chenoa shuddered at the thought of moving the thing into her new house. "I think I found a perfect spot for it out on the curb."

Chante chuckled. "Yeah, right. Zearl loves that chair. He'll never go for that."

As if he knew he was the topic of discussion, her brother-in-law strolled into the room. "Did I hear my name?"

Chante glanced over and gave him a loving smile. "Hey Zearl."

"Hi, Chante." He moved forward and kissed his sister-in-law on the cheek. "Let me guess, my wife is talking about getting rid of my chair again."

"Uh-huh," Chante admitted, sensing his teasing mood.

Chenoa chuckled softly. "Baby, you know I love you."

"You better," he said seconds before capturing her mouth in a passionate kiss.

Chante watched the love between the two, and felt cold and empty. Then she quickly brushed the feelings away and drank her bottled water. As much as she wanted someone special in her life, she didn't feel she was ready yet to risk her heart again. However, she was glad her sister had taken a chance on love. Bald head, goatee, with dark chocolate skin, Detective Zearl Sinclair was a handsome man and a wonderful husband.

"Baby, I want pizza tonight," she heard her sister say, breaking into her thoughts.

"Again?" When she nodded, Zearl chuckled then glanced over at Chante. "For two weeks, all my wife has wanted is ham and pineapple pizza with anchovies."

She frowned. "Yuck."

"When it isn't pizza, it's pickles. I guess it's true what they say about pregnant women having cravings."

Chenoa playfully slugged him in the arm. "You've got a lot of nerve. What about you? Whenever you're sick, you crave peppermint ice cream."

Chante laughed. "I heard an old wive's tale once that sometimes men have cravings and also sleep a lot when their wives are pregnant. You having any cravings yet?"

Zearl and Chenoa glanced at each other and smiled in unison before he responded. "I'm having cravings all right." He told her as he wagged his eyebrows suggestively. "You think maybe you can entertain yourself while I take my beautiful wife upstairs to satisfy an afternoon craving?"

Chenoa gave him a playful look. "You need to quit." She turned and grinned at Chante. "He's just nasty."

Envy mixed with embarrassment flared her face. She felt like she was intruding on a private moment. "Y'all ain't right," she said while Zearl drowned his wife with kisses. "You're wrong for acting all lovey-dovey around me when you know I don't have a man," she scolded, although she couldn't help smiling.

Raising his head slightly, Zearl looked at her with surprise. "Not a problem. Chante, I have this friend I'd be—"

She held up her hand and shook her head, tactfully turning down Zearl's offer at finding her a man. "No, thank you. The last thing I need is another man." She pursed her lips as silence flooded the kitchen.

Zearl kissed his wife once more then released her and retrieved a beer from the refrigerator. He moved over to Chante and leaning closer, whispered, "You're too good for any of my friends." He gave her a loud kiss on the jaw that caused her to laugh, then headed back outside where he was watering the new lawn.

Chenoa waited until he closed the sliding glass door before she spoke. "You know he was just trying to be nice."

Chante sighed. "Yeah, I know."

Leaning closer, her eyes darkened with emotion. "You really should start dating again."

She groaned. "Not that again."

Chenoa held her hand up in surrender. "Sis, hear me out. Now take me for instance. If I hadn't opened myself up again, I wouldn't now be married to Zearl. You were the one who encouraged me to give him a chance."

"That's because he's a good guy," she replied calmly.

"And there are other good guys out there if you'd just give it a chance. I know the right one is out there for you."

Chante sighed again. "Maybe I've already had my shot at love."

Chenoa's mouth flattened. "Please, he was not your soul mate and you know it."

Chante wished she believed it but she didn't. Instead, she had grown accustomed to her current celibate lifestyle. She doubted a soul mate existed for her. "I don't want anything serious and you know it."

"So don't look for serious. Have some fun. How about just living for the moment?"

"Because I'm not the live-for-the-moment type." She fisted a hand at her side and sent her a warning frown. "I'm fine, really." When Chenoa's eyes narrowed, she continued. "I don't need a man to make me happy. I just can't go through that type of pain again."

When she noticed her sister's eyes darken with emotion, she wished she could take her words back.

As a detective, it was Chenoa's job to serve and protect. She blamed herself for not suspecting that something was wrong with Chante's marriage.

Feeling responsible for putting the painful look on her sister's face, Chante moved around the island and embraced her. "Don't worry. If love comes calling, I promise to at least answer the phone."

Chenoa leaned back and gazed at her. "I can have Zearl make sure your phone rings."

Her big sister gave her a threatening look. "You do and I swear I'll tell your baby you used to eat dirt."

"You wouldn't," she countered with a wide grin.

"Yes, I would," Chante insisted while trying to keep a straight face.

Chenoa laughed and her sister joined in. "I was getting ready to make myself and Zearl a sandwich, you want one?" she asked and moved across the shiny new linoleum floor.

Chante sobered and was grateful she had changed the subject. "Sure."

Chenoa finished her water and tossed the empty bottle in the trash. She then reached inside the new stainless steel refrigerator and removed mustard, sliced roast beef and Swiss cheese that she had bought from the deli, and carried them over to the island.

Chante moved and leaned across the blue ceramic countertop. "Guess what Pops got me for Mother's Day?"

Chenoa's head flew up with a look of sheer panic. "Mother's Day?"

Chante's eyes brimmed with laughter. "No, Pops just gave me mine a week early. He's sending me away next weekend."

"Oh, God, you scared me," she said with a sigh of relief. "For a minute I thought I forgot to get Mama a gift." She reached for a loaf of bread off the counter and carried it over. "Where to?" she asked, eyes burning with curiosity.

"Philly for a weekend of rest and relaxation."

Chenoa waved a knife in the air. "Good. You need it. I've been telling you you work too hard."

She gave her a frown. "Look who's talking."

Chenoa met her sister's amused gaze. "My situation is different. I'm one of two female detectives on the force. I've got to always be a step ahead of the game." She rolled her eyes and reached for the jar of mustard. "Although, now that I'm on desk duty for the duration of my pregnancy, I don't see much of that happening."

Chante smiled. "Cheer up. It could be a lot worse."

Sergeant Lawson, her boss, was also a dear friend of the family who watched out for Chenoa. His concern for her welfare was how she and her husband ended up together in the first place. Lawson had assigned Zearl to keep an eye on Chenoa. The stubborn pair butted heads from the start.

The Campbell's had known Zearl Sinclair since grade school. He had come to live with their family after his mother abandoned him, making him a legal ward of the state. Chenoa and the rebellious teenager bumped heads for years until he graduated and left to pursue a career with the FBI. Last year, following a painful divorce, Zearl returned to Delaware and joined the Wilmington Police Department. And to everyone's amusement, Chenoa was assigned as his partner. She fought him every step of the way as they tracked a serial killer. However, in the end, love prevailed. The couple recently celebrated their one year anniversary. They married last May, and were now expecting their first child.

Chante stared at Chenoa's delicate profile as she prepared the sandwiches. During the last year, she had watched her sister transform into a beautifully happy woman, and she had Zearl to thank for that. He was her soul mate. Everyone could see it in the way the two behaved with each other. It didn't matter who was around. Zearl was always showing Chenoa affection, and when he wasn't close by, he was admiring her from across the room. She loved watching the two of them together. Sometimes she felt envious and wished for the same, then she would quickly return to the real world and remind herself that love just wasn't meant for everyone. Even if there was a man out there, she was too afraid to take the risk and find out.

"Let me get this straight . . . you proposed to a woman you have never met?"

Antonio Marks looked up from his dinner plate and, ignoring his brother Dominic's question, glanced over at his younger sister Germaine, who was avoiding eye contact. He should have known when his brother had called and asked him to meet them for dinner at their favorite steakhouse that something was up, especially since they hadn't gotten together in weeks. It was obvious by the expression on Germaine's face that she had repeated the conversation he had shared with her in confidence to their twice-burned older brother.

"Yo, Tony. Is it true or what?" His brother's heavy baritone voice pierced the silence surrounding the table.

Antonio tore his eyes from Germaine's guilty expression and met the quizzical golden-eye gaze across from him. He then simply shrugged and said, "Yeah, something like that."

"Have you lost your mind?" Dominic barked as he raked a frustrated hand through his thick raven curls. "Do you know how many psychos surf the Web? There's no telling who this woman may turn out to be."

Antonio stabbed his house salad with his fork and filled his mouth before speaking. "I'm quite aware of the risks of meeting someone on-line, but Chante is not like that."

Dominic gave a cynical laugh. "You don't know that for sure."

Antonio filled his mouth again and slowly chewed his steak. He usually loved the mouth-watering steaks at Diane's Steakhouse, but suddenly the meat had lost its appeal. "I feel it in my gut. She and I have been corresponding for months, and I find her to be a caring and compassionate woman, who's raising a little boy."

His older brother leaned across the table. "Yeah, but marriage? You don't even know what this woman looks like."

His eyes stole over to his sister again who was nibbling on her french fries, then back to his brother again. "Chante asked that we not exchange phone numbers or photographs until we had a chance to really get to know each other. After a while knowing what she looked like and hearing her voice no longer mattered."

"How convenient for her," Dominic murmured under his breath.

Antonio jabbed his fork into his steak. "Germaine, since you made it your business to blab my business to Dom, maybe you can shed a little light on what you're thinking."

Germaine stared down at her plate as she spoke. "I told you before how I felt about meeting someone over the Internet." Her eyes raised and he met the worried look on his sister's face. Unlike Dominic, she had every reason to be concerned. A little over two years ago, she had tried her own hand at Internet dating and met with one disaster after another. After the last one tried stalking her until Dominic stepped in and threatened to break a few bones in his body if he ever tried it again, she decided to leave the Internet alone. He'd have to agree,

Internet dating was probably something she would not be trying again. However, for him it had been a less painful experience.

"I understand and appreciate both of your concerns," he said, looking at one and then the other, "but I'm a big boy and I am allowed to make a few mistakes from time to time."

Germaine's eyes grew wide behind her glasses. "So you are admitting that this is a mistake?"

He shook his head and gave an offhanded chuckle. "No, but if it turns out to be, although I don't feel that it will, then I'm prepared to live with that. The both of you need to quit worrying about me so much."

"We worry because we love you," she added softly.

"And I appreciate that but I'm gonna be just fine."

A tense silence enveloped the table. Germaine finally glanced over at Dominic and shrugged before reaching for her glass.

Antonio sighed and bit into a slice of garlic bread. As much as he loved his siblings, there were days when he wished they would leave him alone. After their parents died in a house fire five years ago, the three pulled together and began making time for one another. When his wife Julia died three years ago the siblings became even closer, realizing all they had were each other. He was grateful for Germaine and Dominic. He didn't know what he would have done without their love and support. However, over the last year, the two had become so overprotective at times, like now, that he wanted to simply pull his hair out.

"Is your reason for trying to find a wife that you're lonely or are you just that desperate?" Dominic said, while pointing his fork and chewing on a coconut shrimp.

Antonio leaned back in his chair and frowned. Loneliness had not been a factor in his decision to find a companion. He would never marry a woman he didn't love, and more importantly, he definitely couldn't love a woman who didn't meet his standards. His reason for wanting to be with Chante was because even without meeting her, his heart told him she was the one. "Of course not. I assure you my reason for wanting a wife is not sexual or out of desperation. However, unlike the two of you, I like having someone permanently in my life."

Germaine leaned back in her chair wearing a mask of skepticism. "I like having someone in my life, too. But I don't want just anybody."

"Yeah, but as picky as you are you're going to be old and gray and still be looking."

She shrugged and pushed thin, fashionable frames over her short, upturned nose. "Then that's a chance I'll have to take."

Antonio tossed his brother a furtive glance. "And what about you Dom? After Camille you seemed to have given up on relationships."

He gave a bitter laugh. "After the stunt she pulled, can you blame me?"

Antonio stroked his mustache. "No, I guess I can't."

Two years ago his brother was the walking billboard for being in love. He had met and fallen in love with his chiropractor. They'd dated less than four months when he had proposed. On the night before his wedding, he caught his fiancé in bed with his best man. The incident had left a bitter taste in his mouth when it came to women. Nevertheless, last year he decided to give love one more try only to be dumped six months into the relationship without any type of explanation.

"Life does go on. The last thing Julia would have wanted me to do was stop living. I loved my wife and she will always hold a special place in my heart, but I know it is time for me to move on."

"And I agree it is time for you to move on, but why do you have to use such unconventional methods. Whatever happened to good old fashioned dating?" Germaine pointed out.

"I still believe in good old fashioned dating, but times have changed. Unlike you I don't hang out at nightclubs."

"Hey, there are some fine brothas in those joints," she countered defensively.

Dominic arched a sweeping eyebrow at his sister. "Women that hang out in clubs are not at all what decent men are looking for."

Antonio nodded his head. "I agree with you big brother. Nothing but a bunch of gold diggers hang out at night."

Dramatically, Germaine dropped her fork onto her plate with a loud clatter, then glanced at one and then the other with a pretty pout. "And what does that make me?" she asked.

Dominic gave her a teasing smile, then answered, "Well, if the shoe fits . . ."

She rolled her eyes while her brothers roared with laughter.

She inhaled and counted to ten before answering. "There are a few exceptions, namely, me. I go out on the weekends to relax and to listen to some good music. If I meet someone, good, if not, it's no big deal. Believe me there are just as many scrubs in the clubs as there are gold diggers. Last week I met some busted rotten-tooth brotha that had the nerve to step to me like I was really gonna give him some play. I don't understand what in the world could have made him think he had a chance at hookin' up with me."

While chewing, Dominic erupted with laughter. "And that's the point I was trying to make to my little brother here. Who's to say Chante is gonna be anything worth looking at?"

Antonio shook his head because he knew there was no way the conversation was going to end that easily. "I have confidence." He didn't know how, but he could feel her gentle beauty in her responses to his e-mails.

Dominic's expressive eyes were shining. "I sure hope you know what you're doing because if she's ugly you know I'm going to be the first one to tell you I told you so."

"She won't be."

"How about we put a wager on this?" Dominic challenged.

"You're on," Antonio countered without hesitation.

His brother patted his mouth with his napkin then grinned. "If the weekend's a flop I get to hook you up on a double date with one of Tara's friends."

He scowled openly. Tara was Dominic's flavor of the month. She had more gold teeth and weave in her hair than he cared to associate with. If she was any indication of what her friend was going to be like, then he was definitely in trouble. However, remembering the last e-mail Chante sent that said seeing him in Philly would be worth the wait, he felt confident that he wouldn't have to end up double dating.

He reached across the table and decided to shake on it. "You're on. And if you lose, you have to post a profile on an on-line single's site and make a serious attempt at meeting at least two women."

Antonio stared at Dominic, recognizing the faraway look in his eyes, and wondered if he was remembering the pain he had gone through with Camille. For a moment he thought his big brother was going to say no, but he should have known better. Dominic had never been one to back down from a challenge.

"It's a deal."

Chapter Three

By Thursday afternoon Chante was actually looking forward to a weekend of rest and relaxation. Even though she planned to spend a portion of her weekend reading a manuscript by an unpublished author with great potential, she promised she would also take some time for herself.

Andrea Harris was pleased to hear that her partner finally planned to take some time off. "I'll cover the office over the weekend under one condition . . ."

As Chante met the sparkle in Andrea's espresso-colored gaze the corners of her mouth turned downward in a frown. "And what's that?"

Leaning over Chante's desk, the voluptuous woman rested a hand on her ample hip and said, "You hand over your cell phone."

As Chante stared up at her close friend of ten years, her brow rose in amazement. "You're kidding, right?"

Andrea shook her head. "Nope, I'm dead serious. As long as you're carrying that phone, technically, you'll still be working."

Chante leaned forward, resting her elbows on the desk, and glared at her partner. "You're beginning to sound like my grandfather."

The cinnamon-haired beauty looked down at her with

determination. "I know. He and I had a long talk this morning. Now hand it over."

Chante glanced at her outstretched hand for a full ten seconds, contemplating her decision, before she finally released a ragged sigh. "You are so . . ." she began, then instead of finishing the sentence, threw her hands up in disgust. Reaching down into her purse, she retrieved the phone, and placed it in Andrea's outstretched hand.

Andrea gave her a triumphant smile. "Good. Now you're officially on vacation."

Chante rolled her eyes as she took in her friend's attire. As usual, she was dressed to impress. Andrea was wearing three inch pink-and-white Jimmy Choos and a fuchsia double-breasted suit. The color was striking with her dark good looks.

"Promise me you'll have some fun."

Chante gave her a reassuring smile. "I promise. I even bought a new book just for the trip."

She raised a perfectly sculptured brow. "That's not what I'm talking about and you know it."

"If you're asking if I plan to hang at one of those single's bars, the answer is no."

Andrea smacked her palm against the shiny wooden surface of Chante's desk. "You don't have to hang at a bar to meet men. There could be one right in your hotel. Just be open-minded to the possibility."

Chante's eyes grew large. "To the possibility of what? Having a weekend fling?"

"Exactly."

Chante looked at her as if she had just grown a horn at the center of her forehead. "Girl, puhleeze! I don't have the time or the need."

"Who are you trying to fool? You've got the same needs as the rest of us. You just need to knock away some of those cobwebs," Andrea said as she lowered onto the chair across from her.

Chante couldn't help but laugh. "You are too much!" Her friend had always been a bit irreverent. It was one of the things she liked most about her.

Tugging on one wild curl that swirled and bobbed about her head, Andrea didn't look the least bit amused. "I'm serious. It's time for you to meet a nice man and have a relationship," she said gently.

Chante sent her a warning frown. She was beginning to sound like her sister.

Her job and Devon gave her more satisfaction and fulfillment than she could imagine receiving anywhere else. What could possibly be more important than her family and her career? Well, there was a man, Andrea would always argue, seeing that Chante didn't have one, and had little to no life outside of work. Chante had to constantly remind her partner that work and Devon were her life, and she enjoyed it very much. She had a full and satisfying life without playing games with a man.

"I'm not saying I don't ever want another relationship, but after what Dorian put me through who could blame me. I just know that I am content with my life the way it is. For the first time I'm taking care of me. It's not my parents. It's not my ex-husband. It's me. And that's a wonderful feeling, I don't know if I am ready to give that up."

"Who said you had to give it up? I just want you to be happy."

Nodding, she leaned back in her chair. "I know girl. It might be hard for you to believe, but I am happy."

Andrea didn't look convinced. "If you say so."

Chante dropped her gaze to her desk. "Don't worry. I plan to have a wonderful relaxing weekend. I am looking forward to a full body massage and reading a book."

"Uh-huh."

Chante looked up and decided it was as good a time as any

to change the subject. "You all up in my business, what about you and Alan?"

Andrea groaned. "Yuck! Why'd you have to bring him up?"

"Because . . . So what's up? You haven't mentioned him in a while." Chante swung around in her chair with a satisfied smile.

Her partner rolled her eyes. "Girl, puhleeze. Let's just say his fiancée wasn't too happy."

"What! Oh, my God! What happened?"

"Girl, on Friday night, homegirl was waiting at my house when I got home." Chante gaped. Andrea crinkled her brow then continued. "She told me who she was then started bawling like a baby. I invited girlfriend in and we drank apple martinis while we compared notes."

Too stunned for words, all Chante could do was shake her head.

Laughter illuminated Andrea's toffee face as she continued. "Yeah. It was a trip. At Donna's insistence, I called and invited Alan over. He almost shit in his pants when he found his fiancée sitting on the couch. She went upside his head, and I sat back and enjoyed the show."

Chante suddenly burst out laughing, envisioning the whole pathetic scene. "I guess he won't be getting married any time soon."

"That's what I thought, too, but yesterday I got a fancy cream envelope in the mail. I looked inside, and there was a thank you note and an invitation to their wedding. Apparently, I brought the couple closer together," she said, as if the entire thing was ridiculous, then gave a dismissive wave. "Anyway, I'm taking a break on men until June. By then I'll be too horny to hold out."

Chante was still laughing when Andrea rose from the chair. "You are too much."

"Yeah, I know. Anyway, pack your things and get out of here.

I'll see you on Monday." With a finger wave, she turned and left Chante's office before she had a chance to change her mind.

Long after she left, Chante sat and stared at the dark screen of her desktop computer monitor, thinking about what she had said. It was time for her to get on with her life. It had been over six years since she and Dorian had split, and three years since their divorce. She knew it was time for her to move on. But she was scared.

Chante chewed on her bottom lip, trying to ignore the tightening of her stomach. It still hurt so much to think about what might have been. It had been a while since she had thought about Dorian, and thinking about him always brought back too many painful memories. Somehow it was hard to re-member the good times they had once shared.

They had dated since their freshman year in high school. He was everything she had thought she wanted in a man and she had given him her heart and body, willingly. They had married right after she had graduated from Delaware State University with a bachelor's degree in business. For the next three years she thought she was the luckiest woman in the world. Then Dorian lost his father to alcoholism, and every-thing changed.

Dorian became abusive. He started hitting her for just about anything, whenever he felt like it. However, he knew how to hit her in areas that were not visible to others. He had her so afraid that she allowed him total control of her life. She was ashamed to admit that, and it took her two more years before she ended their marriage. It wasn't because she en-joyed being his punching bag. She stayed because she prayed and hoped that some day her love would be enough to make him change. She had given him her heart, her body, and de-votion, but it had not been enough for him. It took a trip to the hospital, where she discovered she was pregnant with Devon, for her to finally wake up and realize that she and her unborn child's lives were in danger.

Chante's eyes flicked to the photo of Devon on the end of her desk. She had ended her marriage for the sake of her precious little boy, because what Dorian felt for her was not love, and she did not want her son to endure anything remotely close to what she had experienced. Tears clouded her eyes. Chante brushed them away then decided to banish her ex-husband from her mind and think about the wonderful weekend ahead.

She was grateful when her assistant buzzed her phone, breaking into her thoughts.

"Chante, Lana Lindsey is on line two."

"Thank you, Kayla," she told her. Getting into her professional mode, she took a deep breath and picked up the phone. "Lana, how are you girl?"

"Anxious. I got your message."

"Well, I've got some great news," she began as she swiveled around in the chair. "I spoke to Katrina this morning. They're offering six-figures for *Mimosa Heights*." Chante pulled the phone away from her ear at the high-pitched scream and chuckled. This was the best part of her job. "Congratulations."

"Oh my God! I can't believe this is finally happening. Thank you, Chante. Thank you so much."

"No problem. It's a wonderful book and the offer is well deserved. They'll be sending over a contract in a couple of days and as soon as I've looked it over, I'll get it right out to you." She then went over a few other details and fifteen minutes later returned the phone to the cradle with a smile on her face. *Damn, I love my job!* It always made her feel good to hear that one of her authors had finally made it. It was why she had quit her job as a junior editor for a local newspaper, and had gone into the business in the first place.

Four years ago, Chante read a book written by a self-published author that touched her so much she was determined to get her story read by millions. She set out on a quest to find her a publishing house and after months of being persistent, she got the author an unheard of six-figure deal. Her first release made the Essence best seller's list. Shortly after that, Chante decided to become a literary agent and now represented a handful of national best-selling authors. Three years ago, she teamed up with a college friend, Andrea Harris. With her strong marketing background, she was eager to add a publicity side to the business. The Dynamic Duo was now one of the hottest agencies in the business.

Anxious to get a few more things done before officially starting her weekend vacation, Chante reached into her top drawer for a pen. It wasn't until she was about to close the drawer that she noticed the small gold package.

She frowned. It hadn't been there this morning, because earlier she had gone in the drawer looking for a large butterfly clip. So whoever had left it had done so while she was gone for lunch. It was a small square box tied with a pink ribbon. It was apparently a gift, but instead of being excited, a wave of apprehension flowed through her. She abruptly pushed her chair back then rose and strolled out into the reception area where Kayla was just finishing up a call.

"Kayla, did someone drop by my office while I was at lunch and leave me something?"

Kayla lowered the phone to the cradle then swung around on her seat, wearing a puzzled look. "No, not that I remember. Unless they came while I was in the supply room making copies."

Chante nodded and pivoted on her heels. "Thank you."

"Is something wrong?"

She halted abruptly, the heels of her pumps sinking into the thick, plush carpet. Chante glanced over her shoulder and registered the concern in her expression, and shook her head. The last thing she wanted to do was to worry her assistant. "No, nothing." She then smiled. "Why don't you go ahead and leave a little early today and beat rush-hour traffic."

"You sure?"

She nodded. "Yes, I'm sure. Andrea and I are both getting ready to leave ourselves."

"Thanks, Chante," Kayla said with an appreciative smile.

"You're welcome. Have a wonderful weekend."

"You too."

With that said she moved into her office and sank into her chair again. Leaning forward, she slowly removed the box, and sat it on top of her desk.

This was the second time she'd found a gift in her drawer wrapped in the same pink ribbon. As before, she looked for a note and once again there wasn't one. And that bothered her.

The first time she had received a gift, it had been two weeks ago. When she had returned from lunch, she found a small, round box in her drawer beneath a yellow legal pad. She had opened it to find a beautiful gold pin of a book no bigger than a postage stamp. It was the appropriate gift for a literary agent, and she had immediately removed it and pinned it to the lapel of her paisley suit. Even then she had looked for an accompanying note and was puzzled not to find one. However, she was certain that the gift had come from either Kayla or Andrea. But when asked, neither knew anything about it. The pin had been tucked away in her desk ever since.

As the days passed, Chante had expected a phone call, an e-mail or something identifying the giver, but so far no one had come forward. She had tried to convince herself that perhaps there was supposed to have been a card but it had gotten lost somehow. And she had almost believed it until today, when she received a second gift, and it too did not have a card.

As she eyed the box, feelings of uneasiness accompanied her pleasure. She told herself that she was being silly.

What if you have a secret admirer?

That would definitely be something since she hadn't had

one of those since junior high. She remembered finding a Snickers bar tied with a red ribbon on her desk in science class every day for two weeks before she had finally caught Oliver Holmes arriving to class early and leaving it at the middle of her desk. She had been flattered and had even allowed him to walk her to science class for a month before she ended their so-called boyfriend/girlfriend relationship.

Chante gave a weary sigh then reached inside the drawer and checked one more time to see if there was a card or note, but just as she suspected, she found none. So, inhaling a deep breath, she tucked her finger under the pink ribbon, and slowly slid it off the box. Then she carefully lifted the lid, and pushed aside the folded tissue paper.

"Ooh!" she said softly, when she saw what was inside. A gold name badge winked at her from its cushion of tissue in the box. It clearly said in an elegant script font CHANTE CAMPBELL on the first line and LITERARY AGENT in a smaller font on the next.

It was a lovely gift. Still, she thought, as she gingerly fingered the badge, it would be nice to know who had been leaving the gifts. If nothing else just to satisfy her curiosity. Chances were it was just someone having fun at her expense. She just wished she knew who so that she could shake the sensation that there was something eerie about receiving anonymous gifts.

Putting the badge back into the box, she returned the lid. She would proudly display it at her next literary conference. It definitely beat the one she'd had Kayla whip up on the computer. Whoever bought it knew that she would put the gift to good use. Nevertheless, hopefully long before then, someone would step forward and take credit for purchasing the thoughtful gift.

"What are you still doing here?" Andrea's exclamation from the doorway prompted her to look in her direction as she entered and said stiffly, "I thought I told you to go home."

Chante frowned, then mumbled, "I'm leaving now."

"Good, then we can walk down together." She stepped into the room and noticed the box. "Ooh! Who sent you a gift?" she asked, her eyes sparkling with glee.

Chante hesitated before telling her friend. "I don't know."

"You mean you got another anonymous gift?" When she nodded, Andrea dropped her purse on the couch near the door, and returned to the chair across from Chante's desk and took a seat. Chante slid the box toward her friend, and Andrea looked inside. "Oh, this is nice. Well, at least he's got good taste."

"Who said it's a he?"

"Let's hope it's a he," she was saying as she admired the gold pendant. "Because if these gifts are coming from a female you are into some stuff you haven't bothered to tell me about."

"Andrea," she scolded. Her partner always had a way of making everything into a joke, even when it was no laughing matter.

"All right, all right. I'll try to be serious." She removed the badge and ran her fingertips across the engraved lettering. "You didn't see who left it?"

Chante shook her head. "No, and neither did Kayla. I think whoever left it, waited until she was in the bathroom." She paused and gave a long thoughtful look. "This is really starting to bother me. I mean, why would someone leave gifts without letting me know who he is?"

Andrea held the badge a few seconds longer, then almost reluctantly returned it to the box. Her gaze locked with Chante's. "Who do you think it could be?"

Chante lifted one shoulder and shrugged. "I don't have the foggiest idea."

Andrea eyed her curiously for a long moment before saying, "What about Marvin?"

She stared across at her. "Marvin? The guy who runs the coffee stand downstairs?"

"Why not? He always goes out of his way to make sure he has the perfect looking banana just waiting for you every morning. Now I've been ordering from that man for over a year, yet he still can't remember that I like my coffee black. While you on the other hand, he remembers that you like a squirt of half and half and one package of artificial sweetener in your cup before adding the dark roasted coffee," she said by way of an explanation. "Personally, I think he would be a prime candidate."

Chante looked doubtful. Although sweet, Marvin appeared to be a little on the slow side. Besides, someone working a coffee stand couldn't afford such exquisite gifts. "Nah, he's not the type to be buying a perfect stranger such an expensive gift."

Andrea met Chante's gaze. "Then there is someone else in this building who likes you. We'll just have to find out who it is."

That still didn't help much, Chante thought. The six-story building had hundreds of employees that were in and out at all hours of the day. That kind of tracking would require a lot of time. "Why should I waste my time trying to figure out who it is? If he wants me to know, then he'll need to come forward."

Andrea sighed and closed the box. "You're better than I am because it would drive me crazy trying to figure out who it is."

You don't know the half of it. "It doesn't matter since I'm really not interested in the first place."

"Are you kidding? This is so romantic."

Chante's brow furrowed. "Romantic?" The word sounded strange for someone who only believed in short-term, no-strings-attached relationships. "Since when did you become a romantic?"

Andrea blushed a little at the question, which Chante also found strange. "I am when it's someone else's life. You know I read at least one romance novel a week. I'm all about other people living happily ever after."

"Maybe it's some psycho sending me this stuff. He might even be a stalker."

She paused for a thoughtful moment then quickly shook her head. "I don't think so. The person who is taking the time to buy you personalized gifts has to like you."

Chante exhaled a slow, unsteady breath and told herself that she was being foolish. Whoever was doing this was harmless. She had nothing to fear.

"You really think I have a secret admirer?"

Andrea thought about it then smiled. "Yes, I do. A secret admirer . . . I like the sound of that."

Chante did too. An admirer was a much better possibility than a stalker—although they could be one and the same. Somehow though, she just wasn't convinced that it was an admirer. The gifts were much too personal. Her instincts were good, and something told her there was something more to this gift giving. She just had to figure it out.

Chante reached for the box and put it safely back in her drawer. "Oh, well, I'm not going to worry myself about it. Hopefully I'll find some answers."

"Where's the first gift he gave you?"

"Still in my drawer."

"Well if you're not going to wear it . . ." Andrea added with a smile, while pointing her middle finger at her chest.

"No thanks. I think I'll hold on to it." She wasn't sure why she wanted to keep the gifts since they made her feel uncomfortable, but she did. Maybe, because deep down she hoped that she was wrong, and it was someone who admired her that was giving her the gifts. And maybe deep down it made her feel good to know that someone thought enough about her to buy her something so nice. She'd never had anyone admire her before. Just the mere thought made her feel quite special.

Andrea looked down at her watch. "All right, it's time for us to leave."

"Just a second. I've got—"

"Chante, now!" she said in an impatient tone. "That work can wait until you get back."

"Okay, I'm leaving in five minutes," she assured her.

Andrea rose abruptly then reached for her shoulder bag, slinging the strap over her shoulder. "Good, then I'll wait."

Chante closed her eyes and bit back a groan. She had no choice but to pack up and start her weekend.

Chante made it home just in time for dinner. The house was filled with the distinct aroma of spaghetti. She left her briefcase on the chair in the entryway then hung her purse and suit jacket on a nearby coat tree. Stepping into the large kitchen, she found Pops and Devon sitting at the kitchen table having dinner. "Hey you two."

"Mom!" Devon sprung from the table and threw himself into her outstretched arms. She gave him a wet kiss on the cheek before he pulled away.

"I've got something for you," he informed her only seconds before he dashed down the hall to his room.

"Hi Pops," Chante said as she slipped out of her heels and left them in the corner, near the back door. As gorgeous as the Donna Karen pumps were, nothing beat padding around on cool mosaic ceramic tiles in her stocking feet.

Pops looked up from his plate. A smile played at the corner of his mouth. "It's good to see you're home early for a change."

She turned away from the cabinet where she had reached for a plate to meet his expression. "Andrea didn't give me much choice. It appears that the two of you have been discussing me," she added dryly.

"That girl never could keep her mouth shut," he grumbled good naturedly.

"That's because she knows where her loyalty lies." She chuckled as she moved to the stove and fixed herself a hefty serving of pasta and meat sauce.

Pops reached for his glass and took a thirsty swallow before saying, "Well at least you're still going. Have you packed yet?"

Chante grabbed a slice of garlic bread then lowered her plate to the table. "Nope. I have all morning to do that."

He raised a dark brow. "O-o-o-kay. I don't want to hear any excuses."

She smiled at her grandfather as she took a pitcher of lemonade from the refrigerator and filled a tall glass. "I promise." Chante pulled out a chair and took a seat at the table just as Devon ran back into the room.

"Here Mom." He handed her something decorated in homemade wrapping paper. Opening it, she found a clay mold of his right hand. It had been baked then painted green. Devon's name was scribbled across the glazed palm.

"You like it?" he asked.

"I love it." She leaned over and kissed his forehead.

"We made it in art class for Mother's Day," he said proudly.

"It's beautiful," Chante told him as she placed it on the table beside her plate. "I'll have to find somewhere special to put it."

Devon returned to his seat, beaming with pride.

"So what will the two of you be doing while I'm out of town?" Chante asked as she took a bite of garlic bread.

"Ooh! I want to go roller skating," Devon said.

She glanced over at him, brow raised. "We'll have to see about that."

Devon had been hooked on skates ever since she'd taken him to the roller rink three weeks earlier. Growing up, she and her siblings used to spend many Friday nights skating with their friends. She still liked to go whenever she had the time. However, thinking of her grandfather with his bad hip, slipping on a pair of skates at his age, she knew skating was not going to happen.

"Mildred and I are planning to take a certain young man to Baltimore to see the d-o-l-p-h-i-n-s." Pops spelled between chews.

Chante looked to see if Devon was aware they were talking about him. He wasn't. He was too busy shoveling his mouth full of spaghetti to notice.

She smiled. "How's she doing?" she asked, as she took a bite of her bread.

Pops took a sip from his glass before saying, "Fabulous. She's just started another water aerobics class."

Chante adored Mildred. At first she had been skeptical about her grandfather meeting a woman over the Internet. However, once she met the sixty-nine-year-old water aerobics instructor, she found her heart to be as pure as gold. Pops was a new man since she had come into his life.

While they ate, the adults engaged in idle chatter. Devon, not one to be ignored, jumped into the conversation with an animated tale of Cynthia Edwards, a girl in his class. Chante was certain he had a crush on his classmate, since she was the topic at the table at least four out of the seven days of the week. Apparently, little Ms. Edwards snuck one of her newborn kittens to school.

"Mom, can I have one?" Devon asked in a pleading voice.

She looked to Pops for help. He simply shrugged as if saying, that's a decision you have to make. After a long pause, she finally said, "We'll see."

Devon seemed all right with her answer for now. Last week he had wanted a dog because Jamise Janson has one, the week before it had been goldfish. She would consider getting him a pet when he became old enough to take care of it himself.

"Why don't you run to your room and get ready for your

bath?" she suggested after finding his second helping of pasta had been licked cleaned from his plate. The kid loved spaghetti.

"Aw'ight." Rising from his chair, Devon moved over to the cookie jar. He grabbed a handful of chocolate chip cookies before he dashed out of the room.

Chante glanced down at her Mother's Day gift that she would cherish forever, and considered herself lucky. Devon loved school and was an excellent student. He was also very well behaved. A child any parent would have been so proud of and she was no exception. Too bad Dorian never got a chance to know how wonderful a child he had. A wave of sadness flowed through her stomach as she thought about how much he'd missed these last six years. What kind of father could abandon his child? She asked herself that question time and time again. However in Dorian's case, it was probably for the best that he chose not to be a part of Devon's life. By now, if he even thought about showing his face, either of her brothers was bound to rearrange it, and possibly break a few bones as well.

Not able to eat another bite, she rose and carried their plates to the sink.

"Don't worry about the dishes."

Chante shook her head. "Pops, you do more than enough."

He rose and shooed her away from the sink. "That's why I'm here. If I didn't have anything to do I'd go nuts," he informed her as he rolled up his sleeves. "Now go."

"I love you." She kissed his cheek, inhaling the faint scent of Old Spice on his skin.

Happiness beamed from his elderly face. "I love you, too."

Chante reached for her shoes and traveled through the living room and down the hall. She moved into the bathroom to run Devon's bath then stepped into her room to change clothes.

Stepping over to her bed, she unzipped her peach linen skirt and allowed it to fall to the floor then took a seat and carefully removed her pantyhose. They were her third pair in the last week. Since she would be away over the weekend, she hoped the pair would at least last until Monday. During her lunch hour she could run out and pick up a couple more pairs.

She then padded across the carpet toward a large walk-in closet. By the time she stepped inside, she had unbuttoned her ivory blouse and tossed it in the hamper in the corner of the closet. On the inside of her door, she removed her robe and slipped it on, and secured the belt at the waist. Turning on her heels, she moved back across the hall to tell Devon it was time for his bath.

"The End," she said an hour later at the close of a bedtime story.

She was returning *The Gingerbread Man* to the bookshelf in that corner, when she heard Devon say in a sleepy voice, "I can't wait 'til Mr. Tony becomes my new daddy. He's gonna take me fishing."

Chante glanced over her shoulder at him and asked, "Who's Mr. Tony?"

Devon was suddenly wide awake. He looked stunned as if he'd realized he had made a mistake.

"Devon, I asked you a question . . . Who's Mr. Tony?" she asked gently.

"I can't tell you."

"Who said?" she asked as she reclaimed her place on his bed and looked her son in the eye.

Light from a lamp on his nightstand permitted him to see her questioning expression. He blinked several times before he finally said, "Pops."

She stared at him, her brow rose in amazement. "Well, if Mr. Tony is going to be your new daddy, don't you think I should know about it?"

"But you will," he blurted. "Mr. Tony is going to Philly."

"He's what! Uh . . . I mean, he is." Chante forced a grin. "Well, I can't wait to meet him."

"I like his letters, Mommy. Pops talks to him on the computer all the time."

Chante pressed her lips firmly together. "He does, does he? Well I guess Pops and I have a lot to talk about."

There was a long moment of silence before Devon asked, "Is . . . Is Pops in trouble?"

Chante saw the worried expression on his face and pasted on a smile. "No sweetheart, he isn't." She leaned forward and kissed him on the nose as reassurance. "Don't you worry."

After listening to him recite his prayers, she dimmed his light and pulled the door shut behind her.

She moved to the kitchen that was already spotlessly clean to the family room at the back of the ranch house. The large room was quite cozy with two black leather couches, and a recliner her grandfather had since she was a little girl. There was a large big-screen television in the corner. A built-in bookcase was along one wall, filled to capacity, and a stone fireplace on the other.

"Pops is there something I should know?" Chante asked, trying to mask her annoyance.

He glanced up at her with a look of confusion wrinkling his forehead. "No, nothing I can think of."

"Then who's Mr. Tony?"

Pops briefly lowered his eyelids and chuckled absently. His great-grandson never could keep a secret, although he was proud Devon had managed this long. "I was going to tell you in the morning."

She strolled into the room and sat down on the couch across from his chair. "What is this about him being Devon's new daddy?"

Pops observed her fearful expression. Since her divorce, Chante had behaved as if her life had ended. It was time for her to move on. He was her grandfather so he knew what she needed even if she didn't—to love again.

Meeting her eyes, he answered softly, "It probably has something to do with the fact that the two of you are engaged."

Chante started to laugh then saw the seriousness of his expression. Her own became incredulous. "Pops, what do you mean, we're engaged?"

He glanced at her with amusement burning in his dark eyes. "I've discovered this fascinating thing called the Internet."

Her head was spinning, and in an instant, it hit her. "Pops, you didn't!"

He gave her a boyish grin. "I'm afraid I did."

"Oh no! How could you?" she asked quietly, trying to absorb it all. She knew her grandfather meant well but this time he had really done it. It was one thing for him to find a female for himself on the Internet, searching for her a husband for her was another thing altogether.

"It's time you let the past go and get on with your life."

She shook her head, clearly dazed. "I have gotten on with my life."

"Devon needs a father."

"He has a father," she countered. "And he isn't worth two nickels rubbed together."

"You know what I mean."

Tears clouded her eyes. "He doesn't need a father. Not when he has positive men in his life like you, dad, and my big-head brothers. It's my life Pops, not yours, and I don't appreciate you meddling in it." She felt frustrated, disappointed, and madder than hell.

"He's been asking about his father."

She met his solemn expression with one of her own. "I know. He asked me last week."

"And what did you tell him?"

"I tried to explain to him that some daddies aren't ready to be fathers. And that hopefully someday Dorian would realize how wonderful his son was and decide to be a part of his life."

She paused long enough to swallow the lump in her throat. "I don't think he really understands—at least not yet."

"Devon asked me to help him find you a husband."

She shot him a glance. "He did?"

He nodded.

"I just don't know if I am ready to go through that again."

Pops sat there as tense silence enveloped the room, the only sound her rapid breathing. Grief filled the air. He wanted to go to her, to comfort her. Only she wouldn't want that. Chante hated to appear weak. Her strength was one of the things he admired about her the most.

"You're a young beautiful woman with her whole life in front of her. You deserve to be happy."

She glanced across with a hollow look in her eyes. Dorian had been everything to her and look where it had gotten her—bruised both internally and externally. She never imagined her life would have turned out this way. Instead, life had played a cruel joke on her. Pops was right. She had stopped living. For so long, she had shouldered her burdens, and deep in the night sometimes she wished she had a man to lean on besides the men in her family. She couldn't though. She couldn't risk falling in love and hurting that way again.

"I think you'll like Mr. Tony if you give him half a chance," she heard her grandfather say.

Chante's mouth tightened and her tired eyes took on a doubting expression. She stole a look at his profile. The only signs of aging on his chocolate face were the wrinkles around his eyes and the age spots that covered his receding hairline. She adored her grandfather and since her grandmother's passing, the two had grown closer. Nevertheless, Pops had no right sticking his nose in her personal life.

Mr. Tony.

She could just imagine what this guy thought of her. He probably thought she was a woman that was so desperate that the only way she could find a man was by using the Internet.

A woman so desperate she was willing to accept a proposal from a man she had never seen. *Hold up! Wait a minute!* What kind of man would propose to a woman he'd never seen before? Chante dropped her face to her hand and groaned. Talk about desperate. Mr. Tony was probably some homely looking computer nerd. She had heard the horror stories. A close friend from college had met several eligible bachelors on the Internet and it had been one disaster after another.

Chante raised her head and met her grandfather's worried expression. "Pops, I need to call this Mr. Tony and cancel."

He shook his head. "It's too late."

Her forehead bunched in confusion. "What do you mean it's too late?"

"I mean he caught a plane after work today and should be arriving in Philadelphia any minute now."

"Then what's his last name so I can call the hotel and tell him it was one big misunderstanding."

Pops paused while he scratched his salt-and-pepper hair. "I can't seem to remember what it is." There was a hint of laughter in his voice.

Her jaw clenched with frustration. "Pops, this isn't funny. That man is expecting to meet a fiancée that he doesn't really have. I don't know anything about this man."

He gave her a reassuring smile. "His wife passed away three years ago."

Great, a lonely widower.

"He's also a pediatrician."

Her brow rose. "A doctor?" she repeated.

Pops couldn't help but smile.

She gaped. A doctor? Did her grandfather think that bit of information was supposed to make everything better? Instead it made matters worse. What would a doctor be doing on the Internet trying to find a wife? "This is ridiculous. It doesn't matter if he's the President of the United States, I'm not going to meet this man. Pops, you got me into this mess, so you're going to have to get me out."

He nodded. "Okay. I'll drive up and talk to him."

Noticing the mischievous look on his face, Chante felt a wave of uneasiness. "On second thought, never mind." Throwing her hands up in surrender, she retreated to her room where she took a seat on a chaise in the corner near the window. As she stared out at the dark sky lit by a sliver of a crescent moon, she tried to figure out how she could get herself out of this mess without having to meet Mr. Tony. After several minutes she realized there was absolutely no way without knowing the man's name. She released a heavy sigh. After her divorce was finalized, she had invited her grandpa to live with her and never regretted it until now.

Grandma, I need you. Delores had passed away four years ago. She had been one tough cookie. While she was alive, she had a way of keeping her husband on a short leash. Chante had loved watching her grandparents. Dragging her knees up to her chest, she contemplated calling her mother then thought better of the idea. She was certain Betty would find the entire situation quite amusing.

This is all your fault.

Chante had to admit that it was. If she hadn't insisted her grandfather find a hobby, he wouldn't have ever discovered the Internet. She knew he spent a lot of time surfing the Web but she had thought it was good for him. Now she knew he had been on the Internet trying to find a man for her.

She didn't need another man. Not after what Dorian put her through. She tried to force away thoughts of Devon's estranged father. He was no longer worth the time or the tears. Nevertheless, she stared at the ceiling thinking about Dorian. She would never risk loving that much again. It had hurt so much to lose the man she'd come to depend on. The man she considered her soul mate, the father of her child. She shook away the pain and regret. All she had now were the painful memories, and her darling little boy.

For a moment, Chante immersed herself in melancholy memories, recollections of the few good times spent before the abuse when they seemed happy. Before things had gotten ugly and the idea of happily ever after had become an illusion.

Chante knew she needed to let go and get on with her life. Try as she might she was unable to banish feelings of hurt and betrayal their marriage had left behind. Maybe a casual relationship was what she needed. It had been years since she'd had any form of intimacy. Her bed had become a cold and lonely place. She had always been a loving and affectionate woman, capable of giving her all without expecting anything in return. Dorian had been her first and only lover so she never had anyone to compare with. As an avid romance reader she had often wondered if maybe she was missing something. She and Dorian had had a passionate relationship, but it had never been the way she read about in those novels.

You won't know unless you find out.

She took a deep breath and let it out slowly, allowing her annoyance to fade away. Staring off in the darkness, she wondered if she was ready to date again. Nothing serious. Definitely not marriage. She couldn't risk those feelings again. But maybe something casual. She had undergone several months of therapy to get where she was today. She had learned to cope with the abuse. And for the first time she had learned how to be independent and loved it. There was no way she was about to give that up.

Why was she even thinking about this? She groaned with frustration. How could her grandfather do this to her? Now she had no other choice but to drive up to Philadelphia tomorrow afternoon and explain to Mr. Tony that it had been one big mistake.

* * *

Antonio stared off into the dark sky where what moon there was played hide-and-seek. He had missed his plane and was scheduled to catch the red-eye. He was supposed to have caught an eight o'clock flight but as he had prepared to leave the hospital, a nurse came rushing through the door and said, "Dr. Marks, Baby Girl Conley is crashing!"

Instantly he dropped his bag and rushed down the hall through the NICU doors to observe the neonatal surgery team jump into action to save the life of the critically ill infant. An hour later, they had pulled the baby girl through yet another crisis.

With a sigh of relief, he went to meet the infant's frazzled parents and reassure them that their daughter was a fighter. He had then moved down the hall toward his office to reschedule his flight.

As usual there was a flurry of activity on the unit. Sounds of periodic alarms and the hiss of ventilators rang in his ears. Rows of incubators held critical infants, some so small they could barely be seen among all the wires and the tubes. A few parents were around dressed in paper gowns and face masks. They sat near the small cribs, trying so desperately to bond with their children, praying for a miracle.

Antonio had seen it so many times that he often left work with feelings of sadness. He didn't know how he managed to do it day after day, dealing with the stress of caring for sick infants. He just knew why he did it.

Antonio stepped away from his bedroom window. He had returned home barely an hour ago after making sure that the Conley baby was out of any immediate danger. Carol and Alvin Conley were good friends of his. They had all grown up in the same neighborhood. The loving couple had tried for years to conceive, and after three miscarriages, Carol had almost given up hope when she discovered she was pregnant again. She spent the duration of her pregnancy on bed rest, but even then had delivered her daughter at twenty-nine weeks. The baby was barely two pounds.

Antonio raked a frustrated hand across his face. He hated to leave them during such a trying time but he knew that Dr. Santiago was more than capable of covering for him. However, even knowing his colleague was as dedicated as he was, did nothing to calm the emotions swirling through him. He was no stranger to the feelings. He experienced them each and ever time one of his little patient's lives were left hanging by a thread. Thank goodness, fewer than most patients eventually lost the battle. And each time he was reminded of his well-guarded memories, a time that he preferred not to remember. The child he had lost fourteen years ago.

He took a seat on the end of his bed and leaning forward, rested his forehead in the palms of his hands as the memories he wanted so badly to forget came rushing back.

He and his wife were second-year medical students when she discovered that she was pregnant. Julia had been working long hours in the ER, and one night after getting off the night shift, she had fallen asleep at the wheel. She had swerved into another car and had gone into premature labor. Their son had been barely twenty-seven weeks. He was a fighter but his lungs weren't strong enough, and after forty-eight hours, he had passed away.

Antonio had then buried himself in his work, driven by the need to never let another couple go through the suffering of watching their child die. Through the years, although there had been many success stories, the failures still hit him hard.

They never had another child. At first Julia was too afraid to try again and then they both became so consumed by their work there wasn't enough time to raise a child. It wasn't until Julia left the hospital and opened a small free clinic in the city's rural neighborhood that she had come home one evening and announced that she was finally ready. But it was too late. At thirty-six she was at high risk, so she decided to have a complete physical and make sure she was healthy enough to carry a child to term, and that was when they discovered she had a brain tumor.

He swallowed a lump from his throat as he remembered his beautiful, devoted wife. Being the compassionate woman that she was, she had tried to reassure her husband that as soon as she had the surgery and her doctor gave her a clean bill of health, they were going to have a baby. Only she never survived the surgery.

For almost two years he had grieved after losing his first and only love. And then one night his wife had come to him in a dream and told him it was time for him to move on and love again.

Antonio rose from the bed and moved into the kitchen for something to quench his thirst. He grabbed a bottle of orange soda and removed the cap. He was engaged. He still had a hard time believing that he had honored his wife's wishes and had moved on, and because of it had fallen in love with a wonderful woman. Now he couldn't wait to meet her.

Glancing up at the clock over the sink, he realized it was time to leave for the airport. He finished the last of his soda then headed down the hall to retrieve his suitcase. He brushed aside the feelings of heartache he had felt earlier for the Conley baby and finally allowed excitement to flood his heart.

Chante Campbell.

He couldn't wait to finally meet her. Despite everything his brother and sister may be thinking, he was certain that this was going to be one weekend he would never forget.

Chapter Four

Chante pulled into the circle drive of the Westshire Hotel where a valet was waiting to assist. She climbed out and allowed him to retrieve her rolling suitcase from the trunk of her navy blue Nissan Altima. After handing him her keys and a generous tip, she stepped through the double sliding glass doors. Her gaze swept around the space, impressed with the surroundings. A large brass chandelier illuminated the lobby while a copper-colored marble floor shined like a brand new penny. Sixteenth-century furnishings gave the hotel a touch of elegance.

She checked in, then with her keycard in hand, strolled down the decorative taupe-carpeted hallway and rode the elevator to her suite on the twelfth floor. Sliding the key in the door, Chante stepped into the spacious foyer and immediately a huge smile tilted her lips as she murmured, "Thank you, Pops."

She moved into a spacious living room that was tastefully decorated with sixteenth-century furniture in shades of hunter green and beige. There was a couch and two large armchairs conversationally arranged around a mahogany coffee table and a gorgeous armoire with a thirty-six-inch cable television inside.

She dropped her bags in one of the chairs then moved through a dining room to a large bedroom where she found a king-size Louis XVI bed and matching chiffonier of dark, hand-carved mahogany. Chante dived onto the bed and giggled as she bounced. The light green comforter was stuffed with goose down feathers and felt heavenly. She was going to have a fabulous weekend.

Rising from the bed, she moved to open the heavy green drapes. Staring out her expansive window at the towering buildings along the commercial district, Chante shook her head at the excitement below. Already the newest summer fashions were on display in the storefront windows below. Spring was finally in the air. The leaves had turned green and flowers were in full bloom. After a long, rough winter, warm temperatures were finally a part of the weekend's forecast.

Concentrating intently, she pulled her lower lip between her teeth. She had become so wrapped up in the comfort of her surroundings that she had almost forgotten the real reason for her being in Philadelphia.

How in the world could her grandfather have accepted a marriage proposal? She had asked herself that same question several times during the hour and a half from Dover to downtown Philadelphia and still couldn't believe it. It was like something out of a soap opera. What had Pops planned to do, hit her over the head when it was finally time for her to walk down the aisle? She shook her head. The entire thing was too ridiculous for words. She would never marry a man she didn't know or, more importantly, love.

Chante pulled her shoulders back and took a deep breath, trying to renew her confidence. As soon as she explained everything, she could get her weekend started. She just hoped this Mr. Tony was a man with a sense of humor. Although, she had to admit, if the shoe were on the other foot, this situation would be no laughing matter. With a sigh, she turned away from the window. Since she didn't know his last name, all she could do was wait for him to contact her.

Strolling over to the chair, she reached for her briefcase

and moved to a small desk in the corner. She lowered onto a small rolling chair and pulled out her laptop.

"Might as well get some work done," she murmured, needing something to do to help pass the time.

She was reviewing the final pages of the rough draft when the phone rang, breaking her concentration. Chante took a deep breath. Only two people knew where she was. Pops and Mr. Tony. Moving over to the table beside the couch, she answered the phone by the fourth ring.

"Hello?"

"Hi Chante. This is Antonio Marks."

She took in a gasp of air at the sound of his low, husky voice. "Hello, Antonio." She managed to say. Closing her eyes, she allowed herself a few seconds to indulge in a fantasy of a man that looked every bit as sexy as the voice sounded on the other end of the phone.

Yeah, right.

"It feels really weird to finally hear your voice after communicating over the Internet for so long."

She gave a short nervous laugh. Antonio didn't know the half of it. Until he had called, all she had known was his nickname. "Yes, it does feel quite strange," she replied as she took a seat on the couch.

"Well, I want you to feel completely comfortable around me. How about we meet in the café downstairs in a half hour?"

She tightened her hold on the phone and took a slow breath. "Sounds good." *Might as well get this over with.* She could then spend the rest of the evening watching a pay-per-view movie. "How will I know it's you?"

Antonio gave a deep seductive laugh. "You'll know, just as I'll know. See you in a few minutes."

Chante hung up the phone and sat there for a long time trying to put a face to the voice. He didn't sound like Magilla Gorilla but that didn't mean anything. Her insurance agent

had also sounded sexy on the phone, and when they had finally met, she had to force herself not to laugh. He was a foot
shorter than she and about one hundred pounds overweight.
Please Lord, let Antonio be easy on the eyes. It would make
breaking the news that much easier. Suddenly her confidence
began to fade and she found herself wishing she had brought
her grandfather along. After all, he was the one who had
gotten her in this mess in the first place.

Reluctantly, she rose and moved into the other room carrying her tote bag. With it in hand, she entered a bathroom decorated in green and gold. She glanced at her reflection in a
large mirror over the sink. A growing curiosity about the man
on the phone made her suddenly want to look her best without overdoing it.

Chante retrieved her brush and ran it across her dark brown
hair, smoothing down the sides. She'd had it professionally
cut a couple of weeks ago and was still getting used to the
way she looked. Her thick, chemically relaxed shoulder-
length hair now had henna highlights, and had been cut in
layers. Studying her café au lait face, she reached for her
make-up bag then repainted her lips, and brushed on a little
mascara. She glanced down at a pair of faded blue jeans and
her favorite red button-down shirt, and debated changing,
then thought against it. For what she was about to do, she
needed to feel as comfortable as possible. She was glad she
had worn her tennis shoes just in case she needed to get away
before Antonio tried to strangle her. She had a strong suspicion that he would probably resent being the victim of what
he might consider a very cruel joke. After taking a deep
breath, Chante moved into the living room, grabbed her purse
and key, and headed for the door.

On wobbly knees, she stepped into the café, then scanned
the area looking for a man that fit the voice. A handsome red-
boned man looked her way and she smiled only to discover
he was looking at someone else. Who was she trying to fool?

A good-looking man like that wouldn't need to use the Internet to find a date. He would have women falling at his feet.

With a wave of apprehension, Chante took a seat at a small table in the corner. When her waitress came by, she ordered a tall glass of lemonade. While waiting, she tapped her painted nails nervously on top of the table. She had no idea how she was going to begin. Maybe have a bite to eat first and warm up to the conversation or preferably just get right to the point and be on her merry way. By the time the waitress had returned, she still had not figured it out. Because no matter how she did it, telling him the truth wasn't going to be easy.

While sipping her drink, she had a strong sensation that she was being watched. She glanced to her left to find a man standing at the front of the café and her breath caught in her throat. With him heading in her direction, their gazes locked and her cheeks warmed. It didn't take him saying, "My name is Antonio Marks" for her to know who he was. Only someone who looked like *that* could be a doctor. Oh, brother. She was in deeper trouble than she'd ever thought possible. The dream of Magilla Gorilla faded and was replaced by reality. With each step he took, came a rapidly hammering heart, and a distinct feeling of light-headedness. Antonio was handsome, and oh, so sexy.

"Hello, Chante."

She tilted her chin to get a better look at the man standing before her. He was tall, not quite as tall as her six-foot-three-inch brothers, but he came close.

"Antonio . . . hi." Damn, she wanted to sample those thick lips, accented by a mustache that looked so silky she had to resist the urge to reach out and touch it. Taking the hand he offered, she gasped at the sensation his touch evoked. It sent sparks flying all the way down to her toes.

"Please, call me Tony," he said, displaying a mouth filled with even, white teeth.

It was obvious he was trying to get past the formalities and set the tone on a more personal level. As he lowered to the seat beside her, his appreciative smile told her he was clearly impressed with what he saw. He wasn't the only one impressed. Chante returned his smile and tried to ignore the fact that his own good looks had caught her totally off guard. He was not at all what she had expected. She was mesmerized by the paper bag-brown brother who was wearing black jeans and a Chicago Bulls' sweatshirt, both which hinted at a strong muscular physique.

When Antonio released her hand, she reached down and held on to the edge of the table. For some reason she felt if she let go, she just might float away. *Stay focused!* a voice screamed in her head. Chante blinked a couple of times as if she had suddenly remembered where she was. Clearing her throat, she met his direct gaze. *Big mistake.* His dark ebony eyes were gentle and intelligent and pulled her within their depths. They were so assessing she could have stared at him for hours. Wasn't it enough that her body was still tingling from the handshake? Knowing this was not the time to lose sight of what she needed to do, she shifted in the chair and dropped her gaze to her trembling hands. "Uh, Mr. Tony . . ."

He erupted with laughter. "At this point in our relationship we should be way past the formalities."

"Uh, yes of course, Anton—I mean Tony. I . . . I have something to tell you. This is hard for me to say but our . . . our engagement is . . ."

". . . a mistake."

Her head shot up. She was caught off guard by his choice of words. How did he know? Had Pops contacted him? She tried to speak, but he interrupted.

"You don't have to explain."

"I don't?" The words floated from her throat as a whisper.

He reached over and rested a hand on her arm then shook his head. "No, there is no need to explain, so relax. I see the fear in your eyes, the uncertainty."

A slight frown appeared between her eyes. "You do?" Was she that readable? She shifted an eyebrow and caught a look of genuine concern.

"Yes, and I have to say I don't blame you."

"You don't?" She knew she was beginning to sound like a broken record.

He nodded. "I've had time to think about it and I think proposing to you on-line was a mistake."

"You do?" She let out her breath in an audible sigh. Her prayers had been answered. "Yes, a mistake," she repeated absentmindedly.

Antonio smiled. "Yes. That's why I suggested we finally meet and spend time this weekend getting to really know one another. A woman deserves to be wined and dined first. Roses, dinner, the whole nine yards." Finding her staring at him strangely, he stopped to laugh. Chante could have sworn he was blushing. "I apologize. I'm an old fashioned kind of guy whose common sense was taken over by modern technology. Chante, I want to learn everything there is to know about you. I want to do this right."

"But—"

"No buts," he interrupted. "How about we spend the weekend exploring our feelings and really getting to know one another?" He was looking at her, waiting for some kind of reaction other than the stunned expression on her face. "Neither of us will even mention our engagement until breakfast on Sunday. How does that sound?" he suggested, trying to put her mind at ease.

Chante was touched by the tenderness on his face and the smile that tipped his lips. Antonio wanted an opportunity to court her properly. She was flattered by his proposition. His actions stirred the deepest part within her. It was all she could do to keep from leaning toward him as if pulled by a magnet. "Well," she began after a moment of silence. "I . . .

I don't know what to say." Things were not going at all how she had planned.

Antonio reached up and stroked her cheek with his thumb and Chante found herself speechless. A warm sensation shot through her body and frazzled her nerves.

"Just say yes," he whispered.

The moment he cupped her chin, she opened her mouth to protest, but his lips covered hers, absorbing the sharp intake of her breath. What she thought would be a simple kiss changed so suddenly she didn't have time to think. Need consumed her as his tongue slid inside her mouth, stroking, exploring, and melting her into a trembling mass. She would have thought it were the Fourth of July instead of Mother's Day weekend with all the fireworks she saw. His kiss was dynamite, her reaction explosive. Her entire body tightened with desire as the heat of his lips penetrated through any need to resist. She kissed him eagerly, each stroke of the tongue becoming more demanding and passionate. She was losing it. *This can't be happening.* It was too real. Too intense. *Enough!* Finally, she pulled back. When Chante opened her eyes, she found Antonio grinning.

"Mmmm. You taste every bit as sweet as you look," he murmured.

She stared at him. Though she knew he'd said something, she hadn't heard him. Her heart thumped, her ears rang. She was still suffering from the aftereffects of their contact. Chante inhaled deeply, forcing her mind to concentrate. Only it was useless. What was supposed to have been an open and shut case suddenly became virtually impossible. Every cell in her body vibrated with awareness. As she gazed up into his eyes, she realized he had felt it too. Theirs was a mutual attraction.

Antonio glanced down at the watch on his wrist then back at her. "How would you like to go on a carriage ride before dinner?" he asked, the words bursting with enthusiasm.

The deep tone washed over her like a warm breeze on a cool spring day. Chante drew in a shuddering breath when his questioning eyes came up to meet hers. She couldn't take her eyes off him. This is crazy, she told herself. This is impulsive and dangerous, and . . . so exciting. It had been a long time since a man had stirred more than a simple smile. Yes, she had to admit she was intrigued by his proposition and although she knew it sounded a bit crazy, there was something about him that was so damn appealing. Not to mention, hard to resist. And at that moment *no* wasn't even a possibility. A ripple of excitement had raced through her body. She didn't know what happened except that the feelings stirring inside overrode her common sense. All she knew was what she was feeling right now, this instant. And it felt good. Damn good. Besides it had been a long time since she'd had any fun.

Antonio was handsome but it wasn't just his appealing looks that had her interest. It was her curiosity about him. He was intriguing. There had also been an instant attraction between them that she felt compelled to explore further. A smile softened her lush mouth as she said, "Yes, that sounds nice."

Antonio's shoulders relaxed. "Good. How about we meet in the lobby around six? I'll have a cab waiting."

Gaping, Chante felt a wave of heat suffuse her face as Antonio pushed back his chair and rose, offering her his hand. Successfully masking her excitement, she placed her hand in his, sealing their evening together.

After they separated at the elevator, Chante returned to her room, feeling as if she'd been ravaged when in fact Antonio had barely touched her. What was she thinking agreeing to have dinner and share a romantic ride with the handsome doctor?

With a groan, she threw her body across the bed. That was the problem. She wasn't thinking, or rather couldn't think, when he was around. Just the mere sound of his voice implied intimacy. She found herself catatonic. She had been unable to draw a normal breath. Although it had been a few minutes, she still remembered everything about Antonio; the fabric of his shirt strained against his firm chest and broad shoulders, and his smell. The familiar scent of his cologne had wrapped itself around her. As much as she tried to deny it, she found him tempting.

She'd had every intention of telling Antonio the truth before she lost her mind. Never before had a handsome man affected her that way, so why now?

She closed her eyes and could still feel the gentleness of his kiss. She regretted allowing him to kiss her, but the softness of his lips, and the sweetness of his taste made her keep right on kissing him. No one had ever kissed her that way. Not even Dorian. She was stunned by the level of electricity that had raced through her veins. She had felt as if someone had stuck her finger in an electrical outlet. His lips had been warm, skilled and inviting. Antonio had managed to make her feel alive from the top of her head down to the tips of her toes.

Then there was also that tingle at the pit of her stomach. It had to be gas or something. No matter how undeniably sexy he was, there was no way she could be physically attracted to a man she had known for less than an hour. It just wasn't possible. Though she was smart enough to know that the stir of heat between her legs had not been a figment of her imagination.

"This is not happening," she told herself aloud as she rolled off the bed and headed for the shower. She was a thirty-four-year-old mother, not a giggling teenager. However, as she reached inside her bag and removed a scarf to tie her hair, her heart rate increased at the excitement of seeing Antonio again in less than two hours. *Why am I so intrigued?* she asked herself. His presence represented everything she had been avoiding for years. There was no way she could even consider falling for the handsome Dr. Antonio Marks.

So why wasn't her heart listening?

* * *

Antonio climbed out of the shower, reached for a large white towel and wrapped it around his waist. While moving into the bedroom, his smile reemerged. Not that it had ever really gone away. He could not stop thinking about Chante Campbell or her large brandy-colored eyes, surrounded by the thickest lashes he had ever seen. She was the color of his morning coffee with cream. She had high cheekbones that any fashion model would die for, and succulent full lips that tempted him too much. No way could he have resisted pressing his mouth against them. And he wasn't at all disappointed. The kiss they shared proved that she was a passionate and sensual woman. Even when the kiss had ended, a look of wonder filled her eyes. Neither of them could deny the heat that had radiated between them. He felt it. Chante had felt it too. Now his body yearned for more. As he reached for his garment bag and selected something to wear, he continued to go over every detail of their first encounter.

If he hadn't seen her shiver or the spark of interest in her eyes, he might have believed that his presence had absolutely no effect upon her. He would have thought that all their weeks of corresponding and the connection they felt for one another had been a figment of his imagination. Instead, he had witnessed a woman who shared an equal attraction with him. Lowering onto the bed, Antonio chuckled. Their first in-person encounter had been quite amazing, and everything he had hoped for.

When they had first started writing, he had no idea what to expect and really hadn't thought much about it since he had never expected it to be more than two people communicating by e-mail. But when the e-mails became more personal and Chante began to talk about herself and her son, he found himself wondering about the woman behind the words. She was unlike the other women that corresponded. Most wanted to know right off what he did for a living, where he lived, and what kind of car he drove. Yet, Chante didn't ask any of those things. Instead, she had suggested that they not exchange phone numbers or personal attributes. He had been stunned yet had agreed. But as the weeks passed he began to fantasize about her appearance. Nevertheless, he never approached the subject again because for once he wanted to learn to appreciate a woman from the inside out.

Without conceit Antonio knew he was a handsome man and he had his share of women pursuing him. However, because of his medical degree, most of the women he met were only after his money. Since his wife's death, all of his relationships had been based on a physical attraction, and as a result, he met a lot of women whose beauty was purely superficial. But with Chante it was different. He found that they had a lot in common. They had both lost their first loves. She was also a Laker's fan, and she, too, enjoyed reading a good mystery. Most of the women he had encountered didn't even read.

Still smiling, Antonio stroked his chin. Now that he had finally gotten to see her, he was stunned. Her smile was enough to heat his blood with anticipation. Past experiences had taught him to trust his gut feeling. And he had a strong feeling about him and Chante. A part of his body stirred, and he knew he wanted to know her in the most intimate way possible.

Antonio rose then walked over to the closet and pulled out the ironing board. As he plugged the iron in, his smile deepened. He wanted to look extra special this evening.

Chapter Five

Chante's hands shook, her stomach fluttered. It had been years since she had gone out on a date, so she didn't have the foggiest idea what she was doing. All she knew was that she was supposed to meet the gorgeous doctor in less than thirty minutes and her stomach still hadn't settled down.

Deciding what to wear was quite simple since she hadn't bothered to bring much. After a long shower, which was intended to calm her nerves, Chante changed into a pair of navy-blue dress slacks and an ivory cashmere sweater. She glanced in the mirror at a woman with flush cheeks and sternly reminded herself she was no longer a virginal teenager getting ready for her first date. She was definitely old enough to separate fantasy from reality.

Lust from love.

You can do this, rang through her mind several dozen times while she finished preparing for her date.

Chante pulled her curling iron out of the bag and plugged it in. While she waited for it to heat up, she decided to give her face a little attention. After brushing on a thin layer of mascara, she applied her favorite red shade of lipstick. She thought about adding a little eye shadow but decided against it. She didn't want Antonio to think she was trying to impress him. Instead, she lightly brushed her face with translucent powder then added a stroke of blush to her cheeks. After one final look, she smiled, pleased with the total affect, and headed into the bedroom.

While taking a shower, she had come to the decision to tell him the truth just as soon as they boarded the carriage. She figured Antonio couldn't strangle her if there was a witness. The one-hour tour would give her plenty of time to express her apologies. Feeling confident that she had her emotions better under control, Chante reached for a jacket and her purse, and headed toward the elevator.

She arrived in the lobby to find Antonio standing near the main entrance with his massive arms crossed over his chest. His face lit up when he noticed her coming his way. His gaze swept from her head to her feet in seconds. Approval illuminated the depths of his eyes, causing her pulse to take a giant leap. *Oh boy, here we go.*

Antonio closed the distance between them and stopped in front of her. "You look lovely." Leaning forward, he lightly pressed his warm lips to her cheek, then leaned back. He gave her a direct stare, his gaze taking in the details of her face. "Ready for a fabulous evening?" he asked with a sexy smile.

The top of her head reached his nose. She tilted her chin and met his intense gaze then nodded. His high cheekbones, chiseled jaw, and lips were so masculine that she wanted to reach up and stroke his face. There was a glimmer in his deep set eyes that held her mesmerized. Her body tingled as she realized she was going to spend the rest of the evening in the company of Dr. Antonio Marks. The hunger in his gaze told her there was more to this man than meets the eye, and that more was enough to make her face flush with anticipation.

He extended his arm to her, crooking his elbow. She threaded her arm through his, following his lead through the lobby and out to a cab waiting in the circular driveway. Antonio opened the door and aided her in, then slipped onto the seat beside her. After Antonio gave the driver their destination, he shifted slightly and stared at her delicate profile. "I assume you've done this before." His deep, resonant voice knifed through the silence with the finesse of a finely edged blade.

Chante nodded and replied softly, "I used to take a carriage ride at least once a year. But I've only gone once since Devon was born." What she didn't tell him was that when she and Dorian first started dating they would spend romantic getaways in Philadelphia. She was certain that Devon was conceived during one of those weekends.

"Well, it's my first time, so please excuse me if I act overly excited. I really have a thing for American history." He laughed softly, the sound rumbling in his wide deep chest.

She inclined her head, smiling. "That's okay. This is one tour I could never grow tired of."

His excitement was quite evident in his smile. "Good. I want us to both have a wonderful time tonight." When he reached over and clasped their fingers together, Chante didn't even consider pulling her hand away.

As he stared out the window, fascinated by the view, she shifted on the seat so she could study his enchanting profile. She admired the cut of his angular features, and his high dimpled cheeks that gave his face a distinct character. Her gaze moved to his mustached mouth and she found herself reliving how wonderful the hairs on his upper lip had felt against her mouth. Anxiety spurted through Chante, her heart racing wildly against her breasts. She took several deep breaths in an attempt to calm her nerves. The enticing scent of his body swept over her. God, he smelled good! He should have been labeled hazardous to her health. There was something about the doctor that disturbed her more than she wanted to be. Antonio was truly sexy. How could a man like that be single? Chante was certain she would ask herself that same question several times before the night was over.

A cab delivered them to Fourth and Chestnut where the carriages were lined along the street. Antonio paid the driver then climbed out of the cab. Extending a hand, he assisted her to her feet, then curved a protective arm around her slender waist, and led her up the sidewalk.

Antonio was as excited as a little boy in a candy store as he carefully chose the friendliest horse. Chante had to suppress her laughter. This was a trait that she found she truly liked about him. When he finally decided on a horse named Kirby, they boarded the carriage.

The temperature had dropped to about fifty-eight degrees, with a light gentle breeze in the air. Even with her jacket on, Chante was grateful for the wool blanket at the foot of the carriage. She unfolded it and spread it across their legs. Once they were both comfortable on the seat, the horse backed away from the curb and began a slow trot.

Antonio glanced around, fascinated by the sights and sounds. "I can't believe how nice it is here with all this history surrounding me. I have always dreamed of living in a historical neighborhood, buying a large old house, and restoring it."

Chante glanced over at him with stunned amazement. "Oh my goodness! I want the same thing with two rocking chairs on the porch."

He looked pleased by her response. "I'm surprised. Most women want a brand new house with all of the upgrades."

She shook her head and shifted on the carriage seat. "Oh no! The fun would be in doing it yourself; stripping wood, repainting, laying new tile. I've taken quite a few classes at Home Depot. I know how to use most power tools."

"I'm impressed. My wife believed that men and women have roles. Women weren't supposed to use power tools while men were supposed to stay away from knitting needles and sewing machines."

Disbelief marred her forehead. "You're kidding right?"

He gave a hearty chuckle full of memories. "No. I'm afraid not. Julia wouldn't even screw in a light bulb."

She giggled lightly. "I used to be that way, but after my husband was gone, I learned how to be quite handy. If not, my grandfather would have tried his hand at fixing things, and that would have been a disaster."

He chuckled along with her. As the carriage pulled onto the next street, the guide's robust voice drew their attention. As he explained their surroundings, Chante thought about what Antonio said about women's roles. Her mother had taught her a long time ago that although there is nothing wrong with a woman being independent, they should never forget that men like to feel needed. Just like Antonio's wife, as long as her father was around, her mother also never screwed in a light bulb. That job was reserved for her personal handyman. A smile touched Chante's lip as she remembered when she was around thirteen and the door knob to her bedroom was loose. She dashed to the tool shed for a screw driver to tighten it. Her mother stopped her as she stepped back into the house, and told her, "Let your father do it." She had thought it stupid at the time because it was an easy enough task she could have done herself. However, the look on her father's face when she asked him to fix it made it quite clear. Afterwards she gave her father a big hug and told him, "What in the world would we do without you?" He rewarded her with a bear hug and a kiss, then told her, "I hope you never have to find out."

As she thought about the way her mother always thanked her father with a kiss, she couldn't help wondering if Julia used to do the same thing with her husband. Maybe Antonio also liked to feel needed. She doubted with his good looks that he had felt unwanted at any point in his adult life. The man could come over and screw in her light bulb any day of the week. Just watching would send her blood racing. Goodness, she was getting ahead of herself. There was no way she could possibly be thinking or feeling this way about a man she had just met. He just looked so incredibly handsome and sexy, she hadn't been able to help herself.

She shifted her weight and thought about the attraction that had exploded between them the first time they looked at each other. *Impossible.* However, not only had it occurred but it was still happening. Her pulse was racing. She didn't want to stop looking at him. She wanted him to kiss her again.

As if he knew she was watching him out the corners of her eyes, Antonio reached over and took her hand in his. A shiver ran up her arm and her nipples tightened beneath her bra.

"Are you cold?" he asked in a tone she found both comforting and unsettling.

She took a deep breath trying to bring her self-control back in place then finally shook her head.

She noticed that he studied her intently before he leaned over and whispered near her ear, "Don't worry. I'm nervous too."

Oh, dang, his eyes were sincere. Light from an overhead street light radiated across his face outlining a lean cheek with an irresistible dimple. Why did he have to be such a heart-stopper? She felt herself softening toward him.

This was exactly the trap Pops intended her to fall into. Damn him!

Chante swallowed and wondered if he heard the faint sound from her throat. She tried to relax again, however the feat was close to impossible. She felt herself weakening again. Feeling the need to quickly pull herself together, Chante turned away from the warmth of his breath and stared off to her left. How was she going to survive the evening with so much sexual tension between them? If she told him the truth now, would it make the rest of their evening more bearable? She wasn't sure. Besides, something told her now just wasn't as good a time as she had originally thought. Antonio was having such a good time, she hated to ruin the moment.

Yep, she convinced herself, it would be better to discuss their impending union over dinner.

The setting sun had turned the sky orange-red. She managed to take a moment away from her racing thoughts to appreciate the beauty of their surroundings.

Antonio draped an arm across her shoulders which she found quite comforting. As the guide took them along one cobblestone street after the next, she found herself relaxing with every breath and, without realizing it, had nestled her head against Antonio's shoulder while they listened to the driver's narrative tale of the area's history. By the time she realized what she was doing, she couldn't bring herself to remove her head. Instead it felt quite natural. His chest felt large and solid under her touch, just right for resting her head on.

Antonio was fascinated by the entire thing. He didn't hesitate to ask questions. She closed her eyes. She didn't need to see to know where they were going. She had done this tour so many times, she could buy her own horse and carriage and give tours. Instead, she'd listened to the harmonious sound of Antonio's voice. He probably had no idea how tranquil the tone was.

"Armani," she blurted in a low voice as she finally remembered the fragrance he was wearing.

A slow, sexy smile flattened his upper lip against the ridge of his teeth. "You're familiar with my cologne?"

She raised her head and nodded. "Yes, my brother Dame wears the same brand."

He gave her a long thoughtful look. "Let me see if I remember correctly . . . Dame is your youngest brother, right?"

"How—" She was about to ask him how he had known that when she caught herself and faked a sneeze instead. "Excuse me. I had something in my throat. Yes, Dame's the one that rides on the back of a garbage truck all day. We always tease him that he smells like trash, so he started wearing cologne whenever he comes around."

They shared a laugh, then realizing they were being rude, resumed listening to the rest of the tour. As the carriage traveled down the quiet streets, Antonio continued to hold her hand with his thumb grazing across her knuckles. They were slow sensual strokes that she felt clear down to her toes.

When they moved down South Street, the street that never sleeps, Antonio turned and directed his attention to Chante. "Are you enjoying yourself?"

When his eyes locked upon hers, the rest of the world faded. Her breath caught in her chest as she continued to stare and remembered the last time she'd seen that strange simmering quality before.

It was right before he had kissed her.

Their gazes remained locked. "Yes, I am." She blushed, her bright eyes crinkling with a smile. "Since I've done this before, I should be asking you that question."

"I'm having a wonderful time just being here with you." Then, just as she thought, his head came down and his lips covered her mouth.

Chante didn't struggle. She thought about resisting then the taste of him got through, tempting her, and once again, she gave in to the impulse. Her brain was screaming one thing, while her body said something else. As his lips parted, she couldn't help opening her mouth. When his tongue thrust past her lips she forgot about staying in control. All she thought about was what she felt, and what she felt was out of control. She felt young and new to the experience although she had been kissed before. She felt alive in ways she hadn't felt in years. *My goodness, what am I doing?*

She pulled back.

Gazing up at him, Antonio gave her a look that said he understood then draped a comforting arm around her shoulders again and drew her near. She lowered her head to his chest and her eyes drifted closed as she sank under his spell. He was strong and warm and smelled wonderful. Her attraction for

him flowed through her veins [...]
heart beat steadily against her ear.

"I'm glad you agreed to spend th[...]

"So am I," she heard herself say. [...]
Worrying her lower lip between her teet[...]
she'd had since childhood, she tried to ma[...]
The entire situation was truly unbelievable.
hard she tried to stay focused, to stay in con[...]
seemed to make her forget everything, includi[...]
name.

What was she doing? She tried to stop her body
throbbing but she could hardly think straight sitting so c[...]
to him. They were not only sitting close and holding hand[...]
but taking a romantic ride around the city. She had to find the
nerve soon to put a stop to this before she did something foolish like invite him back to her room. Inhaling deeply, she
forced her mind and body to get a grip. For the duration of the
ride she tried to regain control of her emotions by taking a
stab at a casual conversation in regards to their surroundings.
Only it didn't work. The feelings continued to battle within
her. Then finally, exactly one hour from the time they departed, the carriage came full circle and pulled back to its
original spot.

"Stay right there," Antonio said quietly. He jumped down
from the carriage and held out his arms for her. Seconds later,
Chante found herself being lifted out of her seat. Instead of
lowering her to her feet, he held her effortlessly, her shoes
dangling several inches off the ground. Her arms circled his
neck as she attempted to maintain her balance. His fingers
tightened around her waist, bringing her breasts in contact
with the solid wall of his chest. She felt the heat of his flesh
through the layers of clothing. Her head, leveled with his,
eased forward until she felt the whisper of his moist breath as
it swept over her mouth. Desire burned in his eyes.

Chante smothered a groan and resisted the urge to kiss

er sensitive nipples
the blood through
tle was left of her
ided to savor the
oked at her that
em she had no
night.

"hungry yet?"

RST SAW YOU
nd pooled at her center. His
e weekend with me."
What was happening?
h in a nervous habit
ke sense of it all.
No matter how
rol, Antonio
g her own
y from
lose
ds,

cked for a
ning behind
gry she truly was, An-
er into his arms and carried her
Maybe a consummation would put an end
raction once and for all, she thought. However,
Chante sensed that it wouldn't be quite that simple. If anything, it just might make matters worse.

"Yes, I'm starved," she simply stated.

"So am I." He took her hand and held it protectively as they
strolled along the crowded sidewalk toward the corner and
caught a cab.

They were on their way back to the hotel when Antonio
heard her ragged sigh. He turned and glanced at her stunning
face, her expression impassive, and wondered what was going
on in her head. Tenderness slid through him. He wanted to
soothe away the confusion, to calm the nervousness that made
her hands tremble. Reluctantly, he swallowed against the need
to kiss her again. Nothing would please him more than to take
her in his arms and press his lips to her mouth again. Two
stolen kisses were not enough. He was in danger of losing his
restraint around her. His loins hardened merely thinking
about it. Chante was quickly becoming addictive. He was
trying to take things slow and give her a chance to realize that
their emotions were real. The only thing that stopped him
from carrying her back to his suite and making love to her

was that he wanted her to trust what was truly happening between them. He had felt the emotion in her e-mails and he felt it now even more.

Antonio continued to stare at her, feeding on her beauty. Barely four hours had passed since their first face-to-face encounter, yet he was more than certain he had made the right choice to have her in his life and in his bed. He was a good judge of character and so far he hadn't found anything to change his decision to make her Mrs. Antonio Marks.

The sun was sliding lower, and darkness would soon descend. When they arrived back at the hotel, he placed a hand at the small of her back as he steered her to the restaurant up on the third floor. As they stood near the front and waited to be escorted to their table, he leaned over, and whispered close to her ear, "I remembered that you love seafood. This restaurant is supposed to have some of the best crab cakes in the county."

She glanced up at him curiously. "How did you know I . . ." she stopped suddenly realizing that Pops had told him that as well. *What all has he been telling this man?* She forced a smile. Her long thick lashes hid the bewilderment of her eyes. "How do you know I want fish? I might be in the mood for steak tonight."

Squeezing her hand gently, Antonio winked when she glanced up at him. "Sweetheart, you can have whatever your heart desires."

Her heart soared. The sound of the endearment sounded so natural one would have thought them to be truly in love.

A formally dressed young man with short blond hair came over to greet them. "Your table is ready. Please follow me."

Again, Antonio placed a hand lightly at her back as they followed the maitre d' to a wonderful spot near the window. The table was covered in white linen, with a lighted candle in the center.

The maitre d' placed their menus on the table. "Your waiter will be with you shortly. Enjoy your meal."

Chante was pleased when Antonio pulled out the chair for her and made certain she was comfortable before he took the seat across from her. It was the kind of thing Dorian had never done, and that was why she appreciated the gesture so much. Thinking about him and the pain he had caused her, she turned her head and stared out at the evening sky as she felt the threat of tears. Taking a deep breath, she stared above at the brilliant cloudless star. She rested her chin in her hand and forced the feeling away. She was not going to waste tears on Dorian. He wasn't worth it. Remember the happy times and hold them near and dear to your heart is what her mother had said when their marriage had finally ended. Below was a view of downtown nightlife. She watched the streets filled with people as she attempted to brush aside the memories. Putting on her happy face again, she reached for her menu, and opened it.

Antonio shrugged out of his jacket to reveal his broad chest covered by the fabric of his silk shirt. Chante stole a furtive glance, then cleared her throat and resumed concentrating on the menu.

He waited until a white-coated waiter poured them each a glass of water and departed before he asked, "Since you're in the mood for steak, how about crab cakes as an appetizer?"

She simply nodded.

Antonio gave the menu one final glance then angled his head, and asked, "How'd Devon do on his zoo project?"

She tried to hide her surprise. Was there anything her grandfather hadn't told him?

"He actually did very well. After spending a week cutting out elephants and pasting them on a poster board, he earned a gold star."

He laughed freely. "That must mean he got an 'A.'"

Nodding, she continued, "He was so proud. I found a tape

cassette with jungle music and his teacher played it while he did his presentation. Pops attended and videotaped the whole thing."

"That's wonderful. I can't wait to see it."

She raised a brow. His words had taken her by surprise. He was speaking of them as two people with a future. His choice of words reminded her why she was here in the first place and what she still needed to do directly after dinner. Why was her heart no longer in it?

"What does your family think about us finally meeting?"

The only ones that knew were Pops and Devon so that made her answer easy without having to lie. "They think it's time I learn to love again."

"And what do you think?"

The excitement on Devon's face when he left for school this morning almost brought tears to her eyes. He so badly wanted a father. "I agree."

"And now that you're seeing me for the first time, am I anything at all like you imagined?"

More than you'll ever know. She dropped her gaze and blushed. "I think you're quite the catch, Dr. Marks."

"And I think you're equally intriguing. Every time I read your e-mails I used to try and think of the color of your hair, and even your eyes."

"Did you come close?"

His eyes twinkled excitedly. "I imagined that you were light skinned with short dark hair and big beautiful brown eyes. I also thought you would be short and very petite."

Her brow rose. "That sounds like Halle Berry to me."

"That's probably where I got the image," he admitted with a boyish grin.

"I hope you're not disappointed."

His gaze darkened intensely as he shook his head. "Not at all." He paused to chuckle. "My brother is going to have a cow. He was so sure you were going to look like Wanda from *In Living Color.*"

She covered her mouth and chuckled along with him.

"Instead I couldn't have selected a more beautiful woman to spend the rest of my life with." He reached across the table and brought her hand to his lips.

Her look of surprise had not gone missed. Antonio knew he was moving a bit too fast but he didn't seem to have any control of his functions when he was in her company.

Antonio stared at Chante, seemingly deep in thought. "What would you like to drink?"

She blinked as if she'd just come out of a trance. "I don't drink—"

"Alcohol. I remember," he finished for her, then winked before turning to their waiter who had returned to take their orders. "We'll have two iced teas please and crab cakes as an appetizer."

Chante rested her chin in the palm of her hand. She had to admit Pops was definitely thorough. However, she was certain he didn't bother to tell Antonio the reason why she didn't care for alcohol. After being married to an abusive husband and seeing the way alcohol affected him and his father she wanted to have nothing to do with it.

Their waiter returned within minutes with their drinks. As he took their dinner orders, Chante listened to Antonio order them both a steak.

She was acutely aware of him, but who wouldn't be aware of a man like that. All six-feet-two-inches and in lean, perfect condition. She glanced over at him after their waiter had left with a smile. "I like a man who knows what I like."

Tilting her chin, she smiled up at him through her lashes, unaware of the seductiveness of the gesture. The look made him hot and turned him on so much he tried to control the rage brewing at his loins. He was tempted to ask her what else she liked but thought better of it. Instead Antonio raised his glass with a wide grin splitting his face. "I would like to propose a toast."

Crossing her slender legs beneath the table, she smiled at him. "What are we toasting to?"

As he visually examined her through long, dark lashes, he wanted to take her mouth there and then, but brushed the impulse aside. "To us and what the future holds."

They touched their glasses then shared a smile before they both took a sip. Chante glanced up, magnetized by his intense gaze. There was a gleam of interest in his eyes. He reminded her that she was a woman and he was a man. She had no intentions of getting romantically involved with him but her racing pulse refused to listen. She wasn't sure how long they sat there staring at each other. The waiter returned with their crab cakes and the spell was broken.

After he departed, Chante looked at Antonio over the rim of her glass. "How's work?" she asked as she placed her glass on the table. Suddenly she wanted to know everything there was to know about him.

"Well it depends on if you're talking about my appointment at the hospital or the free clinic?"

"Both." *Especially since this is the first I've heard about them.*

"Well, both the pediatric and neonatal units are currently occupied by more infants than any of us would like to see. Lots of premature infants and chronic illnesses."

Chante could tell by his expression that sick babies saddened him. She listened intensely as he spoke about several of his patients that he'd been caring for since birth.

"And what about the clinic?" she asked when he paused long enough to take a sip from his glass.

She noticed his smile reemerge. "For our fourth year, the clinic is going quite well. Like I had told you in my e-mails it's a small free clinic in a low-income neighborhood. We have come a long way in such a short period of time." He then went on to explain the limited services that they provided.

She was drawn to everything about this man. Now she knew what it was about him that drew her so deeply—Antonio's compassion for anything and everyone around him.

Her eyes lit up. "That sounds fantastic," she said, her gaze on his sensual lips as he sipped from the glass.

"I hate that Julia never got a chance to see the clinic's success. She had gone into family practice with the intention of reaching out to her people. A lot of sweat and time had gone into getting funding for her project. She had just gotten it off the ground when we had discovered she had the brain tumor." The sadness in his voice gripped him.

Brain tumor. She'd had no idea. She tried to mask the look of surprise, hoping he hadn't noticed. "You still miss her, don't you?" she asked, genuine concern etching her face.

He leaned back in his seat. "Yes, I do," he admitted softly. "Julia was a caring individual. She dreamed of giving back to the community by helping people who couldn't afford health care. She had such big plans. Not many doctors accept Medicaid patients because of all of the restrictions on billing. We lose a lot of money because Medicaid discounts the services so much that sometimes we get nothing at all. But Julia didn't care about that. She came from a well-off family and most of the money in her trust fund was used to start up the business. The rest comes from grants and government-funded programs."

She could tell he had loved his wife deeply. It was the way she wished Dorian had felt about her. "Why Chicago's west side?"

He shrugged. "Why not?"

"Why not the suburbs?" she said forcing herself to focus on his broad nose. It was much safer to look at than his eyes or lips.

"Because my wife's grandmother lived on the west side

until she finally passed away. Julia grew up there and wanted to give back to her old neighborhood. A woman that she had known all her life had died a couple of years earlier due to kidney failure. She was sick and didn't want to go to the hospital because she didn't have any insurance. As long as she could help it, Julia was determined to never let anything like that happen again."

"How sad." She was intrigued by everything that came out of his mouth. So far she had learned that he was an old fashioned type of guy, who was sexy, with a warm personality, and educated.

"So what kind of services does the clinic provide for free?"

"Checkups, immunizations, contraceptives, and diabetes and hypertension testing. The clinic also accepts patients with no insurance based on a sliding scale. Most of the time, we generally ask the patients to pay whatever they can afford."

His compassion for the others less fortunate than he blanketed Chante's heart with warmth and true admiration. "That's wonderful."

"It's not about the money. My parents died five years ago and left me a large chunk of change. Also, all the insurance money I received after Julia's death, I poured into the clinic. I'm one of the rotating doctors on staff, and like all the others, we donate our time for free." He gave her a look that sent her pulse racing and for an instant she was lost in the depths of his eyes. She could see that medicine was his life. She could also see that the clinic probably saved his life after the death of his wife. If he hadn't had it, grief would have probably destroyed him.

As if he'd read her mind, Antonio nodded then said, "I grieved for so long until I realized Julia wouldn't have wanted that. I have since learned that the memory of my wife will live in my heart forever."

Without thinking about what she was doing, Chante reached across the table and patted his hand in a comforting gesture.

Antonio stared across at her and as they looked at each other, she couldn't seem to move, she couldn't breathe. His eyes held her in his gaze.

He leaned closer while the finger of his right hand lightly stroked back and forth across her knuckles. "Julia would have liked you."

She smiled. His compliment pleased her. "Thank you."

She stared at him recognizing the faraway look in his eyes and knew he was thinking about his first love. There was a long, pregnant silence. She didn't know what else to say or do because thinking about her first love only caused unnecessary heartache.

The waiter arrived with their food, then after asking if they needed anything else, he disappeared.

Chante removed her hand from the table and after draping her napkin across her lap, reached for her fork. Everything looked and smelled wonderful.

For the next hour they talked about everything from the weather to childhood memories. They debated why the Lakers' best two players hadn't been able to get along and what it was going to take for the team to get back on top. They also had a winded conversation about the effects of rap music on today's youth, and that they don't make music like they used to.

Slowly she began to unwind and found that she enjoyed talking with Antonio. He was bright, full of information, and had a humorous wit about him that kept her laughing throughout the main course.

"You never told me how you got into the literary market."

Chante dropped her shoulders in relief. *Finally, something he doesn't already know.*

While they shared a slice of strawberry cheesecake, she told him about her first client and how she had joined forces with her closest friend. Antonio watched her mouth when she spoke. Her lips were painted with a lush ruby red. His warm gaze lingered over her face. He could tell she was more at ease. She appeared relaxed and comfortable. She wasn't hesitant.

Chante blushed when she realized she was rattling on. "I'm sorry. It feels as if we've known each other forever."

Antonio nodded. "I can't put it into words but I've sensed it from the first. A connection with you that had nothing to do with how long or how deeply we've known each other. All that matters is that it seems so right."

Seeing her nervous smile, Antonio felt a protective pang in his heart.

"I feel that . . ." He paused as her tongue darted out the corner of her mouth to capture a crumb, and Antonio realized he had stopped talking. "Sorry. My mind wandered. What was I saying?"

Chante's brow arched while her gaze filled with curiosity. "What were you thinking about?" she asked softly.

"You," he said, turning her hand in his and leaning closer. "Your smile. Your kiss . . . wanting to make love to you."

She inhaled sharply. Antonio stared across at her and for just a moment, sensuality quivered between them. "You're embarrassing me."

"Sorry, but you asked." His voice was husky.

She tried to disengage herself from a spell that he seemed to weave, and sliced into the cake, allowing herself a smirk. "Let's talk about something else."

"That wouldn't be nearly as much fun," he said with a teasing smile.

"But it's safer." She hoped her cheeks weren't as flushed as they felt.

"Scared, Chante?"

Their gazes collided. "Not at all." She said in as calm a voice as she could manage, especially since her heart was racing a mile a minute.

She took another bite of the cake and again graham cracker crumbs took possession of the right corner of her mouth. This time Antonio was unable to resist. He rose from his chair, leaned toward her and kissed that portion of her lip, allowing his tongue to flick the crumbs into his mouth. He then lowered back in his seat and watched with fascination as she quivered, her cheeks flushed, and her eyes opened wide.

Why did he want more than anything to take her to his bed and make love to her and forget about everything else? He already wanted her in his bed, his lips tasting her skin, her body warm and naked beneath his—

Down boy. He was tempted to keep flirting with her but instead he leaned forward in his chair and enjoyed the scent of her perfume. It was fun to tease Chante, watch the tiny lines at the corner of her mouth.

After she recovered from the surprise, he smiled and she did the same. While they sipped coffee, she found herself charmed and entertained. Antonio kept her laughing with stories of growing up. When he laughed, amusement flickered in his eyes and softened his mouth. He lightly stroked the top of her hand. Every stroke fueled her desire, but she was still determined not to lose her focus.

After Antonio took care of the check they followed the sound of piano music to a small lounge down near the lobby. He offered his hand and a smile. "Let's dance."

Chante left her jacket and purse on a chair close enough to the stage that she could keep an eye on, then walked with him to the dance floor that was at the center of the dimly lit room. When she stepped into his embrace, she could feel his warmth, smell the light tantalizing scent of his cologne. As they swayed from side to side together, he pulled her even closer into the circle of his arms.

"You feel wonderful in my arms. I like holding you."

She looked up at him. "I like having you hold me." Their eyes met and it was several seconds before either of them spoke again.

"It's been a long time since I've been dancing. I've been so busy with my patients I barely have time for fun anymore. That's was one of the reasons why I had suggested this weekend."

"What was the other reason?"

"To get a chance to know you better."

She felt a warm rush flow through her midsection as his piercing gaze met hers. "You're trying to make me blush."

"Good," he said as he leaned forward and brushed her forehead with his lips. She closed her eyes and he pulled her close again. "As long as you're blushing I know I'm saying and doing the right things." He leaned down to trace her ear with his tongue and she shivered.

It felt heavenly to dance in his arms and be held close. For the moment, she might as well enjoy feeling like Cinderella, she thought. The stroke of midnight would come soon enough when she'd have to tell him the truth about their relationship.

The song changed and Antonio began to two-step and Chante followed his lead. She had never mastered the moves but moving with Antonio was easy.

In such a short time, she had come to realize that there was so much more to this man, he was absolutely nothing like the desperate nerd she had originally envisioned. Antonio Marks was a handsome, fun-loving, and dedicated doctor, and any woman would be lucky to have him.

The next song was a fast number, and Antonio was skillful and sexy as he moved, spinning her around, and pulling her back into his arms. Fast and slow, they went from one dance to another. They finally left the floor when the piano player announced in a small handheld microphone he was taking a fifteen minute break.

"You really are an excellent dancer," Chante remarked after she retrieved her belongings, and they moved slowly across the lobby to the bank of elevators.

"Thanks, you're not half bad yourself," he said, and pressed the up arrow.

She shrugged. "I do okay. My girlfriends and I used to

hang out at the clubs back in the day and party until the sun came up." She laughed, lost in her thoughts. "Gosh, that was so long ago."

"You sound like me and my boys. We were the first ones in and the last ones out. We used to compete in dance contests."

"I can tell that you really like to dance," Chante said as she stepped onto the elevator. Antonio followed and turned to face her.

"What I like is touching and holding you," he said in a low, sexy voice that made her heart skip a beat. "To me, dancing is a form of foreplay."

"Stop trying to turn me on," she managed around a smile.

"I merely said what was on my mind."

Her pulse drummed as she said in a breathless whisper, "At least you're honest."

"I try to be."

She groaned inwardly. *Too bad I can't say the same.*

He pushed the button sending the elevator up to the twelfth floor and then turned to put one hand on the wall beside her while he leaned close. "I try to always be honest. It was the way my parents raised me. Besides, I couldn't dream of lying to you." He was too close, his mouth too tempting, and thoughts of her deception, swam through her brain. She was getting in way over her head.

Chante placed a hand against his chest, "Anto—"

"Hush," he whispered and leaned down to cover her mouth with his.

Her heart thudded as his lips touched hers. She willingly opened her mouth to him, practically melting when he pulled her in his arms. As their tongues mated, she was only aware of Antonio's mouth against hers, his solid body molded with her own. She heard the bell and then twisted as the door opened. Antonio didn't seem to notice.

"Antonio."

At the sound of her voice, he raised his head. The blatant

need in his eyes sent her body temperature soaring. It wasn't until they had gotten off the elevator, and were standing outside her door when she started to feel nervous again. Antonio had a way of making her lose all restraint. He brought out the impulsive side of her. Continuing to deceive him was wrong but she could not deny the emotions she was feeling.

Antonio turned, his eyes on her.

She swallowed. "Well, I guess this is it."

Slowly he drew closer and shook his head. "No. It is far from it. This is only the beginning."

Chante's throat tightened at the meaning. His words were ridiculous yet she was unable to resist them. "Y-yes. The beginning." She gulped. The look in his dark eyes was filled with unspoken promises of passion.

"I think this good old fashioned courting is off to a good start. Don't you agree?" Antonio asked, tilting her chin so she had no choice but to look at him, his large dark eyes examining her. She gazed into his eyes and fell into the fire burning behind their ebony depths. She tried to tear her eyes away but it was useless. It was as if one side of her brain refused to listen to what the other side was saying.

Then something happened.

Somehow, Antonio took her key card from her hand and maneuvered her inside the room and pushed the door shut behind them. Gently he pulled her into his arms, but this time was different. Somehow the tone of his embrace had changed. He looked down at her; masculine intent gleamed in his eyes.

Chante was certain she heard the wedding march as his hand stroked the hollow of her cheek then moved slowly down her arm. And as if the pastor had said, "You may now kiss the bride." Antonio's head lowered and she found herself meeting him halfway.

Antonio wanted to feel Chante's lips on his again more than he'd ever wanted anything before. The pressure of her soft moist lips washed away any lingering doubts he had that maybe their relationship would never develop any further than an Internet romance. What he felt for her, she felt for him, and that need was profound when she leaned forward and melted in his arms. An overpowering rush of desire surged through his body when he heard her softly whimper his name. He tried to take things slow and respectfully, but he discovered that with Chante it was going to be next to impossible.

Chante felt the earth tremble beneath her feet. Her senses reeled as he continued to kiss her in such a way that was purely sensual. The warm pressure of his chest against her aching nipples was enough to make her melt. She longed to get rid of the barrier of clothes, but knew she needed to guard her heart against the charismatic man. Antonio was making her want something she hadn't wanted since Dorian— intimacy. She slid her arms around his neck and pulled his mouth down to hers. Antonio was an experienced kisser and he aroused something in her that she had never felt before.

Your heart knows what the mind has been hiding all these years.

Her lips parted, inviting him deeper, kissing him in a way that was totally different than before. His mouth on hers, fiery and magic all at once. Not a soft, gentle, seductive kiss but a hot, deep, ravishing kiss that filled her with heat and need. She could lose herself in his warmth, his promise. The feel of Antonio's arms around her, his body pressed to hers, left no room for memories, for ghosts, only for the here and now. She was hot, aching for him. Her knees went weak and she held on tighter to keep from melting onto the floor. The incredible way he brought her back to life. Her body. Her heart.

No, not my heart.

That was only loneliness speaking. How could she be so drawn to a man she had just met? Things were spiraling out of control. The walls she had built to protect her heart began to crumble. It had never been like this with Dorian. Never.

And that scared her. Antonio Marks was the man to bring her to her knees. Shocked, she wiggled free.

Chante took a step backwards and drew in a deep breath. "Antonio, I have something to tell you." She figured the easiest way to put the brakes on their developing relationship was to tell him the truth. "Things are not as they seem."

He placed a finger to her lips, silencing her words. "There's no rush. We've got time."

She searched his face and felt the deep intensity of his gaze.

"Plenty of time," he whispered then bent his head once more and brushed his lips with hers in a seductive bid of good-bye.

He raised his head, his eyes on her face. The hot look burning from their depths told her that this was only the beginning. The mere thought stole her breath away.

"I know you're still grieving over your husband's death, so I promise not to push until you're ready."

Grieving? Death? What in the world was he talking about? Before she could question him, he leaned closer to kiss the corner of her mouth, touching her lips with his tongue, then pulled away.

"Good night," Antonio said huskily before he opened the door and departed.

Chante stared at the closed door. Her pulse raced, her body tingled and her mind was in chaos. With trembling fingers, she touched her swollen lips. The kiss had shaken her to the core. It had been heated and passionate, and tremendously satisfying.

She moved into the bedroom and took a seat on the bed and removed her shoes. Momentarily closing her eyes she recaptured the moment in Antonio's arms when she knew she had never before in her life felt so filled with desire for anyone. When she was around him she was powerless, something inside her ruptured, spilling heat and fire throughout her body. But even with all of that heated excitement she had felt something more, something deeper. She sensed some sort of need that went beyond anything physical.

Chante took a deep breath while she collected her thoughts. Now was not the time to start losing her mind over Antonio. She had just met the man and it was best that she not forget that. She tried to close her mind against the sensual need rocketing through her body, but it throbbed on, ignoring her wishes. Despite everything, she still hadn't told him the truth. Now she had dug an even deeper hole. What was he going to think when he found out?

How will he ever know?

She thought about that question for a moment. Maybe he wouldn't figure it out and maybe he would, but unless she knew more about him, chances were not good.

As soon as she changed into her pajamas, she took a seat on the bed, reached for the phone, and dialed her home number. It didn't matter if it took all night. Pops was going to tell her everything she was already supposed to know about Dr. Antonio Marks. Most importantly he was going to tell her why Antonio thought her ex-husband was dead.

Chapter Six

Antonio rose the next morning with a silly smile on his face that he couldn't get rid of no matter how hard he tried. Not that he was really trying. In fact he hadn't felt this good in a long time.

There was something about Chante that ran straight through his system like a shot of Hennessey, impairing his train of thought. He just hadn't put his finger on what it was about her that he liked the most. So far he was impressed by everything. However, if he had to claim one thing he enjoyed the most, it would be just holding her. Nothing had ever come close to the soft comfortable feeling of Chante in his arms. The way her head had rested lightly on his shoulder. The feel of her soft round breasts against his chest.

Last night, all through dinner all he could think about was touching her, the taste while sampling her sweet breath on his tongue, and hopefully some day very soon, being inside her. He couldn't get her off his mind. Her mouth had been everything he had imagined and more. Even now he could still taste her on his lips and the faint scent of her perfume still clung to his skin. She was a passionate woman. The single kiss had awakened sensations within him that had torn at his control. He didn't want to think about what would happen the next time he kissed her. When he took her in his arms again, he was likely to whisk her off to bed, slowly undress her, and then make love to her through the night. Antonio mentally groaned and reprimanded himself for letting his imagination get out of hand. He needed to back off in order to prove his love, his honor.

But it isn't going to be easy, he thought, running a hand over his face.

He wanted her like he had never wanted a woman before. He didn't realize until this morning when he woke up alone just how much he wanted her to be a part of his life, and to share his bed. Even now, he felt the cool touch of her cheek and wanted more than anything to feel that touch elsewhere on his body. After all, he decided, his feelings were understandable, considering it had been more than six months since he'd been intimate with a woman.

Almost two years after his wife's death, he had engaged in a casual relationship with an OB/GYN on staff, Dr. Tiffani Ross. With their busy schedules, they both found the relationship convenient and physically satisfying for the time being. Before Antonio had joined the Internet site, he had pondered the possibility of the two of them becoming serious, but realized that although Tiffani satisfied his needs, she was not at all what he wanted in a wife. Tiffani lacked compassion and sometimes came across as selfish and aloof. To top if off, she had no desire to have children.

He needed a woman who wanted a family and set his blood on fire. A woman who he enjoyed talking to and being with outside of the bedroom, who was selfless and compassionate. He was certain that compassion was something Chante had plenty of.

Fantastic. Things were coming along better than he could have ever hoped for.

Tipping his head back, Antonio paused then frowned. He did, however, find it strange that she repeated things to him as if she was telling him for the first time. When he had mentioned seafood she had appeared stunned he knew that bit of information. It was as if she had forgotten that she had told him. And when he had spoken of Julia dying from a brain tumor, it was as if he had forgotten to mention it to her earlier, that he had lost his spouse. However, despite how puzzling it may seem, he was certain there was a logical explanation.

Again Chante's image came to mind and Antonio felt his body harden. He cursed under his breath. He was hard and straining and he honestly didn't think he could wait another day to bury himself in her body. Man, he wanted her. But it wasn't just physical. He desired her body but he wanted the whole woman more. He cared deeply for her. From the first time he laid eyes on her he felt this overwhelming need. Did she feel it too? he wondered. He sure hoped so, otherwise this could very well be the hardest weekend he ever spent with a woman.

After a two hour phone conversation with Pops, Chante had gone to bed hoping that when she woke up everything would make sense. Only it didn't. It was worse.

Antonio thought she was a widow.

Apparently, her grandfather had set up her ad on a lost love Web site. So, naturally the widower assumed she was widowed, too. Then to make matters worse, once questioned further about her husband, Pops informed Antonio that Dorian died in a car accident while away on business. Once caught up in the lie, he felt he had no other choice but to continue it.

Chante rolled out of bed, feeling sleepy and agitated. She didn't need this kind of confusion in her life. Things were just fine before Pops had decided to meddle in her life.

Shuffling into the bathroom, she moved to the sink and splashed water on her face with the hope that the icy cold water would shock some sense into her. She sighed heavily when it did not. *Man, I'm in trouble.* As she moved into the dining room, she asked herself for the hundredth time how in the world could she be drawn to this man? It wasn't just physical. What astonished her most was that she'd had any type of physical reaction at all. She thought she was dead inside. For over five years, she had met an abundance of men but not once had she felt anything or even considered getting involved, yet Antonio had awakened feelings she'd buried deep inside. Sure she had gone out on an occasional date, but none had ever come close to making her feel the way she had after her evening with Antonio. To further complicate matters, she had spent the night hungering over a man she barely knew.

The in-depth phone conversation with Pops had painted a picture of a compassionate, intelligent and giving man, who was ready to love again. Even after she had hung up the receiver, she stared up at the ceiling thinking about Antonio. His image appeared, strong and handsome.

Face it—you're sexually attracted to him.

Okay, so maybe she was attracted to him. Chenoa and Andrea had been telling her for years that she needed to start living again. That she needed to get some before she dried up like a shriveled old prune. But that wasn't a reason to marry somebody. A relationship had to be based on more than just sex. Even though she was certain the sex between them would be out of this world. Nevertheless, she was old enough to know that what she was feeling was lust and nothing more.

So why are you missing him?

That was a good question, considering she was still reliving every moment of their last kiss. The soft feel of Antonio's lips, the silken glide of his tongue, the strong yet gentle way he had held her. And she had willingly enjoyed every second of it. No matter how hard she tried, she couldn't figure out what had happened to her mission to set things straight. Somehow she had experienced a temporary lapse of sanity.

Or maybe you want this to be real.

She quickly shook her head. That was ridiculous. Her attraction was nothing but her body talking. Long ago, she had learned that sex and lust did not lead to love. At one time, she had made that mistake and it had done nothing but lead to heartache. Giving yourself to someone didn't mean that that someone would give themselves emotionally to you. Gosh, how was she going to face him?

Like a mature adult, of course.

She moved to the coffee pot in the corner then turned on the faucet and filled the pot. While the coffee brewed, she asked herself, why now? Why after more than six long years was she allowing a man she had known less than a day to affect her this way? And not just any man. A man who was looking for a wife. A man who had proposed to her. A man she longed to have tasting her lips as well as every other part of her body. A man she had unintentionally deceived.

She strolled to the window and glanced down at the early morning activity going on down below. After a while everything became a blurry swirl of colors as she stared off in a trance while trying to make sense of what she was feeling.

Antonio's dark, hungry looks brought to life emotions she hadn't experienced and she feared trusting them. What she was most afraid of, was her reaction to him. He reminded her of the fact that she was a woman who had been alone for too long. A woman who longed for someone to fill a void in her life. Since Dorian, she had felt dead inside, and despite every effort to fight it, for the first time she felt alive again. Yet every time she even dwelled on that fact, she remembered the pain of loving Dorian. She had vowed to never love that way again. She wasn't strong enough to go through that type of hurt again. Antonio was doing things to her no man had done in a long time . . . okay, never. She'd barely known him twenty-four hours and already she was thinking things she should not be thinking, considering things she shouldn't be considering. She would just have to keep reminding herself of her mission and remember that her grandfather, bless his heart, had gotten her into this mess in the first place.

The phone rang, startling her. Chante took a deep breath and reached for the receiver. "Hello?"

"Good morning, beautiful," he greeted softly.

"Good morning." Why did Antonio's voice have a way of flowing through every nerve in her body, making her ache with longing?

"How did you rest last night?" he asked.

She slowly lowered onto the couch. "Uh, I slept well," she lied. "What about you?"

"Not well, not well at all."

At the seriousness of his tone, she gripped the phone tightly. "Why, what's wrong?"

"You baby. I couldn't get you off my mind."

Her eyelids fluttered shut. The sincerity of his words touched her in ways that made her speechless.

He chuckled kind-heartedly. "Have breakfast with me?"

Oh, that wasn't a good idea. Not now. Not with the way she was feeling. She needed to keep some distance from this man until she could figure out how to tell him the truth. Antonio made her feel too many emotions.

"I can't," she blurted.

"Why not?

"Be . . . because I have a massage scheduled for"—she quickly glanced over at the clock and saw that it was a little after nine—"ten." She had a massage but it wasn't until noon.

Antonio paused for a second and Chante thought maybe he would call her bluff. "All right, then how about we meet for lunch?"

She gulped and drew her knees to her chest. "How about I call you later?"

There was a long moment of silence before he finally answered, "Okay."

She could tell he was a little surprised by her response but she didn't have time right now to worry about that. She quickly said good-bye and hung up the phone before he could start asking questions.

Now what? she asked herself. She had no idea. Instead, she picked up the phone and ordered room service.

Antonio paced around the room like a caged animal as he waited for room service to deliver his breakfast.

Something was wrong. He could feel it. Why else would Chante be avoiding him? And she was definitely avoiding him. He had heard the hesitation in her voice. Now the big question was, why?

Last night there had been a connection. He felt it and he was certain she had felt it too. That she wanted him, too. Why else would she kiss him like that, come into his arms so willingly, so warmly, so eagerly? He also knew she was lonely. He knew because he realized he was lonely too. She was scared, but he planned to help her through her fear.

Lying on the massage table, Chante closed her eyes as the masseuse worked her magic. She hoped that if she released some of the tension she would be able to get Antonio off her mind. Only it wasn't working.

She tried to convince herself the attraction between the two of them was a mistake. It wasn't real. He was drawn to words on a computer screen. Somebody that Pops had invented.

Then, what's your excuse?

She had been caught up in the moment. She had been thinking with her raging hormones and not with her common sense. She didn't have time to dwell in fantasies and allow her body to crave the comfort of a man. She had been doing just fine without one. She had come to Philadelphia to break off the engagement not to have a weekend fling with a man she barely knew.

As the masseuse's hands came to massage the kinks out of her thighs, she found herself envisioning those were Antonio's hands instead. His long, strong fingers traveling slowly up her inner thighs until finally reaching her core where she would welcome him.

Chante released a ragged sigh. She wanted him so badly her body ached, which was another reason why she needed to stay away from him. She wanted him way too much, and the want only seemed to have increased the more time they spent in each other's company. Longing flowed through her chest down to the area between her legs every time he looked at her with those gorgeous ebony eyes. Even now, despite the smell of lemon and eucalyptus, Chante could still smell his cologne that mingled so perfectly with his own masculine scent, one would have thought Armani had been created especially for him. She could have easily spent the night with her head resting comfortably on his chest, lost in the wonderful fragrance. Just thinking about lying in his arms caused her heart to flutter.

Chenoa scowled at the direction of thoughts. She had no business indulging in such foolishness about a man she barely knew. She had a major problem she had yet to rectify—an engagement. She had no right daydreaming about a man who, as far as she was concerned, had been deceived into believing that she wanted to spend the rest of her life with him. If she really thought about it, she also had been deceived, which was why she was in Philadelphia in the first place.

At the masseuse's request, Chenoa rolled on to her back then she closed her eyes and heaved another sigh. She needed to stick to the agenda. She had a job to do and that was break off the engagement. So she didn't have time to fantasize about her fake fiancé.

So why does it feel so right?

That was a question she was unprepared to answer.

* * *

An hour later, Chante walked briskly through the lobby. Every time she heard footsteps, she glanced over her shoulder. Quickly she crossed the hall to the elevator. When the gleaming doors opened, Chante looked both ways before boarding the elevator. She dashed into the empty car, and pressed the button for the twelfth floor. She held her breath until the doors closed, then let out a deep breath when it finally rose.

This is ridiculous. Ever since she had left the masseuse, she had expected Antonio to suddenly appear. Her hands were shaking. Her heart was pounding. Every time the doors opened to pick up or drop off another guest, she thought she was going to leap out of her skin. When she reached her floor she hurried off the elevator and scrambled down to her room as her heart did a nervous flip-flop. One would think Antonio was an axe murderer the way she was acting.

She swiped her card then looked both ways before entering. As soon as she was safely inside her suite, she collapsed in the chair and closed her eyes. She was out of breath. That was how he made her feel, breathless. Somehow, in a course of one day, Antonio had gotten under her skin.

She couldn't take any more. She needed to somehow relax because the massage had not done the job she had hoped. Rising, she moved to her suitcase to find her navy-blue swimsuit. Maybe a little swimming would help. If not, she wasn't sure what she was going to do. Pulling off her clothes, she quickly changed into the suit then tucked her thick hair beneath a white swim cap, grabbed her keycard, and headed down to the lobby.

Fifteen minutes later, with a towel wrapped around her waist, Chante moved across the blue tiled floor toward the edge of the pool. Other than a few kids playing at the shallow end, the water was relatively empty. She removed the towel, slipped out of a pair of pink flip-flops, and dove in. The shock of the cold water was just what she needed to clear her head.

She swam several laps along the width of the pool. After a while Chante floated on her back as she tried to think about the mess she had made. She should have told Antonio the truth from the start. Now she was going to have to find a way to break the news to him before the end of the day. She groaned. Telling him meant seeing him again, and she wasn't sure she could keep herself together or stick to her mission if she did. However, calling and tell him over the phone wasn't even an option. He deserved to hear the truth from her in person.

Her thoughts were interrupted by a soft wolfish whistle. Lowering her feet to the bottom of the shallow end of the pool, she opened her eyes, ready to light into someone for his rude unwanted advances. Wiping the water away from her eyes, she found Antonio standing on the edge of the pool before her. An unexpected bubble of warmth rose within her that she could not blame on the water since the pool was not heated. It was all because of the gorgeous man standing before her.

Every time she saw him, he managed to make her head spin until she didn't know what to do or say. The frown on his face did nothing to lessen the impact of his devastating good looks, which had haunted her ever since their initial encounter.

"You're running away from me."

"No I'm not. I just felt like swimming," she responded unevenly. Her heart was beating erratically. She felt nervous and uneasy.

He met her gaze with a careful, concerned expression. "So why didn't you call and ask me to join you?"

She took a deep breath then blurted out, "Because I needed time to think."

He stared at her for what felt like an hour before a smile of understanding suffused his features. Chante tried to ignore how good he looked standing across from her but found herself conducting a study of his features.

There was no doubt about it, he was a fine specimen of a man. Her eyes moved from his eyes to his lips. The sensual shape of his mouth reminded her of how it had felt molded to hers while driving her crazy with passion. Dropping her gaze proved to be an even bigger mistake. She found a perfect solid chest sprinkled with dark silky hair that arrowed down past his navel and disappeared inside a pair of black swim shorts.

To her excitement, he lowered onto the edge of the pool then dropped inside the water and slowly waded her way. "What are you thinking about?" His crooked smile set her heart to pounding again. Water dotted his moustache and spiked his lashes.

Omigoodness, he is so fine. How did he expect her to think with him looking at her that way?

He stepped closer until only inches separated them. A slight flush rose in her cheeks. At his nearness she swallowed hard. He was too near, too tempting. "You. Us," she finally admitted.

He closed the distance between them. "Us," he repeated. "I like the way that sounds." She lifted her face to his. His eyes met hers again then moved down at her breasts. By the heated look in his gaze, she could just imagine where his thoughts were.

He touched her—a tiny caress of her cheek that spread quickly through her body. How could she ignore him for long? Suddenly she didn't want to. Suddenly, despite everything she had decided earlier, she really wanted to get to know him.

Sensations of awareness coiled through her as he watched her. She couldn't speak, couldn't breathe, and couldn't think. The feelings she had ignored had returned again, the warmth of her body, the tightening of her breasts, the desire to be kissed again.

He lowered his head and captured her lips. The kiss, although gentler than the night before, was just as passionate and possessive. His lips parted, sought, found, and was rewarded with her meeting each and every skillful stroke. Somehow, she felt as if he was trying to tell her something as he kissed her.

She closed her eyes as he drew her close in his arms. The other hand clasped her bottom and pressed her hips against his muscled thighs. She clung to him with all the strength she possessed.

She wasn't sure where this was going to lead but somehow it felt right. For now, kissing him was exactly what she wanted to do. Again and again, he dipped his head to hers. Eventually she lifted a hand to his hair, threading her fingers through his curls, loving the way they felt.

Chante didn't understand what she was feeling. And at the moment she didn't care. Denying herself no longer held any appeal. She just wanted to enjoy what was taking place between them. Nonetheless, she vowed that whatever might happen with Antonio would be strictly physical. She would keep her emotions in check. No emotional commitment. No love. That she could do. After all, it was only a weekend.

Then as if he had suddenly remembered they were standing in a public place, Antonio pulled away and smiled.

"What do you have planned for the rest of the day?"

Her head was spinning, her blood roaring, her body aching with need. Whenever he kissed her, an exquisite weakness seemed to take over her entire body.

He bent his head and brushed her mouth once more with a feather-soft kiss, encouraging her lips to move.

"Nothing," she finally managed to say.

"Good, then you won't object to spending the day together."

His eyes held her captive but she knew it wasn't against her will. He sparked something deep inside her from the moment they first met in the hotel café. No matter how dangerous the attraction might be, a part of her wanted to explore it.

There was no clear reason for her sudden change in behavior, especially since she had spent the entire morning trying to hide from him and the feelings he stirred.

With an eager bob of her head, she accepted his offer to spend the rest of the day together.

Chapter Seven

Chante was falling hard. After they had changed into something dry, they caught a cab to Independence Hall. They viewed the Liberty Bell, strolled to the Visitor Center then visited the African-American museum.

It was a beautiful afternoon. Because of the man beside her the sky seemed bluer, appeared clearer. Colors were bright and vivid. Walking hand in hand, they joined the up-beat crowd of visitors to the district, wandering the historical streets.

Chante felt happy and alive. Antonio's smiles were warm and contagious. They stopped along the way, reading historical facts and to take pictures. After seeing a folk dance, they caught a cab to Jasper's for a couple of Philly cheese steaks.

They arrived at Penn's Landing in time to listen to an up-and-coming R&B group perform an original single as well as a few songs made popular by others. Chante took a seat on the grass beside Antonio. Antonio curved his strong arms around her and held her close. Resting her head on his shoulder, she closed her eyes as the music vibrated through her. She took a deep breath loving the way he smelled, the way he felt, and wished the afternoon never had to end. Chante thought she might as well be in a dream because being with Antonio was like nothing she had ever known before.

He kissed the side of her neck then traveled up to her ear and whispered, "Are you enjoying yourself?"

A soft enchanting smile touched her lips as she said, "Yes."

"Good, so am I."

She looked over to the right under a tree where a teenage boy seemed more interested in making out with his girlfriend than watching the show, and frowned. "Maybe you should go over there and tell them to go get a room," Chante mumbled close to his ear.

Antonio glanced in the direction of her eyes, and after watching the boy slide his hand underneath the girl's shirt, chuckled lightly. "Kids nowadays don't give a damn what they do in public."

Chante shook her head. "I know. I can't say that I've ever been quite that carefree."

"You mean to tell me you've never ravished your man in public?" he asked with a teasing grin.

Her lips curled upward. "No, have you?"

"Nope. However, I'll admit I've thought about doing it on more than one occasion."

"What about the movies? When you were that young did you ever take a girl to a movie and spend so much time kissing that you had no idea what the movie was about?" From the way he chuckled, Chante knew she had hit home with her comment.

"Yeah, I guess you got me there. Although even in the dark movie theater I wasn't doing anything close to what those two are doing. I think he's about to suck her tonsils from her throat."

She chuckled and squeezed his hand.

When the show was over, they caught a cab back to the hotel. They made plans to meet at seven for dinner. After a light brush of the lips, they parted in the elevator.

Once back in her room, Chante took a quick look through her clothes only to remember she hadn't brought anything fancy to wear. *I guess because you hadn't planned to spend your weekend with him.*

She rushed back down to the lobby and out the door, to a small boutique she had spotted across the street. Her choices were limited but in a few short minutes, she found a dress that she thought would be perfect.

Once back in the room, she showered then dried off and moisturized her body with a peach-scented lotion. She added a few dabs of perfume behind her ears and at her wrists, then spent the good part of an hour curling her hair. A sensual smile softened her mouth as she gazed at the result in the mirror.

There wasn't much time left, so she quickly slipped into the dress and her favorite mules and moved to stand in front of the full-length mirror on the back of the door. She smiled as she took in the body-hugging garment that framed every curve perfectly.

Wait 'til he sees me in this dress!

She had just put in a pair of one-carat diamond studs when she heard a knock at the door. She paused at the door, took a deep breath then opened it. There he stood, grinning.

Taking a good look at his attire and the gorgeous smile on his face, her breath caught in her throat. He wore a tweed dinner jacket and a cream silk shirt with a two-tone brown tie. Her gaze moved down to his pleated chocolate slacks then down to a pair of dark brown wingtip shoes. He looked so good a tremor flowed through her body.

"Don't you look nice." She returned his smile with a dazzling one of her own.

"I was going to say the same about you. You look marvelous."

The compliment was more intoxicating than a bottle of champagne. Usually she ignored such a remark but from Antonio the words sounded sincere. Deliberately he allowed his eyes to travel over her body from head to toe, then back up again. The smile playing with the corners of his lips left little doubt that he liked what he saw. She loved the way his gaze traveled appreciatively over the length of her body. Awareness flowed through her veins as she watched his eyes dance.

"Thank you." She smoothed down the front of her form-fitting red dress that stopped just above her calves. She had complemented it with a black shawl.

She glanced up to find his eyes drawn to her mouth. It was no telling how long they would have stayed there staring at each other if she hadn't cleared her throat.

"Are you ready to go?" he asked in a deep masculine voice.

She nodded then said nervously, "Yes. Let me grab my purse." As she walked to her room, she could feel his eyes watching her.

Alone, Antonio finally took a breath. Chante moved with the kind of feminine grace that had been fascinating men for centuries. It was a crime for a woman to wear a dress like that. The red dress hugged every curve and teased him by what it revealed and hid. The slits on the sides showed long, shapely legs. It took everything he had not to scoop her in his arms and carry her back to her room.

He wasn't sure what it was about her, all he knew was that he wanted her more than he'd ever wanted a woman before. By the time she had returned he felt he had gotten himself under moderate control.

"Ready?" she asked as she slid her purse strap over a slender shoulder.

"Do you mind if I take a picture first?" He asked then removed his cell phone.

"No, I don't mind," she replied, flattered that he wanted to take her picture.

She struck a pose and waited for him to snap two pictures before he returned the phone to his hip.

"Ready?" she repeated.

"More than you'll ever know." Pulling her hand into the curve of his elbow, he led her out the suite and down the hall.

As they stepped off the elevator car and sashayed through the lobby, she was aware of people watching them. Chante felt a surge of warmth as she glanced over at him. Antonio was tall, dark and sensual in the way he moved as much as in the way he looked. She had to admit he was very intriguing. What woman wouldn't look at the tall man who exuded confidence? She thought, then her eyes traveled to his profile. Dimpled cheeks, dark serious eyes, and a prominent chin, there was no way she could keep from smiling. She felt so proud to be on his arm.

They stepped out into the star-studded night to find a cab waiting. Antonio helped her into the back and took the seat beside her. The driver pulled away from the hotel, and Antonio reached over and clasped her hand again. Chante glanced up at him, and then to her pleasure he leaned forward lowering his mouth to hers. This kiss was gentle, yet passionate, and although it only lasted for mere seconds it was quite consuming. When he pulled away his eyes were still glued to hers.

"That should hold me until after the meal. Then I'll be ready for dessert."

She tried to keep calm yet it was impossible. His words held a couple of different meanings, and one in particular made her heart race.

They were quiet the rest of the ride, and within minutes the cab pulled up in front of Zanzibar Blue. The restaurant had a distinctly upscale atmosphere. Everything had class, from the fine linen tablecloth to a vast repertoire of smooth jazz. It was barely seven o'clock and already the small intimate restaurant was full. Many other well-dressed men and women were sitting at the bar waiting for a table. It was a good thing Antonio had made a dinner reservation. It wasn't long before they were escorted to a small table that was both intimate and very romantic. Antonio seated Chante then took the seat across from her.

"Everything okay?" he asked after their waiter took their drink orders.

She nodded, joy bubbled inside her like fine champagne. "Everything is fabulous."

He took a few moments to gaze across the table at her. Thick curls were looped and pinned on her head. The tendrils that had managed to escape made him think about running his fingers through her hair. She smiled and her exquisite face lit up. The soft light from a candle at the center of the table flickered. The flame made her eyes sparkle in a face so exquisite it might have belonged to a goddess.

He had to force his eyes away. He reached for the menu and studied it then looked across at her doing the same. "What are you going to have?"

Glancing up from her menu, she shook her head. "You decide." She was too nervous to make a decision even as simple as dinner. The entire evening was so romantic. She felt like Cinderella with her prince. Even though she tried not to think about it, she couldn't help wondering where the evening would lead. Feelings for Antonio had begun to creep deeply into her heart and soul. Feelings for the man she was beginning to understand him to be.

"How about mahogany Long Island duck, apple glazed sweet potatoes, and lemon currant asparagus?"

He stared across at her, waiting for a response, and all she could do was gaze at him. "Uh, that would be great."

Antonio closed the menu and lowered it to the table. Staring across at her, he returned her smile. The candlelight caused her skin to glow against the shadows. His gaze was glued to her mouth. She had painted her lips with a fabulous color that emphasized their shape. He took a deep breath when her mouth curled into a delightful smile. Desire flowed through him down to his loins. He wanted to savor her sweet lips, to once again delve into their depth and taste her. He wanted more than a kiss but right now a kiss would do.

Chante was as beautiful as the dress she wore. He wasn't sure what he loved most, her lips or her eyes. There was a sort of innocence that radiated from them.

He was proud that she'd agreed to spend the weekend with him—all the more reason not to scare her off by pushing too hard or too fast. It was his goal to make sure to prove she hadn't made a mistake by accepting his engagement.

In the meantime, he needed to find a way to control his desire. Unfortunately, her lips were something he couldn't seem to get enough of. And if she returned his kiss again the way she had, he couldn't promise anything, because around her he had no control over his actions. He'd almost lost it last night. Two more minutes, if she hadn't stopped, she would have found his pants around his ankles and his hands all over her body. Perhaps if he was drinking something stronger, he'd forget his devilish thoughts. That, or act upon them. He knew how he wanted the evening to end. However, the ball was now in her court. He wasn't going to push her. He was going to sit back and let Chante and fate direct the rest of the evening. No, he was lying. There was no way he was going to sit back and do nothing. He was going to do everything it took to make sure she came to the same conclusion he already had.

Their waitress returned with two glasses of lemonade. Antonio gave her their dinner selections. When she left, he leaned back in his chair, with his glass in his hand. He took a swallow then noticed Chante staring at him over the rim of her glass.

"What's wrong?" he asked.

She blinked once then lowered her glass to the table, smiling. "I'm curious. Maybe I asked you this once before, but I want to ask again now that we are face to face. Why would a man of your caliber try to find a wife over the Internet?"

He chuckled softly. "I knew that question would come." He rested his elbows on the table and leaned towards her. "I'll answer only if you do the same."

She hesitated, dropping her eyes briefly to the napkin draped across her lap. What would she say? *How about the truth!* She slowly lifted her gaze to him again and nodded. "All right."

Pleased with her response, Antonio took another sip before replying, "I was tired of women wanting me for my good looks."

"Poor thing," she mocked.

Antonio chuckled. "I'm serious. Women want me for my looks as well as my medical degree. For once I wanted to meet a woman who wanted to know the real me. That was what had first attracted me to you. You didn't need to hear my Barry White voice. You didn't want to see my bedroom eyes." He paused long enough to join in on her laughter. "Okay, so maybe I don't sound like Barry White, but regardless of what I sounded like it was not of great concern to you. I knew then you had to be someone special."

She swallowed, feeling a second of guilt. This was her chance to come clean and tell him the truth. Only she couldn't seem to find the words. What would he think of her? She pushed her nervousness aside. Even though she knew Pop's reason for discretion was because he was role playing, she had to admit that it worked out perfectly. If not, they wouldn't have ever met, and she wouldn't be having such a wonderful time.

Closing her eyes, Chante let out her breath slowly. "After Dorian, I didn't know how to get back into the dating scene. To be honest I didn't want to. So I found comfort in the computer. I've heard horror stories about people pretending to be someone they weren't, and the disappointment, so I thought I'd just be discrete and cautious. I never expected to meet you or for things to go this far."

"Are you disappointed?" Antonio asked as he caught her hand and brought it to his lips.

She shook her head and answered honestly. "No, I'm not."

"I feel as though we've known each other forever. I can't put it in words, but I've sensed it from the first, a connection with you. You feel it, too, don't you?"

Chante nodded. "Yes, I feel it."

Their eyes were saying all that their words couldn't, and despite her best effort to keep him at a distance, she was drawn to him.

The meal was exquisite as well as the conversation. Several times she glanced up in time to find Antonio staring at her. He even reached across the table and placed his hand over hers. Both actions made her warm and tingly inside.

By the time dessert was served, the lights dimmed, and the band moved to the stage. A beautiful chocolate woman stepped before the microphone. Her rich clear voice evoked memories of Gladys Knight.

After the performance, they decided to walk back to the hotel. Chante felt the protective warmth of his hand at her back as they stepped out into the cool night air. A soft breeze ruffled her hair. The streets were streaming with people coming in and out of stores and others in search of Philadelphia's nightlife. They walked several blocks in silence. Chante peered into store windows admiring the latest fashions and some expensive shoes.

Antonio took her hand and laced their fingers together as they took in the sights and sounds. He adjusted his longer strides to a leisurely pace. A few blocks from the hotel, he stopped and met her eyes. "When I proposed . . . what made you say yes?"

She was caught off guard by Antonio's question and the flash of desire in his penetrating eyes. As she gazed at this beautiful man she tried to think of an answer, while trying to make sense of what she was feeling. Everything about him turned her on, from the sparkle in his sexy eyes to his fabulous body. Heat flowed through her, stimulating her senses. He was a wonderful person with a loving heart. He was confident, charming, and handsome. What was there not to like? She liked being around him. She liked his smile. The way he made her feel like the most beautiful woman in the world.

"How could any woman say no?" Emotions rocketed through her and she realized at that moment that she already cared more than she would have ever imagined.

The smoldering gaze Antonio leveled at her melted any further resistance Chante might have been clinging to. A deep heat stirred inside her. She wanted him.

He moved in closer and her entire body came to life. Reaching out, he caught her fingers, holding them in a firm grip he pulled her closer. Antonio crushed his lips down over hers before she could draw a breath. Instinctively, she opened to him inviting the mating of his tongue. He was equally deliberate, launching a searing exploration of her mouth. He tasted of heat and mystery—the essence of desire. A fiery passion rushed through her blood washing away her inhibitions, consuming her heart and mind. The world whirled out of focus, out of her control.

Her fingers dug into his back and held on tightly. She clung to him, letting his kiss deepen and swell, filling her with her own needs. One of his arms circled her waist while he allowed his other hand to cruise across her breasts. Through her dress and bra, she could feel the heat generating from his fingers. Her nipples were already tingling, but his touch made them hard even through layers of clothes.

At last he leaned back, their lips parting. Her body throbbed with unsatisfied desire. "I want to make love to you," he whispered breathlessly.

Chante inhaled deeply. Common sense told her to decline but why should she when they both wanted the same thing. There was no mistaking the blatant need in his eyes. He gazed at her with a hunger that made her breathless. There was no way to fight off the strength of this overwhelming power he had over her defenses, or the tremor passing through her body. She reached up with her forefinger and traced his lower lip. He inhaled deeply, and she was still amazed at the effect she had on him. Why should she continue to deny herself when she knew she wanted him as badly as he wanted her? Reality faded along with all those other reasons she had to keep this man at arms length. There was only need and heat. He was special and she needed to show him that she wanted him as she had never wanted anyone else.

"I want that too," she said softly.

It was finally time to return to the hotel.

Instantly, Antonio hailed a cab that got them back to the hotel in record time. Chante giggled because as short a distance as it was, they could have easily walked. However, overwhelmed with desire, she too was anxious to lie in his arms.

Chapter Eight

They boarded the elevator with Antonio holding her close to him, his fingers brushing lightly against her arms and shoulders. Anticipation bounced around the paneled car as they were both eager to reach his suite on the tenth floor. As soon as the doors opened they hastily covered the distance to his door. As soon as he closed the door behind them, he hauled her against him. She put her hand against his chest.

"Alone at last," he murmured. His mouth then came down on hers demanding, possessive. Her heart thudded as his lips touched hers. She returned his kiss passionately, feeling the bond between them.

She was hot, aching for him. Her fingers drifted up and down his back then she brought her hands around front again and went to the buttons of his shirt. She freed them, then broke the kiss and pushed the shirt off his broad shoulders. Leaning back, she took a moment to get a better look at him. She growled deep in her throat. The mat of dark hair narrowed down to a fine line that disappeared below his belt. Reaching up, she ran her hand across his chest, tangling her fingers in the thick curly hair, then brushed her hands across his flat nipples. At her touch, he gasped and dipped his head to claim her mouth again. He kissed her passionately and she slid her hands over him feeling his hard body and corded muscles. Excitement exploded in every nerve in her body.

His kisses continued a magical seduction that made it so easy to accept what was happening between them. As he trailed kisses along her throat, he slid his hands down her back, pulling the zipper of her dress down at the same time. He tugged at the material and the dress pooled at her feet. All she wore was a demi bra, a matching thong, and high heels. From where he was standing he could see the tops of her breasts and the barest hint of her nipples. When she tried to turn away, a hand to her waist stopped her.

"I want to look at you." When she gave him a puzzled look, he added, "I want to explore you. Tonight I plan to learn everything that pleases you."

His words caused something to clench deep inside of her. She wanted to know him tonight as she had never known a man before. Then he kissed her again, drawing her attention.

One of his arms circled her waist while he shifted enough to be able to let the other hand cruise across her breasts. Her nipples strained against the fabric. He ran the tip of one fingertip around her aroused flesh and she shook uncontrollably. She clung to him, feeling the thick muscles of his upper arms. His strength was exciting, his touch electrifying.

She nibbled at his neck, kissed his shoulder, and ran her fingers once more over his flat muscled stomach down past his belly button stopping at his belt. She unfastened it, then unzipped his slacks. They fell to his ankles, then she tugged at his boxers, and freed his erection. Her breath caught at the size of him. Taking a deep breath, she reached out and stroked him with the palm of her hand. He was thick and hard and ready for her.

"Tony," she whispered while still stroking him.

"Chante," he ground out her name when her hand closed

tightly around his thick shaft and sensual heat leaped to his ebony eyes.

He trailed warm kisses on her throat as he undid the front clasp of her bra and pushed it away. He lowered his head, seeking her chocolate, pouty nipple and letting his tongue circle then lock gently. At the first tug of teeth and tongue, she tilted her head back, gasped his name and ran her hands along his strong shoulders. She was still stroking him, but was barely aware of what she was doing. All her attention was focused on the need he had created.

"You're beautiful," he whispered hoarsely and her heart thudded. His words made her feel like the most desirable woman on earth.

While he continued to kiss her breasts, he slid his hands down her smooth skin over her stomach to push down her thong and reveal the thick brown curls at the juncture of her thighs.

Chante gasped and released him as he neared her wet center then sighed when the tender play of his fingertips brushed over her most sensitive area.

Antonio knelt in front of her, his fingers feathering along the inside of her thighs while he spread kisses across her stomach. His tongue made burning paths on the inside of first one thigh and then the other. She closed her eyes, letting him caress her, wanting his hands all over her. His mustache was tickling her. Sensations rocked her. His fingers moved to her most intimate places, sliding through her brown curls to caress her.

She bit down on her lower lip when he increased the pressure of his fingers finding the bud that was supremely sensitive. She moved her hips, gasping with pleasure. While he kissed and rubbed her, his other hand glided down. His forefinger slid inside her and she cried out. She hadn't known she could want a man sexually to the extent she wanted him, yet she strained toward him wanting to feel every bit of the pleasure that was building inside of her.

When he stopped, she cried out, wanting more. Opening her eyes, she watched him as he tried to balance on one foot, tossed his shoes aside then discarded the rest of his clothes. The entire time, his gaze never left hers.

He swung her into his arms and crossed the room in a few long strides and lay her on the bed. She was dimly aware of his room and the large king-size bed. Right now everything was dreamlike and so unreal. What was real was warm flesh against warm flesh. Kisses that sent her temperature soaring. Looks that made her tremble.

Placing his knee on the bed, he lowered her gently and leaned over to kiss her breasts again. Beneath his mouth, her nipples pebbled, turned diamond hard as he rolled them around on his tongue. He cupped them almost reverently, massaged them as he claimed her mouth again and took her deeply with his tongue. Desire washed through her. He was driving her mad with his mouth and fingers.

"Chante, I've wanted you so badly," he whispered in her ear, his warm breath tickling her as his tongue followed the curve of her ear. "Let me love you."

He whispered erotic words of longing in her ears. He reminded her that she was a desirable woman. It also reminded her that she'd been without a man for too long. She wanted him with everything she had. Tonight she wanted to have it all.

His hand caressed her leg sliding to her inner thigh and she opened her legs to him. While she caressed him, his fingers trailed high then touching her slick folds, found her center. He aroused the bit of flesh between her legs with his forefinger, taking her to a new height.

"You like this?"

"You're driving me crazy!" she said, all inhibitions gone.

"You ain't seen nothing yet."

His tongue followed where his hand had been. She clutched the sheets and held on tight. He caressed her breasts and stomach. She felt his mouth on her belly, his tongue in her navel and waves of pleasure washed over her. He moved lower, pressing his mouth into the curls at the apex of her legs. She gasped as he parted her slick, womanly flesh and began to taste her there. He was nipping her now, the hairs on his upper lip tickling her.

He was between her legs watching her as he kissed her. She closed her eyes and continued to writhe against his tongue. Sliding his palms beneath her buttocks, he brought her closer to his mouth, holding her still for his thrusts. He caressed her until her body was on fire for him until she began to whimper his name.

"You like this?" he asked, his breath warm against her inner thigh.

She'd never known desire until now. She couldn't answer until the need to climax tore through her. "Tony!"

"I'm right here, baby."

He held her immobile as he laved and tasted, stroked her again and again. She rocked with spasms that only made her want more. She was weak and sobbing with pleasure when it ended. "Please, baby, I need to feel you inside of me!"

Stepping off the bed, he took his billfold from his slacks and removed a foil packet. She put her hands behind her head and watched him rip it open and roll on a condom. Standing there he looked primitive, fierce, a male counterpart to her passion. Just watching his beautiful body made her tingle with anticipation.

As he moved back over to the bed, he lowered into her arms and gave her a passionate kiss, his tongue moving deeply and slowly. With a cry, she wrapped her legs around him and arched beneath him pulling him closer. As the kiss deepened, she wound her arms around his neck.

Antonio finally broke the kiss and rose. "Spread your legs," he commanded.

She obeyed and he locked his fingers at her hips, holding her still as he entered her, withdrew, then slid into her again. She clung to him and thrust her hips. Desire thundered in her as they found a harmonious rhythm. In minutes she could tell her control was slipping away. She thought she would come apart if she didn't climax soon. *This is love-making,* she thought, surprised at the passion and heat burning within.

"Chante!" he chanted as he filled her hard and hot. He kissed her again while all she knew were wild sensations tearing her apart. Against her, Antonio's heart raced, his body pulsing within her.

She burst with release and held on, moving with him as their hearts pounded in unison and welcomed the oncoming tide of pleasure that burst over her. Rapture exploded in her carrying her further into oblivion while he shuddered with satisfaction. While his thrusts slowed they both tried to catch their breath.

As she struggled to breathe, those dark ebony eyes studied her. He held her and she snuggled close. The warmth of his arms gave her comfort while she tried to calm the tremors traveling through her body. Chante's mind churned, shocked by the passion she'd never before experienced. Lost in the cocoon surrounding them there was no need for words, which was a relief because there was no way she could have found the words to express what had just happened between them, except to say, magical.

Chante ran her fingers across his chest. She was certain before she gave in to sleep, she heard Antonio whisper, "I love you."

* * *

Chante awakened and found herself propped against Antonio's muscled chest. His arm was draped across her, holding her close. His leg was thrust between hers. She snuggled against him content to lie beside him for a long as possible, but sunlight brought reality to her consciousness and tears to her eyes.

What in the world was she thinking sleeping with a man she barely knew? Although in her mind, it felt like she had known him forever. Why did it feel so right to be with him? She closed her eyes tightly trying to block out the fantastic memories of last night.

He's your fiancé.

She groaned inward as reality struck. She still had the lies hanging over her head. What was she doing getting involved with this man? A fiancé was the last thing she needed. She enjoyed her life the way it was and didn't need or want a man complicating things for her. The only explanation she had for the last several hours was that she had been blinded by physical attraction and it had overshadowed her common sense.

Gently, she turned in his arms and found herself within inches of his sleeping face. Awed by his handsomeness, she smiled and then tried to etch each detail into memory. Lord, she wanted to stay. She had never felt so complete. But it was impossible. She had vowed to never risk her heart again. Besides, she still hadn't managed to tell him the truth. Gazing at him, she felt torn by emotions. He had given her a night that would be forever with her, but now it was time for the fairy tale to end.

Slipping out from under his arm, she carefully rose from the bed and gathered her things. She disappeared inside the bathroom, and a short time later came out completely dressed.

Chante looked down at Antonio. He was still sleeping peacefully. Gazing at him, she studied his relaxed features, the way his brown skin gleamed, defining his slashing cheekbones, the silkiness of his neatly trimmed mustache. As she studied him, she remembered the intimacy and the passion between them. She still couldn't believe how uninhibited she had been with a man she barely knew. Dorian had been her first and only, and she never considered herself the type of girl to have a weekend fling with a total stranger. But as she nibbled nervously on her bottom lip, she realized that he wasn't a stranger, not really. Not only was he her fiancé but he was the man she had spent the last day and a half with, and in honesty, about whom she had learned so much and felt so connected to.

Okay, then what's the problem? The problem was their relationship was based on a lie.

She held her breath as Antonio shifted slightly with his arm tossed across his face. The sheet was low across his waist. For a moment she allowed her eyes to roam over his beautiful body and remembered how well the two of them connected. Longing tugged at her. She was torn with conflicting emotions, hating that they had gotten involved yet she couldn't completly categorize what happened between them as a mistake. However, she did know that their relationship was based on a lie, and anything with false pretenses was destined for disaster.

A sob filled her throat. She had to get away long enough to sort through her emotions and figure out what was real and what was not. They would have to talk later. There was no avoiding that, but right now she just needed to put as much distance between them as she could.

After one final glance, Chante shoved aside the longing she felt, and strode quietly out the room.

Antonio awoke with memories of their night of passion. He had never felt so complete, his body blended with hers, as if she was the other part of him. He snuggled deeper into the pillow, inhaling Chante's scent.

He loved the way she'd suckled him in all of the right places, and the way she had sounded when she begged for release.

He knew it was a bit premature to be thinking about wedding vows and a honeymoon vacation, but he knew it was going to happen sooner than later. As he had instructed her, they would not discuss their engagement until Sunday. Now that the day had finally arrived, he planned to properly propose.

Antonio stirred and stretched, then reached over only to find the other side of the bed was empty. He sat up and gazed around, then listened to see if she was in the bathroom. His eyes dropped to the floor where his clothes were in a heap and he noticed that the only ones there were his own.

"Chante!" he called, but the only voice he heard was his own. He threw back the covers and stalked into the bathroom. To his disappointment, it was empty.

She was gone.

Met by a wave of disappointment, he rubbed his forehead as he returned to the room. He reached for his boxers and slipped them on then lowered onto the bed. Raking his fingers through his hair, he became more aggravated by every passing minute. Why was she running away from him? Unless he was imagining things, last night she had kissed him with enough fire and desire to brand him for life. He had expected to wake up beside her and make love to her again, then order room service and lie under the covers and talk about their future together.

No way in hell was he letting her slip away, not when she felt so soft and right in his arms. Not when he loved her.

Staring down at the floor, for the next few minutes he allowed his thoughts to consume him as he found himself lost in the memories of their time together. Frustrated, he stroked his mustache and cussed under his breath. He couldn't understand why she had walked out on him. Last night he had finally thought they had reached a comfort level with each other. That she had finally put her fears aside.

He remembered one of her e-mails in particular where she had expressed her fear of falling in love again because the emotion was too painful. He understood, hell he was also afraid but he refused to let his fears stop him from being with the best thing that could have happened to him since Julia. He had grieved long enough and knew it was time to get on with his life which was why he had posted the ad in the first place, looking for someone else that had lost a loved one. Someone who would understand what it felt like to lose a part of yourself. However, with Chante, he believed that he had found the woman to fill the emptiness in his life and make him feel whole again.

From the very beginning he had been intrigued and after meeting her, he was even more attracted to her. Everything from her beautiful smooth skin, to her long legs, and radiant smile. There was no way he could lose her. Not now. He loved her. Couldn't she tell? He was deeply and unequivocally in love with her.

Chante was his and there was no way he was letting her slip away.

Chante ordered room service but after it arrived found that she had very little appetite. She played with her eggs and ate a few pieces of fresh fruit but nothing seemed to settle her stomach. Rising from the table, she moved to stare out the window.

From the exact moment she had left Antonio she felt so alone.

Why did you leave?

Because she felt vulnerable around Antonio. He made her

want to risk her heart again. Her goal was to enjoy him for the time they had together. There was no risk as long as her heart wasn't involved. But after last night, she wasn't so sure she could do that. Her attraction for Antonio was quick and unexpected, so unlike the gradual development from friend to lover she'd had with her ex-husband. Antonio had affected her deeply despite her vow to protect herself from feeling again for any man. She had made a pledge to guard her heart. But it wasn't working anymore. Her heart was now involved. For the first time since her loss, she felt like herself again. Capable of loving another man.

Chante let her breath out slowly. Why did she react to him so quickly? After years of struggling to be strong and independent, scheduling her every move, how could she trust and want a man so much who she had known less than forty-eight hours? Was she so desperate for a man that she accepted him so easily? No, that wasn't the case. There was a tangible bond between her and him that was so apparent it was startling. He had sensed it from the beginning and now she felt it, too. And that scared her.

For the longest time, she stared out at buildings across the street as tears fell from her eyes. She cried for that trusting piece of her that Dorian took away from her. She cried for Devon who had a father who never took an interest in getting to know him. Despite everything Dorian had done to her, she would have never denied him his right to be a father to his son.

Damn you, Dorian!

For the next few minutes she allowed her mind to travel back to one of the most painful times of her life.

They had just returned from seeing a movie, when Dorian started drinking and accusing her of flirting with the man behind the concession. Chante had learned that the best thing to do when he was in a jealous rage was to ignore him, however, the more he drank the worse the accusations became.

She finally lost her patience and decided for once to stand up to him. Big mistake. Dorian punched her square in the jaw and even after she hit the floor he kept sending blows to her face. At some point, she wasn't sure when since she had long since blacked out, he must have panicked and driven her to the hospital. She had woken the next morning with her husband by her side, teary eyed and remorseful, swearing he would never touch her again. As always, she felt sorry for him and was seconds away to accepting his forgiveness when the doctor came in to tell her how lucky she was that her husband had walked in on her assailant when he had. Discovering Dorian had lied to cover his alcoholic rage, left her cold and bitter. And when the physician revealed she was pregnant, there was nothing else to consider, except herself and her unborn child. She asked the doctor to call the police and have her husband removed from her room, then called her family.

Only hours after being released from the hospital, she had gotten a restraining order and had him banned from their apartment. Dorian had called numerous times begging for her to take him back and even tried once to come to her job. However, security had been alerted and he was escorted off of the premises. From that day on, she never saw or heard from him again.

By the time Devon was born, her heart had softened. Chante dropped all the charges, as well as the restraining order against him. She had called Dorian's mother, who had never cared for her daughter-in-law, and left a message about the birth of his son. To her disappointment, he never came to the hospital to see her, he never called and asked about the baby, instead, Dorian seemed to have vanished from the face of the earth. It took her three years and a private investigator before she tracked him down living in Las Vegas. When she had the divorce papers served at his job, he signed them without contest, giving her sole custody of their son. The impression she had gotten was that as far as he was concerned, if he couldn't have his wife then he didn't want his son either. It bothered her that he didn't want any part of Devon's life although with his temper, she believed it was probably for the best. However, now that Devon was older, her heart ached for him because he'd asked her numerous times why he didn't have a daddy like his friends. She had tried to explain, although at his age, she knew he didn't really understand. Pops tried to fill the void, as well as her brothers, Dame and Martin, but she knew it wasn't the same. Devon wanted a father.

She moved and took a seat on the side of the bed, reached for a tissue and blew her nose. Maybe Pops was right. It was time to let go and allow herself to love again. But how could she? She was scared. One, because she didn't know if she could find it in her heart to trust another man; two, she didn't think she could possibly survive that kind of hurt again; and three, if she did give their relationship a chance it would first mean coming clean and explaining everything. What worried her most was Antonio's reaction to the truth.

Wrapping her arms around her body, she closed her eyes and swayed side to side. If she had told him the truth from the beginning then maybe they would have had a good laugh together. But instead she had allowed the lie to continue and even went as far as adding more fuel to the fire. And to make matters worse she had slept with him while knowing good and well she had betrayed him. She wasn't sure he would forgive her. And she couldn't blame him. If the shoe was on the other foot she wouldn't have forgiven him either.

Hearing a faint knock at the door, she brushed the tears away from her eyes and moved to answer it. She opened it, expecting to see Antonio standing outside her door. Instead, it was a bell boy delivering a bouquet of spring flowers.

"Ooh! They're beautiful," she said as she took the vase

from his proffered hand. "Hold on a minute and let me get my purse."

The young man shook his head and grinned. "No need, it's already been taking care of." From the look on his face she could tell he'd been given a generous tip.

Chante nodded. "Okay, well then, thank you." She closed the door then moved over to the couch and lowered the vase onto the coffee table. Inhaling deeply, she took a seat then removed a purple envelope and retrieved the card. It was from Antonio.

To the most beautiful mother on the planet, Happy Mother's Day.

Her eyes fluttered close as a smile touched her lips. Her pulse raced in response to the compassionate gift. Antonio was sweet and had proven to be a romantic. How else would he have known such a thoughtful gesture would mean so much to her?

Lowering the card to the table, she leaned back on the couch and took a deep breath as the tears slid down her cheeks. There was no way she could ignore him. There was no way she could just pack up, and check out of the hotel without seeing him again. Warmth spread through her chest as she remembered him telling her he loved her only seconds before she had fallen asleep. As much as she tried to pretend she hadn't heard his confession, she had. And the feeling of warmth that cocooned her, had left her speechless.

She shook her head. Avoiding him was not even an option. Despite her protests and denial of her feelings, something was happening to her.

There were too many "what ifs." What if turning her back on him turned out to be the worst mistake of her life? What if fate meant for them to meet? How often in one lifetime could a person expect to find the perfect mate? And here she was turning her back on a fabulous man.

In the next hour, she convinced herself that she needed to take a chance and follow her heart no matter how scary things may seem. All she had to do was make things right between them. All she had to do was tell him the truth and then it would be up to him as to which direction their relationship headed.

She wanted the handsome doctor with all her soul. If she didn't follow her heart, she might be walking away from her last chance at happiness.

She dashed into the bathroom, showered and dressed. Suddenly, she needed to see Antonio again. He made her feel alive, she thought with a giggle. He made her feel good. God had given her a second chance at love and she was going for it.

She ignored the warning bells ringing in her head, blocked out her vow of never falling in love again, and just gave in to the magic which engulfed her when she was with Antonio. "Follow your heart," a voice whispered. "Give everything you got." And God help her, she planned to do just that.

Chapter Nine

Antonio wondered if Chante had received the flowers yet. Shortly after ordering breakfast, he had called down to the flower shop, and ordered them. Glancing down at his watch, he determined it had been two hours since the order. Chante should have received the bouquet by now. As anxious as he was to climb up two flights of stairs and find out for himself, his pride wouldn't let him. He wasn't going to call her. The ball was now in her court. She had to make the next move. Chante was the one having doubts, not he. He was secure with his feelings. Now he just needed her to realize she felt the same. He needed her to accept that he was the exact same man she had been corresponding to via e-mail over the last several months, the same man whose proposal she had accepted. He completely understood that things were moving fast between them. That was why he had agreed to back off a little and give her the opportunity to get used to the idea. He just hoped that after last night, he hadn't scared her off.

There was a knock at the door. It took everything he had not to run to answer it. He paused long enough to take a deep breath, then opened it to find Chante standing in the hall.

"Hi," she greeted with a nervous smile.

"Hi, yourself."

Her eyes caressed him. "Thank you for the flowers."

His stomach fluttered nervously. "You're welcome."

There was a prolonged silence before she asked, "May I come in?"

Without answering, Antonio stepped aside and allowed her to enter his suite. As soon as he shut the door, he turned around and faced her. They were standing only inches apart. He folded his arms across his chest and waited as she surveyed his bare feet, faded jeans that rode low on his slim hips, and his black T-shirt.

There was a long moment of silence before Chante finally cleared her throat and said, "I didn't mean to run off this morning. I just . . . I mean . . . I needed some time to myself."

Their eyes met and it took everything he had not to take her in his arms and carry her back to bed and kiss all her fears away. "I'm glad you decided to come back." A slow smile parted his lips.

"Me, too." Tears welled in her eyes and began to slip down her cheeks. She reached out and touched him, then went up on her toes and kissed him softly on the lips.

No longer able to resist, Antonio wrapped his arms tightly around her, pressing her into his chest. He inhaled her scent, felt the brush of her hair against his cheek. Her breasts pillowed against him. He couldn't help thinking about their weight and the softness, the way they filled his hands. He remembered how good it had felt last night to be inside her.

"I'm scared," she replied in a shaky tone against his shoulder.

Antonio lowered his voice, and said in a rough whisper against her ear, "You have nothing to be afraid of as long as you have me in your life."

There was a pregnant silence before Chante spoke again. "I need time. I'm so afraid of loving again."

Antonio cupped her chin so that she had to look up as he stared down into her eyes. "Baby, you can take all the time you need. Just promise you'll never run away from me again."

"I promise," she whispered close to his lips.

Antonio took her mouth with urgency that didn't even begin to alleviate his frustration. He held her close and rejoiced when she participated in the kiss with the same intensity. When she moaned and leaned in even closer, he thrust his tongue between her parted lips and met hers with sensual strokes.

Without breaking the kiss, he led her into the other room and to the bed. Within a matter of minutes they had freed each other of their clothes. Chante removed the foil packet from his hands and put the condom on him, then they climbed beneath the cool sheets. Antonio moved between her legs, sliding an arm beneath her to hold her while he pushed inside her. He moved slowly at first, thrusting and withdrawing. Within minutes, she thrashed beneath him, urging him to move harder until she lost control. Shortly after, light exploded beneath his eyelids, while release sent shudders coursing through his body. Breathing heavily, he rained light kisses across her forehead until they both drifted off to sleep.

Chante woke up around ten-thirty and stretched under the warmth of the blanket, inhaling his scent. The spot on the bed beside her was empty, and she listened to the sound of the shower. Lying there she tried to prepare herself for how to react after the passionate morning she had spent coming apart in Antonio's arms. She stretched, her whole body aching from Antonio's possession. Her breasts were sensitive, her body aware that it had been shared intimately with a man. The intensity was so overwhelming she had no idea it could be like that between two people.

She shivered and fought for a grasp on the morning. Things between them were moving so fast. But every time he kissed her she became helpless putty in his hands with no will to fight.

She was falling in love.

Curling into a ball, she pondered the possibility of falling in love with a man that fast. She had read dozens of romance novels, many written by authors she represented, and even though the stories left her breathless, she knew it was only fiction—or was it? She just wasn't sure anymore.

She drew the sheet against her naked body as Antonio stepped out of the bathroom wrapped in a towel. His burning gaze told her that he had no regrets.

"Good morning, sleepyhead," he said in a soft, soothing tone.

"Good morning," she returned.

He lowered his head and rained feathery kisses from her forehead to her mouth where he lingered thoroughly before stepping away. "Why don't you take a nice hot bath while I order room service?" he suggested.

"Isn't check-out at noon?" she queried.

"Since my plane doesn't leave until four, I've requested a late check-out for the both of us."

"But—"

He kissed her once more. "No buts. I've already taken care of everything."

She forgot what she was going to say when she saw that Antonio had dropped his towel. She rolled to her side and rested her head in her hand. He reached for a pair of gray boxers and drew them over his firm hips. Chante watched and admired how beautiful he was with hard muscles sliding beneath dark, sleek skin. Watching him, she wanted him again. Since last night they had made love three times and yet that still wasn't enough. What in the world was happening to her?

You're falling for him, that's what.

She found Antonio staring at her as well. She was going to have to get it together. Relaxing in a tub of hot water was too good an offer to ignore especially since they had more time to spend together. "A bath sounds like a good idea." Suddenly putting a little space between them sounded like a good idea, before she invited him back to bed.

She threw back the covers then sprung from the bed and walked naked into the bathroom and closed the door. She leaned against it and shook her head. She was going to have to find a way to get herself together long enough for the two of them to have a long talk.

Glancing into the vanity mirror, she saw another woman, one tousled and thoroughly loved. Her heart tumbled. There was no turning back at this point. Despite her mixed emotions, ending things between them was the furthest thing from her mind. She liked Antonio. She liked him so much she knew she was falling in love. She wanted to give their relationship a chance.

She moved over and tried to pull herself together while she poured herself a tub of hot water. She lowered the toilet lid and took several deep breaths. Somehow, some way, she needed to tell him the truth before check-out.

Hearing the door open, she glanced up as Antonio stepped in. He draped a robe over the sink then moved and dropped down on his knees in front of her. She watched his eyes darken possessively as her hands came up to cover his.

"Don't tell me you're still having second thoughts?" he asked as his thumb caressed the back of her hand.

She dropped her eyelids and blushed. "No . . . although, I never knew it could be like that."

"It's only the beginning." He kissed her forehead then turned and tested the temperature of the water the way she would for Devon. Antonio reached for a complimentary bottle of vanilla-scented bubble bath and poured a capful of the liquid into the flow of water. When he finally turned around, Chante was slipping into a robe, trying to adjust to this new feeling. A cowardly part of her still wanted to retreat but the look in Antonio's eyes said he sensed it and wasn't going to make that easy.

While the water ran, he sat on the edge of the tub and she leaned against the vanity. Steam and the sound of running water filled the room, and Antonio gazed up at her, stirring the bathwater with his hand.

Her body seemed to have a mind of its own as she felt a throb down low, a hunger within. She remembered his big hands running gently over her nude body. Already she was ready for him to take her again.

A woman who had planned and controlled every day of her life had suddenly decided to live for the moment, and what a wonderful moment it had been. She couldn't tear her eyes away from his strong gaze. She felt herself heating, waiting and aching for him. The look was intense—both physical and emotional.

Antonio rose and moved toward her. He gazed possessively down at her robed body. When he stopped in front of her, he took her hand and raised it smoothly to his lips.

"I think your bath is ready."

She swallowed. "Yeah, I guess it is."

His thumb cruised slowly across her sensitized lower lip. "Want me to join you?"

Her expression was guarded. "That might not be a good idea."

He traced her hair, his fingertip following a strand over her ear. "Why not?"

"Because I can't think straight when you are around."

"Guess what? Neither can I." His eyes locked with hers. "You're in my blood. You're in my heart. You're a part of me now." He grabbed her and pulled her close against him so that she could feel the affect she had on his libido. "That's evidence of what you do to me." He kissed her soundly on the lips then left the room.

Oh, brother, Chante thought as she disrobed and gingerly lowered her body into the hot, soothing water. *That brotha is definitely playing for keeps.*

Chante leaned back against the tub and tried to think of a way to tell Antonio about the deception. No way was easy and even now that she had gotten to know him, it didn't in any way make the task any easier. In fact, it had made things harder because now she found that she cared enough about him that if he decided he wanted nothing further to do with her, although she'd understand, she would be genuinely hurt.

Lathering her body, Chante's thoughts were filled with Antonio and their future together. And she so badly wanted a future with him. The only thing standing in the way was the truth, and her fear of losing her heart.

Chante had just adjusted to her privacy and her thoughts when Antonio strolled in again carrying two cups of coffee. He winked as she sank deep into the mound of bubbles.

"Thank you," she said as she took a cup from his proffered hand. The dark, rich brew smelled wonderful.

He lowered onto the toilet with a boyish grin. "You're gonna have to sit up or get burned."

She furrowed her brow and ignoring his comment took a cautious sip. "Delicious," she said with a grin of her own.

He shook his head. "You're hiding from me. Tell me why you're ashamed of your body?"

Her eyes widened. "I'm not ashamed."

"Then why are you blushing?" he asked softly, watching her reaction.

"I-I'm not blushing" she said quietly, avoiding his eyes as she sipped her coffee.

With his free hand, he reached past the bubbles and cupped one of her heavy breasts and lifted it out of the water. She looked at him, but self-consciously her gaze lowered to the bubbles below. "Okay, maybe I am blushing."

Carefully, Antonio lowered his cup to the tiled floor then kneeled down in front of the tub and cupped the other breast. "Why? You're beautiful." He leaned forward and captured a nipple around his tongue and suckled it. She gasped on contact. Sensual heat leaped through her chest. When he finally pulled back, he murmured, "There is nothing to hide." Antonio's voice was deep and uneven and when she forced herself to look at him, sexual hunger leaped to life, quivering on the steamy layers in the room. He brushed his lips with hers, enough to curl her toes, and pulled away. His eyes lowered again to her breasts, surrounded by bubbles. "If I don't leave now, I'll be in that tub with you."

"There isn't enough room."

"You should see your face." Antonio chuckled as he reached for his mug and rose from the floor. "Breakfast will be arriving shortly." He then turned and closed the door behind him.

Chante sunk lower into the tub. Oh, brother, she was definitely in way over her head. She was falling in love with him, or already had. Or maybe she was just infatuated. Common sense told her it was too soon, yet at that moment she didn't care. And that's what scared her the most.

Antonio brushed his lips against her forehead. "Hey, sleepyhead."

She couldn't believe she had dozed off, and wasn't sure how long she would have stayed inside that tub if Antonio hadn't come in looking for her. "Is breakfast here?"

He winked at her. "Yep."

She shifted slightly beneath the lukewarm water, the bubbles were long gone. "All right," she managed around a yawn. "I'll be out in a second."

"Now."

Antonio must have read the resistance to his order in the stiffness of her body because before she could protest, he leaned down slightly, scooped her out of the water, and swept her up in his arms. Afraid she was going to slip onto the floor, Chante looped her arms around his neck.

"Antonio, I can walk," she insisted.

He pulled back enough to see her face. "I know you can but I prefer to carry you. Now hush up."

Chuckling, she relaxed against his bare chest and allowed him to carry her into the room and gently lay her across the bed. Chante pulled the sheets against her cold chest and pulled up comfortably against the pillows as Antonio pushed a cart in front of her.

The wonderful smell hit her nose. "What have we here?" she sang merrily.

He lifted the cover on the first plate and her stomach growled at the sight of an omelet stuffed with mushrooms, green peppers and tomatoes, and smothered in cheese. There was also a side of thick sugar-cured bacon and hash browns.

"Yum." She grabbed the plate and dug in hungrily.

Antonio reached for a similar plate and sat on the bed beside her. "You forgot a plate," he said, tilting his head toward the cart.

"What's on it?" she asked between bites.

"Why don't you look? I'm sure you won't be disappointed."

She lowered her fork to her plate then reached across and removed the lid. Underneath was a Belgium waffle covered in strawberries, whipped cream, and—

Chante's mouth dropped opened before she snapped it shut. On top of a soft pillow of cream was a startling platinum three-carat diamond ring. "Is that what I think it is?"

Her shocked expression apparently pleased him because Antonio was grinning. With a shaky hand, she reached for the ring and held it between her fingers.

"Yes, it's an engagement ring. If my memory serves me right, we had agreed that we would wait to discuss our engagement on Sunday."

She shook her head slightly. "I know, but—"

He must have sensed he hesitation because he interrupted with, "Listen, don't say anything just yet."

Before she could protest he had slipped the ring onto her third finger. Glancing down at the sparkling diamond, she didn't know what to say or even how to say it. She had to find the courage to share with him how she felt, and also be able to face the possibility of being rejected after she told him the truth. "I need a little more time."

Antonio moved his plate away. "Come here," he whispered.

She leaned forward which was all the encouragement he needed. He slid her onto his lap then cupped her chin and turned her face toward him. "I don't need any more time. I knew from the moment I read your first e-mail that you were the one for me. But if you need more time to adjust to this entire idea that's okay." He paused long enough to brush a kiss to her lips.

"Nevertheless, I still want you to wear my ring," he whispered, and caught her bottom lip between his teeth. "It doesn't have to be official. You don't have to make a decision about our engagement yet. Instead, consider it a promise ring. Just wear it and the next time I see you, you can give me your answer." Antonio knew what he was challenging Chante to do, but his stubborn pride wouldn't have it any other way. He wanted her in his life and he wasn't going to be happy until he had her.

Chante leaned a fraction away and studied him. He gazed at her and their eyes met and held. He could see his reflection in their depths. After a long pause, she finally answered, "Okay." She then leaned forward and pressed their lips together. When she opened her mouth, his tongue instantly slipped inside. The slight suction of her mouth caused his body to harden instantly. He ran his hand along the smooth curve of her leg and trailed his fingertip upward across her lower belly and down her other thigh. He enjoyed the slow hiss of her indrawn breath, a sign that she reacted instantly to him.

"Can breakfast wait?" he murmured against her cheek.

"That depends on what you have in mind," she returned as she leaned in for a long and intimate kiss.

"I can show you better than I can tell you," he teased against her lips. Antonio then leaned her back against the cool sateen sheets and covered her with his aroused body.

Chapter Ten

Chante decelerated, maneuvering her car off the highway. As she reached the stop sign, a smile curled her painted lips.

After Antonio had slipped the ring on her finger, they spent the next couple of hours eating too much and falling into each other's arms for the wildest most satisfying lovemaking imaginable. He had a way of pushing her to the surface, leaving her exhausted, clinging and smiling against his damp chest. She had never felt so complete. It was almost like a dream for Chante to feel again. She didn't want anyone or anything to take this moment away from her.

Antonio made her want things she'd promised herself that she would never risk again. Love. Commitment. When he held her, she allowed herself to let go and trusted in his big strong arms and the way she felt. With him she risked losing her heart again.

Which is why you need to tell him the truth.

Chante scowled inwardly. She had planned to tell him once they had arrived at the airport. She figured with all of the people around, away from the tempting bed, she could finally get a word or two in. However, taking Antonio to the airport had turned into a passionate experience. They stood kissing in the terminal, creating a storm of need within her. She trembled with each final kiss, wanting him with all she had, wanting another passionate night. And when they finally pulled apart, he had less than twenty minutes to get through security in time to catch his plane.

As she watched him move through security, her mind raced over her weekend spent with a man with a heart of gold. A man who had won her over since the moment they first met.

Then, just as he was about to turn the corner, Chante caught Antonio's gaze, and as if he had known what she was thinking, he raised his hand in a wave and mouthed, "I love you." He then moved out of sight and headed toward his gate.

Long after he was gone, she stood, afraid that once she turned her back and climbed in her car, she would discover it had all just been a wonderful dream. But it wasn't a dream, she reminded herself as she glanced down at the brilliant diamond on her finger. Antonio Marks was for real.

As she pulled into her subdivision, she shivered, remembering how he watched her bathe . . . how those dark ebony eyes had stroked her body beneath the sudsy water. She was on dangerous ground and knew it. She also knew she still had yet to tell him the truth. It wasn't that she hadn't tried. Antonio had a way of straying her focus and then when she was ready to tell him, the time just seemed to be all wrong.

That's just an excuse and you know it.

Okay, maybe she wasn't being completely honest. If they had any chance of having a future together, she needed to find a way to tell him the truth.

Glancing down at her finger again, Chante exhaled. The ring was beautiful and much too expensive to be considered a promise ring. As soon as she got home, she was putting it safely away in her jewelry box. For some reason that she was not ready to explore, the thought of taking it off saddened her.

Chante turned onto Eastview Drive, a wide, tree-lined street, and gasped. Her parents, Chenoa, and Martin's cars were lining her driveway. Dame's motorcycle was parked in front of her house. What was going on? she thought, as she pulled in behind her father's Lincoln Towne Car and killed the engine.

"Oh, no! Pops!" Panic took over as she rushed out of the car and hurried up the driveway. She quickly prayed that he hadn't had another stroke.

She pushed through the door. "Mama! Daddy! Where is everyone?" Her eyes darted into the living room.

"We're in the family room!"

Quickly, she followed her mother's voice down the hall. "What's going on? Is Pops . . ." her voice trailed off as she spotted six pairs of eyes smiling at her from across the room. Pops was sitting in his favorite recliner with a newspaper in his hand. Her shoulders sagged with relief. Thank God, he was okay. So then why was her family at her house?

She glanced from one to another. "What's going on?"

Betty Campbell, who was sitting on the couch next to Chenoa, clasped her hands together and said with glee, "We heard the news."

Chante stepped farther into the room and gave her mother a puzzled look. "What news?"

"Oh, my God! She's wearing an engagement ring."

Before she had a chance to comprehend what her sister had just said, Chenoa rushed over to her and grabbed her hand. "Wow! Mama, look at the size of that sucker." The family quickly crowded around to take a closer look.

Dame leaned forward and whistled. "Well at least we know the brotha ain't cheap."

Chenoa dropped a hand to her protruding waist and met her stare head on. "So when were you planning to tell us about your fiancé?"

Chante's jaw dropped. "M-my fiancé?" Had she heard her right? Her lips parted to speak, but nothing came out.

"Yes, dear, the man you ran off to spend the weekend with?"

She glanced at her mother. Someone had told them about Antonio. "How do you know about that?"

"My grandson told me all about it. Naturally I rushed over here to find out for myself." She frowned. "Shame on you for keeping something so important from us."

Mouth gaping, she glanced over at Devon's smiling face as he sat on her couch and groaned inwardly. She was in way over her head. Everyone started talking at once, and she wasn't exactly sure what was being said. She loved her family, truly she did, but sometimes they were a little smothering. A long moment passed before Chante found the mental resources to join back in the conversation.

"So how was your weekend?" her sister asked, eyes sparkling with curiosity.

"We—"

"When is the wedding?" Chenoa interrupted.

"I—"

"What's he do for a living?"

"Quit getting all in her business!" Dame barked.

Chenoa punched her brother in the forearm. "She's my sister. I can ask if I want."

"The two of you stop bickering like a couple of children. You're ruining my daughter's moment," Mrs. Campbell scolded.

Chante's head was starting to spin. The entire incident had spiraled completely out of her control. She took a step back and decided now was as good a time as any to tell her family the truth. However, before she could open her mouth, her older brother Martin stepped out of the kitchen, holding an open bottle of chilled imported champagne. He poured two fingers of the amber liquid into a half dozen fluted glasses and handed one to her.

"Congratulations, Chante."

"I, uh . . . you know I don't drink champagne," she said, trying to say something, anything.

His dimple deepened. "I think this is one time you can make an exception."

"Thanks, Marty." She managed a strained smile.

He pressed his lips to her cheek. "I'm happy for you, sis."

Carlos Campbell draped an arm around his daughter's waist then cleared his throat and raised his glass in a toast. "To you, Chante, for being a survivor."

A chorus of voices agreed as they gently tapped their glasses together.

Tears pushed to the surface as Chante remembered the pain and suffering she had endured for years at the hands of an alcoholic. In time she had come to realize, her pain had also been felt by her family as well. Now they were happy because they all believed that she had finally moved on and was getting ready to spend her life with another man. How in the world was she going to be able to tell them the truth?

She had barely taken a sip before Chenoa, the only one besides Devon not holding a glass, took her hand and led her into the kitchen. As soon as they were alone, the interrogation began.

"Okay, sis, what's the deal? Last we talked you weren't thinking about a man. Now I find out that you've been seeing someone on the DL. What's up with that?" The look she gave was a combination of surprise and disappointment. "I thought we were closer than that."

Chante stared over at her little sister, leaning against the counter with her arms crossed. She looked genuinely hurt. With a sigh, she tilted her glass and gulped down its contents. She rarely ever drank. However, she did manage to have a glass of wine from time to time for special occasions. This would definitely be considered a special occasion.

She waited until Chenoa had retrieved a bottle of water from the refrigerator and took a seat at the kitchen table before speaking.

"Noa, before you get all bent out of shape things aren't quite like they seem." She lowered her empty glass to the counter.

Chenoa cocked her head at an angle. "What do you mean?"

Chante glanced over her shoulder into the other room to make sure no one was listening. Apparently, Pops had popped in a home video he had put together of his and Mildred's trip to Cancun last month. She moved and took the seat across from Chenoa and whispered, "I'm not really engaged."

Chenoa looked completely confused. "What do you mean by, *not really*?"

"I mean . . ." her voice trailed off because she didn't know what she meant. She was sporting a large diamond that signified her engagement to a wonderful man, yet it was all a lie. He had proposed to Pops, not her. Shaking her head, she tried to free her brain of the confusion. "What I mean is, Pops thought since he had found Mildred on an on-line singles Web site that I could be just as lucky, so he set up a personal ad for me."

Chenoa choked on her water, spraying the liquid onto her sister's neck and face.

"Hey!" Chante said with a start as she tried to mop her face with her blouse.

Chenoa lowered the bottle to the table and rose. "My bad. You caught me off guard." She paused long enough to grab each of them a paper towel then returned to her seat. "Okay, you need to explain this to me."

Chante nodded then took the next few minutes to explain everything that had happened as well as the reason why she was wearing the expensive diamond. As soon as she was done, Chenoa threw her head back and erupted with boisterous laughter.

Chante's mouth tightened slightly. "It's not funny."

"Yes, it is," she countered smoothly. "You got played."

"I wouldn't say that."

Chenoa shook her head in amusement. "Well at least there

is a bright side to this story. You're now engaged to a fine doctor. That's every woman's dream."

"Not my dream." She rose from the table. They both knew she had dreamed of spending the rest of her life with Dorian.

Chenoa swung around on her chair. "Actually this is better than a dream."

A slight frown marred Chante's smooth forehead. "It's not real," she said, moving to lean against the counter.

Her sister's penetrating eyes crinkled as she smiled. "Why isn't it? You just told me how wonderful he is."

He was wonderful, and she wanted him. There was no denying that. But did she want more? And what was more? She didn't have a clue. Maybe more weekends together. Maybe putting the brakes on things and starting over the right way. But being his wife, it was just too soon for that. She had too many trust issues to be ready to spend the rest of her life with him. "Antonio is wonderful, and I like him so much, but our relationship is built on a lie." Feeling defensive, she crossed her arms in front of her. "Besides, I'm not engaged, I'm promised to him."

Chenoa gave a dismissive wave. "Promised, engaged, it's all the same. Apparently he would have called it anything just to get you to wear his ring."

That was probably true. When she tried to tell him she wasn't ready to get married, he still had insisted that she wear the ring. The entire situation was getting harder by the second.

Leaning forward with her hands circling the bottle, Chenoa smiled. "Did you give him some?"

She started to lie, but realized Chenoa would see right through her, as she always did. "Yeah."

"And?"

Was she asking what she thought she was asking? "And what?" she teased, enjoying the look of pure outrage that raced across her face.

"Sis, don't play. How was the man in bed?"

Chante blushed then giggled. "*Wonderful*," she sang. "It was something like I've read about in one of those romance novels." She moved and gave her sister a high five then returned to her seat.

Chenoa's eyes sparkled. "He-e-ey, then I guess the man is worth keeping."

Chante leaned over and rested her elbows on the table. "Sex complicates things."

"Does it have to?" Chenoa questioned.

Vertical lines appeared between her eyes. "It already has. Noa, I experienced something with this man that I've only read about. Now I'm feeling things that I'd never expected to feel again." Making love to him had brought about the realization that something had been missing from her life. And that something happened to be Antonio. He was perfect. Almost too perfect, if that was possible, and that's what scared her. At one time, she had thought Dorian perfect.

"Don't fight it. Enjoy it. And let what's supposed to happen, happen."

She wished it was that easy. Tired of being the topic of discussion, Chante decided to turn the tables. "You've got a lot of nerve. I remember how even after you had slept with Zearl you were still trying to deny your feelings."

Chenoa couldn't keep from blushing. "True. But in the end everything worked out. I married my soul mate and now we're getting ready to have a child created by love. I couldn't be happier." She rubbed her stomach. "Now it's your turn to find happiness again."

Guilt clamped down on her heart. "Maybe, maybe not. Our relationship is nothing but a lie that I can't continue."

"Don't you think it's a little late for that," Chenoa asked. "Especially since now you are technically engaged to this man."

With an elbow on the table, Chante rested her chin in her hand. "I'm *promised*, and so torn between my feelings."

There was a long moment of silence before Chenoa finally asked, "So what are you going to do?"

She exhaled deeply. "I don't know. How do I know it's right? I mean, I've only known this man one weekend yet I feel things for him that I've never imagined possible."

"I'll admit it takes longer than a weekend to really get to know someone, but I don't think it takes that long to know if something is right."

Chante gave her sister an impatient look. "How do I know if I've gotten it right this time?"

Chenoa's smile was gentle. "Only time will tell that, but it sounds to me like the relationship is definitely worth exploring."

"I don't know. This is like some kind of soap opera." Her soft sigh floated across the kitchen as she continued, "Antonio thinks I'm a widow. Pops told him Dorian was dead."

Chenoa snorted rudely. "He *is* dead, as far as everyone in this family is concerned."

Chante frowned at her words. "But it doesn't make it right."

Her sister gave her a long serious look. "Does he love you?"

"He told me he does."

Chenoa was silent before she asked the question Chante was dreading, "Do you love him?"

Oh, goodness, how could she answer a question that she had trouble understanding? To her relief, her father stepped into the kitchen, carrying a tray of empty champagne glasses. She was grateful because love was a topic she was not ready to discuss.

Swinging around on her seat, Chante met her father's wide smile. His dark eyes shone with pride. At sixty, Carlos Campbell was a handsome man with large, walnut colored eyes, a broad nose and curly hair with only a sprinkle of gray. He was a few inches shorter than Dame yet managed the same bulky build. He still ran a mile every morning and played tennis with other retired firefighters on Wednesdays.

"Daddy, you can just leave those there on the counter."

He lowered the tray beside the sink. As he passed he placed a dark, wrinkled hand on her shoulder, leaning down to kiss her lightly on the cheek. "You made an old man mighty proud this evening. I'm so happy for you."

She simply nodded and smiled. With that he turned on his heels and rejoined the others. Chante and Chenoa stared at each other for several silent seconds.

Her sister rested her hands on top of her inflated belly. "So what are you gonna do? Dad is expecting to walk you down the aisle."

Chante nodded her head knowingly. She couldn't forget the look on her father's face when she and Dorian had run off to Las Vegas and eloped. He had been hurt and disappointed that he hadn't been given the opportunity to give his daughter away.

Her sigh came out rough, frustrated. "I need to tell them the truth."

Chenoa frantically shook her head. "You can't do that! Didn't you see how happy you made Daddy? You know he still blames himself for not protecting you from Dorian's physical abuse. We all blame ourselves."

She grimaced at the reminder. When she had shared with her family the details of her abusive marriage, her dad had blamed himself for not protecting his little girl. She had told him countless times that there wasn't anything any of them could have done differently because she'd made sure that none of them found out, yet he still had felt responsible.

She was trapped in a lie. Realization rocked her. "So what am I supposed to do, go through with this?"

Chenoa shrugged. "Why not? At least for now you can plan a long engagement and get to know the guy a little better."

Chante noticed the smirk on her sister's face and frowned. "This isn't funny. This is quite serious."

"Oh, I agree," Chenoa said with a slight chuckle. "Your engagement to a total stranger is quite serious. He could be a fake."

"Antonio is not a fake," she stated in Antonio's defense. "He is the most caring and compassionate man I've met in a long time. He doesn't deserve to be deceived."

Chenoa rubbed her stomach. "It sounds like you care about this man." She then released a long peal of laughter.

Chante sighed. She should have known that Detective Chenoa Sinclair was setting her up so that she could discover the extent of her feelings.

"I do," she finally admitted.

Chenoa quickly sobered. "Then go for it. Like you used to tell me, life is too short for games."

"I just don't know. Our relationship is built on a lie that I don't know how to fix. I get a feeling that the truth is gonna come crashing down on my head."

Her sister brought her water bottle to her lips and took another swallow then said, "Well, it seems to me you have two choices, either tell Daddy the truth or open up your heart to Antonio and take a chance."

Neither choice was going to be easy. "I could just strangle Pops for getting me into this mess," she said with a pout of frustration.

"You can't blame the old guy for trying," Chenoa chuckled. "He has always been unpredictable."

Despite herself, she found herself laughing along with her. "That's for sure."

The phone rang and before she could rise from the chair someone in the other room answered it.

Chenoa continued. "All I ask is that you tread lightly. As much as I want to see you happy, I don't want to see you hurt again."

She read the compassion in her sister's eyes. "Neither do I."

Her mother strolled into the kitchen with the cordless

phone on her ear. Chante's eyes grew large as she listened to the tail end of the conversation.

". . . we can't wait to meet you, and again, congratulations."

Congratulations! Oh, no. "Mom, who are you talking to?"

Betty handed her the phone. "Antonio."

Her heart fluttered as she put the receiver to her ear. The two had been discussing her engagement.

Out of the corner of her eyes, she saw her mother and Chenoa eyeing her with interest. She took a deep breath and said, "Hello?"

"Hey beautiful," Antonio said in a velvety tone that made her heart melt. "My plane stopped in Memphis. Thought I'd call and make sure you made it home safely."

She swallowed to relieve her constricted throat. "I made it in one piece."

"Good." His words sounded sincere. "I just had a brief conversation with your mother. She invited me to your sister's housewarming party."

"She did what?" Chante squeaked. Stunned was an understatement. She glanced over at her mother and Chenoa who were both nodding their heads and mouthing "yes." With a roll of her eyes, she turned so her back was to them.

"I'll be glad to come. That's if you're ready for me to meet your family."

Her heart thumped with anticipation. She couldn't believe this was happening. She was inviting a man home to meet her family. "Sure, I'd love to have you."

"Cool. I'll make sure to clear my schedule and make a three day weekend of it," he said. The pleasure in his voice was quite apparent.

"Okay." There was a moment of silence. However, she was sure he could tell she was also smiling.

"Your mother mentioned the ring. Is there something going on I should know about?"

Chante sighed. "I'll have to tell you later. Let's just say, everyone saw it."

"Oh, man. Sorry about that."

She gave a strangled laugh. "It's not your fault. Let's talk later when my family is gone."

"Okay." There was a short pause. "I miss you already."

A slight tremor swept through her. "I miss you too," she confessed.

"I'll call you when I get in."

"All right." She hung up to find her mother and sister both smiling up from the table. "What?"

Mrs. Campbell clapped her hands together, merrily. "I think we have a wedding to plan."

Chenoa's eyes danced with amusement. "Count me in."

Chante was ready to tell her mother the truth, when she spotted her brothers stepping into the kitchen.

"I want to know who this guy is you're supposed to be marrying," Martin demanded.

"Yeah," Dame chimed. "Especially since tonight is the first time we've heard anything about him."

Chante rolled her eyes toward the ceiling and groaned. She was in for a long night.

"Did you ever get around to telling Antonio the truth?"

She stared across at her grandfather's curious expression. She was curled up on one end of the couch with her legs tucked beneath her. Pops was on the other end with his feet propped up on a padded foot rest, sipping a mug of chamomile tea. The family had been gone barely ten minutes when Pops insisted she take a seat and share all the details.

Chante shook her head. "No, but I plan to tell him."

He gave her an uneasy smile. "At this point, what would be the point of telling him?"

She frantically shook her head. "I have to tell him especially now that the family knows about my fiancé. Pops this has gotten way out of hand. Everybody thinks I'm engaged, but me!" She interjected, then began relating the details surrounding the ring on her finger.

Pops shot her a glance. "Would it help any if I apologized again?"

She released a weary sigh. There was no way she could stay angry at the dear old man no matter how big a mess he had made of her life. Besides, if it hadn't been for him, she would have never met Antonio. "Apology accepted. Now I just need to find a way to tell him the truth."

"I think you should do it in person."

She agreed. Wasn't that the reason why she had driven to Philly in the first place, so that she could tell him the truth in person? Instead she had made a bigger mess of things. "He's flying in for Chenoa's housewarming party. I guess I'll break the news to him then."

"That sounds like a good idea."

She gave him a look that said she wasn't too sure.

"Since I got you in this mess, if you want I can explain everything to him."

Chante took a moment to think about his offer then shook her head. "I've had several opportunities to make this all right and I didn't. No, I think he needs to hear the truth from me."

"Well I'm here if you need some help."

"I know, and I appreciate it." She slowly rose from the couch. "I'm going to go and get ready for bed. I'll see you in the morning."

He smiled as he raised the mug of hot tea to his lips. "Good night."

Chante moved down the hall and stopped outside Devon's room. She knocked twice before entering. Even though he was only six, she respected his privacy. Her son had already taken his bath. He was sitting on the end of his bed in his pajamas playing his PlayStation.

"Time for bed."

"Aw, Mom!" Devon groaned.

"Aw, Mom, nothing. You've got school in the morning and you know it."

Reluctantly he shut off the game and moved to get ready for bed.

"Mom, I can't wait for Mr. Tony to be my daddy," he said as he slipped underneath the covers. "He likes PlayStation, too."

"He does, does he?" She smiled and envisioned the doctor finding the time to play video games.

Antonio tossed his keys on the table in the hall and closed the door. It was good to be home. With a sigh of relief he carried his duffle bag upstairs to the last room on the left. He dropped the bag on the floor then stepped across the plush carpet and took a seat on his bed and removed his shoes. He was tired and had an early day tomorrow but he wasn't complaining. The weekend had been well worth it.

A faint smile tugged his lips as he remembered the conversation he'd had with Chante's mother, welcoming him into the family. He hadn't met her yet and already he felt part of their family.

His thoughts returned to Chante. He couldn't wait to see her again. The reason that he was hopelessly in love after a weekend came as no surprised because he had always known what he wanted. He had known for quite some time, he wanted Chante. Memories of their first night assailed him, and he grew hot just thinking about making love to her. It went beyond physical desire. More than ever he knew he had made the right decision. He wanted Chante to be his wife.

A sudden overwhelming sensation caused him to pause and evaluate. What was it that made her so different from the others? Why did he have this heavy weight in his chest and this strong urge to tell her how much she already meant to him? He wasn't sure if he'd ever know the answer to that.

The phone at his bedside rang. Climbing across the bed, he grabbed the receiver.

"Hello?"

"So, how was she?"

His eyes closed as he chuckled. He should have known it was Germaine.

"Who are you talking about?"

She clicked her tongue. "Don't play dumb. You know who I'm talking about."

She had always been pushy. He chuckled again. "Don't you have something better to do?"

"Nope."

He hesitated a moment longer but hearing the impatience in her voice he decided to tell her what she wanted to hear. "Chante is everything I thought she would be and more."

"So she must be pretty."

Her face came to mind. "That's an understatement."

Germaine sighed through the receiver. "I'm so relieved. I was afraid your experience was going to be like mine."

Unlike him, Germaine asked for a photo up front because she refused to take any chances. Unfortunately the picture, Dante Carver had sent her was ten years and eight-five pounds earlier. Then, after her encounter with the psycho, she refused to give Internet dating another chance. Antonio would never say it, but he was pleased to know she had decided to leave it alone. There were too many crazy people out there preying on young woman and he'd hate to have to rearrange some brotha's face.

He lay back on the bed and used his arm to prop his head up. "No, quite the opposite. She is a wonderful woman who I still plan to marry."

"When do I get to meet her?"

He should have known that was coming. "Soon. We're taking things slow."

"Slow!" she bellowed. "I thought she'd accepted your proposal?"

"She did but we decided to step back and take our time. She's wearing my ring, and right now that's good enough for me. I'll propose again when I think she's ready."

"Hmmm. I still want to meet her."

"You will. I promise."

He talked to his sister a little longer then hung up. Feeling hungry, he moved into the kitchen to find something to eat. While he popped a TV dinner in the microwave, he thought about how proud he was of his little sister.

She had graduated last year from Loyola University and was now a school teacher at Susan B. Anthony Elementary School. He wished his parents had lived to see her success.

He quickly ate then rose and decided to go ahead and take a shower. He would then call Chante as soon as he was comfortable beneath the sheets.

Antonio had just gotten out of the shower when the phone rang. He prayed it wasn't the hospital. Dr. Bailey was the pediatrician on-call this weekend but sometimes his colleagues would call to give him a heads-up if they were treating one of his patients.

With a towel wrapped loosely around his waist, he took a seat on the end of his bed, and reached for the phone. It was Chante.

"I see you made it safely."

"Yes, and my bag was even there."

"Well, that's always a good thing," she teased.

"So I'm dying to hear what happened. I got the feeling wearing my ring got you into trouble."

She exhaled deeply. "I had planned to put it away as soon as I got home. Unfortunately, my family was already here waiting for me. Apparently, Devon had already shared the news of his new daddy."

"Oh boy."

"Yeah, I guess passing it off as a promise ring is out of the question."

Absentmindedly, he drummed his fingers against his lips. "What do you want to do?"

"Nothing," Chante began. "You should have seen the look on my father's face. There is no way I could bring myself to tell him it was a promise ring. He didn't get to walk me down the aisle the first time. Dorian and I had run down to Vegas and gotten married at one of those drive-in chapels."

He gasped with disbelief. "You didn't tell me about that."

She groaned. "Something I'm not too proud of. We were young and in love and didn't want anyone to stand in the way of our happiness. I knew my mom wanted to plan something big and elaborate, and we didn't want to wait."

"I'm sure your mother was disappointed as well."

"She was more hurt than anything. I ended up regretting our decision. My family is really close and we believe in sharing special moments together. I swore to never do anything like that again."

"I guess whisking you off to Jamaica is out of the question?" he said jokingly.

"Fine if you don't mind the Campbell clan tagging along."

"I don't mind. As long as you're by my side, we can invite the entire state of Delaware for all I care." They shared a laugh. As soon as he sobered, Antonio leaned back against the cool sheets. "Baby, just because your family found out about the ring doesn't mean you need to feel pressured in any way. As far as I'm concerned, as long as you wear my ring you have promised to consider spending the rest of your life with me. Take as long as you need. When you're ready I'll buy another ring, and we can make it official."

"I don't need another ring," she insisted.

He shifted comfortably on the bed. "We'll see."

"Thanks, Antonio," she said with laughter in her voice.

"You're welcome."

He heard her yawn through the receiver. "I guess I better get ready for bed. I just wanted to hear your voice before I drifted off to sleep."

"Good night, sweetheart," he said softly.

"The same to you."

Antonio returned the cordless phone to the base, then lay there for the longest time with a wide grin on his face.

Chapter Eleven

"I can't believe your grandfather did that!" Andrea chuckled only seconds after Chante shared tidbits of her Internet engagement. "Then again, yes I can."

Chante tented her hands beneath her chin. "It was a pretty awkward situation . . . at first."

"At first . . . what happened?" Andrea smiled at her expectantly, waiting for her to give the juicy details.

"I don't kiss and tell."

Andrea's smile faded. "I tell you about my dates."

Chante stared up at her. "Because you want to. Not because I ask."

Her partner crossed her arms over her chest and rocked back on her heels of her Prada pumps in what she could only interpret as a challenging gesture. "Keep your little secrets. With that big smile on your face, I've got a pretty good idea how well your weekend went." At her continued silence, her brown face twisted and she groaned, "Come on Chante! Can you at least tell me what he looks like?"

Visions of Antonio's scalding gaze swept through her and made her heart pound. "Tall, dark, and gorgeous."

Andrea's eyes grew rounder with each delectable description. "He definitely sounds fine," she remarked.

"He is, and with a body that is out of this world." Her mouth went dry as she mentally remembered the way he looked standing over her with nothing on.

Andrea studied her face. "So when are you going to see him again?"

"At Chenoa's housewarming." She made a mental note to call a caterer for the event. This was one time she didn't plan on having to cook anything. She would be too busy entertaining.

Andrea pointed a finger at her. "Then add my name to that guest list because I'm definitely going to make meeting him a high priority. I can't remember the last time you've been this excited over anything."

Chante gave a faraway look as she admitted, "I can't remember the last time I've enjoyed myself as much."

"And this is coming from a woman who planned to spend her weekend reading a book. I thought you weren't interested in a relationship?" she teased.

"Don't misconstrue my words," Chante retorted playfully. "I didn't plan on getting engaged. This . . . this was all so unexpected."

Lowering her arms, Andrea splayed her fingers on her waist, smiling. "What did Antonio say after he found out the truth about your engagement?"

Chante hesitated before saying, "I didn't tell him."

Her expression stilled and grew serious. "Why not?"

She mulled that over for a moment while Andrea continued to scrutinize her. She honestly no longer had a legitimate excuse. "I don't know why I didn't tell him. Either the timing wasn't right or I was afraid at how he was going to react." She paused and shifted on the chair uncomfortably. "Pops doesn't think I should say anything, and after tossing and turning all night, I agreed."

"Sounds like an excuse to me." Andrea shook her head. "What's going to happen when he finds out the truth?"

Chante disagreed. "How would he find out? Besides, I really don't think it matters now."

"Then if it doesn't matter, why not tell him?"

She frowned. "Don't worry. I got it under control."

Andrea opened her mouth as if to reply but then shut it abruptly, and Chante's gaze narrowed. "Go ahead and say it."

She shook her head. "Say what?"

"What you were going to say."

"I wasn't going to say anything," Andrea denied.

Chante's right eyebrow arched. "Yes, you were, so you might as well say it."

Andrea paused a moment longer then leaned across the desk to reply in a softer voice, "If you really like this guy, I think he deserves to hear the truth."

Chante pursed her lips together at her friend's persistence. Andrea never did know when to leave well enough alone. "I got myself in this mess. I promise you I will find a way to work everything out."

"Uh-huh."

Chante rolled her chair up to the desk and reached for a pen. "What did I miss around here on Friday?"

Andrea frowned at her attempt to change the subject but decided to let it slide for now. "Trevor's signing at Barnes & Noble was a sold out event."

The glint returned to her eyes. "That's wonderful news. I'm sure he's beside himself."

"He is. I spoke to him just before he was heading back home to Atlanta. I had Kayla check and three boxes of his newest release arrived at the bookstore last week."

Nodding, she was quite pleased with the information. Trevor was doing a reading at a literary event at Morehouse College on Wednesday, then signing at Niama's Books on Thursday night. Chante made a note to call him on Friday and see how everything went.

"Anna Devine's release date has been pushed up four months."

"Wow!" Chante exclaimed.

"I'll have Jared update her Web site, then I need to have Kayla start setting up her book signing."

Jared Lewis, a senior at Delaware State University who was majoring in computers, worked part-time in their office, designing and maintaining Web sites for several of their clients.

Chante scribbled notes as they spoke. Andrea gave her the rest of the information then told her about a potential new client she had met on Saturday for cocktails.

Long after Andrea had returned to her own office, she read over her notes, then began preparing a to-do list for the following day. After her agenda was put together, she sat and unconsciously began drawing little hearts all over the paper. She hadn't done anything like that since grammar school.

Antonio brings out the kid in you.

Chante stared down at the yellow legal pad, and finally admitted that she wanted her engagement with Antonio to be real.

Last night while staring up at her ceiling fan, she found herself thinking about what Pops had suggested—not telling Antonio the truth about their engagement. And after hours of deliberation, she finally agreed. At this point, what did it matter if Pops had hooked them up? Who cared if he was the one who had accepted the marriage proposal? All that mattered was that they were now together. They had spent a glorious weekend that ended with her wearing his diamond, and now that her family had seen the ring, she was officially engaged. Everything was exactly the way Antonio had expected things to be, the way Pops somehow knew they would turn out. So if everyone was happy, then why did she feel so guilty?

Dorian isn't dead.

Dropping her pen, she swiveled around in her chair. It was approaching noon and the warm spring sun was shining outside her window while she sat there thinking about her estranged ex-husband. As far as she knew, he wasn't dead, yet Antonio thought he was because Pops—correction, she—had lied to him. Chante groaned. That was going to be a problem. She hadn't heard from Dorian in years and as far as she was concerned, he was dead to her. Only it wasn't the truth. Dorian was out there somewhere.

It was also unfair for her to allow Antonio to think that she was a widow when she was not. No, she was going to have to tell him the truth about Dorian. The question was, how was she going to do that without causing him to question the legitimacy of everything else that she had told him?

Putting down the manuscript, Chante stretched and yawned. She had gotten home in time to have pizza with her family. After putting Devon to bed, she'd taken a shower and spent the rest of the evening making a few comments on a manuscript.

She always took the time to proofread every one of her client's manuscripts before submitting them to an editor for consideration. As a result she had a reputation as an agent who believed in her client's work. If she didn't think a manuscript was ready, she had no qualms about suggesting to her client that they have the material professionally edited first.

Dropping her ink pen onto the night stand, she again stretched her arms over her head and yawned. She was tired. She didn't sleep well last night, and was certain tonight wouldn't be any easier. Ever since her return, her mind and emotions were in turmoil. After one night together, she realized just how much she missed sharing her bed with a man. Sex had never been a problem in her marriage. The warm, gentle Dorian Hunter had been a wonderful lover. The abusive Dorian took it out on her even in the bed. However, with Antonio he had been a patient lover who made sure she had gotten hers before he got his. A smile curled her lips as she thought of his body against hers.

Why hasn't he called today? she wondered. She had anxiously been watching her phone all day, hoping to have heard from him. She had even checked her bedroom phone twice to make sure it was working. Chante dragged her left leg to her chest and sighed. She had it bad, which was what she had been afraid of. Loving a man made you do crazy things. It was why she was so afraid of trusting. But despite her apprehensions, she was yearning to hear his voice. She could have picked up the phone and called him herself, but she didn't want to come off too strong by calling him two nights in a row. No. She would wait and let him make the next move. Part of her was disappointed that she hadn't heard from him today, but she quickly reminded herself Antonio was a doctor and some things just couldn't be helped. She released another sigh. It was amazing how after just one weekend together she had gotten used to him being around.

While sitting on the bed in sweats pants and a T-shirt, another thought came to mind. She rose from the bed and moved over and retrieved her purse. Reaching inside, she pulled out the business card he had given her only minutes before his final kiss good-bye. She raced down the hall. It took all of five minutes for Pops to supply her with the information pertaining to the free e-mail account and password he'd used to correspond with Antonio. As soon as she logged on, and opened her mail, she was pleased to see that Pops had saved all the weeks of correspondence. Kicking back under the covers, she spent the next several hours reading one romantic e-mail after another.

What woman wouldn't fall in love with him? she thought as she read the last one.

Are you in love? She pushed the laptop away and reached for her bottled water then took a long thirsty swallow. She suspected that she was in love but wasn't prepared yet to admit it. She did know, however, what she felt was too soon to put into words. All she knew was that it was something she didn't want to give up. It was something she wanted to continue to explore.

Wrapped in that warm feeling, she sat back onto the bed and reached for her laptop again. She put her hands on the keys and raked the back of her mind. *What do I say?* She didn't want to sound like a lovesick fool so she decided not to tell him she was lying across the bed thinking about him. Even though it was true, and the reason she was writing him in the first place. Ten minutes passed before she finally composed a simple e-mail thanking him for a wonderful weekend. Chante clicked SEND, then sat there with a silly grin on her face.

She couldn't wait to receive his response.

Chapter Twelve

Antonio tore the prescription from the pad and held it out to his patient's mother. "Give him Tylenol and plenty of fluids and he should be fine in a couple of days. If not, make sure to call my office." He smiled down at the eighteen-month-old's sad little face. "Cheer up, little man," he said as he rubbed his head.

"Dr. Marks, thank you so much."

He nodded. "See you soon." As she dressed the little boy, Antonio departed and moved down the hall to his office. Once there, he took a seat behind his desk and put his feet up. It had been a busy morning filled with runny noses and ear infections. There was something apparently going around. He still had an afternoon scheduled with patients with similar symptoms.

Deciding to take a few minutes to himself, he twirled around in his chair and logged on to his computer. While he waited for his computer to warm up, he leaned back in his chair thinking about Chante.

Last night he had planned to call her as soon as he'd gotten home. Unfortunately, there had been so many emergencies that he had felt it necessary to stay and assist. He didn't make it home until almost three o'clock this morning, which gave him just enough time to take a quick nap and return to the hospital for morning rounds. Hopefully tonight would be a little less eventful. If not, he'd find the time to call her before the night was over, even if it was for five minutes.

With a click of his mouse, he discovered he had three new e-mail messages. Bubbling with anticipation, he clicked on his inbox. Two were junk mail, but a smile touched his lips when he discovered the third was a message from Chante.

Thank you for a weekend that I will hold close to my heart forever.

Moving his keyboard closer, he quickly typed a response. By the time he had sent the message, another idea came to mind. He picked up the phone and made a call. Ten minutes later he hung up, then leaned back in the chair and folded his arms behind his head with a smile.

Hearing a light wrap at the door, he glanced up at his nurse of ten years, Blanche Conway. "Your eleven-thirty is here."

He rubbed his forehead and scowled. So much for a few minutes to gather his thoughts.

"Are you okay?" She stepped her round figure dressed in pink-and-blue-striped scrubs into his office.

He glanced up with an amused look on his face. He was used to the fifty-nine-year-old grandmother doting over him.

"Yes, I'm fine, really. Just didn't get much rest these last couple of nights." He stifled a yawn.

Blanche rested back on her heels. "I know about last night. Do you care to explain why you didn't get much sleep over the weekend?"

Leaning forward, he rested his elbows on the desk and met her curious look. "I flew to Philadelphia."

Her eyes grew large. "You finally met your mystery lady?" He nodded. "And?"

"She's wonderful." He explained how he had suggested that they meet in Philadelphia. Before he realized it he was pouring out his heart. "And I . . ." he allowed his voice to trail off when he noticed Blanche grinning at him. "What's so funny?"

She looked genuinely happy for him. "You, that's what? I haven't seen you this happy in a long time."

He nodded in agreement. It had been a long time. "Chante makes me happy."

"Does she want more children?"

He paused and frowned as he realized that was something they had never discussed. They had spoken extensively about her and her son. He knew Chante was a package deal. One he was more than willing to accept. As a stepfather, he would treat Devon the same as any child of his own—with love and devotion. He could tell Devon meant the world to her, but the discussion of having more children had never come up.

Children had been a sore spot with him and Julia. He wanted kids and she had wanted to wait until their student loans were paid off. After that, she wanted to wait until after she had started her private practice, and then it was something else, until they had put it off for so long, it was too late. Even though they had never discussed it, he knew the reason why Julia kept putting off starting a family—she was afraid of losing another child. By the time she had found the courage to try again, they had discovered she was ill.

Antonio rubbed his chin. "I don't know. I never asked her."

Blanche's expression grew serious. "I think that's something the two of you need to discuss."

He nodded. She was right. They needed to talk. What if Chante doesn't want any more children? That was something he would have to think about because if she wasn't interested in having another, he wasn't sure if he was willing to give up his desire to have a child of his own.

He reached for his stethoscope from his desk and draped it around his neck then followed his nurse down the clinic corridor. He and Chante were going to have to talk soon. But it would have to wait until he saw her again. Something as important as having a family was meant to be discussed in person.

Chante was reading a book proposal when Kayla knocked lightly on her door. Glancing up, she found her holding a beautiful bouquet of yellow roses.

"These just arrived for you."

She quickly rose from her chair and moved around her desk. Taking the large vase from her assistant's hands, she moved over to the small table near the window, and set the flowers at the center.

"Hurry, who's it from?"

She gave Kayla a weird look. "Aren't we being nosy?"

"Yes, now hurry up and read it," she whined impatiently.

Chante chuckled as she reached for the small pink envelope and removed the card inside.

Sweetheart, the pleasure was all mine.

The flowers were from Antonio. Her heart fluttered at the endearment.

"They are beautiful. I didn't know you had anyone special in your life."

She pretended she didn't hear her. Kayla was fishing and she had no intention of taking the bait.

Finally, her assistant gave an impatient sigh. "Are you going to tell me who they're from or not?"

Chante closed the card then slipped it in the breast pocket of her suit. "I'm not." Her smile belied her sharp tone.

"Suit yourself." Kayla looked disappointed but tried to hide it before returning to her desk.

Chante adored her assistant. The twenty-four year old recent graduate was a gem. She kept a close eye on her and Andrea's calendars and charmed all of their clients. The only complaint that she had was that Kayla liked to spend a great deal of time gossiping. Whether it was about celebrities or local neighborhood gossip, Kayla always had to be the first to know and made sure that, to Chante's dismay, she repeated every juicy detail to all the other secretaries in the seven-story building. And that was why she chose not to be the topic of discussion for the day. Kayla was just going to have to find someone else to spread rumors about.

Moving behind her desk again, she lowered into her seat then removed the card and glanced down at it. Antonio had already managed to become quite special to her. She looked forward to seeing him at her sister's house next weekend.

With the housewarming party fresh on her brain, she picked up the phone and dialed a dear friend of the family, Candace Price.

During her senior year, Chenoa was paired with Candace as part of a big sister/little sister program. It had been her sister's responsibility to be a positive role model, and to help make the freshman's transition from junior high to high school as easy as possible. The two became fast and close friends. Candace often spent weekends with the Campbell's and it wasn't long before the fourteen-year-old had fancied herself in love with Martin. Twenty at the time, Martin spent most of his time trying to ignore her advances. Chante chuckled at the fond memories. Candace now lived in Missouri with her younger sister Shanice. She had become her legal guardian when their parents were killed in an automobile accident the day of her high school graduation. Taking on the responsibility meant turning down a full athletic scholarship to Morgan State. But she never had any regrets. Last year, to her excitement, Shanice was offered a scholarship to run track. The Campbell family was proud of the two, whom they considered part of their family.

"Good afternoon, Harper and Associates, can I help you?"

"Hey, Candy."

"Chante, what's up girl?"

Absentmindedly, she twirled the phone cord around her

finger as she spoke. "I'm planning a housewarming party for Chenoa."

"Ooh, I was hoping you were doing something! I spoke to her last week and she was so excited about decorating her new home."

Chante crossed her legs. "Yes, she is. She wants to have everything in order before the baby comes."

"I can't wait to see my little goddaughter."

She smiled. "Neither can I." She then told her they planned to have a catered barbecue luncheon at the Sinclair's new home the following weekend.

"I wouldn't miss it for the world. However, I might have to drive if I can't find a couple of cheap tickets." There was a slight pause before she spoke again. "How's Marty doing?"

Chante smiled, not at all surprised to hear her asking about her brother. "Why don't you call and ask him yourself?"

"No thank you. Your brother still tries to treat me like I'm a little kid," Candace admitted with frustration.

"That's because he adores you."

She exhaled deeply. "I don't want him to adore me. I want your brother to see me as a woman."

Chante thought about the way her brother had been looking at her at Chenoa's wedding as she sashayed around the church in a form-fitting red dress. Candace may not have realized it, but the look was anything but brotherly love.

She felt she needed to reassure her. "Just keep doing what you're doing and he'll notice."

They talked a little longer catching up with each other's lives, and when she finally hung up, Chante decided it was time to go to lunch.

Reaching inside her desk drawer for her purse, she noticed a light blinking on her computer screen indicating she had a message waiting. Sliding over in her chair, she clicked her mouse and opened her mailbox. It was from Antonio.

The weekend was only a sample of the weeks to come. I'll call you tonight. Can't wait to hear your voice.

She stared at the words, pulse racing with excitement. Tonight wouldn't get here fast enough.

Antonio finished evening rounds then dropped by his office long enough to hang up his lab coat on the back of his office door then decided to call it a night. He was tired and looking forward to a long hot shower.

He moved out to his silver Jaguar, climbed behind the seat and within minutes was cruising down Roosevelt Avenue toward Oak Park. At a stop sign he turned on his radio and tuned to 107.5 WGCI in time to hear the latest saga of R. Kelly's "Trapped in the Closet." He smiled as he listened to the newest chapter unfold. He had to give him his props. R. Kelly was definitely talented to be able to create a soap opera to music the way he had.

As he pulled away from the curb, he spotted a brotha with a fresh haircut coming out of a barbershop. Running a hand across his head, he decided that tomorrow he needed to call his boy and see if he could hook him up after work on the Thursday before he was scheduled to fly to Delaware to see Chante. Planning to meet her family, he definitely wanted to look his best. Just thinking about Chante caused his pulse to skip and heat to flow to his loins. He couldn't wait to see her.

As Antonio neared his home, his stomach started to growl. Deciding to stop and grab a bite to eat, he made a right at the next corner and headed toward his favorite soul food restaurant, Dominic's. It was a nice cozy spot centrally located in downtown Oak Park.

Antonio pulled into the parking lot behind the back and was fortunate to find a spot not far from the side door. As soon as he stepped out the car, the mouth watering aroma of southern cooking traveled to his nose, and he realized he hadn't eaten since breakfast.

He stepped inside. For a Tuesday evening, the place was packed.

Dominic's was an upscale restaurant that had a comfortable atmosphere. There was a bar at the center of the room surrounded by bar stools. Lanterns adorned the ceiling. Tables with linen tablecloths surrounded the rest of the area.

He waved at the hostess then strolled past rows of occupied tables to an office at the back of the restaurant. He knocked on the office door.

"Who is it?" asked a deep throaty voice.

"Tony."

There was silence then he heard shuffling, and finally the door opened. Tara stood before him, grinning.

"Whassup Tony?"

He stared at the woman with her platinum blond weave and nose ring. She could be a cover model for *Hoochie Mama Magazine,* if there were such a thing. "Hey, Tara."

She patted her head, making sure her weave was still in place, then sashayed past him, swaying her wide hips in a short spandex skirt. Antonio gave her a long look then shook his head and and stepped into the small office. His brother was sitting behind his desk, grinning.

Tony arched his brow. "Did I interrupt something?"

His brother waved a hand in the air, dismissing the thought. "Nah, we were talking."

"Oh really?" Antonio chuckled. "You might want to wipe your face."

Dominic reached for a napkin from his desk drawer then wiped his cheek, removing cherry lipstick. He scowled when he noticed the evidence she'd left behind. As Antonio laughed, he dragged a weary hand down his face.

"What brings you out?"

He moved over to his desk and rested his hip against the corner. "I came to throw my weekend in your face."

"Geri said you had a good time." Glancing up from the chair, he studied him. "Is she really all that?"

Antonio removed his cell phone from his hip and showed him the screensaver of Chante in the red dress.

Dominic whistled. "Damn! She's bad."

"Yes, she is," he said, his chest stuck out with pride as he returned the phone to its case.

"I guess you did have a good weekend?"

Antonio grinned. "Excellent, which means . . ." He made a show of rubbing his palms together, and noticed the exact moment of realization sunk in.

"I lose."

Antonio punched him lightly in the shoulder. "Bingo! I've come to hold you to your end of our deal."

"Huh?" Dominic's voice dropped. "Oh, boy. I can't wait."

"How about you let me have that chair?" He signaled for him to rise. Reluctantly, Dominic rose and stepped to the side. "Thanks," Antonio said as he lowered onto the seat. "Why don't you go and fix me a plate of collard greens and that baked macaroni and cheese that I love so much, while I set up your personal ad."

"I see you've got jokes."

Antonio's eyes twinkled as he reached for the keyboard. "You ain't seen nothing yet."

Chante left work on time for a change. Tuesdays were Pops' bingo nights, and also the one day of the week she insisted on making dinner for Devon. Tonight, however, they were going to McDonald's, which was Devon's favorite place. She wasn't big on fast food, but every now and then she was willing to make an exception.

She pulled into her driveway and climbed out, juggling her

briefcase in one hand and the bouquet of roses in the other. She had considered leaving the arrangement in her office to appreciate all week, but on her way out was unwilling to part with the thoughtful gift.

She climbed the three stairs and before she could stick her key in the lock, the door swung open.

"Well, what do we have here?" Pops asked. He took the briefcase from her hand then stepped aside so she could enter.

"Flowers for me," she said as she moved into the foyer. Stepping over to the dark oak sofa table, she removed a potted silk arrangement and replaced it with the real thing.

"Do I have to ask who they are from?"

She blushed openly. "Tony sent them to me."

His eyes sparkled with amusement. "I guess that means he had a good time over the weekend."

"We both did." She placed the silk plant on a round end table beside the couch. "I thought about what you said the other day and I've decided not to tell Antonio about you hooking the two of us up."

Nodding, Pops moved over to an overstuffed chocolate chair and took a seat. "That's probably a good thing."

"I really don't think he'll appreciate knowing that he proposed to you, not me and this late in the game, I don't see how it is relevant that he knows. I've read all the e-mails. I know everything the two of you talked about." She paused and took a deep breath, realizing she sounded like she was asking him to lie for her. "I don't want to mess this up."

"Young lady, it sounds to me like you're in love."

A long pause hung over the room before Chante responded, "I am." There, she finally admitted how she felt. She had fallen in love with Antonio. And it terrified her. "That's why I don't want this whole thing to backfire in my face." She lowered onto the couch. "The only thing I have to do is tell him the truth about Dorian, and I'm hoping he'll understand."

He nodded. "I'm sure he will."

"Hey, Mama!" Devon came racing down the hall.

"No running in the house," Pops scolded.

"Sorry," he said as he swung his arms around Chante's middle.

"Hi sweetie." She planted a kiss to the top of his head. "How was school?"

"Okay. Can I have a kitty? You said you'd think about it?"

She glanced across at her grandfather then back down at Devon's pleading eyes. "How about we go to McDonald's for dinner tonight?"

"Oh boy!" He started jumping up and down. She sighed with relief. The cat was quickly forgotten and replaced by french fries.

She looked over at Pops again and winked. "Let me go and change my clothes, and then we can go."

"Yeaaah!" Devon was clapping his hands and dancing around the room. Pops chuckled and she joined in on the laughter. Her son was definitely easy to please.

They spent well over two hours at McDonald's. After feasting on burgers and fries, Devon dashed off to play in the large indoor jungle gym. Luckily, Chante had brought along a book to read while she waited. Once they made it back home, she helped Devon with his bath then read to him before tucking him in for the night. She hurried and took a shower, and had just slipped underneath the covers when her bedside phone rang. She checked the caller ID and grabbed the phone.

"Perfect timing," she sang by way of a greeting.

"Hello beautiful. How was your day?" Antonio asked.

She blew out a long breath. "Busy as always. Thank you so much for the flowers."

"Baby, it was my pleasure. Getting your e-mail made my

day. I wanted to do something to show you how much I appreciated you spending the weekend with me."

"I couldn't think of a better way to spend it."

"Neither could I." He chuckled. "I went to Dominic's for dinner tonight."

Thank goodness she had read all of her previous e-mails and now knew his older brother Dominic owned his own business—a restaurant on one side of the building and a barbershop on the other.

"What did you have?"

"Collard greens, mac and cheese and cornbread," he said as he rubbed his stomach.

"Sounds delicious."

"It was. He has really been successful. He took our grandmother's cookbook and opened a restaurant. People can't get enough of his food."

"I can only imagine. Although I ain't too bad in the kitchen."

"That's what you say." Antonio sounded unconvinced.

"And what is that supposed to mean?"

"It means, that remains to be seen."

"Fine, when you come down I plan to prepare you a home-cooked meal."

"I'm gonna hold you to that."

They shared a laugh and then there was a slight pause.

"There's something I want to ask you?"

"Sure, what is it?"

"When I spoke to your mom she introduced herself as Betty Campbell."

"Yeah, that's her name."

There was a slight hesitation before he said, "I was under the impression that Campbell was your married name."

She swallowed and closed her eyes as another lie rolled off her tongue. "No, my husband's name was Hunter. I chose to keep my maiden name."

"How come?" he asked gently.

A long pause hung over the line before she responded, "Although I loved my husband, I believed in keeping my own identity." She took a deep breath. He just didn't know how true that statement really was. After her experience with Dorian she would never give up everything that was hers again.

Antonio gave a playful groan. "Oh boy, another independent woman."

"You better believe it."

"I ain't mad at you."

She released the air pinned in her lungs, relieved at how understanding he was. "You didn't tell me how your day was," she asked glad to change the subject.

"Filled with runny noses and crying babies," he said and faked a groan. She knew that he loved his job. The next few minutes she listened to him tell her about a set of triplet girls that always brightened his day when they came to the clinic. Afterward they chitchatted about nothing in particular for almost an hour then Antonio grew quiet. Chante found it quite comforting holding the phone to her ear, just listening to him breathe.

Antonio finally broke the silence. "Are you still wearing my ring?"

Chante glanced down at the diamond that was still prominently displayed on her ring finger. "Yes," she whispered.

"Good."

"Why?"

"Because if you're still wearing it, then you're still considering being my wife," he replied, his voice both quiet and husky.

She shut her eyes as her heart fluttered frantically in her chest. Emotions exploded within her. Excitement. Pleasure, and most importantly, *love*.

"I better let you get some sleep," he suggested.

She curled up in a ball. "Yes, six o'clock comes pretty early."

"Tell me about it." He settled on the bed. "Good night, sweetheart."

"Good night, Tony."

"Oh, before I forget . . . I love you."

"I love you, too," she said aloud before returning the cordless phone to its cradle.

Chapter Thirteen

She had just gotten off the phone with an editor at Dutton, who had called to offer one of her first time authors a two-book deal. She waved her arms in the air with excitement for the talented woman. Her days couldn't possibly get any better.

There had been no doubt in her mind that they would fall in love with the book. *The Magic Hour* was a powerful story that she had found almost impossible to put down. She couldn't wait to tell Michele Scott the good news.

Thumbing through her Rolodex, she was hunting for her client's phone number when her mother came blazing through her open door.

"What are you doing here?" her mother demanded to know.

Folding her hands on top of her desk, Chante then leaned forward and stifled a groan. She would have to call Michele later. When Betty was around, she demanded attention.

"Mama, last I checked, I worked here."

She gave her a dismissive wave as she flopped down into the seat across from her desk. "You know what I mean. Antonio is coming tomorrow evening. You should be home preparing for him."

She bit back a smile at the mention of Tony's name. The last two weeks had been everything she could have possibly dreamed of and more. Every morning she looked forward to his e-mails. They spent so much time e-mailing, she was shocked either of them got any work done. Then every evening at exactly eleven, she received a call for Antonio and they talked until they both drifted off to sleep.

"Don't worry. Pops has that under control."

Her mother's lips twisted in a look of disapproval that she allowed her grandfather so much control over her life. What her mother couldn't understand was that Chante didn't know how she could function without his help with Devon.

Betty smoothed down the front of a red tunic as she spoke. "There is no way I could trust a man to do my work. If I left it up to your father, nothing would ever get done."

She loved hearing her mother complain about her father. Everyone knew that even after forty years, the two adored each other.

"I think Pops can handle it. He managed to do all right with you. Besides, wasn't it your idea that he move in with me?" she reminded.

Her rose painted lips thinned. "Yes, but I didn't expect him to take over your house."

Chante groaned inwardly. It had been three years since he had first come to live with her and yet they were still always having the same discussion. "He hasn't. Besides, I'm sure I'll have control of my house again before the summer is over. I'm sure he and Mildred are planning to announce their engagement soon. Eventually they'll move in together."

Her mother's face softened at the mention of the woman who had become a good friend. The thought of Mildred trying to replace her mother never crossed her mind. "I sure hope so. Milly really makes my dad happy."

Chante nodded in agreement. "Yes, she is a wonderful woman."

"Okay, getting back to you . . . how about I keep Devon for you tomorrow evening?"

She should have known she wasn't off the hook. "That won't be necessary. Antonio wants a chance to meet him."

"What about afterwards?"

She raised a brow at the idea. "Mom, I appreciate your offer but I've got things under control."

There was a long pause. Betty didn't look too pleased with her decisions. But as soon as the frown arrived it disappeared. "Well, I bought you something."

When she held up a pink bag it was the first time she noticed her mother had something in her hand. Hesitantly, Chante took the bag that she held over her desk. Looking inside, she gasped. Inside was a skimpy black nightie.

She slid the bag across the desk. "Mom, I can't take this."

"Yes, you can," she said then tossed the bag into her lap. "And just to make sure you don't try and take it back, I ripped off the tags."

Chante gave her mother a grim look. "What if it's too small?"

"That's even better." Betty wagged her brow suggestively. At her daughter's frown, she chuckled joyously. "You've got to keep the spice in the relationship. How do you think your father and I have managed to stay together all these years?"

That was something she didn't need to know. "Maybe Chenoa would like to have it."

"She's pregnant." She snorted then crossed her jean-clad legs. "There is obviously nothing wrong with their sex life. However, after that baby is born I'll be sure to get her one also. So, there, you have no choice but to keep it and wear it. I guarantee it works. I have one just like it at home."

That was definitely too much information.

"Everything is set for the housewarming. I've already contacted Aunt Helen, and you know she'll get the word around." Betty released a sigh. "I just wished your sister would let me help with her decorating, but she and Zearl insist on doing it themselves. Although, I'll let you in on a little secret. I did order her some gorgeous paintings to cover her living room walls."

"I bet she can't wait to see them." More than likely they were pictures of daisies.

"I'm so proud of my girls," Betty said then paused and frowned. "I sure hope your brothers can find someone like you did."

No problem. Just ask Pops to put their profiles on the Internet. "I'm sure they'll meet someone nice when they're ready."

Her mother didn't look convinced. "Dame is having fun, but Marty, I think he has never gotten over Tamara Elliot."

During his senior year at college her brother was a guaranteed second-round draft pick. He had it all. A fiancé, and a promising career. Then a knee injury ended not only his chances as going pro, but also Tamara's desire to marry him.

Chante shifted in her chair as a certain redhead came to mind. Candace Price was just what Martin needed to get over the gold-digging wench who'd tried to rip his heart out.

Betty glanced down at her watch. "Well, anyway, I need to get home before my soap operas come on." Her mother rose, then before moving to the door gave her a long, hard look. "Promise me you'll get out of here early."

Chante nodded obediently. "I promise."

With a smile, her mother then turned and walked out the door with the same amount of enthusiasm in which she'd arrived.

Leaning back in her chair, a smile tipped the corners of her lips. Her mother was definitely something else. She could be annoying at times. Nevertheless, she loved her just the same. Her mother was right. She needed to get ready for her weekend. The mere thought of lying in Antonio's arms again, caused a tingle to run through her and settle at the pit of her stomach.

Glancing over at the clock, she decided to end her day by three o'clock. That left her two hours to finish her work before rushing home to prepare for Antonio's visit.

She pushed aside her thoughts and returned to her professional mode. If she was going to leave early, she needed to finish a few things first. Thumbing through her Rolodex again, she found what she was looking for, and dialed Michele's phone number.

Chante left exactly as scheduled and headed straight for the grocery store. Pops was planning to make his famous lasagna tomorrow. He tried to shop, but with his bad hip he moved so slow, it was easier for him to make a list and have her do the shopping. She was grateful that he loved to cook because that saved her from rushing home every night to prepare dinner. Not that she minded cooking. She was a fabulous cook. However cooking was something she never liked to rush through. With Pops handling most of the meals, she was able to enjoy cooking over the weekends.

She pulled into the Acme Shopping Center and was lucky to get a parking spot at the front of the lot. It was a beautiful spring afternoon, she thought as she moved toward the automatic doors. She moved into the store and went down aisle after aisle as she checked off each item. It was funny that after a weekend together she had learned so much about Antonio's likes and dislikes. He loved broccoli but he hated carrots. He was allergic to peanut oil. His favorite meal was meatloaf and mashed potatoes. And he loved soul food. Since she had informed him she was an excellent cook, Chante decided that she was going to make his favorite meal on Sunday before it was time for him to catch his plane. Her stomach tingled at the possibilities of where the weekend would bring them. Deep down, she hoped that it brought the two of them even closer.

* * *

By the time Antonio called, it was thundering and lightning something fierce. Chante was just getting out of the shower when the phone rang. She dropped a bottle of lotion onto the bed and reached for the phone. When she heard his voice, a smile curled her lips.

"Antonio, you sound exhausted. Is everything okay?"

He sighed. "I had a long, eventful day."

"You want to talk about it?"

"One of my teenage patients came in complaining of a stomachache. It took an hour of poking around before she finally admitted she had faked the illness just to come see me, then she confessed her love."

Chante gasped. "How old is she?"

"Thirteen."

"What did you do?" she asked with a grin playing at the corners of her mouth.

"I gave her a lollipop and sent her own her way."

"I'm sure you're every teenager's dream," she said then laughed.

He chuckled along with her and she realized that she'd been doing a lot of that lately. All because of him. Things got quiet, and still wrapped in a towel, she leaned back on the bed and reached for her scented lotion.

"What are you wearing?" he dared to ask.

"Nothing," she answered.

Antonio groaned. "Damn, I didn't need to know that."

"Then you shouldn't have asked," she retorted with a soft chuckle while she rubbed cream over her thighs.

Antonio laughed then quickly sobered. "I miss you."

She stopped oiling her legs, dropped her lashes and smiled to herself. "I miss you too. I can't wait until you get here tomorrow. The family has been going on and on about us."

"I can't wait to meet them."

She reached for the bottle again then shifted the receiver to her other ear as she oiled her arms. "You didn't tell me what time your flight is coming in so I can pick you up at the airport."

"I'll arrive in Philadelphia at four-fifty. As anxious as I am to see you, it's not necessary for you to come pick me up during rush hour. I'm gonna rent a car."

"You sure? I don't mind, really."

"Yes," he answered.

She smiled against the mouthpiece. "Okay." She didn't care how he got there just as long as he came.

"I'm not making any promises about keeping my hands to myself around your family."

"Good," Chante said, "I'd hate to be responsible for broken promises."

His laughter was soft against her ear as he told her good night and disconnected. Chante hung up the phone, then pulled her knees up beneath her chin and hugged herself. It was becoming obvious that what was happening between her and Antonio was happening so fast, she barely had time to think straight. She knew that she needed to slow things down a bit until she had time to adjust to being in love, but she had no control over what she was feeling. That scared her because what she felt for Antonio surpassed any feelings she'd ever had with Dorian. Her love for Antonio was exciting and scary at the same time. She wanted him to be a part of her life so badly. Because for the first time in a long time she felt like she had found a man worth holding on to.

Chapter Fourteen

Friday dawned cool and breezy after a night of heavy thunderstorms and high winds. Chante woke slowly, coming to her senses before opening her eyes. The air was refreshing as she took several deep breaths. Her grandmother's old quilted bedspread cradled her comfortably as the ceiling fan directly above her bed circulated cool air through the room. Without even glancing over at the alarm clock on her bedside table she knew it was late, but her sleep last night had been restless. Only shortly after she had dozed off, she had awakened again. She had dreamed that someone was in her room watching her sleep. Even when she had gotten up and had gone to the bathroom, she remembered the feeling and flicked on the light but no one was there. She had even gone down the hall to check on Devon and Pops who were both snoring loudly as usual. When she had returned to her room it still had taken her a while to fall back to sleep. When she finally had, she slept hard, and now she had no desire to move.

Chante released a deep breath. She could have easily rolled over and gone back to sleep. Who would complain if she decided to take the day off? It was indeed one of the pleasures of being your own boss. Nevertheless, Andrea would call certain something was wrong with her best friend, considering she was a workaholic and not to mention, always the first to arrive to work. The notion was still on her mind when suddenly she remembered it was Friday. Her breath quickened. This evening Antonio would be arriving. When she offered to pick him up at the airport, he had declined her offer. She frowned, slightly puzzled by his decision, thinking traffic was just an excuse. However, he had mentioned in an e-mail the other day that he didn't want to inconvenience her and intended to rent a car. He insisted that it would make things easier when he left for the airport to catch the red-eye late Sunday night.

She smiled. Antonio was such a thoughtful and considerate man. She couldn't wait to see him again. The thought of spending another weekend in his company made her shiver with longing. She tried to convince herself that it was crazy to feel so attached to a man that she had known less than a month, that she was setting herself up for another disappointment, but she felt that way just the same.

Without giving it another thought, she flung back the bedspread and sat on the side of the bed. As she did her eyes went toward the clock that was blinking, indicating that the power had gone out some time during the night. She wasn't sure what time it was, but judging by the sky outside, it was well past six o'clock.

She stared out the window a few seconds longer and what she saw made her heart quicken. The screen was missing. Remembering the feeling of being watched the night before, her mind began to race with the possibility that maybe someone had climbed through her window last night before she shook the thought away and convinced herself she was being ridiculous.

With a puzzled look, she rose from the bed and moved over to the window and peered out into the damp flowerbed and saw the screen lying below.

How the hell did that happen? she asked herself as she reached down to grab the screen and pull it through the window. Examining the frame she noticed that one of the brackets that held the screen in place was loose. One good breeze had possibly pushed it through. And after last night's storm it was definitely a strong possibility. Feeling a sense of relief at what possibly had happened she leaned the screen against the wall, then reached up and shut the window. Even though she could have easily fixed it herself, she would ask Pops to fix it. She always tried to think of ways to make him feel needed, and this was one.

Spinning on her heels, she headed for the shower, stripping out of her nightgown as she went. Later, as she was dressing, she heard Pops and Devon in the kitchen. An early riser, her grandfather had taken on the responsibility of getting Devon ready in the morning, which allowed her more time to get herself ready.

She gave herself a quick glance in the mirror, eyeing the pale yellow spring suit she had spotted on the clearance rack at the mall last summer. It was the perfect attire for today's weather conditions. The suit would definitely brighten up any dreary day. She moved over to her closet, and removed a pair of cream pumps to match the scarf knotted loosely around her neck. Satisfied with her appearance, she left the room and followed the scent of bacon and fresh coffee permeating the air.

"Good morning," she said as she entered the kitchen. Pops and Devon were seated at a large walnut table. "Something sure smells wonderful."

Devon glanced up and smiled. "Pops made pancakes."

Chante lightly dropped a loving hand to her son's shoulder, then she moved over to the coffee pot. "Just what you need this early in the morning—an overdose of sugar."

Pops finished a bite of his food then swallowed. "A hearty breakfast is the best way to start your morning off. Why don't you sit down and join us."

She grabbed her mug and declined. "Pops you know if I eat

that many carbs this early in the morning, I'll be falling asleep at my desk before ten."

"How about a slice of cinnamon raisin toast?"

She grinned. "Now, that I'll do."

Before she could do it herself, he rose from his chair. "Coming right up."

Chante filled her mug with vanilla cream-flavored coffee then took a seat at the table across from Devon.

"Don't you have a field trip today?" she asked.

He stuffed the last of his bacon into his mouth then nodded as he chewed. His class was going to the Brandywine Zoo.

"I already packed his lunch." Pops dropped a slice of bread in the toaster then pointed to the brown sack setting on the edge of the counter.

"Pops made me peanut butter and jelly and chocolate cake," Devon announced proudly.

She pretended to frown. "That sounds like a bellyache waiting to happen."

"He'll be fine. Kids' stomachs are made of iron these days," Pops said then winked. He turned, his eyes alight with curiosity. "What time is Tony arriving?"

Dropping her gaze, she blushed. "Around six."

He nodded with a grin then turned around and reached for a plate for her toast. "I'll get the spare room ready for him. If you have somewhere else in mind for Tony to sleep let me know and I won't even bother getting the room together."

She glanced at the laughter in his eyes. He was trying to find out if she was planning to have him share her bedroom. As much as she wanted to wake up in his arms, she had a child to consider. She lowered her mug to the table. "No, go ahead and get the room ready. Also if it isn't too much trouble can you put the screen back in my bedroom window? For some strange reason it fell out sometime last night."

Pops returned to the table carrying her toast and put it in front of her before returning to his seat. "It was coming down pretty hard last night. I'm surprised I managed to sleep through it all."

Reaching for her knife, she buttered the bread. "I didn't sleep well at all, which is unusual for a rainy night. I'm usually out like a light."

Smiling, Pops reached for his mug. "Maybe the reason why you couldn't sleep was because a certain person was on your mind last night."

She blushed then chuckled. "Maybe."

Chante had finished her breakfast then dropped Devon off at school. She arrived at the George Washington Building shortly before eight o'clock, and pulled her car into the parking garage underneath the building. After climbing out, she reached for her briefcase on the backseat and closed the door. She was amazed to find Andrea's Mazda Miata already in the spot beside her. Her partner usually came late and left early. That could only mean one of two things: she had a marketing idea that she was dying to get down on paper, or she was having men problems and needed her work to preoccupy her mind. Either way, she was bound to hear about it only seconds after sliding behind her desk.

She moved down the row of cars that ranged from a beat-up Volkswagen to several BMWs. She stopped at the elevator door and pushed the button.

"Good morning, Chante."

Chante swirled around clutching her chest. The man standing before her had practically scared the living daylights out of her. "Gordon, I didn't hear you."

He gave her an apologetic look. "Sorry, didn't mean to scare you."

She met his gaze as she forced her heartbeat back to normal. "No problem. I guess I was preoccupied."

Gordon was an underwriter for Nationwide Insurance Group, located on the third floor. He was a good-looking guy, if she chose to ignore the way he stared at her with his somber puppy dog eyes, and concentrated instead on his pleasant features, and slender, athletic build. But she couldn't ignore it. Nor had she given it much thought that he was forty and single. However, despite his staring problem, she actually liked him. He was intelligent and talented. His talent was what brought them together.

The doors opened and he waited until she boarded the elevator before following.

"How's the literary business going?" he asked.

Gordon was standing closer than necessary and making her feel uncomfortable. "Fine," she said politely, then took a step back. "I've been quite busy."

He gave her his usual shy smile and said, "That's good to hear. I made those revisions you had suggested. As soon as I have my manuscript edited, I'll be ready to submit it."

She nodded. "Like I said before, I'll be more than happy to recommend a couple of agents."

He looked pleased. "I really appreciate your help."

A couple of months ago, Gordon had waited for her in the parking garage then personally handed her a science fiction manuscript he'd been working on for over three years. She didn't represent science fiction because for one she wasn't as knowledgeable about the market, and most importantly, she didn't care for the genre. She had never been into *Star Wars*. Nevertheless, she did take the time to edit the first chapter and give him some valuable advice.

The elevator stopped on his floor, and before the doors opened, he turned to her and asked, "Would you like to go out to lunch with me sometime?"

Chante could tell he'd been working up to asking her that question. She hated to hurt his feelings. He was a nice guy and she didn't want to lead him on. Besides, one man was all she could handle at one time. Not that it would have made a difference in her decision.

She replied as gently as she could. "I'm seeing someone."

"Okay, well, I'll see you around." He quickly turned and exited the car, but not before she witnessed the look of disappointment on his face.

Chante sighed and pushed the button, closing the elevator doors. As she rode up to the seventh floor, she asked herself if there had been a better way of handling his invitation. She knew he was interested. He went out of his way to speak to her, and she had run into him on too many occasions in the elevator for it to be just a coincidence. It was as if he'd been waiting for her. Like today.

Arriving on her floor she got off the elevator, pondering another possibility as she strolled into their suite and unlocked the door. She stepped into the small reception area and switched on the light. Bright light blazed the pale yellow walls and grey charcoal carpet. The Dynamic Duo Literary Agency had a break room with a fully stocked refrigerator for those days they were just too busy to go out for lunch. There was also a restroom, supply closet, and two offices, one each on opposite ends of the reception area.

Instead of going to her office, Chante moved to the office on the left, directly behind Kayla's desk. The door was closed but light glowed from underneath the door. She knocked lightly then turned the knob. She found Andrea sitting behind her desk.

She leaned against the doorjamb then asked, "Why are you in so early?"

Andrea met Chante's gaze. Held it. "Your brother. That's why."

Chante gave her a puzzled look. "Dame?" She nodded. "What has he done now?"

She noted the lines of discomfort as Andrea spoke. "I'll tell you what he's done. He refused to take that old recliner that I decided to get rid of. I put it out on the curb yesterday, and how about it was still there when I got home last night!" she complained. "You better believe, I hopped in my car and drove over to Dame's apartment and cussed his behind out, then after he slammed the door in my face, I told him I was calling his boss."

Chante rubbed her temple and groaned. She'd been hearing the same song and dance ever since Dame started working his new trash route, which happened to include Andrea's subdivision. Every month it was one thing after another. She complained that Dame forgot to put the lid back on her trash can or that the wind had blown her cans down the street because he had forgotten to put them back where he found them. It had gotten to the point that Dame had started calling her up to complain about Andrea. The battle was starting to get on her nerves. As much as she hated Andrea calling Dame's boss, in a way she thought it would probably be for the best if he did move to another neighborhood. Only Dame refused to let Andrea have her way.

Glancing at her friend, Chante decided that the firetruck-red suit she was wearing was a perfect reflection of her mood this morning. Andrea was definitely on fire. When she was in one of these moods, Chante knew to tread lightly, otherwise she would never hear the end of it. Pushing away from the door, she took a cautious step forward, and asked, "Isn't there some kind of rule about leaving furniture on the curb? I believe you're supposed to call for a special pick-up."

Andrea looked appalled. "For what? A broken chair? With all those muscles your brother has, he can lift that chair with one hand and toss it onto his truck." She leaned across the desk and met her eyes with an intense stare. "Well, he's not getting away with it. I called his boss last night and left a lengthy message and told him if he doesn't call me this morning by nine, I am going over his head."

Chante shook her head. "Aren't you getting a little carried—"

She held up a hand cutting her off. "Absolutely not! As much as they charge for trash service, I think it wouldn't be asking too much for them to carry the trash cans back up to the house. There is nothing worse than coming home to find my cans in the middle of the street. Last week I had to replace one because some idiot had run over it with his car."

"Oh, brother." She swung her purse strap over her shoulder and turned on her heels. "I'll talk to you later."

Before she could depart, Andrea called after her. "Was there something you wanted to talk about?"

"Oh, yeah," she murmured. In all the excitement, she had almost forgotten why she had come to her office. Swinging around, she faced her again. "I think I know who's sending me those gifts."

Anger quickly departed Andrea's face and was replaced with curiosity. "Who?"

"Gordon."

It took five seconds before the name registered. "The science fiction geek?"

Chuckling, she nodded. Andrea had given him that name after he had dropped by twice to discuss his manuscript. "Yes, I just ran into him in the elevator and he asked me out to lunch."

Andrea leaned forward in her chair. Chante had managed to grab her attention. "You go girl. He is kinda cute. What did you say?"

"I told him I was seeing someone."

"How did he take that?"

She pursed her lips slightly as she answered. "He looked disappointed."

"You think he's the one who's been giving you the gifts?"

She shrugged matter-of-factly. "Who else could it be?"

Andrea took a moment to think about it then finally said, "I don't know, but I guess if he was the one you don't have to worry about getting any more gifts after today."

She gave a frustrated laugh. "Yeah, I guess you're right."

"So since you told him you're seeing someone, does that mean that you and Antonio are officially an item now?"

She wiggled her finger. "I'm wearing his ring, remember."

Andrea giggled along with her. "So does that mean you've decided to make your engagement official?"

She was quiet for a long moment before she finally answered. "We'll see."

Chante checked her watch. It was almost seven. Antonio should be pulling into her driveway any minute and she felt a nervous flutter at the pit of her stomach. The thought of spending the weekend together had her pulse racing. If he did any of the things that he had warned in a lengthy e-mail this morning, she was in for an unforgettable weekend.

When she finally heard him pull up, it was all she could do to keep from dashing out into his arms.

"Mama, he's here! He's here!" Devon called as he dashed down the hall and into the living room.

She turned and looked in the mirror. Brushing back a strand of hair, she blotted her painted lips then took a deep breath and moved down the hall.

Chante stepped out onto the porch just as Antonio was shutting the car door. Her heart raced as she gazed at a pair of broad shoulders straining against the fabric of a red polo shirt. A baseball cap bearing the Bull's logo covered his head, and faded loose-fitting jeans hung low on his hips. As he moved up the driveway, she stared at the flexing muscles in his upper arms as he carried his duffle bag. As soon as he noticed her standing there, his lips curved into a full grin. The gorgeous smile made the muscles of her stomach contract and her eyelids flutter.

Antonio strolled up the walkway with Devon by his side, chattering a mile a minute. In a matter of seconds the two had already formed a bond. When he reached the sidewalk, he stopped in his tracks. Chante looked absolutely gorgeous in a pair of hip-hugging jeans and a mock sweater. When their eyes met, her face lit up. The warmth from her eyes touched him. He didn't truly realize how much he missed her until now.

"Hi," she said, smiling. She closed the gap between them. With each step she took toward him his heartbeat quickened. She continued to move forward until they stood toe-to-toe.

He curved an arm around her waist and tugged her closer. "Hey baby."

"Miss me?" Her moist breath feathered his chin.

"Let me show you how much." He lowered his head and kissed her.

He felt the stirring of desire that only she could arouse in him so quickly and easily. He kissed her with all the love he felt in his heart. He leaned forward, their bodies drawn together. A passionate moan escaped her lips.

His lips were soft yet insistent, his tongue persuasive yet nonintrusive. He tasted like mint gum, a flavor that set her senses on fire. His hand slid along her back and down to her small, round butt covered by jeans. He traced the seat of her jeans as his mouth moved on hers making her feel like the most desirable woman in the world.

Chante's fingers held on to his forearms, feeling the heat radiating through his shirt. A wave of desire swept through her. Her nipples hardened against the soft cotton of her sweater. She wanted to rub her bare skin against his chest. The urge was stronger than anything she'd ever experienced.

"Aw, Mom!"

She heard giggling. Slowly, Antonio lifted his mouth from hers.

Feeling suddenly embarrassed she stepped back out of his arms and blushed openly.

"I'm sorry, I forgot we had an audience," Antonio whispered with a sheepish grin. "We'll finish this later." The look of desire in his eyes took her breath away.

Chante then moved over beside Devon and ruffled his hair then leaned down and kissed him on the cheek.

"Mom," he groaned as he wiped off her kiss. "Yuck!"

She made a face. "Since when don't you like my kisses?"

He lifted his shoulder in a self-conscious shrug.

"Chante you're embarrassing that boy," Pops said coming up from behind. A smile was on his face as he held out a hand to Antonio. "So nice to finally meet you."

He reached for his proffered hand. "The same here. I've heard so much about you."

Chante had to stifle a chuckle. Pops always managed to talk about himself in *her* e-mails to Antonio.

"Come on in. I have lasagna cooling on the stove."

Antonio reached for her hand and she laced her fingers with his, then they strolled into the house together. When they stepped into the kitchen Mildred was setting the table. Her eyes lit up with interest when she noticed their guest had arrived.

Still holding Antonio's hand, Chante pulled him forward. "Mildred, this is Antonio. Antonio this is Mildred, a dear friend of the family."

Antonio gave him a warm smile. "It's such a pleasure to meet you."

"Same here. I've heard so much about you," she said, grinning broadly.

The meal was accompanied by nonstop chatter and lots of laughter. It didn't hurt that Antonio seemed to have endless patience with her son. He was relaxed and abounding with good humor in the face of Devon's numerous questions. Chante found herself drawn even closer to him.

She took a sip of her soda and looked around the table. When she glanced to her left, Antonio winked. When he squeezed her hand beneath the table, warmth flowed through her body. They were a family. She felt it in her heart and she knew by the looks they received from Pops and Mildred, they could sense it too.

She leaned over until their shoulders were touching. A smile softened her lush mouth as she said softly, "If you keep looking at me that way I'll be forced to kiss you."

He moved and whispered against her ear, "That's nothing compared to what I plan to do to you." The low seductive tone held a promise that momentarily swept away her ability to breathe.

After dinner, all of them watched a movie in the family room. Sitting together on the couch they held hands. Halfway through the movie, she glanced over at him and saw a familiar heat burning in his eyes. She couldn't wait to be alone with him.

They didn't have long to wait. Shortly after ten, Devon had fallen asleep. Pops was spending the night with Mildred. As soon as he heard Devon snore, he and Mildred said good-bye. Chante walked them to the door. After she turned the lock, Antonio rose and, carrying Devon, followed her down the hall. She tucked Devon in the bed and dropped a kiss to his forehead, then took Antonio's hand and pulled him down the hall to her room. As soon as she shut the door behind them, she moved into his outstretched arms.

Antonio pressed his mouth to hers. "I've been waiting all night to have you to myself." He deepened the kiss, his tongue slipping between her parted lips. She moaned as a shudder shook through her body.

"Mmmm . . ." she murmured against his lips. "I missed you too."

Antonio pulled back slightly, and chuckling, pressed his forehead against hers. "I guess I need to slow it down a bit."

She laughed along with him. "It's okay. I didn't think Devon would ever fall asleep. He was determined to spend the evening hanging with his new friend." She pressed her cheek against his chest.

"He's a good kid."

"And you're good with him," she complimented.

He simply shrugged. "I love kids."

"I can tell. Is that why you decided to become a pediatrician?"

He nodded. "Children are so sweet and innocent. Sometimes they say the most amazing things."

She pulled back and met his stare. "Don't I know."

"I love putting smiles on their faces and making things all better. The only downside to my job is the kids that I can't help no matter how hard I try."

She squeezed his arm. He didn't have to explain any further, she knew the pain he was talking about. She saw it on his face.

Taking her hand, he led her over to the end of the bed. He took a seat then lowered her onto his lap. Antonio looked so serious, it scared her.

"What's wrong?" she asked.

He tightened his hold on her. "I want to talk to you about something."

Her heart thundered against her chest. *Oh, God. He knows!* "Sure, w-what do you want to talk about?" she stuttered.

"Children."

"Children?"

Tightening his hold, he nodded slowly. "I need to know if you want to have more children?"

Her shoulders sagged and she sighed then started laughing. Oh gosh, she was losing her mind. *He wants to talk about me carrying his child!*

Antonio's brow rose with amusement. "What's so funny?"

She shook her head and sobered quickly. "Nothing, nothing at all. I was thinking about something else." She then threw her arms around his neck, knocking him back onto the bed and smothered his face with kisses. When she finally came up for air, she folded her arms on top of his chest and rested her elbow. "Yes! I always wanted to have at least three."

"Three? Wait a minute. I was thinking about having maybe one more." A smile tilted the corner of his lips. "Why three?" he asked curiously.

"Well, one child has a tendency to be spoiled. Two, one kid is sweet and the other is usually a wild child, but three seems to keep order. " She paused and smiled with fond memories. "I know that sounds crazy because three is an odd number. Growing up there were four of us, two boys and two girls and it was always the boys against the girls and each always taking sides, but when Zearl came to live with us, he kept things off-balance. Sometimes he sided with the girls and other times he sided with my brothers."

"Sounds like at our house. My parents thought they were gonna pull their hair out with my brother and me. Ella Mae said she prayed the entire time she was pregnant, hoping for a girl. After my sister was born nothing was ever the same. Dom and I doted on her, still do. My mother always said Germaine balanced the scale. My brother stood on one side, me on the other and Geri in the middle."

"I like that." Her brow quirked. "How come you and Julia never had any children?"

Chante watched as the smile on his face coolly vanished. Realizing she had touched a sensitive subject, she quickly apologized. "I'm sorry. You don't have to talk about it if you don't want to."

"No." He closed his eyes briefly then opened them again and rolled her over on to her back. He propped a pillow behind his head so he could look down at her as he spoke. "I need to talk about it." He reached up and stroked her cheek. "We lost a child several years ago."

"Oh, Antonio, I'm so sorry." She tilted her head and brushed her lips over his.

"Thanks, baby." He gave her a painful smile. "After that Julia was too afraid to try again." He told her about the car accident that took his son's life and the years following that lead up to Julia's death. "She would have been a wonderful mother." He blinked twice like he had just come out of a trance and gave a curious look. "How come you and your husband never had any more children?"

She inhaled deeply, wanting to tell him the truth. But she knew that she couldn't. She didn't want to risk his reaction. She knew that she had to tell him, and she would. Just not today.

"We waited too late to start a family." That part was true. She had been on birth control, and after the abuse started she didn't think having a child was a good idea. However, during the stress of the last three months of their marriage, she had missed a pill or two, but thought she was still protected. Instead, she discovered she was pregnant.

Reaching up, she stroked his stubble cheek. "How do you feel about having children?" she asked softly.

Antonio's eyes were fixed on Chante. He swallowed. "I would love having a child . . . with you."

The thought of his baby growing inside her womb brought tears to her eyes. "So would I," she whispered.

He then kissed her in a way that made it impossible for her to think. Her blood was racing through her body. Her nipples were hard and aching for him. And her center was wet with desire. As he kissed her, he ran his hands along her back, tripping along her ribs one by one. Everywhere he touched, he set off little fires of desire.

Now, she thought as she pulled her mouth reluctantly away from his. She wanted him now. She turned her back on him and reached for the button of her jeans. Before she had the chance to unfasten it, though, Antonio stepped forward, pushing his body flush against hers, sending a shiver of excitement rushing through her.

"Let me undress you," he whispered close to her ear.

Before she could answer, he dipped his head to the curve of her neck and brushed his open mouth over her sensitive skin. Chante's eyes fluttered closed at the contact, and she was so wrapped up in the enjoyment that she barely noticed him pushing down the zipper of her jeans and spreading the fabric open wide.

He slipped his hand beneath the satin fabric, pressing his palm against her flat belly, pointing his fingers downward, toward the heart of her femininity. His hand traveled downward until the position of her blue jeans hindered his progress.

Unconsciously, Chante spread her legs, giving him freer access. When she did, he drove his fingers deeper, until he found his way between the damp folds of flesh and began to explore.

"Oh," Chante gasped when he touched her so intimately. "Oh, Antonio. That feels . . ."

"What? Do you like that?" he asked softly, his voice a whisper against her ear.

"Oh, yes," she managed to say. "Please . . . I want . . ."

"What?" he asked.

He didn't give her a chance to answer. He teased her with one long finger, reaching up and pressing on her sensitive flesh. Her fingers tightened around his strong forearm, silently urging him to continue his erotic journey. To her pleasure, again and again he stroked her with his fingers, and finally after what felt like forever, he thrust one finger inside her and she clenched around it.

Chante moaned, then told him breathlessly, "I want you there. Antonio, I want you inside me again. Please," she begged.

She didn't need to ask him twice. He removed his finger, then without warning, he jerked her blue jeans and panties down over her hips. After struggling to remove them, Chante finally sprang from the bed and stepped out of them, kicking them aside. Antonio rose also. She tried to turn around to face him, but Antonio caught her hands in his and moved them to grip the chair instead. Reflexively, she clung to it, but looked over her shoulder to see him struggling with his own jeans. While he yanked down his boxers, she pulled her sweater over her head, followed by her bra, and tossed them aside. He reached for his billfold, removed protection and quickly slid it on. Antonio stepped behind Chante and gripping her hips, entered her from behind with one long deep thrust.

Feeling him penetrating her the way he had, she was overcome with passion. He filled her so deeply, she felt they really were one. He fit so perfectly, as if he and he alone had a right to be there. As if he belonged there. As far as she was concerned, Antonio was a part of her. Because she had fallen in love with him. Totally, irrevocably in love. Maybe even from the first moment she'd laid eyes on him she was unconsciously in love with him, she thought vaguely as he withdrew himself, and then pushed more deeply into her. Maybe that was why she had made love with him their second evening together.

He pulled out of her again, then entered her once more, and Chante pushed herself backward against him, until she felt as if he penetrated her to her very core.

"Antonio," she managed to gasp. She didn't want him to stop what he was doing, because it just felt so good, but she had a problem. "Antonio."

"Yes, baby?" he asked breathlessly against her neck.

"I-I got a cramp in my leg," she told him softly.

Chuckling, he carefully pulled out of her. He then kissed her softly on her shoulder before he swung her into the comfort of his arms. "You're killing me baby," he told her as he lowered her onto the bed and moved beside her.

He pulled her into his arms and kissed her deeply again. After one final kiss, he clasped her forearm and pushed her up until she was kneeling over him, her legs on each side of his torso.

"You set the pace this time," he said. And then he grasped

her hips and urged her up on her knees, positioning her over him. Inch by inch he brought her back down again, entering her slowly. "Fast or slow, however you want it. As long as you ride me, Chante."

Slowly, she pushed up then brought herself back down over him. Antonio closed his eyes and cupped her breasts, massaged her nipples. Chante lifted herself up again, repeating the motion.

Antonio returned his hands to her hips, helping her pump fiercely against him until both of their bodies were dripping with sweat. Again and again he plunged into her, until she thought they would both melt from the heat their bodies were generating. A hot coil of pleasure began to tighten inside her. Just as she was on the edge of exploding, Antonio flipped Chante on her back then draped her legs over his shoulders. He took control of their roller coaster ride to ecstasy, driving himself deep inside her. Finally with one last, fierce penetration, he cried out, going rigid and still above her. Mere seconds later, Chante also reached climax. Then he collapsed on top of her, their damp bodies entwined, his breathing as labored as her own.

They kissed and touched some more until Antonio rolled over onto his back with Chante still wrapped in his arms and eventually drifted off to sleep. She kept her head resting on his chest and listened to his deep breathing. Making love with Antonio had brought about the realization that something had been missing from her life for so long. And that something was Antonio.

Chante woke hours later to find Antonio sleeping soundly with his head turned facing her. With a smile she propped her head up with one elbow and studied him.

She took in every detail, starting with his face. Dark brown lashes fanned below his closed eyelids. There was a small faint scar that sliced right through the corner of his left eyebrow. As he breathed, the hairs covering his upper lip blew slightly. She studied his arms covered with thick dark hair, contrasting with his paper bag-brown skin. She visually scanned his broad back and kept going right down his spine to his incredible butt. Watching him she found herself growing aroused again. She didn't know where he got the energy. He had awakened her twice during the night and she had welcomed him inside her body with open arms. Goodness, she couldn't get enough of this man! She should be totally satisfied yet she felt the familiar stirrings of wet heat between her thighs. Shifting slightly she found that she was sore from last night and definitely needed a few more hours and a hot bath if she planned to make love again tonight. With a wicked smile she rose from the covers and decided to go soak in a hot tub of water and allow him to sleep a while longer.

By the time she exited the bathroom wrapped in a large fluffy bath towel, she noticed that he had barely moved an inch. He looked so peaceful, she hated to disturb him. He had a long week with young, sick patients. However, spying the clock on the wall, she realized that she probably needed to get him up if they were going to get him out her room before Devon came looking for her.

She took a seat on the bed beside him and smoothed her hand across his forehead and cheek. "Sleepyhead, time to get up."

Antonio's eyes slowly drifted opened and he greeted her with a smile. "You smell good." His voice was gruff and sounded so darn sexy Chante considered shedding the towel, hopping back under the covers and forgetting about everything else.

"What do you want for breakfast?" she asked.

He rolled onto his back. "You."

She swallowed. Everything from the top of his head to the middle of his thigh was staring up at her. Antonio was totally comfortable with his nudity. He ran a hand across his chest then reached up to caress her cheek.

"How about eggs and bacon?" she suggested.

"That's not what I want." He glanced down and she followed the direction of his eyes. In a matter of seconds, his needs had grown very obvious. "Why don't you climb in bed and find out." His grin deepened as he slid his hand past his belly as if to taunt her.

Feeling herself weakening, she quickly rose from the bed. "I don't think that's a good idea."

Crooking his finger at her, he chuckled. "At least give me a good morning kiss."

As much as she yearned to do just that, she didn't dare go anywhere near him. Not if she intended to make it out the room in time. "I'll give you one after you hop in the shower. Otherwise, Devon is gonna catch us."

Antonio laced his fingers behind his head. "I'll be quick, I promise."

Her heart raced. She knew his quick. Round three was supposed to have been a quickie and instead it had lasted until the wee hours of the morning. Chante knew if she gave in and climbed back in bed with him, it would be hours before the two of them came up for air.

"Sorry, not enough time. Devon will be waking up any minute," she reminded him as she reached for a bottle of cocoa butter lotion. "I left some towels out for you."

He wasn't ready yet to give up. "I would love it if you'd join me."

She considered his words but once again logic won. "I already took a bath. Now get up."

Following an exaggerated groan, Antonio climbed out of the bed and strolled into the bathroom. She admired the way his muscles flexed with every step. As soon as she heard the shower, Chante blew out a sigh and realized she had been holding her breath. If he'd taken one step toward her, her resolve would have weakened and they would have ended up back in her bed.

Chapter Fifteen

After a light breakfast of cinnamon rolls and orange juice, the three loaded into Chante's car and took Antonio on a tour of Dover. Antonio was impressed with the First State. Although small, the state's capital was rich with history. State Street was lined with blooming pear trees and large Victorian homes. Legislative Avenue had been preserved. The historical buildings in the circular cobble-stone road were now dominated by law offices.

At Devon's insistence from the back seat, Chante took Antonio to see his elementary school and his favorite park. As she talked about her quiet little city, he heard the pride in her voice.

Watching her, he pondered another question. How would she feel about leaving and moving to Chicago? They never discussed that. He scowled. In his haste to propose he had forgotten two important things. Children and living arrangements. No wonder she had insisted they slow things down a bit. However, despite the fact they still had a lot to learn about each other, there was one thing he was certain about, and that was that he loved her and still planned, if she'd have him, to make her his wife.

As they drew near, Devon started bouncing up and down

in his seat. "We're going to see Aunt Noa and Granny!" he exclaimed with excitement.

Antonio gave her a sidelong glance. "He must love going to visit your family."

Chante glanced through her rearview mirror to make sure Devon wasn't listening. He was staring out the window with his lips pressed against the glass. What she had to say wasn't for little people's ears. "That's because they spoil him rotten," she replied in a low voice. "No matter how much I complain, whatever Devon wants, Devon gets."

"He's the only grandchild, right?"

"Yes, and that's the problem," she groaned as the subdivision came to view. "My mother insists that we hurry up and give her some more grandchildren before she dies a lonely old lady."

"I guess her kids should take her advice," Antonio replied, laughing.

Chante made a right at the next corner and said, "Thank goodness Chenoa's finally pregnant. Now if we could just figure a way for my brothers to slow down and have a family, she might give us girls a break."

Antonio grinned. "Your brothers sound a lot like Dom. Settling down is the furthest thing from his mind."

As soon as they turned onto Nita Drive, Antonio noticed all the cars and SUVs lining both sides of the street. Chante slowed and pulled in behind a gray Lexus with personalized plates that read MARTY. The moment she shut off the engine, Devon dashed out of the car and into the house. They climbed out. Chante grabbed the housewarming gift from the back seat then came around the car and offered Antonio her free hand.

"Ready?" she asked.

He met her gaze and smiled. "I'm always ready." Antonio snaked an arm around her waist then tilted forward and pressed a tender kiss to her lips. After he felt she had been properly kissed, he pulled back slightly, and staring down in her eyes, whispered, "I love you."

"I love you, too." Rising on her tiptoes, Chante kissed him again, slipping her tongue between his parted lips. Her mouth ignited the already simmering flames inside him to a roaring blaze. He was tempted to drag her back into the car and return to her house so that he could make love to her again. He loved this woman. His woman. However, as much as he wanted her to himself, he was looking forward to meeting her family.

After one final kiss, Chante lead Antonio up to the house and through the front door. From what he could see, it was a nice two-story house with all the comforts of home. In the foyer, early spring flowers filled a vase on a table against a freshly painted pale green wall. The scent of baked apple pot-pourri filled the air.

"Anyone home?" Chante yelled.

Seconds later, a pregnant woman came around the corner. Antonio instantly knew it was Chante's sister. Although her complexion was darker, they shared identical small noses and large, brandy colored eyes.

"Hey, sis," she greeted.

Holding his hand, Chante pulled him forward. "Antonio, this is my sister, Chenoa."

He returned her warm smile. "Nice to finally meet you."

Chenoa ignored his hand and embraced him. "No need for formalities. By the time my husband and brothers get done interrogating you, you'll feel like part of the family," Chenoa added with a winked as she moved away.

From the expression on her face, Antonio didn't know if the detective was serious or playing until her face split with laughter. "Gotcha!"

He gave her a weary smile.

Chante looped her arm through his and headed toward the kitchen. "You have to excuse my sister. She decided to quit her job on the force and become a comedian."

Antonio chuckled. He liked her already.

They moved into the kitchen where a comfortable-looking woman was standing at the island, icing a cake. Betty Campbell wore her gray-specked dark hair very short, but curls made it look soft. She had brandy colored eyes that resembled her daughters', and clear, almost wrinkle-free skin. Dressed in black slacks and a royal blue blouse, it was apparent that even at her age, she could still make heads turn.

"Well, this must be my future son-in-law. Welcome to the family." She wiped her hands across her apron then held her arms out to him.

"Thanks, Mrs. Campbell," Antonio replied as he stepped into her warm embrace and hugged her in return.

"We will have none of that," she scolded as she stepped back, still holding his hands in hers. "Please, call me Betty."

"Betty," he repeated.

"And this here is my husband Carlos," she replied as a tall, dark man with curly salt-and-pepper hair came in through the sliding glass door.

Mr. Campbell moved forward with his outstretched hand. "My boy, I hear you plan to make my daughter an honest woman."

Antonio glanced at Chante's glowing face then met her father's large walnut-colored eyes, and nodded. "Yes, sure. That's my intention."

Mr. Campbell assessed Chante's fiancé, nodding and smiling. He didn't think he'd ever see this day come. "Then that's good enough for me." His large arms pulled him into a strong bear hug. When Carlos finally released him, he seemed to have tears in his eyes. "You made an old man very happy."

"Hi, Daddy." Chante moved over and draped an arm around her father's waist.

Carlos brushed a stray tear away from his eye and beamed down at his oldest daughter's lovely face.

"Young lady, when have you known this family to cater a barbecue?"

"Never, but there's a first time for everything. Although Mama still felt she had to bake something." She pressed a kiss to her father's wrinkled cheek. "I know you love cooking but this was one event where I wanted everyone to be able to kick back and relax."

Antonio stood back and listened to the exchange admiring the relationship between the two. It was obvious the two were very close.

Minutes later, Chante led him out onto the deck and introduced him to her brothers, dozens of cousins, uncles, aunts and close friends. More names than he would ever remember in one sitting. Nevertheless, he smiled, feeling completely welcomed.

"Very nice," Chenoa mouthed, giving her a thumbs-up sign as she and Antonio moved across the wooden deck.

Her family and friends were sprawled out across the yard eating and relaxing. A long table at the corner of the deck housed large pans of side dishes covered by aluminum foil. Chante walked over and made sure that everything she ordered from *Delaney's BBQ* had arrived and was pleased to find potato salad, cole slaw, baked beans, corn-on-the-cob, ribs, barbecued beef, hot dogs, hamburgers, and chicken.

Devon was at the other end of the yard playing tag with two cousins his age. It would be a while before he'd come looking for food. However, she and Antonio reached for Styrofoam plates and dug in.

Martin was on his way back from the guest bathroom when he heard the doorbell ring. He strolled down the hall and opened the door, and immediately felt like someone had punched him in the stomach. Standing on the porch was Candace Price, wearing tight-fitting, low-riding jeans and a scoop neck pink shirt that didn't quite meet her waistband, providing a glimpse of bare flesh at her belly.

"Hey, Marty," she said in a deep sultry voice that did strange things to his insides.

He stood there for the longest time staring at the young beauty. Auburn locks curled slightly around her face and spilled onto her shoulders. Their deep color held highlights of gold. He itched to run his fingers through its thickness.

Thickly lashed, large, stormy gray eyes met his. He didn't recall ever meeting another woman with eyes the same shade or that had the same effect on him. It was something more than the color that always left him breathless. Besides her eyes, she had an upturned nose, full pouty lips and high cheekbones.

"Are you gonna let us in or what?"

The rough tone of her voice brought him away from his runaway thoughts and back to the present. "My bad. Come on in," he muttered as he stepped aside. It wasn't until she stepped in leaving behind the sweet fragrance of her skin that he noticed she wasn't alone. "Shanice, I didn't see you."

"Hey Marty." The nineteen-year-old launched herself into his arms.

"I missed you," she whispered against his ear.

"I missed you, too, squirt." He lowered her back to her feet and made a show of looking her up and down the way an overprotective brother would do. Shanice wore her auburn hair short and spiked with blonde highlights. She was wearing a jean mini skirt-outfit that left very little to the imagination. He glanced over at her older sister with a dumbfounded look. "You let her come out dressed like *that*?"

Candace raised a hand to her hip. "You know how teenagers are today. You can't tell them nothing. They all want to look like them hoochie mamas in the music videos."

Shanice sucked her teeth. "Everyone dresses like this."

Candace pushed out her very attractive mouth. "Whatever. The only thing you need to worry about are those books."

Marty nodded. "I agree."

He closed the door and turned to the two standing in the foyer. "Well, go ahead and make yourselves at home. Everyone is out back."

Candace nodded then he watched as she surveyed her surroundings in awe. "This house is gorgeous." She strolled into the partially furnished living room and admired the pale green and lemon walls.

He tried to divert his eyes from her backside, but it was easier said than done. "I'm sure Chenoa is anxious to give you a tour."

"Where's the bathroom?" Shanice asked then rolled her eyes. "Someone refused to stop and told me I had to hold it until we got here."

With narrowed eyes, Candace studied her younger sister's face. "Nobody told you to drink thirty-six ounces of orange soda on the ride over from the airport."

Used to the sisters' constant bickering, Martin quickly pointed to the bathroom down the hall. Finding himself alone with Candace, he was suddenly at a loss for words again.

She slipped her purse strap off her slender shoulder and tossed it onto the lemon-yellow couch. "How's it been Marty?"

"I've been well, and yourself?"

Gray eyes studied him intently, searching his face. "Can't complain. Columbia is nothing like Wilmington but I'm learning to adjust."

"How long are you staying?"

"Until Tuesday."

"Hopefully you'll let me take you out to dinner before you leave."

She smiled, a single dimple creasing the corner of her mouth. "You know I never turn down a free meal."

They stood there saying nothing yet the air between them started to vibrate and sizzle. Their eyes held for a long moment, suspending Martin between a strong yearning to kiss her and caution buzzing around in his head. Everything about her was young and refreshing.

"So what have you been up to?" The question was the kind you asked when your brain refused to function.

A smile tilted the corners of her mouth when she said, "I've finally enrolled at Columbia College."

"Good for you."

She shrugged a slender shoulder. "Yeah, it's their evening program but anything is better than nothing."

"I agree. Those four years will be over before you know it."

As she told him about the accounting program she was taking, he found himself watching her full lips. They had a seductive shape to them. They looked so soft. As much as he hated what he was feeling, he yearned to feel them against his. All it would take was for him to ease his mouth to hers and push between her lips with his tongue and—

"Why are you staring at me?"

Candace's words jarred him from his thoughts. Martin took a quick step back and ran a hand down his face. "My bad. You have truly grown into a beautiful woman."

The compliment brought a smile back to her face. "Thank you."

He suddenly felt warm and inhaled deeply, trying not to stare at her mouth. Yearning was beginning to win out when, thankfully, Shanice strolled back into the room.

Candace cleared her throat. "Well, I guess we'll go out and join the others."

He nodded and watched the sisters' retreating backs. Once they were out of sight, he took a deep, calming breath and slowly moved toward the backyard as well.

He had first met Candace when she was fourteen. Over the years he had watched her grow from a budding teenager to a beautifully seductive young woman. One he had been trying for years to resist. As he watched the sway of her hips as she moved through the sliding glass door, it was apparent he was starting to lose that battle.

An hour later, Chante and Antonio were relaxing on a double chaise lawn chair in a shaded corner of the yard.

Chante rubbed her stomach and groaned. "I think I ate too much."

"So did I." He draped an arm around her shoulders.

She closed her eyes and rested her head against his chest. "I don't think I'll be able to move the rest of the afternoon."

Lowering his head, he whispered close to her ear, "I can think of a wonderful way to work it off."

Her eyes snapped open. She looked up at him, his gaze flooded with desire. Her lips parted and they could have been the only people in the yard. The air seemed to sizzle and all she cared about was being in his arms. Tilting her head, she pressed her lips to his. Antonio returned the kiss with so much tenderness, tears burned beneath her eyelids. As the kiss deepened, the flame between them ignited, causing her body to ache for him once again. Hearing children's laughter reminded her they were not alone.

"I guess we got a little carried away," she said moments later, after breaking off their kiss.

"You little tease. Just wait until I get you home," Antonio warned playfully against her hair. "I plan to make love to you all night."

Her heart pounded as he continued to whisper erotic threats that were for her ears only. With the growing ache between her thighs, she didn't know if she'd be able to last that long. Every part of her body was ready to receive him.

Dame had set up a stereo out on the deck. He turned up the volume on Mariah Carey's "Shake it Off" and encouraged the family to get up and shake a leg.

"Come on, baby girl. Let's dance."

Chante gazed up at her father standing over them. "Daddy, I'd love to." She took her dad's hand and followed him out onto the deck. Chenoa, Zearl, Pops, and Mildred were already in full swing.

Antonio sat and watched her voluptuous body swaying sensually alongside her father. He was totally mesmerized by her long legs in brown leather mules.

As the song changed to another, the rest of the family joined in, leaving Antonio no choice but to escort Mrs. Campbell out on the deck. He made his way over to where Chante and her father were dancing and she gave him a heart-thumping smile.

The compilation CD played one jam after another. Voices and laughter floated around the deck as they swung their hips with dance steps that ranged from old school to new. One thing for sure—the Campbell family definitely knew how to party.

The next was an old favorite, "Let's Chill." Mr. Campbell tapped Antonio lightly on his arm. "Young man, I'm gonna steal my wife away."

He nodded and watched as he curved his arm around her waist and pulled her close.

Antonio turned to face Chante. "Can I have this dance?" he asked.

"Yes, I'd love to dance."

Antonio curled an arm around her and pulled her against his middle. Chante rested her head on his chest and closed her eyes, listening to the strong tune of his heart that was beating as heavily as hers. She breathed in the essence of the cologne that, as far as she was concerned, had been made just for him. She tightened her hold on his body. If possible, she sought to absorb him into herself.

Halfway through the song, Chante asked, "Are you having a good time?"

"Very good." Easing back slightly, she gazed up at him, staring down at her. "You think I passed the test?"

She chuckled slightly. "You passed. I overheard my mother telling my aunt that she needed to start planning another wedding."

He lifted a thick black eyebrow then chuckled along with her. "I guess we need to sit down and talk about us. You are, after all, still wearing my ring." He reached for her hand and placed it onto his chest. She gazed at the glittering diamond and a shiver coursed through her.

Looking up at Antonio, she blushed when she saw the heartfelt tenderness in his gaze. Tilting his head, he captured her lips with that skillful tongue of his, kissing her deeply as his tongue swirled around in her mouth. When he finally broke the kiss, he pulled her against him and she closed her eyes. She couldn't remember the last time she had ever felt this happy.

"Don't you two look nice," she heard a familiar voice say as the song ended.

She opened her eyes and a smile curled her lips when she spotted Andrea. As usual she was dressed to kill in a pink cat suit and fuchsia Jimmy Choos.

Chante raised her head from Antonio's chest. "I see you made it." She glanced up at Antonio. "This here is my partner in crime, Andrea Harris."

He held out a hand. "It is a pleasure."

She took his proffered hand and stared up at him flirtatiously. "No, the pleasure is definitely all mine."

Chante groaned. "Antonio, I'll be back." She then dragged her friend to the other side of the deck to talk in private.

As soon as they were out of range, Andrea cooed, "Girlfriend, please tell me he has a brother, 'cause I definitely got to get myself one of them."

It was after five when Antonio looked up and spotted Chante talking with Andrea and her sister from across the yard. He went perfectly still for several seconds as he let himself drift back along the night they'd shared. A pleasurable night during which all he'd cared about was pleasing his woman. He remembered the way she had shivered against his touch, how her eyes had widened in astonishment and delight when she climaxed. Tonight he planned to take it up a notch.

"Yo, Tony, man, you playing or what?"

At the sound of Martin's low baritone voice, his mind returned to the spades game. They were sitting at a small card table under a large shade tree. Martin was his partner and it was his turn. He tossed down a king of clubs and won the first book.

"I want to know what your intentions are with my sister."

Antonio groaned inwardly. He had known the moment he agreed to join the brothers and Zearl for a game of spades, the trio were planning to drill him. He started to tell him it was none of his business but then he remembered how he acted with Germaine's dates and decided to let her brother have his moment. He glanced across the table at Martin, then down at his cards. "I plan to marry her as soon as she'll set a date," he answered as he tossed a queen of hearts onto the table.

"You know I'm a cop," Martin reminded as he slid a three of spades onto the pile.

Antonio met his partner's intense glare. "Yep, I know."

"If you even think about putting your hands on my sister you'll have to deal with me," he threatened without a blink of the eye.

Dame tossed a ten of hearts onto the top of the pile then slid the book over to Antonio. "And me."

"You'll have to deal with all three of us," Zearl added, slouching low in the chair.

Antonio's eyes traveled from one to the next. If they were trying to scare him they picked the wrong man. "Only wimps beat up on women. My mama raised me better than that. I treat Chante the way I would expect a man to treat my sister."

Martin slapped an ace of diamonds on the table. "Good, then we shouldn't have a problem."

"No problem at all. So relax. I've been waiting my whole life to be blessed with a woman like your sister. Chante's my soul mate. I promise you, I will treat her like a queen, and protect her with my life."

Zearl smirked as he covered Martin's card with a three of diamonds. "Dog, you're all right with me."

Dame chuckled. "Me, too. Although that sounded kinda corny."

The table erupted with laughter.

"Yo, Tony, welcome to the family." Then Martin reached across the table and tappped his fist against Tony's.

As soon as Andrea went inside, Chante gazed across the yard at Antonio and frowned. She had a strong feeling her brothers were giving him the third degree. She considered rescuing him but had a strong suspicion that he could handle his own.

"I can tell he is exactly what you need," Chenoa said, while leaning across the picnic table.

She gave her sister an inquisitive look. "How do you know that?"

"A brotha that fine. Girl, he's what we all need," she purred.

Chante felt an unfamiliar tinge of jealousy as she turned and glared at her sister. "Don't forget you've got a husband."

Chenoa gave her a dismissive wave. "I'm married. Not blind."

"Looks ain't everything," she reminded.

"No, but that man has more than looks. Pops shared with me a couple of his e-mails." She wagged her brow. "Very romantic."

Oh brother.

Chenoa slapped her playfully across the knee. "Girl, quit

trippin'. You can't tell me that you aren't crazy about him. I saw the way you looked at him."

She took a deep breath, remembering their unforgettable night. He made her want to forget her insecurities about relationships.

Giving a slight shake of the head, she clamped her lips together and shifted on the bench. "Noa, I am crazy about him, but at the same time I'm scared to risk my heart to another man. Been there, done that, and still got the scars to prove it."

Her sister pursed her lips. "Sis, if you let that good man slip away I swear I will never let you hear the end of it. Get past your insecurities and marry that man. You do love him don't you?"

"With all my heart."

"Then quit tripping before you lose him," Chenoa warned with a scowl.

"I know. It's just gonna take some time to adjust to the idea."

"All you have to do is look down at that rock on your finger and that is all the adjusting you need." Chenoa leaned back in the chair and rested her hands on her stomach. "My sister is gonna marry a doctor. Hot damn!"

"You are too much." Chante looked over at the card game again. Antonio's gaze lifted then, almost as if he had heard their conversation. Her heart flipped automatically whenever he did more than give her a casual glance. She registered the simmering passion lurking beneath his impassive expression.

"Did you see the way Martin was looking at Candace?"

Chante stopped staring at Antonio long enough to frown at her sister. "What did you say?"

"I said, look at the way Marty is looking at Candy. He can't keep his eyes off of her."

She gave her a skeptical look. "That baby is killing your brain cells. He's not staring at her," she replied, shaking her head.

"Yes he is. Watch."

Leaning back slightly, Chante folded her arms across her chest. She followed the direction of Martin's gaze. Sure enough Martin was more interested in watching Candace and Devon playing catch than what was going on around the card table. The look on his face was priceless.

"Oh, my God! You might be right." Chante laughed, put her hand over her mouth and laughed even louder.

Chenoa propped her feet up in the chair beside her. "I am right. I thought he was acting a little strange at my wedding. Now I know it for certain. He's got the hots for my girl." Her impressive brandy-colored eyes were shining. "About damn time." She chuckled. "Remember when Candy was so in love with him?"

How could she forget? Candace was so in love, she had the balls to tell her dad she had a twenty-year-old boyfriend. She remembered when Mr. Price had come over to the house with his shotgun. Thank goodness Martin had been at work, and their father had been able to defuse the situation. "She was a kid then. Now Candy is all grown up."

Shanice trotted across the lawn to retrieve the ball that had been thrown out of Candy's reach, and tossed it to Devon. As soon as the two began to play, Candy relieved herself, and twirling on her heels, moved across the yard toward the deck. Marty practically fell out of his seat trying to follow the sway of her hips. The two sisters shared a laugh. Martin definitely was attracted to her.

"Hey, you two." Breathing heavily, Candace took a seat on the opposite side of the picnic table. "Chante, that little boy of yours was trying to wear a sistah out."

"Don't I know, but at least he keeps me in shape."

Resting her arm on the table, Chenoa leaned closer. "So what do you think of our brother?"

It was Candace's turn to arch an eyebrow. "Excuse me?"

Chenoa frowned. "Girl, don't play dumb. Remember

when you had the biggest crush on Marty and your daddy came over?"

Chante noted the revealing twitch of Candace's jaw before she said, "Noa, I was a kid. I've grown up since then. We're just friends."

She snorted rudely. "Yeah, whatever. I saw the way y'all acted at my wedding."

Candace looked to Chante for help and all she could do was nod her head in agreement. She opened her mouth to protest but set her teeth together instead. At that exact moment, Martin rose from the table and moved over to the cooler for another beer. Both Martin and Candace turned their gaze to each other. Chante saw something that looked like a lot more than just simple friendship.

"We can help you hook Martin if you really want him," Chenoa sang.

Candace's eyes sparkled with curiosity. For someone who wasn't interested, suddenly she was very interested. "Hook him, how?"

"All you have to do is get his attention. I mean really get his attention before you leave."

"He asked me to dinner."

Chenoa slapped her palms together. "That's perfect. I've got a plan that is sure to bring my big brother to his knees."

The three women spent the next few minutes devising a plan they were certain was foolproof.

I need to get my head examined. The thought flashed through Dame's mind as he slipped on another forty-five minute compilation CD.

Two weeks without sex had to be the reason. It had nothing whatsoever to do with the fact that his sister's pain-in-the-butt friend looked sexy as all get-up. He didn't know why he'd even noticed. Andrea Harris was nothing like the women he usually dated. But in that pink cat suit everyone noticed, the envious women in his family, his male cousins who were cocky enough to let their interest be known, and especially he. He took a deep breath. Following a two-week abstinence this was not the right time for his willpower to be tested.

He had a healthy sex life like any good-looking man his age, however, lately he hadn't felt the need to sleep with just any woman. He hadn't felt the desire for sex. Yet for some particular reason Andrea made him feel otherwise. Why hadn't he felt the need before her arrival?

It's the attire, he tried to convince himself. In those stiletto heels, all he could think about were them and the long legs attached wrapped around his waist. The pink cat suit showed off one helluva figure. The white tank beneath told him that no matter how many college degrees Andrea had, she was still a take-no-nonsense sistah.

He inhaled deeply. There was no reason why he should be feeling all giddy inside, and he wished he could stop the intensified heat flowing to his loins. The stunning woman would get under his skin if he wasn't careful. And that was the last thing he needed from his sister's crazy friend. Andrea Harris was a thorn in his side. Calling his boss, complaining about the way he does his job. She had the audacity to expect him to empty her trash and roll her cans up to the side of her garage. The woman was crazy.

He moved over to the cooler and, finding no more beer, went through the side entrance and entered the kitchen. He stopped in the doorway. There, sitting at the kitchen table was Andrea chatting away on her cell phone. Finding her alone was like a sucker punch to the chest. His skin suddenly felt overheated as he looked at a profile too beautiful for words. Juicy red-strawberry lips moved a mile a minute. He wanted to walk over, take that phone out of her hands and kiss the lip gloss off her lips. Then there was that wild curly hair that he was dying to run his fingers through.

You need your head examined.

That thought made him take a deep breath and forced him to get it together—quick.

The terrifying thoughts that had flooded his mind since she strutted across the backyard were abruptly drowned out by one shrilled question: *What the hell has gotten into you?*

He wasn't a teenager anymore. He was a thirty-year-old male and it was only natural to respond to an attractive woman. But he couldn't let a great body and a gorgeous face make him lose his sanity. All he had to do was remember who that woman was sitting in his sister's kitchen.

She-zilla herself.

As quietly as he could, he stepped into the kitchen and moved over and opened the refrigerator, and removed a beer.

"Well, if it isn't my friendly neighborhood garbage man."

He turned around as Andrea snapped her phone shut and slipped it on her hip.

On a sigh, he dared to glance her way. "Whassup, Andrea?"

"Well let's see . . . I just had to go out and buy another garbage can."

He chuckled and popped the tab on the can. "I guess you need to stop buying those cheap metal cans."

"Cheap!" Andrea exclaimed as she rose from the chair and stepped in his direction. "I'll have you know I spent good money on those cans and what do you do, you empty my trash and leave them out on the curb with the lid half on," she barked.

Dame took a thirsty swallow then frowned. "I always put the lids back on," he said in response, not the least bit angry. He had heard this several times before.

"No, you don't," she began and he savored the way Andrea's perfectly plucked eyebrows rose in sudden surprise. "By the time I get home my cans have rolled out into the street and some truck has run over and smashed them."

She had stepped forward. The closer she got, the sexier she

looked, especially with those succulent red lips, high cheek-bones, and cute button nose. He was suddenly jolted from his lust-filled gaze when a finger shoved against his chest.

"You owe me thirty dollars!" she sneered.

"What?" Dame laughed with only a touch of bitterness then rested his can on the counter and again met her narrowed glare. "Andrea, you're crazy."

"The only one who's crazy is you!" She was still ranting and raving but for some reason he didn't hear anything else. All he could do was watch how her mouth was moving beautifully, looking good enough to kiss.

And that's exactly what he did.

"Has anyone ever told you you talk too much," he murmured only seconds after he pulled her into his arms. Before she could utter a word, he pressed his lips to hers.

She didn't have time to prepare for the urgent kiss, much less prepare for Dame raising her up and setting her down on the counter when he moved between her parted legs. He refused to give her a chance to object. She was all talk and he was about action. And to keep from grabbing her by her thin slender neck and strangling her, he did the only thing he could do to shut her up. Nothing could stop the kiss, at least from his standpoint. Except the sound of his sisters' voices. He yanked his mouth away and found both of them standing in the doorway.

"Oooooh! I saw y'all kissing." Chenoa cupped her mouth with the palm of her hand.

"What the heck is goin' on in here?" Chante demanded to know.

Andrea took a deep breath, refusing to give in to her feelings. *How dare he kiss me,* she thought staring at him, trying to keep the heat of her desire from showing on her face. *And in front of his family.*

The minute he pulled her into his arms, just as soon as the lightning bolt of anger had hit, his touch had caused it to vanish. And when his lips touched hers, her body slumped as all of her energy seemed to drain away. There was nothing gentle about his kiss, nothing tender. She had been on fire, melting under the crush of his mouth against her.

Damn his whiskey-brown eyes.

She knew the reason why she had gone off was that she could not afford to succumb to her feelings. Even with his bad attitude she had to admit that Dame was handsome as sin. His cornrows and goatee took her breath away. His tall muscular body almost brought her to her knees. Watching him tossing trash, dripping a sweat drench, in his tight fitting T-shirt was more than she could bear. However the last thing she needed was to be attracted to him. For almost a year, she had resisted him, refusing to give in to temptation, to give in to her feelings. Dame was not only her partner's brother, but they were complete opposites. Nope, it would never work. She drove a Miati, he drove a motorcycle. She wore Jimmy Choos and Donna Karan suits, while Dame wore Rocawear and Timberland. She had a Master's in public relations. He was taking night classes at a local community college. She owned a large five-bedroom house, while he rented a studio apartment. Besides, he drove on the back of a trash truck all day and each week he thought of some way to infuriate her. And the worst of it all was that he was younger than she, five years to be exact and she never ever dated younger men.

"What's going on in here?" Chante asked again, breaking into her thoughts.

Dame looked like he'd gotten caught with his hand in the cookie jar.

Andrea slid down off the counter and rushed to explain. "Uh . . . Your brother couldn't reach the glass on the top counter so I had climbed on the counter trying to help."

Her eyebrow rose with humor. "Uh-huh, and your legs just happened to fall around his waist." Her brother was over six-three, reaching something on the top shelf of the tall cabinets was no problem for him.

Chante took one look at the uncomfortable expression on their faces and she and Chenoa tossed their heads back with laughter.

"I'll holla at you on Monday," Andrea said then stormed across of the kitchen and out the front door.

Chante slugged her brother in the arm.

Dame jumped out of her reach. "Ow! What you hit me for?"

"What were you doing slobbering all over my girl?"

Dame gave her what looked like a cross between a scowl and a laugh. "I wasn't slobbering. She just doesn't know when to shut up."

Chenoa cackled. "So you helped her? I am too through with you!" She tossed her hands in the air and exited the room.

Chante shook her head as she gave her baby brother a disappointed look. Andrea was never going to let her hear the end of this. Stepping out of the kitchen she strolled out to the front to speak to Andrea before she pulled off. Unfortunately, she got there in time to hear her burn rubber.

Chapter Sixteen

An hour after the gifts had been opened, Chante and Tony said good-bye to Pops, Mildred and Devon as they moved toward the door. The three were spending the evening at Mildred's to give the lovebirds some time alone.

Chante kissed Devon good-bye then went to find her sister to say good-bye. She found her in the kitchen helping her mom and Candace put the rest of the food away.

"You sure you don't need me to help?" she offered.

Betty intervened. "No, you go on home with Antonio. We've got this under control."

"She's right. You did more than enough." Chenoa came from behind the island and gave her sister a quick hug. "Thanks for everything. Now go," she added, pushing her toward the door.

"All right. Good night everyone," she called over her shoulder. "Candy, I'll talk to you before you leave."

She gave her a finger wave. "I'll make sure to tell you how dinner goes."

"Sounds good." She then exited the kitchen and went in search of Antonio.

After finding him out front admiring Dame's motorcycle, they climbed into her car and headed back to her house. The ride was relatively quiet as they listened to music. Both were caught up in the moment, anticipating what was going to happen now that they were alone.

As soon as they stepped into the house, Chante lifted her arms around his neck. "Are you going to kiss me, or not?" she asked.

Antonio lowered his face to hers. While his tongue invaded her mouth, his hands slowly moved down her back, fingertips stopping to cup her buttocks. When she nibbled the tip of his tongue, his fingers dug into her buttock moving her close against him. By the time she broke away from the kiss, his face was flushed.

The phone on his hip vibrated. Antonio stepped out on the small deck off the kitchen to take a call from his answering service. When he ended the call he leaned against rail and stared into the thick blanket of darkness that surrounded the small fenced yard. The sky was clear with the sparkle of thousands of stars.

He had enjoyed the evening. Chante had a wonderful family. Watching her interact with her son, he found her to be a terrific mother. As the day progressed, he was even more certain of his love.

"Dr. Marks, is everything okay?"

Antonio turned to face Chante, her eyes luminous in the moonlight that spilled down. "Everything is fine. Come here." He opened his arms, his heart sending the blood slamming through his veins as she moved to stand in the circle of them. Instantly the sizzle was back. Her scent and the heat of her body surrounded him.

She pulled back and stared up at him. "I've missed you, Antonio, these past two weeks."

"Not as much as I've missed you." His hands came up to her cheeks. "I've thought of you every night. I've dreamed of touching you." His hands shook as he framed her face between his palms, bent his head and kissed her softly. When he finally pulled away, he dropped down on one knee and cupped her hand in his.

Her heart started racing against her chest. "What are you doing?"

He stared up at her with the most serious expression. "Chante Campbell, I love you so much. I know I've asked you this once before but this time I want to do it face to face. I want to give you babies and love you until the day you die. Sweetheart, will you marry me?"

She gave him a puzzled look. "I thought we were already engaged?"

"No that was a misunderstanding. The first proposal was an impulse. The second engagement announcement was an accident. This time I want to ask you the right way."

"Oh, Tony," she whispered. "Yes, I'll marry you."

He smiled, then rose from the floor. He lifted her off her feet and carried her into the house. Antonio kissed her long and deep. Her love for him was so strong it nearly made her weep.

"Bed?" he suggested.

"Now," she demanded.

They raced down the hall toward the bedroom. As soon as they were there he kissed her again and began to rid both of them of their clothes. He then peeled back the covers and lowered her onto the mattress.

"I'll go slow," he said.

"Don't."

His gaze was as hot as molten steel as it led the way down her body, followed by his hands and then his lips. He kissed her eyelids, ears and her nose. She could feel the heat of his mouth, the softness of his lips, and an ache throbbed inside her. The pleasure he gave was nearly unbearable. He kissed the sides of her neck, trailing kisses over her shoulders, and took her breasts into his mouth, using his tongue and driving her wild.

"Please . . ." she wanted him inside of her. Then her fingers raked over his slick shoulders, dragging him up to where she wanted him. "Please," she begged.

"Just a second, baby," he said.

Never had a second seemed so endless, while he ripped open a packet and protected them. He kissed her again. On his knees and one elbow, he guided himself in place, and thrust. He moved, with his face buried between her breasts, stroking her with his tongue as he sucked her nipples. He whispered her name, his voice sounding as if in pain. He thrust faster, harder. Antonio didn't slow until she reached release and even then he went on until she came again. Finally, he allowed his own climax to come, his big hands tightening around her hips, his body going rigid. Completely spent, he rolled over onto his side, taking her with him. His eyes were closed and he was breathing as if he'd just run a marathon. As she curled against him, he smiled with pleasure, and eventually drifted off to sleep.

They finally rose around noon after Pops called to warn them they were on their way home. While Antonio showered, Chante moved into the kitchen to make a late breakfast.

She reached into the cupboard over the stove and removed a mixing bowl and a box of pancake mix. A smile tipped her lips as she prepared the batter.

She whipped a spoon through the batter as she remembered after only a few hours of sleep, Antonio kissed her until she stirred. She then felt him roll her onto her back. He parted her legs and wrapped them around his legs then entered her again. They found a rhythm that they both now knew as their song. *If this is a dream then don't wake me.* With a sigh, she moved over to the refrigerator and removed a pack of bacon and a carton of eggs.

She heard Antonio come up behind her. He placed his

hands at her waist and turned her around. "There is something we need to discuss."

She stared into the depths of his eyes. "Okay?"

"I want to know what your feelings are about moving to Chicago?"

As his question registered, she nibbled on her lower lip. He was a doctor so she couldn't expect him to walk away from his appointment at the hospital. Her company was mobile. She could work out of her home if she wanted to. Andrea had mentioned once or twice of them relocating. So moving was definitely a strong possibility. "I hadn't thought about that. I guess that is important, isn't it?"

He nodded. "Yes, very important. My life, my job is in Chicago. I want to share my world with you."

"I look forward to being a part of your world." She smiled up at him. "I've never been to Chicago before."

"Then I guess you need to come and visit me."

She gave him a long thoughtful look then nodded. "How about Devon and I come down and visit right after school is out on the thirteenth?"

"Okay," he agreed, although he didn't like the idea of not seeing her again for another three weeks.

Her eyes sparkled with excitement. "I can't wait to see your home."

"I can't wait either." He murmured against her lips, easing up, fitting the length of her body with his. He buried his mouth at the side of her neck and planted a trail of kisses.

"You're starting something. You need to stop." She whispered but with little force behind her words. The warmth of his breath quivered against her neck.

"I know, baby," he murmured. He was drowning in the feel of her. "I just can't seem to get enough of you." He brushed his lips against her skin one last time then stepped away.

He reached into the refrigerator for the gallon of milk just as Devon came through the front door and down the hall.

"Hi, Mama. Hi, Mr. Tony." He rushed over and gave her a hug then moved over and hugged Antonio as well. "Mama, can we have pancakes?"

She nodded. "The griddle is already heating."

He jumped up and down. "Oh, boy! My mama makes the best pancakes."

Antonio ruffled his hair. "I can't wait to taste them."

While Antonio and Devon set the table, she poured batter onto the griddle. Feelings of family life washed over her again. *This is the way it's supposed to be.*

That afternoon, to Devon's excitement, they decided to go roller skating. They had a fabulous time. Chante was amazed at how graceful Antonio looked in a pair of skates. That evening while she made meatloaf and mashed potatoes, Antonio hung out in Devon's room playing his PlayStation.

Long after they put Devon to bed, he held her tenderly in his arms as he made love to her again and again. She knew there would never be a dull moment in their lives as long as the two of them were together.

Shortly after ten, it was time for him to leave.

Fighting back a rush of tears, she watched him walk out the front door, but before she could shut the door, Antonio was there, pulling her around into his arms. He kissed her again, soundly, deeply, until she felt as if she would never be able to let him go.

He smiled down at her. "See you in three weeks."

She nodded her head and felt like her heart had broken into two. "I love you," she whispered hoarsely.

"I love you, too." He then bent down and captured her lips in another searing kiss before heading for the airport.

Chapter Seventeen

Chante relived every sensation—the power of his body in motion, the strength of his back beneath her hands, and his words of praise so soft in her ears. She could still feel him moving over her, in her. She could still taste his mouth, feel his mustache slide across her stomach as he lowered to taste her intimately. She knew his hands, the sound of his voice and the feel of his body so close to hers. A weekend of sweet, exhausting love-making had only increased her hunger. She had thought that heat and hunger would have eased after seeing him again but instead it had ignited. All it took from Antonio was one dark intimate look, and she heated immediately. The way it should be she realized, an adventure with a loving and compassionate man. A man who didn't know the meaning of brutality, but instead knew how to treat a woman.

Glancing over at the clock, she realized she'd been daydreaming for almost an hour. Shifting on her chair, she once again focused on the proposal she was preparing. For the next thirty minutes, she drowned out thoughts of Antonio and proofread the pages. She was halfway done reading when her phone rang. She corrected a typo then reached across her desk to answer her private line.

"Hello."

"Sweetheart, it's me."

All the muscles in her body relaxed as she leaned back in the chair and smiled. "Hi. How's your day going?"

"Better now that I am talking to you."

Her smile kicked up a notch. "I'm glad to know I have that kind of affect on you."

"Baby you don't know that half of it." Laughter rumbled through the phone. "My sister has been hounding me about meeting you. When you come down, do you mind if we have dinner with her and my nosey big brother?"

Tilting her head, she spoke directly into the mouthpiece. "Sweetheart, not only don't I mind, but I would feel honored to meet your family."

"You sure? I don't want you to feel pressured."

"Not at all. I can't wait."

"They want to see if you passed the test. I told them it didn't matter what they thought and that they might as well get used to you because I plan on you being in my life for a long time."

Chante shivered suddenly with longing. His words made her ache for him. "I like the way that sounds."

"I'm not going anywhere," he said softly.

She smiled. "I can't wait to see you."

"Me neither."

They spoke a few minutes longer then she heard voices followed by a heavy sigh.

"I better get back to work. I love you baby."

Her heart tugged. "I love you, too."

"I'll call you tonight."

She hung up reluctant to break the connection and shuddered lightly still feeling the effects of his words. Antonio loved her. He wasn't the only one that had it bad. She loved him as well.

"Was that lover boy on the phone?"

Chante ignored Andrea's comment and pretended to be

going over some numbers. "Where have you been all morning?" she asked without bothering to look her way.

"I was sending out Karolyn's press release this morning and decided to do some work from home," she replied as she stepped into the room.

Chante's head snapped up from the desk with a skeptical look. "Isn't today trash day?"

Andrea flushed. "That doesn't have anything to do with it."

Chuckling, she leaned back in her seat and folded her arms across her chest. "Oh, it has a lot to do with it. You have been ignoring my questions for two days. What's up with you and my brother?"

"Absolutely nothing," she denied with a scowl. "He is a pain in the butt."

"Then why were you kissing him?" she asked with a smirk.

Andrea rolled her neck as she spoke. "Correction, he was kissing me. I was going off about having to buy another trash can when he grabbed me."

"It sure looked like you were struggling." Chante tossed her head back and started laughing.

Andrea gave a dismissive wave. "Anyway I didn't come in here to talk about me. I wanted to talk about that fine man of yours." She moved and rested her hip on the edge of the desk. "It sounds like things are getting serious."

Her smile widened. "They are." Unable to contain her excitement, she wiggled her finger. "We're engaged, officially. He proposed and I accepted."

Andrea clapped her hands together with glee. "I am so happy for you!"

"Thank you."

"I guess this means you told him the truth about Dorian."

Chante looked down at her desk again. "I didn't tell him yet."

"What do you mean, you didn't tell him?"

She groaned. She should have known Andrea would give her the third degree.

"Chante, you hear me talking to you?"

She raised her eyes to the ceiling before looking at her again. This was worse than her own mother. "The timing wasn't right. He was so romantic and compassionate and so damn happy that I couldn't bring myself to tell him."

"Sounds like another excuse to me."

Ignoring her, she took in her partner's attire. She loved when Andrea wore the purple pants suit with the wide gold belt, and matching gold crisscross sandals. Noticing that Andrea was still waiting for an answer, she sighed heavily, then admitted, "I'm afraid of losing him if I tell him the truth."

"How do you know how he's gonna react. You're being unfair by not being honest with him."

Her eyes narrowed. "Like you're being honest about you and Dame?"

"Forget it." Andrea glared at her as she pushed away from the desk, again running away from any discussion that involved Dame. "I've got a phone call to make." She pivoted on her heels and headed toward the door, but not before glancing over her shoulder and replying, "I am being honest about my feelings. Your brother is a toad."

Chante giggled. "Yeah, right."

Long after Andrea had returned to her office, Chante stared down at the proposal, thinking about what she said. Of course Andrea was right. During the entire weekend, she'd had several opportunities to admit the truth and hadn't taken advantage of any.

Closing her eyes, Antonio's handsome image came to mind. His beautiful smile. His trusting eyes. She was being unfair to him and herself. They were engaged and getting ready to spend a fabulous life together. Neither she nor he could be truly happy until she told him the truth.

* * *

Chante glanced over at the clock on the corner of her desk and gasped. "Oh my!" It was almost seven o'clock. Kayla had popped her head in her office to say good night well over two hours ago.

She set aside the manuscript she had been reading and smiled. She had been so absorbed in the story that she had lost track of the time. Maintaining a small-to-moderate clientele allowed her to not only personally read every manuscript but also allowed her to provide constructive criticism and suggestions to tighten up the story before shopping it to acquisitions editors of publishing houses. The book was about a young psychic who was aiding the police in solving a five-year-old homicide. The book was so well written she had been drawn deep into the life of the young woman and the small town charm of Sudlersville, MD.

Time flies when you're having fun.

There were many evenings Chante was still in the office well after everyone else in the building had gone home for the day. However, remembering her grandfather commenting that she worked too hard, Chante decided it was time to call it a night. Reaching into her drawer, she retrieved her purse and then gathered a few things and stuffed them in her briefcase. Hopefully, after she got Devon to bed, she would have the opportunity to finish the manuscript. She planned to have her critique ready by the beginning of the following week.

After locking the office door, she strolled down the black marble hall to a bank of elevators. She pushed the down arrow and waited for the car. Thoughts of Antonio seeped through her mind, not that they had ever really left. Their weekend together had been everything she could have ever wanted and more. An undeniable ache still throbbed between her legs. The last three nights no matter how many times she had shifted on the bed, nothing had been able to ease the discomfort of not having Antonio lying there beside her. There was no use denying it. She loved him with all her heart and wanted to spend the rest of her life with him whether it be Chicago or Timbuktu. She released a ragged sigh. Somehow she was going to have to find a way to tell him the truth. A part of her believed that as long as they loved each other, nothing else would matter. The other part told her that although her feelings would speak for themselves, and he would be able to accept the fact and probably find humor in discovering that Pops was responsible for bringing them together, she wasn't so sure what his feelings would be when he found out she was not a widow. That was something she might have to find a way to repair.

The elevator arrived and she stepped in and pushed the button taking her down to the garage below. One of the things that had attracted her to the building in the first place was the fact that everyone had his or her own personal parking space below. Although there was plenty of public parking on the street for guests, it was nice to know that her spot was going to be there regardless of what time she arrived at work. At her last job she hadn't had that luxury.

She stepped off the elevator and navigated through the row of cars, heading toward her own.

Bang!

Chante whirled around toward the noise, a car door had slammed, or so she thought. It sounded almost like a car backfiring, but after few seconds of remaining completely still, she realized she should have been able to hear an engine starting or footsteps. Instead, there was only silence. Feeling apprehensive, she spun on her heels and quickly headed toward her car wishing she hadn't worn the torturous three-inch black sling backs.

Bang! Bang!

Her hands jerked up instinctively, as if for protection. She waited for what felt like forever before she hurried toward her car again.

"Snap out of it, Chante. There is nothing to be afraid of,"

she muttered under her breath as she clutched her purse close to her chest. Quelling the urge to look over her shoulder, she decided to walk faster.

Footsteps, heavy and fierce sounding, were somewhere close by. Chante couldn't resist the strong urge to look back, focusing on the row of cars closest to the elevator, but there was no one behind her.

She took a step backward. "Anybody there?" she asked, her heart pounded heavily against her ribcage. No one answered. Instead the chilling silence enveloped her once more, reminding her that she was all alone. She felt only a small measure of relief when she realized no one else was there, and she was perfectly safe. At least as far as she could tell.

Bang!

Terrible fear raced up her spine. She made an about-face and ran toward her car while rummaging through her purse, searching frantically for her keys. Her chest heaved as she breathed. She reached her car and still hadn't located the set.

She heard footsteps coming, and screamed loudly, then started digging faster and finally she felt the plastic chain and pulled her keys out of her purse. She quickly pushed the remote opener, grabbed the handle and leaped into the car, immediately locking the doors behind her. The minute she got the key in the ignition, she sped out of the parking space. She maneuvered around a corner, and just as she reached the exit, a man stepped in her way.

As they drove back to his sister's house, Martin stole a glance at Candace. He was struck once again by her beauty and the way her eyes darkened with passion as she told him about her job as a legal secretary. She was smart, and beautiful.

And sexy as hell.

When he had asked her to dinner he'd told himself he could handle his attraction to her. However, with her close enough to touch, his entire body tensed as if bracing itself.

And the dress.

When he picked her up at Chenoa's his knees buckled when he spotted her in the slinky black dress that left very little to the imagination. She wasn't wearing a bra and her small breasts strained against the material. Her stiletto heels and short dress made her heart-stopping, never-ending runner's legs appear even longer.

After sharing a meal at the Bamboo House, he couldn't stop staring and wondering how it would feel to have her interested in him.

He scowled as he made a right at the next corner, anxious to get to his sister's house as quickly as possible. The last thing he needed was for Candace to be interested in him again. By thinking about such things, all he managed to do was torture himself. He didn't want her attracted to him anymore than he wanted to be attracted to her, but the fact was that he was experiencing a hard-on whenever he thought of kissing her. He couldn't deny that he felt something for her, despite how much he tried.

He was certain that he was confusing the love that he felt for her for something else. Of course, he loved her, but he definitely wasn't *in love* with her. Nor was he in lust with her. No, what had happened between them had been a mistake when she was young, too young for what she had asked him to do. Then she had been young and naïve. But she wasn't the same little girl, begging him to be her boyfriend. Now she was a beautiful and intelligent woman, who didn't need to beg anyone. Instead she was everything a man would want in a woman.

Everything he'd wanted.

Yes, he found her attractive, but it didn't mean he wanted to do anything about it. They lived in two different states and had been living separate lives for years. Besides, he wasn't interested in starting something that he couldn't finish. He wasn't searching for a long-term relationship. If he wanted sex, he knew plenty of women willing to go to bed with him without strings attached.

Martin tightened his hand on the steering wheel. Who was he kidding? He wanted Candace. He wanted to touch her, wanted a chance to feel her beneath him, to feel himself inside her.

"Martin?"

Realizing she'd asked him something, he shook his head to clear his thoughts. "Yeah?"

"What's on your mind?" Candace asked, leaning slightly toward him, her painted lips parted.

What could he say? That he'd been fantasizing about making love to her. "I was thinking I had forgotten to take Buster out before I left." At least it was partly true. Buster was his one-hundred-pound German Shepherd. He had taken him out before dinner but with the volume of water he had drunk from his bowl earlier this evening, chances were Buster was ready to go out again.

"Oh, yeah, Noa told me you bought another dog. I would love to see him."

He took his eyes off the road long enough to smile at her. They shared a love for animals. Something he hadn't found often in the women that he dated. Most were afraid of Buster or frowned at the possibility of getting dog hair on their clothes. Growing up, dogs were something that had always been a part of the Campbell household. However, after the death of Ginger, a Labrador that had been a member of the family for almost ten years, his parents decided not to revisit the heartache of falling in love and losing another pet, and opted not to replace their furry friend.

"You want to drop by my place and see her?" It was out of his mouth before he had a chance to realize what he was saying.

She simply shrugged. "Yeah, why not."

Leaning forward he clicked on the radio and groaned

inward. What was he thinking inviting her back to his place? The best thing for him to do was to drop her back off at Noa's house as quickly as possible and be on his way. Candace and her sister were leaving first thing in the morning, and as far as he was concerned the sooner she was gone the better. He wasn't sure how much more he could take.

The rest of the ride was quiet. He used music as an excuse not to have to talk, instead he listened to New Edition sing one classic song after another as he tried to keep his eyes on the road and off the beautiful woman sitting beside him.

Fifteen minutes later, he pulled in front of a small ranch house he'd bought a year earlier after his accountant told him he needed a tax write-off.

Candace walked ahead of him and he watched her hips sway in the form-fitting spandex dress. The dress hugged every curve and dipped low in the front and the back. Her proportions would make a less controlled man salivate. Martin swallowed—several times.

He hurried and opened the door. As soon as they moved into the living room, a large dog came rushing down the hall.

Candace kneeled down. "Come here boy."

Buster reacted to her friendly greeting by rising on his hind legs and resting his front paws on her shoulders.

"Get down," Martin ordered. Before he could grab his collar, he knocked Candace off balance and she landed on the carpet with Buster on top of her, licking her face. Martin's mouth went dry. He never thought he would envy anyone like he envied his dog.

Snapping out of it, he scooped Candace in his arms and lifted her off the floor. "Buster, go!" he ordered. Obediently, the dog trotted into the other room.

"Put me down," Candace demanded.

Slowly he lowered her to the couch but he didn't let her go. He continued to hold her close to him, staring at her.

"What are you looking at?" she asked.

"You." He was watching the way she looked into his eyes while she spoke, then he dropped his gaze to her mouth.

"Marty, we—"

He cut her words off with a kiss. Not an innocent kiss. There was nothing innocent about it. Her lips were parted and he took advantage of the opportunity and slipped his tongue inside the warm heat of her frosty mouth. She tasted like the spearmint gum she'd popped in her mouth shortly after leaving the restaurant—cool, sweet and tempting. Candace melted in his arms and her curves fitted perfectly against him.

Moments later, he broke off the kiss. As he stared down at her, he couldn't believe they had shared something so powerful and intimate. A part of him wondered what one should say after such a kiss.

He whispered, "You're one hell of a woman."

"Nice of you to finally notice," she said jokingly.

"Candy—" he started, then someone knocked at his door. He moved to get it. Although not especially pleased that someone had interrupted them, he was grateful because he wasn't quite sure what he was about to say.

Swinging the door open he found his flavor of the month, Valerie, holding a bottle of champagne.

"Hello, Boo," she said as she pressed her lips against his, then entered wearing a long trench coat and navy pumps. Seeing the young beauty sitting on the couch in the living room, her full painted lips, thinned to a line. She turned to Martin. "Who is this?" she demanded to know.

He closed the door and followed. "This is a good friend of the family, Candace Price."

Smiling politely, Candace replied, "What's up?"

Valerie turned her nose down at her and didn't bother to answer. Instead, she turned to face Martin and asked, "Are you going somewhere?"

"We've just gotten back from dinner." He shifted his

stance, curious as to why she was here. "What are you doing over here?"

Irritation touched Valerie's face, then she quickly recovered and pasted on her smile. "I came over to bring you dessert." She purred then tossed Candace a look, challenging her.

Candace cussed under her breath. Certain that the woman's idea of dessert was showing up at Martin's in a coat with nothing on underneath.

Buster came around the corner and started growling. Candace chuckled inwardly.

Valerie narrowed her eyes and gritted her teeth. "Martin, I've told you time and time again, you need to put that animal to sleep."

"We should put your fake behind to sleep," Candace mumbled under her breath.

"And I told you he doesn't like everyone," Martin said impatiently.

The dog growled deep in his throat. Candace leaned down and stroked his coat. "Good boy." Buster didn't care for the prima donna. Good, neither did she.

"Candy, can you excuse us for a moment?" Without waiting for an answer, Martin took Valerie by her arm and led her out onto the porch.

Candace shrugged. What did she care? She rubbed Buster and tried to forget about the kiss. Wearing the dress as Chenoa suggested had worked. After years of yearning, she had finally gotten Martin's attention. Only now things were worse than ever.

Candace had waited almost a decade to feel his lips pressed to hers and she hated to admit it but it had been worth the wait.

What a fool she had been. As a teenager, she had dreamed of someday being his wife and the mother of his children. As she stroked Buster she realized even after all these years, nothing had changed. Martin still made her weak at the knees. He still made her yearn.

"Sorry about that," Martin said as he came back into the living room.

"You don't have to apologize. You're not my man," Candace said flippantly.

He gazed down at her, not giving away anything he might be feeling. "No, but we're friends and I think we need to talk about what happened here."

She waved her hand in the air. "What's there to talk about? We both got caught up in the moment. It's a done deal and already forgotten. Now if you're ready, let's bounce." Candace didn't dare look in his direction as she headed toward the door.

As she moved toward his car, she released a long shaky breath. She couldn't believe how stupid she had been. It had taken her years to get over Martin. She had carried a torch for him for years that had given her nothing but heartache and pain. She had humiliated herself once when she had crawled in his bed only to be rejected by him. She had vowed to never feel that kind of humiliation again.

Yet, when she had seen his guarded expression was gone, and he was staring at her as if finally seeing her as a woman, at that moment caution had been thrown to the wind and all she had felt was desire. Now she knew it was a mistake. On the ride back to Chenoa's she made a promise to herself to never let it happen again.

By the time Chante made it home, she was emotionally drained. She still couldn't believe a homeless man had been hanging out in the parking garage. The loud sound had been him digging in the large dumpster at the opposite end of the gate. When she had slid to a halt and flashed her brights, he had quickly run away. Her heart had slowed down by the time she had made it home. She changed into a pair of green sweatpants and a T-shirt then spent some quality time with her son until it was time for him to get ready for bed.

It was well after ten when she finally finished the manuscript with tears in her eyes. *Never underestimate the power of love,* she thought to herself as she put the papers to the side. *Isn't that what you're doing?* Lying across her bed, she took a moment to think about those exact words and realized that was precisely what she was doing. Without giving Antonio a chance, she had already concluded in her mind that he wouldn't understand. When, in fact he was such a compassionate person that she couldn't see him having an unforgiving bone in his body. *What are you so afraid of?* She was frightened at trusting her love for another man. There, she had finally admitted it to herself. She was afraid that by telling him the truth she would be setting herself up for heartbreak. But Antonio was nothing like Dorian. That much was true and because of it she should be willing to take a chance on him, like he was willing to take a chance on loving her.

At exactly eleven o'clock her phone rang. Excitement shook her hand as she reached for the phone. As soon as she heard Antonio's voice, she knew something was wrong.

"Tony, are you all right?"

He was silent for so long she was afraid of what he might say. "I don't think the Conley baby is going to make it."

Chante's stomach cramped as she struggled for something to say. Something that might lessen the pain. "Is that the baby delivered at thirty weeks?"

"Twenty-eight. The baby is a little over two pounds with too many problems." There was silence over the phone for a few moments. "Sometimes I wonder why I do this?"

Chante closed her eyes and said a silent prayer. The little girl's parents were Tony's good friends. He was doing everything in his power to save the child. She could never dream of seeing someone die. She couldn't even stand the sight of blood. But something drove people who decided on careers in medicine, and that courage was something she would never have.

"Because you're good at what you do," she finally said.

"I guess," he said, then released a long ragged sigh. "Sleep is going to be hard to come by tonight. As soon as I get changed I'm going to the gym for a swim."

"I'm here if you want to talk."

"Thanks."

One thing she knew for certain, he didn't need to be alone tonight, considering his present state of mind. How she wished she was there to comfort him. "I wish I were there so I could give you a hug."

"If you were here, I'd want more than a hug."

She was glad to hear him laugh.

When he sobered, he added, "Although anything from you would be nice right about now."

"I wish I was like the lady in *Bewitched* so I could wiggle my nose and transport myself onto your lap."

Antonio gave a robust chuckle. "That sounds wonderful." He sighed again. "I'll let you get some sleep."

"Okay," Chante replied feeling his sadness return. "Hang in there. When you start feeling down just remember I love you."

"Thanks, baby. I love you, too."

Chapter Eighteen

The following morning Antonio was still fresh on her mind. She had tossed and turned most of the night and had even increased the volume on her phone just in case he decided to call. To her disappointment, he had not.

Chante sat behind her desk unconsciously clicking her pen as she tried to think of some way to show Antonio how much she cared about him.

After a light tap on the door, Andrea entered. "Good morning. I decided to stop and pick up coffee," she said as she moved toward her desk, carrying two piping-hot Styrofoam cups. "Can you believe it? Marvin actually remembered who I was. Go figure." She removed one from the cup holder and sat it in front of her.

"Thanks, I needed this," she said, reaching for the cup.

"I figured as much." Andrea lowered in the seat in front of her and brought her cup to her lips. "You look like you were deep in thought. What's up?"

Chante took a cautious sip before answering. "I spoke to Antonio last night. One of his patients isn't doing too well, and I think he's taking it pretty hard." Tears pushed to the corners of her eyes. "I feel so helpless. I want to do something but I'm not sure what I can do so far away."

Andrea crossed her legs and gave a nonchalant shrug. "So, go see him."

Chante frowned as she said, "You make it sound like it's that simple. I can't go."

"Why not?"

She responded with a dumbfounded look. "Because . . ." She couldn't just pop up on his doorstep, or could she?

She looked at Andrea in time to catch the upward flicker of her mouth. "Look, if he's your fiancé, then you need to get on-line and book yourself a ticket out of here this evening and go to Chicago. I guarantee he will be happy to see you."

Uncertain, Chante continued to sip her coffee as she took a moment to think about what she said. "Maybe you're right," she said tentatively. However, the more she thought about it the better the idea sounded. It was probably better than sending a card and flowers.

She nodded slightly. "Okay, but I'm gonna call him and ask him if he'd mind. I'm not popping up on his doorstep uninvited."

Andrea gave her a pitiful look. "You are better than me. I would just show up and say 'Here I am.' But not everybody likes surprises."

Chante tilted her head forward and narrowed her eyes. "No, I don't. Not that I expect to walk in on anything, but to me it shows a sign of respect."

Andrea rose from her chair and gave a dismissive wave. "If you say so. Anyway, call him, book your ticket, and get out of here." She then turned and walked out of the office.

She swallowed and felt goose bumps on her arms as she reached for the phone and dialed Antonio's cell phone.

"Hello, sweetheart," he greeted.

She closed her eyes and smiled. "Hi. How are you feeling this morning?"

"Tired but I'm going to be okay."

After a momentary silence, she asked, "How's the baby?"

There was a slight hesitation before Antonio finally answered, "She's doing about the same."

Hearing the despair in his voice, she was reassured that she had made the right decision. "I was calling to see if you'd like some company."

"That depends on who the company is," he said softly.

"Me."

"You?"

She could tell he was surprised. "Yep, I decided to fly to Chicago this evening and give you that hug I promised."

"I'd like that very much." She could hear the pleasure in his voice.

She smiled, unable to contain her excitement. "Good. Get back to work. I'll call you back as soon as I book my flight."

"I'll look forward to it."

She ended the call. Anticipation filled her chest as she reached for her mouse and logged onto the Internet. Within fifteen minutes, she had booked a flight to Chicago scheduled for seven o'clock.

Antonio arrived at the airport with barely enough time to park before the plane taxied down the runway. He maneuvered the car into short-term parking then raced down to the terminal to wait outside of security for Chante to disembark.

As he stood off to the side, his lips quivered with excitement. Chante's unselfish decision to drop everything and come see him meant more than she would ever know. It was times like this that he missed his wife the most. Julia had always been there because as a physician, she had a clear understanding of what he was going through. Now that she was gone, he was pleased to know that Chante was more than willing to satisfy his need for comfort during those trying times. The last twenty-four hours had been long, struggling through another episode with the Conley baby girl. Her lungs were beginning to develop but not as fast as he had hoped.

The next couple of weeks were going to be long and hard. If she could hold on, her lungs would grow stronger, and they would finally be out of the woods.

As a crowd of people briskly moved down the runway, he scanned the area looking for Chante. When he spotted her walking behind a very large woman holding a toddler, his chest expanded, then he slowly let out a deep breath. Their eyes met and his heart fluttered as a smile emerged on her lips. Damn, she was gorgeous. Her full breasts outlined by red cotton, thrust forward. Her snug jeans look sensational. He smiled back and before he had a chance to think about what he was doing he moved forward and scooped her slightly off the floor into the circle of his arms. Gazing down at her, he smiled and whispered, "Hey, sexy."

Chante clasped her hands behind his head and stared up at him as he lowered her slowly to her feet. "Hey, yourself."

She then lifted up and met his lips halfway in a searing kiss that sent the blood flowing quickly down to his lower region. The kiss would have gone on for hours if he hadn't had plan that didn't involve an audience.

He pulled back and looked down at her. "Thanks for coming."

"How about you show me how thankful you are when we get to your place," she cooed, looking up at him from beneath thick lashes.

Antonio swooped down for another kiss then said, "You're on."

He took her small duffle bag and swung it over his shoulder, then offered her his hand which she took. Locking their fingers together, he led her through the airport and out to the garage. Once at his car, he helped her into his Jaguar then moved around to the driver's side.

"You hungry?" he asked as he pulled away from the airport.

He looked away from the road long enough to glance at Chante as she said, "Yeah. A little. What about you?"

"I could use a little something." What he didn't say was that what he was hungry for, couldn't be found on a menu. "How about we stop and pick up a couple of burgers on the way? Unless of course, you'd rather sit down somewhere and eat?"

She quickly shook her head. "No, fast food is fine."

Night had fallen over Chicago. Stars were sparkling in the dark sky above, the moon a low hanging crescent. As they left the airport and hopped on the highway, he asked her how Devon was doing.

"He wants a cat."

Antonio twisted his lips in a frown. "I've never cared much for cats. My sister has one that doesn't do anything but leave hair all over the place and stink up the house with his litter box."

She chuckled at his comment. "They're not that bad, although I prefer dogs myself."

He sighed with relief. "That's good to hear." He turned at the next corner. "Are you going to let him have a cat?"

She chuckled then said, "Heck no. I told him he needed to wait until he was more responsible."

"I agree. When I was a kid my parents made us take care of the dog. My brother and I took turns walking him and Germaine made sure he had food and water. Even with the three of us working together it still was a lot of hard work." As they drove toward his home, he told her one animated tale after another about his dogs. Thirty minutes later, while munching on burgers, he pulled into his long driveway.

When the house came into view, her sharp indrawn gasp drew his attention. Antonio glanced at his house and suddenly realized he'd taken the red-brick Colonial home for granted. The house sat majestically against a backdrop of three acres of beautiful land with a perfect combination of tall shade trees and open, spacious area. It had taken him and Julia months to find that perfect home and it had been worth the time searching.

"The A-frame roof makes it appear bigger than it really is."

Chante glanced over with a frown. "Obviously you've forgotten how small my house is."

He chuckled. "I love your house. It's flooding with love and that is something money can't buy."

They shared a smile.

Pushing a remote over his sun visor, he pulled into a three-car garage, then climbed out and reached in back for her bag. Chante stepped out and followed him to the side door. He stuck the key in and stepped aside so that she could enter.

"Wow!" she said as he shut the door behind them. "This is quite a house."

"Thanks." Growing up scrimping he had come a long way. "Let me show you around."

Starting in the large kitchen, he took her through room after room decorated in shades of hunter green and gold. One thing he had admired about Julia was that she was an excellent decorator. Even with her busy schedule she had found the time to make their home quite comfortable. He led her down a wide hall of softly hued carpet.

He took her up an oak turned staircase and down the hall past three spacious guest rooms to the large master suite at the end.

"Wow!" Chante looked around in awe in his large and airy room. "Now I am embarrassed. My house really is small in comparison."

"Yes, but—"

"Yes?" She playfully swatted his arm. "You're not supposed to agree with me."

He rubbed his arm, faking pain. "You didn't let me finish. Like I said before, it's small but there is an element of warmth that mine does not have."

"Oh, yeah. You said that earlier."

"I think you owe me an apology, Ms. Campbell," Antonio said, pretending to be offended.

"How about a kiss instead?" she purred.

He tried to keep a straight face as he answered, "I'd rather have the apology."

"What!" She swatted at him again. Anticipating her move, he jumped out of her way. He ran around the room and eventually allowed her to catch him. In a fit of laughter, he wrapped his arms around her and backed her up until she fell back against his California-king bed.

When he lowered his mouth to hers, Chante moaned. She had to admit she'd never get tired of kissing him. He deepened the kiss, his tongue slipping between her parted lips. She met each stroke for stroke. When he finally drew back, he looked at her with loving eyes.

She raised her hands and cupped his face. "Are you feeling better?"

He smiled down at her and held her gaze. "Lots, now that you're here."

Chante suddenly decided that right now was as good a time as any to tell Antonio about Dorian. She opened her mouth. "Antonio."

"Yes?"

She tried to move her lips but the words wouldn't come out. Instead she cleared her throat and said, "I love you."

He brushed a kiss over her forehead. "I love you, too."

Chante breathed a sigh of relief when his cell phone began to ring.

Antonio groaned. "Hold that thought." He rolled off the bed and stepped into the hallway to take the call. It was the hospital calling.

She sat up on the edge of the bed. Why couldn't she find the words to tell him the truth? She was going to have to find a way before she returned to Delaware. In the meantime, she decided to brush the dilemma aside.

Deciding to give him a little privacy, she rose and wandered down the hall, moving into one room after another, admiring the rich, dark wood furnishings, hardwood floors and bold fabrics. By the time she stepped back into the master suite, she decided that the house was the work of his wife or an interior designer.

Antonio finished his call then stepped back in the room and smiled down at her. "Come here." He signaled for her to join him near the window. "The lake's over there."

She moved beside him and stared out the large window spanning the wall. Just beyond the trees she caught a glimpse of blue water beneath a full moon.

"This is a wonderful view," she said.

"Yes, it is."

She glanced at him to find he wasn't looking out the window at all. Instead he was looking right at her.

A devious grin appeared on his face. Scooping her up into his arms, he carried her into the room. Without formality they quickly shed their clothes and stepped into the shower stall, taking turns lathering their washcloth, washing each other's body with slow gentle strokes, building the tension until neither of them could hold on any longer. They barely dried off before they made a mad dash to the bed. As soon as they were under the covers, Antonio gathered her in his arms. He left no part of her body untouched, loving her thoroughly, caressing and teasing, first with his hands, then with his mouth. They finally came together. Antonio moved slowly, gently with easy strokes inside her body, and together they found a rhythm as he whispered words of love. She came first, and he shortly after. In the aftermath they lay in each other's arms, holding on to each other.

The next morning they were having a cup of coffee when she heard knocking at the front door. Antonio tried to pretend he didn't notice it.

Chante gave him a curious look. "Aren't you going to answer?"

Not if I can help it. He was pretty certain the person knocking at the door was either Dominic or Germaine. He continued to sip his coffee, and stared down at his newspaper, hoping if he pretended he didn't hear, whoever it was at the door would eventually leave.

Fat chance.

Chante lowered the cup to the table. "I guess since you're hard of hearing, I'll get the door." Before he could stop her, she padded across the ceramic floor and down the long oak foyer.

"Wait! Believe me, it's not important." Antonio sprung from his chair. When she spotted him coming up behind, following a giggle, Chante raced him to the door and opened it. Antonio frowned. It was worse than he'd suspected. It was both Dominic and Germaine.

"You must be Chante," Germaine said as she stepped into the house.

"And you must be Germaine. It's a pleasure to finally meet you." She stepped forward and embraced her.

Ignoring the glares of his younger brother, Dominic also stepped in and introduced himself.

"Well, well. It's nice to finally meet my future sister-in-law." Glancing at Antonio, Dominic gave him a teasing smile. "Tony, man, I can see why you snatched this one up so quickly. Chante, you are as beautiful as my brother described." Dominic then took her hand and brought it to his lips, and kissed her, causing her cheeks to redden.

"Yeah, yeah, Casanova, knock it off." Antonio moved and draped a possessive arm around her shoulder. "What are you doing here this early?"

To his annoyance Dominic winked at Chante before responding to his question. "Germaine, told me Chante was flying in, so I thought I'd come check her out."

Antonio glanced at Germaine who was trying to keep a straight face. One of these days he would learn to stop telling her things.

Chante squeezed his hand and smiled over at his siblings.

"We were just getting ready to have breakfast. Would you like to join us?"

Germaine and Dominic glanced at each other then said at once, "We'd love to."

Antonio obviously didn't want to share her with his brother and sister and Chante enjoyed every minute of it. While she and his sister made eggs, bacon and hash browns, the group laughed and talked. She quite enjoyed his siblings who revealed embarrassing tidbits from Antonio's childhood. Her stomach hurt from so much laughter. The Marks were close, like she and her family.

It was noon before Dominic left to play basketball with his homeboys. After his departure, they rose and cleaned the kitchen. Germaine hung around disregarding the many times her brother glanced at his watch.

"Geri, don't you have somewhere to go?" he finally asked.

She shook her head as she followed the couple into the living room and took a seat. "Nope."

Antonio rubbed a palm down his face. "Then find somewhere to go, like shopping. I'll even let you use one of my credit cards."

Her eyes traveled over to where Chante was sitting at the other end of the couch. "Boy, he must really like you because he never lets me use his Visa."

The women laughed just as his cell phone rang.

Chante witnessed the frown on Antonio's face as he moved into the hallway to talk. She knew he had arranged for another doctor to take his calls today. Therefore, his office wouldn't be calling unless it was an emergency.

She nibbled nervously on her lower lip as she thought about the sick baby. Falling in love with a doctor was not her idea. The long hours and priorities of patients over family had destroyed many families. However, she knew the demands of his job would never be an issue for her. She loved him and planned to stand by her man.

When he ended the call, she rose from the couch and walked over to him. The look on his face said he wasn't too happy.

"Is everything okay?"

He shook his head. "No, I need to go in. Some twins of mine just came into the emergency room having severe abdominal pains."

She wrapped her arms around him. "I hope they're okay."

"I hope so, too." He kissed her twice. "I'll make it up to you later."

"I'll be right here waiting."

He started to go, then paused and stared deeply in her eyes. "I'm sorry, I hate to run off on you."

"How about if Chante hangs out with me?"

His eyes narrowed dangerously as he looked over at his sister. "Don't you have to work today?"

"Nope. It's my day off." She rose from the couch. "It'll be fun. I'm sure the only thing you've shown her so far is your bedroom. Unlike you, I'll give her a tour of the city."

"It sounds like a wonderful idea." Chante looked from him to his sister.

"Yeah, okay." He forced a smile. "Have fun."

Chante spent a wonderfully exhausting afternoon with Tony's sister. Germaine played tour guide, taking her to Lake Michigan to see the blue water dotted with boats of various sizes and levels of wealth, everything from sailboats to yachts. Next they went downtown where she photographed the Sears Tower and other tall buildings, then they parked and spent hours at the Water Tower shopping. Chante hadn't felt comfortable using Antonio's credit card and opted to treat herself at her own expense. Whereas with his sister, there was no shame in her game.

Arms loaded with bags, they filled the back of Germaine's Ford Explorer and spent the rest of the afternoon strolling down Navy Pier. Chante was fascinated by the numerous merchants on the pier that carried charming and unique items. After a half hour, Germaine suggested they break for lunch. By the time they were ushered to a booth in the corner of Bubba Gump Shrimp Company, she was famished.

She ordered steak with a rich New Orleans sauce of butter and Cajun spices and mashed potatoes with a side salad. She glanced across the booth. Germaine reminded her so much of her own sister. A no-nonsense type of girl who didn't hold her tongue for no one.

"So what made you decide to meet a man over the Internet?"

Chante practically choked on a tomato. "Your brother told you how we met?"

She shrugged a shoulder as she chewed. "Sure, why not?"

"And you're all right with that?" She answered her question with a question of her own.

Germaine reached for her napkin and wiped her mouth before returning it to her lap. "I'll admit I wasn't too happy about the idea at first, especially since I'd tried Internet dating and it had been a disaster, but I can tell that you make my brother very happy."

A blush colored her cheeks. "He makes me so happy."

She took a sip of her drink. "So what do you think of living in Chicago?"

Chante's eyes sparkled with excitement as she replied, "I can't wait."

On the way back to the west suburbs, Germaine took Chante by Dominic's restaurant where she got to meet the staff, and indulged in a slice of sweet potato pie. She got takeout for Antonio, and shortly after seven, Germaine dropped her back off at the house.

She let herself in and closed the door behind her. It was quiet and obvious that Antonio had not returned yet. Moving down the hall, she put the food on the counter then carried her bags up to his room. She turned on the television and lay across the bed and before she knew it she was wrapped in a program on *Lifetime*.

It was shortly after eight when she heard the garage door open and close. Scrambling to her feet she rushed down the stairs to greet him. When she spotted him standing there, she stopped in the doorway.

Antonio stood with his hands hidden in the pocket of his starched lab coat, the V-neck of his blue scrubs revealing a tantalizing glimpse of his dark chest hairs.

"Hey."

He gave her a tired smile. "How was your outing with my sister?"

"Very nice. I really like your sister."

"I just got off the phone with her. She likes you, too."

She took a step closer. "How are the twins?"

His lips curled slightly. "Home with their parents. I don't think they'll be eating glue again anytime soon."

Her eyes grew large. "Oh, no!" She chuckled. "No, I guess they won't."

For a long moment their gazes held, interlocked by a fierce tension.

"Come here," Antonio commanded.

She moved into his arms. He lowered his head and dropped his mouth to hers, a long, sensual kiss that left them both breathless.

She pulled back slightly. "I brought you some food."

"Food is not on my mind," he whispered against her lips.

He had come home tired, and she could tell it had been a long and exhausting evening. Right now, he needed her. Wasn't that the reason why she was here?

"How about I run you a bath and wash your back?" she offered.

His lips curled upward. "Now that sounds like a plan."

Chapter Nineteen

Three days after she had returned home, Chante was coming back from lunch, when she spotted a large box at the center of her desk.

"Dang, he's at it again," she mumbled to herself as she moved over to her desk. She put her purse in her middle drawer then took a seat and sat there for a long time staring at it. The wrapping paper said, "Happy Birthday."

"A nice-looking man dropped that by."

Chante's gaze shot up to Kayla who was standing in the doorway. "What man?"

She lifted a shoulder. "I've never seen him before. He said he had a gift to drop off. I asked him his name, and he told me he wanted to surprise you."

Chante frowned then glanced down at the box again. This game of cat and mouse was starting to get on her nerves.

The phone rang and Kayla disappeared to answer it. As soon as she was alone, she reached for the box, and pushed back the ribbon. With anger, she ripped off the pretty paper then reached inside the box and pulled out a white teddy bear.

Her mood softened as she brought the stuffed animal to her chest and squeezed it. Whoever sent it, knew she collected teddy bears. That narrowed the list down quite a bit to friends, family and Antonio. Her heart began to race with excitement. Antonio must have delivered the gift planning to surprise her for her birthday. Kayla had never seen him so of course he would be a stranger to her.

Dropping the bear on her desk, she dashed out into the lobby where Andrea was standing over Kayla's desk.

"Kayla, what did the man look like?"

She turned slightly in her chair and after thinking for a second, said, "About six feet, chocolate, dimples, a bald head. . . ."

Chante didn't hear anything else. Her shoulders sagged and her excitement ceased. To her disappointment, her admirer wasn't Antonio after all.

Andrea looked from one to the other. "Who are we talking about?"

"Someone brought Chante a birthday present," Kayla offered. "It's in there on her desk."

"Ooh!" Andrea brushed past her and entered her office. By the time she followed, Andrea had already taken a seat behind her desk with the teddy bear in her arms. "Oh, he is adorable," she sang.

"Yes, he is." Chante moved into the seat across from her desk and took a seat. "Only I still don't know who's giving me these gifts. This person not only knows I love bears, but he also knows it's my birthday this week. I can't seem to figure that part out."

Andrea looked inside the box then finding it empty, tossed it aside. "And no card as usual. Maybe I can have my boy down at the precinct dust it for fingerprints."

Chante rolled her eyes. "I don't think it's that serious. It's not like he's harassing me, although at this point the gifts are starting to become quite annoying."

Andrea pushed herself out of the chair and rose. "Well, I don't know what else to suggest. I guess you might as well enjoy it while you can. At least now we know it isn't Gordon.

No man is stupid enough to keep buying a woman a gift after she's given him the brush off."

Chante let loose a sigh. "I guess."

"Well, I've got work to do," she said, coming around to sit on the edge of her desk. "Denise wants me to schedule a ten-city tour. She is determined to hit the *Essence* best seller list this year."

She tilted her head to the side and crinkled her nose. "That girl has so much energy. I'm certain she'll hit it before September."

The rest of the afternoon was uneventful. Her mother and each of her siblings had called, one after the other, to wish her a happy birthday. She was always amazed at how the members of her family never seemed to forget.

By four o'clock, she finished reading over a contract and then decided it was time to return some phone calls. Chante was on the phone talking to one of her clients when there was a brisk knock at her office door. She looked over and her breath caught.

Dorian!

She met the intense topaz eyes of Dorian Hunter, convinced that she was seeing a ghost. Chante swallowed in shock. "Dorian."

He stepped into her office. "You remember."

"Tanisha, I'm going to have to call you back." She hung up the phone just as Dorian flopped into the chair across from her.

His brown complexion still held features that were rugged, sexy, and mesmerizing. His head was shaved and he had grown a beard. Devon looked so much like his father and for a millisecond, sweet memories slid by her. Then his harsh words slid through her.

"Who were you on the phone with?" he demanded.

The fine hair at the nape of her neck rose. Those deep penetrating eyes continued to watch her. Chante sat behind her desk, thankful for the distance between them. "That's none of your business."

His expression tightened with anger. "That's where you're wrong. As long as you're raising my son, anything you do is my business."

She fought laughing, which would only antagonize Dorian, and he was unpredictable when angry. "How dare you show up here after six years making demands on me? You haven't shown any concern for your son since he was born. He wouldn't even be able to pick you out of a line-up."

He leveled a dark look at her. "That's not my fault. You had a restraining order against me."

Frowning, Chante responded sarcastically, "Maybe that had something to do with the fact that you liked using my body as a punching bag."

Inhaling a deep breath, he held her gaze. "I'm sorry, really I am. That's why I stayed away so long. It's also why I am back." He took a moment to gather his thoughts then continued. "I want to apologize for the way I treated you. Words couldn't begin to express how sorry I am. I was a sick man back then. I had a beautiful wife and no business putting my hands on her."

Chante sat speechless, not sure what to say. She expected a lot of things out of Dorian's mouth, but an apology was not one of them.

"After you dropped all the charges, I checked myself into a drug treatment facility."

A dull heavy pain squeezed her heart. "Drugs? I thought it was alcohol."

He gave her a weary nod. "Yes, I was drinking, but I was also hooked on heroine. But I've been clean now for four years. I made a promise that I wouldn't come back and try to be a part of either of your lives until I cleaned up my act. I'm now living down near the beach, and working construction again."

"I'm glad to hear that you've gotten your life together," she finally said with genuine sincerity.

"Thank you."

Glancing over at the corner of her desk, he spotted a five-by-seven photo. "Is that my son?"

She nodded with pride then watched as he reached for the photo and stared down at it with deep emotion.

"He has my eyes."

Chante had to shrug and smile at that. "And your nose."

There was a long moment of silence, both lost thinking about the past and what could have been.

He returned the photo then met her intense gaze. "I want a chance to know my son."

Chante rose and paced a small path behind her desk. After a few moments she said, "Okay, I just need some time to prepare him."

"Prepare him for what?"

She flung around and faced him. "That his father finally wants to see him."

When he flinched slightly, she regretted her harshness but pride drove her. "You have never been a part of his life, so how can you expect to just pop up one day and say, 'Here I am.' It doesn't work that way."

He rose from the chair and stalked over to the large picture window that took up the entire wall and overlooked the Prince George Bridge. He turned to her and the savage look in his eyes was the one she had seen in her nightmare for years. He took in her blue linen dress that showed every curve she had. Aware of his unsteady nature, she dragged the chair in front of her, needing a shield, some protection.

"Who was that man I saw you with?"

"What man . . . you've been following me?" Chante gritted her teeth. "How dare you!"

"You didn't answer my question," he returned evenly.

She huffed. "And I'm not going to."

Dorian looked angered by her curt response. At another time in her life she would have found herself sprawled across the floor. But she was a different person now. Following months of counseling and self defense training, she was a survivor. No longer a victim.

He took a step forward. "You are a beautiful woman. I would be a fool to think that men wouldn't be sniffing around my wife. But I'm back and things are gonna be different. I promise. I just need another chance."

She smiled at that. "Let's leave the past in the past."

"Why, because you're in love with that cat?" Dorian looked at her coldly.

"Because what is going on between him and I is not your concern, not anymore. It's not your business."

He slammed his hand on the end of the desk. "I'm making it my business." In the next instant he reached out and grabbed her upper arms, jerking her up against him.

"You're mine," he raged huskily against the cheek she turned to him, avoiding his kiss.

"Get your hands off of me!" she demanded as she struggled to get free.

"Not until you agree to have dinner with me."

Chante heard her office door open, relieved that her assistant had come to check on her. Only it wasn't Kayla. There stood Antonio with fire burning from his eyes.

He was wearing dark blue jeans and a windbreaker jacket opened to the waist revealing a red and white T-shirt.

Her senses leaped, not with the fear of Dorian's return but with a burst of pleasure at Antonio's unexpected appearance. He had come to celebrate her birthday. She could feel herself in his arms with her cheek resting against his chest listening to a strong heartbeat so much like her own. She wanted to go to him, to have him hold her, and give her a long, sweet kiss.

Dorian killed the excitement by holding tighter to her forearms making her wince.

He glanced from her to him with a sinister look. "I see your man has come to your aid."

"Let her go—now," Antonio ordered, his words dangerously quiet. Without breaking his stare he stepped into the room.

He sneered. "This is none of your concern. This is between me and my—"

"Let me go!" She cut him off before he could say it.

Chante understood the danger in the set of Dorian's body—that dangerous stare. Not because she didn't believe Antonio could defend himself, but because she knew Dorian played dirty, she decided it was time to take matters into her own hands. She wiggled free from Dorian. "It's time for you to leave."

His shoulders stiffened. "I'm not going anywhere. We're not finished talking."

Antonio's nod was almost polite. "You either leave or I'll make you leave." Chante moved quickly to place her hand on Antonio's arm to keep him from confronting Dorian. His arm bunched beneath her touch and she could feel the anger vibrating off him.

"He's not worth it," she said softly. Chante glanced at Kayla standing outside the door with fear in her eyes. "Please call the police at once." Kayla nodded and quickly disappeared.

Hearing the word police, Dorian suddenly changed his tune. "Okay, I'll leave." He moved past Antonio and paused at the door. She always had to have the last word. "This ain't over." The door slammed behind him, filling the room with ominous silence until Kayla opened it again.

"Do you still want me to contact the police?" she asked.

Chante shook her head. "No, but can you ask security to make sure he leaves the building?"

"I'll get on it," Kayla said then spun on her heels.

Chante turned from the door to Antonio, who was now seated on the leather sofa. He looked tired, dark circles were beneath his eyes. Concerned, she moved to his side. "Are you all right?"

"I think I should be the one asking that question." His hand smoothed her thigh. "Who the hell was that?"

"That was . . ." her voice trailed off as she remembered that Antonio thought Dorian was dead. She was getting in deeper and deeper by the minute. Now what was she supposed to tell him, another lie? "That was someone who refuses to take no for an answer."

"Seems like he wanted you really bad."

She shrugged slightly. "He's never acted like that before, he . . ." She let the rest of her words trail off. She dropped her head and closed her eyes. Her mind screamed at her to lie to make up something—anything. Lies, lies and more lies. She couldn't do it anymore.

"Baby, what's wrong?"

Tears pushed to the surface that she couldn't contain. *No more lies,* she told herself, and slowly raised her gaze to meet his. "That was Dorian," she somehow managed to say.

Antonio's brow bunched with confusion. "Dorian? I thought he—"

"Was dead?" When he nodded she took a deep breath before responding, "I hadn't seen him since the day I found out I was pregnant. As far as I was concerned, he was dead, then today he popped up in my office, demanding to see his son." She then folded her arms on top of her knees and shared with him the embarrassing details of her abusive marriage. While she spoke she allowed the tears to flow freely. After she was done talking, Antonio lowered his gaze and laced his fingers together. For the longest time he was so quiet, he scared her.

"Please, say something." Her voice was barely a whisper.

Antonio's head came up. His eyes darkened as he met her intense gaze. "That man put his hands on you, and I had no idea. Why didn't you tell me the truth?"

This was the perfect opportunity to tell him about Pops and

his matchmaking but she had already made a pledge to never bring it up. She looked down at her hands and smiled a sad smile. "I was afraid to. You assumed I was a widow and I didn't know how to tell you the truth. I was afraid of losing you."

"I love you." He slowly raised a shaking hand and placed his fingertips on her wet cheek. "Did you really think I would have ended our relationship for something so minor?"

She closed her eyes briefly and sucked in a breath. "Yes."

"Baby, you are in my heart." He smiled slowly, warmth smoothing away that hard look. "Do you believe that I love you?"

She swallowed then nodded. "Yes, I believe you."

"Then you need to understand it is my job to protect you. I can't do that if I don't have any idea who someone is or what's going on." He lightly stroked her cheek as he spoke. "Do you trust me?"

Chante closed her eyes. A sob was in her throat when she finally spoke. She was on the verge of crying again. "I'm not trying to make excuses, but you have to understand trust is very hard for me. I trusted and loved my husband and he betrayed me."

He reached under her chin and tilted her face so that she had no choice but to look at him. "But I'm not your ex-husband. I'm your fiancé, your future. At least I hope I am." He smiled sheepishly.

"You are."

With a quick movement, Antonio scooped her into his arms and cradled her against him. "Then that's all that matters. I love you, baby, and I plan to spend the rest of my life proving that to you."

Her pulse raced at his words. Her heart leaped. "I love you, too. I'm just scared, but please be patient with me."

"Baby, as long as you love me, you can take all the time you need." He covered her mouth with his lips. Twisting her in his arms, she locked her arms around his neck as the kiss deepened. She met the thrust of his tongue with her own. Moving eagerly with the rhythm he set.

"Antonio," she began as he rained kisses along her nose and cheeks. "What are you doing here? I thought Devon and I were coming to see you next weekend."

His lips brushed the corner of hers as he whispered unevenly, "I missed you. Besides, there was no way I was going to miss your birthday."

He moved slightly, just enough to bring her closer. He ran his hand along her spine, buttocks, then thigh, following the trail with his open hand. She was amazed at how something so simple as a light touch could make her ache for so much more.

"How long can you stay?"

His whisper against her throat was low and sensual. "Until Tuesday evening."

"Good," she said grinning. That would give her plenty of time to tell him the truth about everything. The charade had gone on long enough. Each week she found herself deeper and deeper in love with this man. But hanging over her head was the fact that she had not been completely honest with him. The last thing she needed was for another slip-up. Like, Antonio accidentally finding out the truth about their hookup. This weekend, she was putting everything out in the open.

"I came to Delaware to ask you an important question," he whispered softly against her ear.

She pulled back, and met his intense gaze. "What?"

He took her hand and placed it on his chest so that she could feel his rapidly beating heart. "Will you marry me before school starts again in the fall?"

The question was so simple and yet layered with complexity. She dreamed of Antonio every night and wanted nothing more than to spend the rest of their life together.

She smiled up at him. "Why the rush?"

He returned her smile. "Because that big house isn't the

same without you. I want you to share my bed. I want to wake up next to you every morning and feel your warm body against me every night."

He pressed a kiss to her hair. "Please say yes."

There was no way she could contain her excitement. "I say yes."

At home, Devon was excited to see Antonio had returned. Pops was there as well. That evening the four of them played *Chutes & Ladders*, and afterwards, Chante let Antonio put her son to bed. As she dressed for bed and waited for Antonio to join her, her mind traveled back to Dorian. Even though he said he wanted to see his son, she knew his return meant trouble. The question was, what was she going to do about it? Dorian was back in her life. She shivered at the thought. Something unsettling rested at the pit of her stomach. She rubbed her temples as she pondered the situation. It was something that was going to take some long consideration. As soon as Antonio returned to Chicago, she would give allowing Dorian a chance to be a part of Devon's life some serious thought.

"He fell right to sleep." Antonio stepped into the room, interrupting her thoughts. He closed the door and moved over to where she was sitting next to the bed.

"That's because he was so excited to see you, he wore himself out." Rising to her feet, she went and stood in front of him.

"He's a great kid."

Tilting her face to his, she kissed his chin. "He's crazy about you."

"I'm crazy about him . . . and his mother," he whispered against his lips.

He skimmed his hands down Chante's body, memorizing every curve. He made love to her mouth with slow, confident strokes of his tongue, causing her to gasp against his lips.

With a few skillful moves, he rid her of her clothes and his as well.

Lying in her bed, he savored the feel of her in his arms. His hunger for her gripped him like a fist. Within seconds he had rolled on a condom and slipped inside, sliding deep into her welcoming body. Within minutes, she was calling out his name. She shuddered over and over, he lifted her hips while he thrust wildly. A climax ripped through him, scrambling his brain, and she held on while they road the storm together. When he collapsed on top of her, she wrapped her arms around him as they both drifted off to sleep.

"Mom, tell Mr. Tony I can shoot a basket." She heard Devon say breaking her reverie.

"I'm sorry did I miss something?" Chante said as she carried over a plate of crisp bacon to the table. All morning, she relived the passion they shared last night. For the first time in what felt like forever, she had taken the rest of the week off to spend with Tony.

Antonio propped his elbow on the table and rested his chin in his hand. "Devon here says he's the next Michael Jordan."

She chuckled. "I have to admit he's pretty good. He gets those genes from his father. Dorian was an all-star and had a full scholarship to Georgetown before he broke his leg."

Antonio glanced over at Devon's smiling face.

"See, told ya."

His mouth quirked with amusement. "All right, smart boy. How about we play a little one-on-one after breakfast?"

Devon nodded eagerly. "We can take my basketball to the park on the corner."

"Sounds like a plan," Antonio said, his lips curling beneath his silky mustache. "You sure you're up for the challenge?"

Again Devon nodded.

Laughing, Chante carried over a stack of pancakes and put a couple on each of their plates.

After breakfast, she insisted on cleaning the kitchen her-self and sent them off to the park. She washed the dishes then moved to her room to make the bed. She brought the pillow to her nose, smelled the scent of him, and held it in her lungs. How wonderful it would be to wake up to him every morn-ing! As she straightened her room, over and over she'd re-played last night in her mind. Every kiss, every urgent whisper. Even now, standing in the middle of her room, her blood warmed with memories.

She picked up his duffle bag and carried it to the corner of the room. Looking down, she noticed that something had dropped out. She spotted a small velvet bag. Curious, she peeked inside and found a small Cartier box. She swayed slightly. *Oh my goodness*! She knew she shouldn't look, but she couldn't help it. She pulled out the small velvet box and opened it. Inside were a beautiful diamond engagement ring and his-and-her matching wedding bands.

He was planning to marry her before he returned to Chicago!

Marriage meant relocating. Antonio was obviously serious about her moving at the end of the summer. Was she ready to sell her home and leave her place of birth? Could she move her business that quickly? All she was certain of was that if he asked her to marry him this weekend, she was going to say yes.

The telephone rang. She returned the rings then moved over and picked up the receiver. It was Chenoa.

"I need you to come over and see the nursery."

"I'll try to come by on Tuesday after Antonio leaves," Chante replied with a heavy sigh.

"He's here again, already? Oh my goodness! Things must be getting serious."

There was a slight hesitation as a blush rose to her cheeks. There was no way she could contain her excitement. "He wants to get married right away."

"What's the rush? You pregnant?"

"Hell no. At least I don't think I am." She did remember on at least one occasion they had forgotten to use protection. "Antonio's just anxious to spend the rest of his life with me."

"Oh, this is too much like a freaking romance novel. Girl, I'm so excited for you!" Chenoa exclaimed with glee.

Chante blew out a long frustrated breath then moved and lowered onto the end of the bed. "Yeah, and because of it, I've decided to go ahead and tell him the truth about everything."

"Uh-oh, I hear problems," she replied with a sighing groan.

Leaning back against comforter, Chante closed her eyes. "No, I just need to tell him the truth before everything backfires in my face."

"What could possibly go wrong? You said yourself Pops won't breathe a word of it."

"Dorian's back in town," she replied smugly.

"What! When?"

"He showed up at my office yesterday and he and Antonio exchanged a few choice words before he finally left." She quickly told her sister about the eventful afternoon.

"How dare he bring his behind in town making demands on you!" Tension crackled off her words.

"I've got everything under control," she assured her. She should have known her sister was going to get upset and in her condition that was the last thing she needed. Chante already regretted mentioning it to Chenoa. "Please don't breathe a word of this to Martin or Dame."

"How can you keep this from them? Each of his arms has their names on it."

Her brothers had threatened to break both of Dorian's arms when they saw him, vowing that he would never put his hands on a woman again when they were through with him.

"Promise me you won't breathe a word of it. It would kill Daddy if he found out," she pleaded.

Chenoa groaned, not at all happy about what she was

asking her to do. "All right, I won't say anything. But what are you gonna do?"

Chante gave a weary sigh. "I don't know. He wants to see Devon."

"He gave up all rights to my nephew years ago! I wouldn't trust him any further than I could spit."

"I agree I just need to be prepared to go to court and fight if I have to."

"Sis, I hate that you have to go through this. You know I'm here if you need me. Just promise me you won't be anywhere alone with that man again. If you need us, Zearl and I will be over there in a heartbeat."

She had no doubt the two detectives would have her back, however the last thing she needed was for either of them to lose their jobs over a lowlife like Dorian.

"I'll keep that in mind. I'll call you on Tuesday."

Antonio had to admit Devon was quite good. Playing ball also told him he was definitely out of shape. After about a half hour of running across the court, he took a seat and watched Devon and a couple of neighborhood boys take it from there. As they played, he thought about his life ahead. He thought about the ring he had in his bag, and chuckled. Chante had no idea but tonight he planned to propose again in front of Devon and whoever else was around at the time. On Monday, they were going downtown and apply for a marriage license. He couldn't wait to make her his wife.

Devon moved to take a seat beside him on the bench.

"Good job," Antonio said as he handed him a bottle of water.

"Thanks." He took a long sip then he glanced up at Antonio with a puzzled expression. "Are you really going to be my daddy?"

"Yep, just as soon as your mom is ready."

"She wants to marry you. Pops said so. He told me it was

a secret, but I told my mama about the computer letters Pops sent you. He promised me you're going to be my new daddy."

Antonio raised his brow puzzled by what he had just heard. "Your mom didn't send me those letters?"

Devon shook his head. "No, Pops did. You said, 'Will you marry me?' and Pops typed y-e-s, spells yes."

Antonio shook his head, certain he hadn't heard him right.

"Pops said I didn't have to keep it a secret anymore 'cause you love my mama." Devon raced back over to join in the game.

His heart shouted that what the little boy had just said couldn't be possible, but his mind believed what the heart refused. He felt as if someone had punched him in the chest. Hurt, betrayal surged through him, and anger pounded beneath his chest. How could she have lied to him? He was going to find out just as soon as Devon finished his game.

Chante warmed up leftover homemade vegetable soup and made ham and cheese sandwiches for lunch. She had already prepared the meatloaf for dinner and had placed it in the refrigerator for later. Close to three, she would pop it in the oven then she would make some mashed potatoes from scratch. She giggled to herself. She couldn't wait for Antonio to taste her cooking.

By the time Antonio and Devon made it back from the park, she had the table set for lunch. Pops returned from spending the night over at Mildred's and joined them.

Devon talked non-stop while she found Antonio quiet. Too quiet. She could tell something was bothering him, but thought it best to wait until they were alone to find out what it was.

Halfway through the meal, Pops lowered his spoon to the table. "I have an announcement to make."

Chante took a sip from her glass. "Pops, what is it?"

Her grandfather glanced over at her and his serious expression turned into a grin as he reached under the table and re-moved a small box. "Tonight, I'm going to ask Milly to marry me." He opened the box and she gazed down at the solitaire in awe. She couldn't help thinking about the rings Antonio had bought for them.

"Oh, Pops! That's wonderful." She sprung out of her seat and came around the table and hugged him.

"Thank you."

"Oh boy! Pops is gonna marry Ms. Milly! Yeaaah!" Devon started bouncing around.

"Congratulations, Pops," Antonio replied as he rose and reached across the table.

Pops was misty eyed. "Thanks, son. Like you, I know a good thing when I see it."

Chante noticed that instead of commenting Antonio low-ered back into his seat and reached for his spoon.

They resumed lunch. The entire time Antonio said little to nothing at all. She waited until after Devon had run next door to his best friend's house, and Pops had gone to his room to call Mildred before she approached the subject.

"Is something bothering you?"

Antonio turned to face her, his eyes a mask of stone. "Tell me something, was this some kind of joke?" His tone was rel-atively calm for someone who was angry and felt betrayed.

A frown creased Chante's forehead. "What are you talking about?"

"The e-mails, my marriage proposal. Was it really Pops all that time?"

Shock flew through her as she wondered how he had found out then realized it didn't matter how, the problem was she hadn't been the one who told him. "I was going to tell you when the time was right."

She watched as his eyes darkened with pain. "At first I thought it was strange that you were asking me questions I had already answered, and telling me things I already knew, but when you were avoiding me I thought something was wrong with me. But now everything is clear. This was one big joke." With each word, anger flowed through his veins.

"Please, let me explain," she whispered, the tightness of her throat made it difficult to speak.

"You've had every opportunity to tell me. Now I'm not sure I want to hear it." The sadness made him almost want to listen to what she had to say but anger quickly hardened his heart again. He loved her. He had planned to spend the rest of his life with her, yet all this time she had been playing some kind of game. He should ask her why, but right now he didn't care.

She inwardly winced at the pain that flashed in his eyes as she responded, "Antonio, you're right. There is no excuse for what I did. Please believe that I love you and never meant to hurt you."

She was pleading now and he couldn't bear to stand there and listen, otherwise he might pull her in his arms. "Did you have any intentions of telling me the truth?"

"Not until Dorian popped up at my office." She exhaled a shaky breath. "I'm so sorry for all of this. I should have told you the truth from the beginning but then it no longer seemed to matter."

His mouth tightened in a harsh line. "Matter to who, you? It matters to me. I don't like knowing I was lied to."

"I'm sorry."

"It's a little late for that," he said, tension crackling off his words. "What else have you been lying about? Seeing Dorian yesterday for the first time?"

"Yesterday was the first time I had seen him in over six years. I swear he popped up demanding to be a part of his son's life."

"Why didn't you just tell me the truth from the beginning?"

Oh, God. She squeezed her eyes shut. "After I fell in love with you, I didn't know how."

He laughed, a loud, unforgiving sound. "Do you really think I'm that stupid? You don't love me. This has all been an act."

She shook her head in disbelief. "How can you say that? You don't know what I feel. I love you whether you believe it or not."

He drew in a deep breath. He wanted so badly to believe her but all he could think about was how she had betrayed his trust. "You've had every opportunity to tell me the truth yet you chose not to."

He was right. There had been numerous opportunities when she could have told him the truth. "I can't make any excuse for that except to say I was scared that you wouldn't believe me. I was afraid of losing you."

"Is that the way you treat someone you love? By being deceitful? If it is, I definitely don't want any part of you in my life."

The phone rang. Chante tried to ignore it but Pops called from his room for her to pick it up. She walked over to the wall and reached for the receiver, then put her hand over the mouth piece. "It's for you. It's your answering service."

Antonio walked over to the phone. She stood back and waited for him to complete the call. The expression on his face told her it wasn't good news.

"There was a fire at the free clinic."

Her eyes widened. "Oh no! Was there much damage?"

"I don't know, but I've got to get back." He turned and walked away then turned again. "We'll finish this conversation later."

She nodded. "I understand."

Chante watched him pack his things, go next door and say good-bye to Devon, then load his bag in the trunk.

Walking to the driver's side he stopped in front of her. "I'll call you when I arrive."

She gave him a weak smile then rose on her tiptoes and gave him a hug and a peck on the cheek. There was a long moment before she felt his hands cup her waist. He pulled her close, and then sooner than she wanted, Antonio released her. When he pulled out of the driveway, her heart sank. Why did she feel like she would never hear from him again?

Several moments passed before she could move. *I deserved that*, she thought, her heart aching. Sensing someone standing behind her, she swung around. When she spotted Pops, she dropped her gaze to the lawn and turned away.

"Are you all right?" he asked.

She wasn't all right in the least. The man she had spent the last couple of weeks with had just walked out of her life. And she didn't know what the hell to do about it. She was torn between running after him and begging him to forgive her, and letting him go, allowing him some time to think. Only problem was she didn't get a chance to tell him how much he truly meant to her. So how would he know?

"Chante, I'm so sorry. This is all my fault."

Glancing up again, she met the worried expression on her grandfather's face and knew he had heard everything that had transpired between her and Antonio. The last thing she wanted was for the kind old man to feel guilty. She pushed past her anguish and forced a reassuring smile. "Pops, if it's anyone's fault it's my own. I should have told him the truth a long time ago."

Moving towards her, Pops shook his head. "No, I should have never taken things as far as I had. It was not my place to interfere in your personal life."

A couple of weeks ago she would have agreed but now she was not so sure. Because of Pops, she had met a wonderful caring man and had fallen hopelessly in love.

"If you want I can drive to the airport and stop him."

She paused considering his offer, but in the end declined. "No, I think I need some time to sort this through on my own. Now that Dorian's back in town, my life is one big mess."

He stilled. "Dorian's back?"

She nodded her head then turned with a weary sigh. "I'm gonna take a nap. Can you keep an eye on Devon? He's next door."

Pops moved forward and reached for her hand. "You know you don't have to ask."

She kissed his cheek then headed back in the house just as the tears streamed from her eyes. Once in her room, she closed the door and fell face first across her bed. She sobbed softly in her pillow as she remembered the hurt look on Antonio's face. He believed it was one big game. Nothing was further from the truth. Instead, she had fallen in love. As she swatted at the tears clouding her eyes, she thought about the mess she had caused. She didn't know how she was going to get him to believe that it wasn't a game. What she felt for him was real. Maybe in the beginning things weren't as they seemed, but once they spent that fabulous weekend together everything had become so clear. She had been lonely and had spent the last six years trying to protect her heart. Afraid to become a victim of love again like she had been with Dorian.

She groaned at the thought of her ex-husband's return and his demands to know his son. Why did he have to show up in her life now after all these years? Now, when she was trying to love again.

Antonio returned home well after midnight, hot, dirty and exhausted. Thank goodness there was only minimal damage to the facility. The fire department gave a preliminary cause as an electric outlet in the back treatment room. The clinic would only be closed for a short period of time. Even shorter, if he could help it. As soon as the insurance company completed their investigation, he would have a contractor on the job.

After a quick shower, he decided to turn in for the night, only trying to fall asleep proved to be a big waste of time. Hurt and anger flared through him every time Chante invaded his thoughts. Yet he couldn't get her out of his mind no matter how hard he tried.

He lay on his back with one arm tucked behind his head as memories of their conversation came flooding back. She had actually had the audacity to try and apologize. That was something that was still hard to digest. Did she really think he wasn't ever going to find out? Obviously, she didn't, otherwise she wouldn't have tried to pull the wool over his eyes like she had. The joke was on him. Not only had Pops and Chante been in on it, but Devon as well. Not only had he trusted her, but had fallen in love.

He raked a hand across his face. Did she actually think he'd believe that she didn't mean to deceive him? For Christ sake, he had been corresponding for weeks with her grandfather while all along he had thought it was her. Where was the humor in that?

The part that bothered him the most was that his anger was the reason why she hadn't leveled with him in the first place. She had known he would have been angry. And she was right. He was angry. She had been playing games with him, so how else could she expect him to act but furious.

It no longer seemed to matter.

On the plane ride home, he could not help thinking about what she had said. Chante claimed that after she had fallen in love, she didn't know how to tell him the truth. He wanted so badly to believe that she really loved him, but how could you love someone and try to deceive him at the same time? First he discovered that Dorian was alive and kicking, then in less than twenty-four hours, Devon revealed he had been corresponding for months with her grandfather instead of her. The part he couldn't understand was why?

If you had hung around long enough she might have had the time to explain.

A nagging part of him said that maybe he was too quick to judge and that maybe, just maybe, she was telling the truth about it no longer mattering how they met. All that mattered was that they loved each other. He couldn't let go of the fact that she had not only agreed to marry him, but she was also willing to relocate to be with him.

As much as he wanted to call and give her an opportunity to explain further, his stubborn pride stood in his way.

Chapter Twenty

"I can't believe you let him just walk away!"

"What was I supposed to do?"

Andrea's jaw tightened and Chante braced herself for verbal abuse. She knew when she had asked Andrea out to lunch that as soon as she told her about Antonio, her partner was going to light into her behind. "You were supposed to hold him down until you had a chance to explain."

Chante simply shrugged a delicate shoulder. "He had to leave."

"I hope you're not just gonna to let this good man go?"

She glanced up from her pasta at Andrea's curious gaze. She was known for being direct and straightforward even when Chante didn't want to hear it. Chante sighed deeply. "What choice do I have? He feels betrayed and deceived."

Andrea lifted a brow as she poured dressing on her salad. "You're in love with him," she said in a simple statement of fact, not a question.

More than you'll ever know. Chante nodded.

"Then you need to show him," her partner suggested while chewing on a tomato.

Chante shook her head, wondering what on earth she was going to do. "I don't know. He was pretty mad."

"Can you blame him?" Andrea pointed her fork at her. "Didn't I tell you everything was going to blow up in your face?"

Her eyes narrowed dangerously. "I'm not in the mood for I told you so."

"You're right." Andrea reached across the table and took her hand. "I'm sorry. I just hate to see you hurting. I know how much you love this man."

This time Chante looked away. "I'm a realist, Andrea. I had a wonderful time with Antonio, but I knew all along what we had couldn't last."

Andrea removed her hand from the table and dropped it into her lap. "Who said so? You told me yourself your parents knew each other a week before your father popped the question. By week three they were married, so anything is possible." She reached for her glass and took a sip. "Girl, I wouldn't dream of letting a good man get away."

Chante lifted a brow as she chewed her food. "You've got a lot of nerve. You still haven't told me what's going on with you and my brother," she said changing the subject.

"Nothing. I told you, love ain't for everyone. Although, as fine as Dame is, if someone hit me over the head, I might be willing to make an exception."

Her eyes grew large. She never for a minute thought her dear friend would be interested in her brother. "One phone call and I can make it happen."

Andrea gave her a dismissive wave. "Girl, puhleeze, he's just a kid."

"He's not that much younger," she retorted, with one brow lifted.

"You know Dame and I don't get along. We have a love/hate relationship." Andrea stabbed her salad with her fork then glared over at her. "And quit trying to change the subject."

Chante gazed down at her glass thoughtfully. "I'm not

trying to change the subject. I've just accepted that it's over between Antonio and me."

"Are you sure about that?"

"I'm positive." However, as she stared down at the glittering engagement ring on her left hand, Chante knew she would never forget him. Not today. Not tomorrow. Not ever.

She was grateful that Andrea finally changed the subject. She actually enjoyed the meal and almost forgot about Antonio for the moment. However, once she returned to her office, she logged onto her e-mail and her heart sank when she saw she had five e-mails and not one was from Antonio.

It was truly over.

Her eyes clouded with tears that she pushed aside. She had to hold herself together and accept the fact that their relationship was over. She had survived six years without a man and she could do it again. She reached for her ink pen and a contract that she needed to review. She was certain she was going to be okay. It was just going to take time, she told herself.

So why wasn't her heart listening?

Antonio was in his office. It was the end of a long tiring day of meetings and people bringing him all kinds of problems. It was actually typical but feeling what he was feeling, it had been a little bit overwhelming, and he had come to his office hoping for a little quiet time.

He flipped opened a file filled with documents that required his signature and reviewed the first on the pile. Halfway through, Chante drifted to his mind. He was a wimp. Chante had played with his emotions and yet he still loved her. Falling out of love wasn't going to be easy, he thought as he reached for another file. Getting over her wasn't going to be easy either.

What angered him most was that he had finally gotten over his wife's death and focused on the clinic, then Chante walked into his life and everything changed. He had fallen helplessly, and foolishly in love. The pull on his heart had been too strong. Now his heart had been broken a second time.

He wondered if she had even cared. He loved her deeply and she had played with his emotions. But why?

If you call her maybe you might find out.

He had promised her he would call when he got home but by the time he'd gotten home his anger had brewed. He had tried to play every scenario possible. Remembering the painful look in her eyes, he had even considered the possibility that maybe she was as much of a pawn as he was, then he pushed that thought away and eventually drifted off to sleep.

When his intercom buzzed, he reached out and answered it automatically.

"Your sister's here to see you," said his efficient medical assistant.

He pulled his reading glasses off and tossed them on the desk. What in the world did his sister want today? Hopefully, not to discuss his return trip from Delaware. As usual, he had shared his plans with his younger sister. She had been happy for him.

Loosening his tie, he willed himself to relax a little before Germaine came in asking for all of the details. He reached over and pressed the intercom button. "Send her in."

He signed one last document and closed the file just as he heard Germaine knock at the door.

Chante had just finished putting Devon to bed when she heard heavy pounding on the door. She moved to look through the peephole and spotted Martin on the other side.

"What's wrong with you?" she said after swinging open the door.

He brushed passed her and stepped into the house. "Where the hell is he?"

Her brow bunched. "Who?"

"Dorian."

Her eyes grew wide. How in the world had he found out? She pursed her lips. Chenoa, that's how.

"I don't know where Dorian is," she said at last.

He rubbed a frustrated hand across his face. "Why didn't you tell me he was back in town?"

She shut the door and moved to clean the kitchen. "Because I didn't think it was something you needed to know."

Martin gasped. "Are you crazy! After what that fool did to you."

She waited until he took a seat at the table before she answered. "He's changed. Or at least he says he has." Although, after the way he had behaved in her office, she wasn't sure.

Her brother regarded her narrowly, long enough to make her sweat. "I'm a cop. People like him don't change."

Chante waved the dishtowel in the air. "Well, maybe he hasn't, but he apologized and I forgave him. End of story." Turning her back on him, she wiped down the stove.

"Are you going to let him see Devon?"

She hesitated. "He is his father."

"You don't owe that fool anything. You don't have to let him in Devon's life."

"I know I don't, but Devon has a right to know his father."

Martin stretched his legs out in front of him. She could tell he wasn't ready yet to let up on the subject.

"He didn't want to have anything to do with him. Why is he back now?"

"I don't know," she answered with a shrug of the shoulders.

He rose from the chair. "Well, I plan to find out. Where is he staying?"

"I don't know. He didn't tell me," she lied. "All he said was that he was back to stay for a while."

"Come on, sis. I know he gave you a number," he interrogated.

"No he didn't. Look, I don't want to talk about it anymore."

There was a brief awkward silence. "You want some dinner before I put it away?"

"Sure. I'm starved," he said with a frustrated breath then moved and grabbed a plate and helped himself to the fried chicken and scalloped potatoes that she had made for dinner.

"There's some lemonade in the refrigerator."

Since there was no point in cleaning up the kitchen until he was done, Chante moved over to the table and took the seat across from him.

"So when's the big day?" he asked between chews.

Just at the mention of Antonio, she shuddered. "We broke up."

He stopped his fork in midair. "What happened?"

She propped her head up with her hand. "Pops."

While he ate, Chante gave him the humiliating details of their engagement. Martin fell over with laughter.

"Ha-ha, very funny." Her voice was dripping with sarcasm.

Martin continued to laugh between chews. "I can't believe he did that to you."

She started to ask him about Candace but thought better of it. Martin could dish it out but he couldn't take it. The last thing she wanted was a heated discussion with her brother.

She raised a hand to her head. "Pops did me a favor. I love Antonio."

Martin suddenly stopped laughing. "You're serious, aren't you?"

Her eyes stung the tiniest bit but she blinked the feeling away. Self-pity was something she was not going to accept no matter how much she was hurting.

Chapter Twenty-one

Still wearing her robe, Chante stood at the window and watched the rain dampening her backyard. She liked the rain, especially on a Sunday when she had nothing else to do but sleep late and read a good historical novel. Gosh, it seemed like ages since she'd last had a day to do nothing but relax. Over the last several weeks her life had changed so much, she had grown accustomed to spending time with a special man.

Now that was all in the past.

She turned from the window, and moved over to the coffeemaker. She replaced the grounds, added water, and turned it on. She figured if she got some caffeine in her system, she just might be able to survive the day on less than four hours of sleep.

The snippets of sleep she had managed were filled with erotic dreams. Antonio was buried between her legs, working his magic, and she was lying beneath him, crying out his name. The dream had felt so real. Somehow, however, she was going to have to find a way to shut out those feelings and pull herself together.

She heard the front door open and close. Pops was back from walking Devon to the corner to catch his school bus.

By the time the coffeepot sputtered, Pops shuffled into the kitchen.

"Are you working today?" he asked.

Chante turned at the sound of his voice. Pops stood in the doorway, his reading glasses on his eyes. "Yes, I didn't get much sleep last night, and decided to go in a little late for a change."

"Your partner is going to have a panic attack." With a smile, Pops moved over to the cabinet and pulled out two mugs.

"Yeah, I know." She took the mugs from his hand. "Have a seat. I'll get the coffee."

"You don't n—"

"Yes, I do. Now sit," she ordered as she steered him over toward the table.

"I could make breakfast while you get ready for work," he offered.

"Nope. Now sit," she said more firmly. "Let me wait on you for a change."

"All right young lady." Pops appeared tickled as he pulled out a chair and took a seat.

Chante filled the mugs with hot coffee and set one in front of her grandfather. Then she set a sugar bowl and spoon on the table and took a seat across from him.

Pops put two generous spoons of sugar in his mug then stirred. "Have you spoken to Antonio?"

Her heart sank at the mention of his name. "No, and I probably won't. He doesn't want to have anything else to do with me."

"You don't really believe that do you?"

With her own cup in hand, she looked across the table at him and nodded. "Yes, I do."

"I think what the two of you have is special and only comes once in a lifetime. You can't let him go."

Chante sighed. "What do you suggest I do? He doesn't

believe me, so how can I get him to sit still long enough to listen to me?"

"Send him an e-mail and explain everything."

Her face lit up and her heart raced. "That's a fabulous idea." That way she could get everything out in the open. Even if he didn't forgive her, at least she would have had an opportunity to tell her side of the story. "I'll type it as soon as I get to work."

"Sounds like a good idea."

"Thanks, Pops." She took a cautious sip. A sudden thought occurred to her and she asked abruptly, "Oh, I almost forgot! What did Mildred say?"

His lips curled upward. "She accepted. We're officially engaged."

Chante reached across the table and squeezed his hand. At least someone was happy.

After fixing breakfast for Pops and herself, she decided to curl up on her bed and type Antonio a lengthy e-mail before going to work. Of course while she tried to concentrate, Andrea called, wondering where she was. It took ten minutes to reassure her friend that she was not suicidal.

After typing what she thought was the perfect letter, Chante showered, changed and rushed off to work. She arrived shortly after ten and immediately logged on hoping to find a reply from Antonio and was disappointed when she did not. She told herself he probably had a full clinic schedule and he would reply as soon as he had a chance.

To take her mind off of him, she buried herself in her work. She spent the rest of the morning responding to query letters from authors seeking representation. Unlike some agencies, she didn't believe in sending out a standard rejection letter. Instead, she liked to take a few moments to personally hand write a response.

When the clock struck six, Chante decided to call it a day.

She still hadn't received a reply from Antonio and at this point she wasn't holding her breath. She packed up her things, angry that she had even allowed herself to think that for a moment they still had a chance. It was over between them and the sooner she accepted that the better.

As she walked across the lot, she spotted Dorian sitting on her car in a green sweatsuit and Nike tennis shoes. She was already having a bad day, and he was here to make it even worse. Angrily she reached into her purse for her keys and walked around to the driver's side.

"Chante, please, hear me out," Dorian said as he slid off her hood.

She stuck the key in the lock. "Dorian, I have nothing to say to you. You popped up after six years and acted a fool."

He held his hand up in surrender. "Okay, I admit I was wrong, but it's hard for me to see you with someone else. Especially since I still love you."

Her head snapped up and she glared at him. "Is that what you call love?" She gave him a bitter laugh. "Leave me alone or I'm going to call the police."

She opened the door and peeled out of the lot before he could say anything else.

Antonio strode down the hospital hallway at a modest pace. It was almost eight and daylight was fading outside. Inside the hallways were quiet. Family and friends were wrapping up their visits, and nurses were busy getting medications ready for patients before they settled down for the night. For the first time in days, he was going home. The Conley baby girl was doing wonderfully. Finally after weeks of praying, she was gaining weight and growing stronger by the moment. Nothing pleased him more than sharing the good news with her parents before he prepared to go home for the night.

He arrived home shortly after nine to a quiet, lonely house. The place would never be the same after being graced by

Chante's presence. How could he forget Chante when his every thought reminded him of her? He paced the length of his living room restless with each minute that passed. He had picked up the phone twice to call her at home then stared at the receiver and finally declined. He hated that he had left things on such a sour note, but didn't he have a legitimate reason? He had worn his heart on his sleeve, confessed his love and had made plans to spend the rest of his life with a woman who had never had any intentions of being with him in the first place. Who was to say what her real intentions were. All he knew was that he felt hurt and betrayed. With a scowl, he dragged a hand across his head. Maybe her grandfather had been the one to throw her into the lion's den. However, she'd had several opportunities to clear herself and had not. Why? he pondered. He slid his hands into his pants pockets. Part of him hoped that the reason why she hadn't was because after all of the time they had spent together, she too had fallen in love. That deep down she really had every intention of becoming Mrs. Antonio Marks. But that couldn't be the case, because not once in all of the time they had spent together had she ever bothered to tell him the truth.

Hearing a knock at the door, he moved to find his nosy sister standing on the other side.

"What do you want?" he said by way of a greeting.

Germaine followed his retreating back into the kitchen. "Is that a nice way to talk to your sister? After all, I came all the way over here to see how you were doing."

He moved over to the cabinet and grabbed a bag of potato chips. "I'm doing swell."

"Yeah, right," she said as she took a seat at the kitchen table. "I have sense enough not to believe you. You look like crap."

"Good, then it matches the way I feel." He reached into the bag and angrily chewed a chip.

"So have you spoken to her yet?"

"Why would I?" he snapped. "So she can lie to me some more?"

She shook her head. "Nooo," she sang. "So that the two of you can work things out."

"What is there to work out? All of this was nothing but a big joke to her. She strung me along for weeks making me think she was interested in spending the rest of her life with me when she never had any intentions of marrying me."

She shook her head sympathetically. "You don't actually believe that do you?"

He no longer knew what he believed. "Of course I do."

Germaine gave him a long impatient look. "I don't agree. I'll admit in the beginning I was a little reluctant about you meeting a woman over the Internet but now that I have gotten a chance to get to know her and have spent time with her, I can honestly say she is the woman for you."

Antonio simply chewed on his chips and said nothing.

Germaine offered him an encouraging smile. "I don't care what you say—that woman loves you. And you love her, too. So you might as well push away that stubborn pride and try to work things out."

There was a long pause before he took a breath and said, "This afternoon she sent me an e-mail."

"What did it say?"

He shrugged and reached for another chip. "I didn't read it."

"Why the heck not?" she barked.

He wasn't sure why he didn't read it except that he wasn't interested in hearing any more lies. "I haven't gotten around to it," he mumbled.

She rose and grabbed him by the arm. "Then let's do it now."

The next day, Chante arrived at work to find Dorian in her waiting room. As soon as he spotted her coming through the door, he rose and moved toward her. Kayla sprung from her chair.

"I'm sorry, Chante, but he insists on seeing you."

She sighed. "It's okay, Kayla. However, call security just in case." She turned and walked into her office. "Dorian, what do you want?" she asked without looking at him.

He strolled over to her desk. "I told you what I wanted. A chance to make things right between us."

She nailed him with a hard look. "There *is* no us. The only chance you might have is getting to know your son." When he opened his mouth to speak, she held up an impatient hand and cut him off. "It's that or nothing."

Dorian didn't look too pleased, but he must have realized she wasn't going to budge on the issue. "All right. When can I meet him?"

Chante's lips tightened. The man had a way of putting her on the defense, which she didn't appreciate. She had worked too hard to eliminate negativity from her life to allow it to seep back in now.

She finally nodded. "All right. Give me a chance to tell him you want to see him."

"You had all weekend to do that!" he snarled.

"And you've had six years to come and be a part of his life," she retorted, pinning him with a penetrating stare.

There was a long awkward silence. "Chante, please, just give me a chance."

She eyed him cautiously. Noting the dejected droop of his shoulders, she finally said, "Okay. I promise to talk to him."

Nodding, Dorian started for the door.

Antonio disappeared in his office at the end of morning rounds. He shut the door behind him hoping for a few moments of peace and quiet while he attempted to clear his head. Moving around his desk, he slumped into his chair, spun it around to gaze out at the rain and felt emptier than ever. Even after seeing over three dozen children, some sicker than others, all he could think about was Chante's e-mail. With his sister standing over his shoulder, he had logged onto his e-mail last night and read the three-page attachment. By the time he had gotten done, Germaine was reaching for a Kleenex while demanding he had been too quick to judge.

She had explained everything that had happened, from the ad Pops had set up, to the evening he had found Dorian in her office. He had read the e-mail twice and had expected to feel better about what she had done but instead he felt worse. Chante had taken the cowardly way out. Instead of calling him or showing up in person to explain, she had sent an e-mail, hoping to make everything all better. And it angered him. The thing that bothered him the most was that he had hoped that by the time he had reached the end of the e-mail there would have been some mention of her feelings for him and yet there was none. He wanted to hear that she loved him. That she truly wanted to spend the rest of her life with him. Only there was no mention of either, just an explanation and an apology for everything that she and her grandfather had done.

"Dr. Marks, your brother is on line one."

He scowled. The last thing he needed was to hear his brother say, "I told you so." By now he was certain Germaine had shared the events of this weekend and he was calling to gloat. Reluctantly, he reached for the phone.

"Yo, bro, what's up?"

Dominic's booming voice came in loud and clear. "Nada, just checking to see if you are up for bowling tonight."

Antonio slouched in the chair. "Nah, I'm on call this evening."

"Okay, then let's hang out this weekend."

"I'm on call." At least this time he wasn't lying.

There was silence for a moment. Dominic asked abruptly, "Why do I get the impression you are trying to avoid me?"

Antonio blew out a frustrated breath. "Listen, just go ahead and say it."

"Say what?" his brother asked.

"I told you so," he said flatly.

"Why would I say that?"

Antonio snorted rudely. "Don't try and pretend Germaine didn't say anything to you."

"She did, and that's why I wanted to know if you wanted to hang out so I can try and cheer you up. Listen, I may have been dead set against you meeting this woman and maybe I gave you a hard time about meeting a woman over the Internet, but I was wrong. At least this time. I only spent a few minutes with Chante but it was long enough to know that she is good for you and you'd be a fool to let her go."

He couldn't possibly be hearing him right. "Are you sure Germaine told you she deceived me?"

"Yeah, and yes, Chante was wrong for not telling you the truth. But I think what the two of you have doesn't come too often. You were fortunate to marry a woman like Julia. You should feel blessed to have the opportunity to find true love again."

He was floored. He didn't even know where to begin with a response.

He could almost see Dominic's smile when he replied, "You know, I just realized that I'm not on call tonight. I guess I can meet you at the bowling alley after all."

"Bet, I'll see you there."

When Antonio hung up, he was still stunned by his brother's sudden change of heart. Maybe there was hope for him yet. Tonight would be as good a time as any to ask him how many responses he'd had to his profile.

Feeling a vibrating at his hip, he glanced down at his pager. It was coming from Chante's house. He couldn't help the excitement bubbling inside his chest as he dialed the number and waited for an answer.

"Pops. This is Antonio. Is Chante okay?"

After seeing his granddaughter moping around for a week, Pops decided it was time for him to do something. He'd promised her he wouldn't get involved but he got her in this mess. He was going to get her out.

Antonio still cared. That was a good sign. "She's fine. Everyone's fine. I called you."

"Oh."

He could hear the disappointment. It was reassuring. Calling him had been a good idea. "I want to apologize."

He then explained his plot to see his granddaughter happy again. "I hope you don't let my mistake stand in the way of the two of you."

Antonio felt the knot tightening in his stomach. "I don't know what to say."

"Say you still want to marry my granddaughter."

He paused to clear his throat. "It's more complicated than that. But I do love her."

"Why don't you tell her yourself?"

"Give me some time and I'll do just that."

"That's the best news I've heard all day."

Chapter Twenty-two

It had been a week since Chenoa's call before Chante finally made it over to see the nursery. Her sister had wallpapered the nursery in Mickey and Minnie Mouse. A beautiful wooden crib had been positioned in the center of the room with Disney bedding. A matching dresser was in the corner. Chante had bought the baby a giant teddy bear that was sitting in a rocking chair near the window.

Chante couldn't help from smiling. "It's gorgeous."

Chenoa turned to her. "I'm glad you like it. We spent the last couple of days getting this together. You'll never guess who came up with the decorating idea."

Chante gasped. "Mama?"

She nodded. "She popped over with the wallpaper and I couldn't resist."

"See, and you were worried for nothing."

"You're right. She has actually had some good ideas for my bedroom. We're going to the paint store tomorrow." She waved for her to follow her. "Come on down. I have cheesecake."

"Ooh! That sounds good."

Chante followed her down the stairs. So far her sister had done a fabulous job of decorating. The décor was bright and cheerful. The furnishings quite comfortable. She moved over to the kitchen table and took a seat.

"What is going on with you and Antonio?" Chenoa asked as she removed the pan from the refrigerator and carried it over to the table.

Chante covered her face with her hands and announced, "Noa, I really blew it."

Chenoa yanked her hands down. "What did you do?"

"Antonio found out everything."

Over cheesecake she told her how Devon had spilled the beans.

"How could you let him just walk out?"

Chante stiffened slightly. "What else was I supposed to do? He didn't want to hear it. Noa, it's too late."

"Too late? You sound crazy. It's not too late. That man loves you," she said while waving a fork in the air. "Are you telling me that you are no longer in love with him?"

"Of course I love him. I love him so much I feel like I'm dying inside without him."

"Okay dummy, then what are you waiting for. Go tell him," Chenoa said softly.

"I already explained everything in an e-mail and he didn't respond."

"Then go tell him in person. He deserves at least that."

How she wanted so badly to make everything right. But since he hadn't responded wasn't it too late for that? "I don't think he wants me anymore."

"You'll never know unless you try. I can't believe you are willing to let that man go. He completes you, sis. Please don't let your future get away."

She considered Chenoa's response further and in a moment she knew exactly what she wanted—a life with Antonio. She wanted to spend her life with him. Maybe he'd gotten over his anger, but as Chenoa said, she wouldn't know unless she tried. She had always loved a challenge and in the last six years she hadn't let anything stand in her way. Now she wanted Antonio with everything she had. She needed to find out how he felt. There was only one way to do that.

She threw her arms around her sister's neck. "Thank you, Noa. You're right. I need to talk to him and make things right."

"Go get him girl."

With a resolute breath, Chante nodded. "I plan to do just that."

"What time is she supposed to meet you here?"

Dominic took another swig of his beer then shrugged. "I thought she said seven."

Antonio glanced over at his brother then exhaled a frustrated breath. The last place he wanted to be on Sunday night was an oldies-but-goodies spot on the West Side. He had never been big on nightclubs, although this spot was more like a juke joint. It was a dark, smoke-filled spot at the bottom of a pizza joint. There was only one way in and one way out, a place he usually tried not to find himself in. But since he was the one who had gotten Dominic into this in the first place he didn't have much of a choice.

For the past week, Dominic had been corresponding via e-mail with Roxanne Hall. Tonight they agreed to meet face-to-face for the first time. She mentioned she was bringing a friend for support, and had asked Dominic to do the same. Reluctantly, Antonio had agreed to go with him.

His gaze shifted to the deejay in the corner, spinning the sounds of Al Green, and back to his brother who was staring at an attractive chocolate brown woman sitting near the bar.

"You sure she's not already here?" he asked drawing Dominic's attention.

"Nah, she said she would be wearing all white." While his brother turned to stare at a woman in the corner, another beautiful woman filled Antonio's mind.

He missed Chante beyond words. Sleep didn't come easy because his mind was too consumed with thoughts of her. Last night he had lay awake wishing she was there so he could hold her. The conversation with Pops had confirmed that what she had told him was true. He told him that he was going to talk to her and even tell her he still loved her but he couldn't bring himself to call her just yet. Something was still making him hold out.

Antonio reached for his glass and took a sip of the warm draft beer. Hopefully, with a few beers sleep would come easier tonight. Although he truly doubted that anything would help except holding Chante in his arms.

So go get her.

He scowled. As much as he missed her, he couldn't bring himself to making the first move. Blame it on his stupid pride but there was no way he was going to be able to go to her without first knowing how she truly felt about him. And that would take Chante telling him in person. Not in an e-mail or over the phone. If she truly wanted to salvage their relationship then all she had to do was make the first move and he'd be more than happy to take over from there.

"Hey, Tony," Dominic called, breaking into his thoughts. "I think that's them coming through the door."

Antonio turned his head and looked over at the door where two women were standing, one was wearing white. Dominic raised his hand, drawing the women's attention. They sashayed in their direction and as they drew closer, Antonio was pleased to see that they were both extremely attractive. While Dominic and Roxanne made their introductions, Antonio turned to the woman standing closest to him.

"Hi, I'm Antonio."

"Hello, I'm Jasmine. Listen . . . ," she paused long enough to take the seat beside him. "I want to let you know I am here because my sister insisted. I am happily married." She made a show of wiggling her ring finger.

"No problem." Antonio's shoulders sagged with relief. He had dreaded having to spend the evening fighting off unwanted advances. "Would you like something to drink?"

She shook her head and smiled. "No, I'm pregnant."

"Congratulations." He asked her about her pregnancy and told her he was a pediatrician. They then got into a long discussion about infants' stages of development. A half hour later, Antonio glanced over at his brother who was staring deeply into Roxanne's eyes and grinned. If his brother could find love, then he honestly believed that anything was possible, including he and Chante working things out.

Chapter Twenty-three

Chante silently entered the medical annex lobby and scanned the board for Antonio's office number. As soon as she found it, she moved with determined steps over to a bank of elevators, pressed the button and entered. On the ride up to the fifth floor, her heart pumped with excitement at seeing him again, while her hands shook with apprehension. What if he no longer wanted to have anything to do with her? He had never responded to her e-mail nor had he called. She gave her head a mental shake. She had come too far now to back down.

The elevator doors opened and she exited and moved down the long corridor toward the Department of Pediatrics. She had made a call on the way over and found out Antonio didn't have clinic hours on Monday afternoon. It was almost four o'clock. She remembered him telling her that he had rounds on the pediatric floors of the hospital at five. She took a deep breath. That would give her just enough time to say what she needed to say.

Once she entered the glass door, she stepped inside the reception area and made her way to the front desk.

The receptionist looked up with a smile. "Hi, may I help you?"

"I'm here to see Dr. Marks."

The woman surveyed her with curiosity. "Do you have an appointment?"

Chante shook her head. "No. I'm a friend of his."

"Okay, I'll let him know you're here." She reached for the receiver. "Your name?"

"Chante."

"Last name?"

"He'll know who I am."

The receptionist hesitated for a second then nodded. "Just a moment, please."

While she dialed his office, Chante stepped away from the desk and glanced around at the beautiful office. However, her heart was beating much too hard for her to appreciate it.

"Chante?"

She swung around and met the receptionist's smile.

"Dr. Mark's office is the last one on the left," she said, directing her down the long hall behind her.

She gave her a nod of thanks then somehow, on legs that felt like rubber, she managed to hold herself upright and walk down the hall. The closer she got to his office, the heavier her feet felt. She had no idea how she was going to handle things. All she knew was that she wanted Antonio back in her life.

Arriving at the end of the corridor, she found his door open and entered. Antonio was sitting behind his desk with his feet propped on the end of his desk and his hands laced behind his head. A fabulous backdrop to the sunny day behind him, only he wasn't smiling.

"Close the door," he said, his voice a low command.

Chante did as he requested then took a step toward his desk, clutching her purse in her hands.

"Hello." Something was in her throat so the single word came out in a raspy whisper.

He looked at her, his expression cool and guarded. "Hello, Chante. To what do I owe this unexpected visit?"

She cleared her throat before answering. "Did you get my e-mail?"

"Yep, I got it," he said without blinking an eye.

"Oh." Her heart jack hammered against her ribs, reverberated in her head. "Well . . . I wanted to come and say how sorry I am in person."

Antonio dropped his feet from the desk, and leaning forward clasped his hands on top. "I'm listening."

A shiver coursed through her as she held his gaze. He was going to make her grovel. And she couldn't blame him one bit. *Here goes nothing.* "I was wrong for not telling you the truth in the beginning. I had no idea Pops was trying to fix me up. He thought because he found Mildred on the Internet that he could find someone for me. The only reason why I found out was because Devon spilled it the night before I was supposed to leave for Philadelphia."

Antonio slowly rose and came around and took a seat on the edge of his desk with his arms crossed and his gaze leveled on her. "Why didn't you tell me the truth when we met?"

Chante closed her eyes unable to hold back the tears that slipped out the corner of her eyes. "I tried. I just couldn't do it," she admitted in a croaking voice. "Then I fell in love with you and I was so afraid of losing you that—"

"Can you repeat that?"

"I said, I tried to tell—"

Antonio held up his hand. "Not that."

"I was afraid of losing you?" she sniffled.

He shook his head. "No, the part about loving me."

She swallowed with difficulty. "I fell madly in love with you."

He rubbed a hand across his face and gazed down at the floor for several long seconds before looking at her again. "Are you sure?"

Tears ran down her cheeks. "More sure than I have ever been about anything in my life." She loved him more than she could ever put into words. She couldn't imagine not spending the rest of her life with him.

Antonio didn't speak, but his expression spoke volumes. It was obvious he didn't know how to respond. She couldn't blame him. Not after everything she had put him through. However, she couldn't stand the silence a minute longer.

"Tony, please, say something, anything. If it's too late then please let me—"

Before she could get the words out, Antonio pushed off the desk and jerked her against him. "Be quiet and kiss me."

Chante dropped her purse then threw her arms around his waist and pressed her lips to his. He deepened the kiss, his tongue slipping between her parted lips.

"You put me through hell this last week," he murmured, his warm breath against her cheek.

Her hands shot up to hold his face. "I'm sorry for everything."

He leaned his forehead against hers, looking straight into those brandy-colored eyes he loved so much. "The truth really hurt."

"I promise to make it all better."

"I can't believe you're here." Reaching up, Antonio cupped her chin and stared intensely into her red-rimmed eyes. "I love you with all my heart, Chante Campbell."

Her heart did a flip-flop. "And I love you, Antonio Marks."

Then his expression turned serious and he took a step back and panic filled her.

"What's wrong?"

Without answering he walked around to his desk and reached inside. When he returned to stand beside her, she noticed he was holding the black Cartier box she had stumbled across in her bedroom. Reaching for her hand, Antonio removed the diamond he had given her their first weekend together, and replaced it with a platinum engagement ring. She had never seen anything so beautiful. There had to be at least five carats.

Still holding her hand, he dropped down onto one knee and met her with an intense gaze. "Chante, will you marry me?"

She would have never guessed hearing those words would make her heart spin, especially since this was the third time she'd heard them. But nevertheless they meant more now than before. Tears spilled over and she allowed herself to cry as she nodded her head, and answered, "Yes, I'll marry you."

"Are you still willing to move to Chicago? Because a long distance relationship is out of the question."

She nodded and brushed tears away. "I can have my bags packed by Friday."

Laughing, he rose and pulled her into his arms again. "Not that soon, but at least you got the idea."

He dropped his mouth to hers and kissed her deeply, until she finally sighed and melted against him.

"I feel like the luckiest woman in the world. I've never had a man propose to me so many times," she replied with a touch of breathlessness.

"And as far as I'm concerned, no one else ever will."

Antonio brushed his lips against hers again and slowly backed her against the door and locked it. He then reached for the buttons of her blouse and had released the third one by the time she realized what was about to happen.

"What are you doing?"

"I'm getting ready to make love to the future Mrs. Marks."

She watched as he slipped out of his lab coat and reached for his belt buckle. She grabbed his hand and stopped him.

"You can't do that here," she scolded. "You're supposed to be on the floor in a half an hour."

He gave her a wicked smile. "Then I guess we better hurry."

"Aren't you worried that someone might walk in?" she cautioned.

"Nope, that's why I locked the door."

Chante stood in that same spot, speechless, and watched as he slipped out of his clothes then moved to relieve her of hers. She didn't care who knocked or even managed to break down the door. All that mattered was what Antonio was about to do to her.

He slipped her blouse off over her shoulders then reached behind her and unclasped her bra. When he unzipped her skirt, she held on to his shoulders and balanced. As soon as the material fell around her ankles, she kicked it away.

When she was down to just her panties, Antonio pulled her in his arms and gave her a deep kiss full of emotion.

"I missed you," he said as he rimmed the edge of her lips with his tongue.

"I missed you, too." She held him tight knowing in her heart that this is where she belonged, in Antonio's arms.

Bringing their lips together again, he led her over to a couch near the window that he had fallen asleep on many times and lay her down. He covered her with his body, and murmured words of love as he explored every inch of her.

Her brown skin was as smooth as satin. Beneath him, he felt her heart beating heavily beneath her chest. With skillful fingers, he moved slowly down her body, tracing the shape of her breasts and peaking her nipples into hard little pebbles. When his fingers kneaded the tight buds of her nipples, she sucked in a slow deep breath.

"Antonio . . . enough! I want you inside of me. Now, baby, please."

He needed no more encouragement. He left her long enough to retrieve a condom, then moved over her and parted her thighs. His entry was hard and fast, robbing him of his breath. For every body-slamming thrust, she met him halfway, winding her legs tightly around his waist and her arms around his neck. Together they loved as if nothing else mattered.

When they were breathless and spent, Antonio rested his

elbow on the cushion and propped his head up so that he could study her beautiful face. He looked forward to seeing her every morning and night for the rest of his life.

"How long can you stay?"

Chante smiled as she responded. "As long as I need to. Why?"

Leaning forward, Antonio whispered against her cheek, "Because as soon as I finish rounds, I plan to make love to you again."

"I'll be right here." And she meant it. Waiting for Antonio was definitely worth it.

The next morning, it was a long while before either of them moved. Chante was so happy she couldn't contain herself. Antonio was back in her life. No more secrets. Only love and trust.

She was lying across Antonio's chest when his bedside phone rang. He reached over and placed it to his ear.

"It's Pops."

With a wide grin on her face, she took the phone from him and cradled it between her ear and shoulder. "Hey, Pops."

"Chante?"

Something in his voice caused her breath to stall. "Pops, what's wrong?" she asked.

"It's Devon . . . he's missing."

Chapter Twenty-four

The next several hours were a blur. Antonio booked their flights, refusing to allow her to travel alone. Chante was grateful for him for taking over because she didn't remember getting on the plane or even the ride home. Cops, family, friends. She couldn't remember who or what, all she knew was that her son was missing, and she was certain that Dorian had snatched him.

Totally distraught over the entire incident, Pops tried to explain what had happened. Apparently, he and Devon had gone to the park shortly after breakfast. He was reading the *News Journal* and had glanced up from the newspaper and saw Devon frolicking around in the grass with a small black puppy. When he looked up again, Devon had followed the puppy into a large bush. By the time he got there, Devon and the puppy were both gone.

Chante tried to hold herself together through all the questions. However, when the police finally left, she insisted that her siblings and her parents leave as well just to give her some time to figure out what was going on and to get herself together. As soon as they were gone, Antonio made her lie down on the couch. She stared up at the ceiling, praying that her little boy was okay. She was confident the police would do their jobs, especially with her brother and sister riding their backs. Knowing Martin and Zearl, they were probably out combing the streets, searching for Dorian.

Antonio walked in carrying a cup of tea. "I thought maybe some chamomile tea would help you relax a little."

Nothing would help her relax except holding her son in her arms again. But when he handed her the cup, Chante accepted it. Without speaking, she slowly sipped the liquid. Her stomach suddenly queasy, she set the cup aside. Feeling Antonio's hand at her back, she looked up, saw the concern on his face, and dissolved into tears as he held her in his arms. She had cried so much, she was surprised she had any tears left.

"Why would he do something like this?" she sobbed. "My son means the world to me and he knows it."

"We're gonna get him back. Just wait and see," Antonio assured her.

Her arms were around his neck, her fingers clutching the fabric of his T-shirt as if he were all that was holding her together. Her voice quivered and her heart ached.

"Oh, Antonio . . . this is so unreal! Just tell me this is a bad dream."

He hurt for her in so many ways and would have done anything to bring her son back to her. Unfortunately, he didn't know where to begin and that angered him because one thing he hated was to feel helpless.

"Baby . . . I would give my life if I thought it would bring your son back."

"I know," she muttered, then hid her face in the curve of his neck. "I just don't know what to do."

She moved from the comfort of his arms and brushed angrily at the tears on her face. "I hate feeling so damn helpless. I don't even know where to begin to look! Dorian's parents are dead. I don't know where he lives. Dear God, that bastard took my baby!"

She rose and fled from the room and out the door with no

destination in mind, just the sudden need to fill her lungs with air, otherwise she would start screaming at the top of her lungs and might never stop. Antonio caught her before she made it past the neighbors' yard, then spun her around and held her close. His breath was warm on her face, his grip firm as he held her close.

"Let me go!" she screamed.

"You need to calm down," he said.

She struggled to get free.

"Damn it, Chante! You've got to hold it together."

"How am I supposed to do that when my little boy is out there somewhere," she yelled. "He needs his mama!" Then the rage was gone as quick as it had come and she went limp in his arms. "My baby needs me," she cried against his chest then her crying became almost hysterical.

"I know, baby, and even if I have to turn over every leaf in the city, we're gonna find your son."

His words must have soothed her because her crying quieted slightly.

Antonio scooped her into his arms. Her head cradled against his shoulder. Once inside the house, he found Pops standing in the living room looking deathly ill with worry. Possessively, Antonio cradled her close to him as the two men exchanged looks. Pops nodded. The message was clear that she was his woman and he had taken on the job of protecting her. Moving down the hall he carried her into her room and lowered her gently on the bed. Her crying had quieted and he continued to hold her close to him. Anger brewed inside. He would do everything in his power to find Devon and bring him home to his mother.

Chante had finally managed to relax long enough to take a nap, when the phone rang. She scrambled off the bed and hurried to answer the phone, while Antonio hurried down the hall and picked up the one in the kitchen.

"Hello?"

"Chante."

A chill ran down her spine. "Dorian? Where is Devon?"

Chuckling, he replied, "He's right here. He's fine."

A sob rose up to her throat. "Give me my son back."

Seemingly amused, he answered, "I can't do that. He's my son, too."

"I-I never said he wasn't your son. I told you, you could see him just to give-give me some time," she stuttered nervously.

"You never told my son I wanted to see him. You lied!"

"I didn't lie. I was going to tell him," she pleaded.

"No you weren't."

She swallowed and tried to stay calm. The last thing she needed was for him to hang up. "What is it that you want?"

"I want my family back." Dorian released a heavy sigh. "What do I have to do to show you I've changed? If I wanted to hurt you, I would have done it the night I slipped into your window and watched you sleep."

Her stomach churned as she remembered the night of feeling that someone was watching her. She was going to be sick.

"I even bought you the gifts to show you how proud I—"

She gasped. "Those gifts were from you?"

Dorian gave a soft chuckle as if the answer was obvious. "Of course. That's what a man does for the woman he loves."

"I—I don't understand. Why now after all these years?"

"Why not?" he snapped. "Look, enough of the small talk. I want you to meet me. No cops. No boyfriend. Just you, me, and Devon."

She had no other choice. Her son needed her. "Okay. Where do you want to meet?"

"On the boardwalk at ten."

Instantly, she remembered him telling her that he lived down near the beach. "Okay. I'll be there."

"I mean it," Dorian warned. "Any cops, and you'll never see Devon again."

As soon as the line went dead, Chante hung up the phone and rushed to change clothes.

"Where are you going?" Antonio asked when he entered the room.

While reaching in her drawer, she replied, "I'm going to meet him."

He grabbed her arm. "You can't meet him. We need to call the police."

Chante yanked her arm from his firm grasp. "No way! Didn't you hear what he said? If I call the cops, I'll never see my son again."

"Then I'm going with you."

"No!" She pushed him away from her. "I can't take that chance. Please . . . understand."

He stood to the side and watched her slip into a pair of jeans.

"How far is the boardwalk from here?"

"Rehoboth is about thirty minutes from here," she answered as she reached for her tennis shoes.

"I'm going with you. Wait! Before you say anything, hear me out. I'll drive down in the rental car."

She stared at him for the longest time not saying anything before she finally said, "Okay. Let me use the bathroom and then we can go."

As soon as she walked into the adjoining room, Antonio picked up the cordless phone and moved into the living room. Reaching into his pocket, he removed the phone number Martin had given him before he left, and dialed the number. To his disappointment, the voice mail picked up. "Martin, this is Antonio. Dorian has Devon." He gave him the number that had showed up on the caller ID then left his cell phone number for Martin to call back.

He moved into the living room to wait for Chante. When the phone rang, he answered it, hoping it was Martin calling back.

"This is Tony."

"If you want to see your fiancé alive, you'll pay close attention."

Antonio's hand stilled as panic twisted his stomach. He raced down the hall into the bedroom and barged through the bathroom door. He felt like someone had knocked the wind out of his chest when he found Chante gone and the window wide open. He heard Dorian chuckle. Clutching the phone, he hurried out the front door and down the driveway where Chante's car was parked. He felt rage when he spotted the car door open and the key in the ignition. Chante had climbed out the window, planning to meet Dorian alone, only he had been outside waiting.

He took a deep calming breath. "Just tell me what you want," he said as he glanced up and down the street, looking for any suspicious activity.

"If you even think about calling her family or the police you will never see her again."

Rage exploded through him. "Listen, you bastard! If you hurt her I won't need to call the police because I'll kill you myself."

Dorian chuckled, not taking his threat serious. "Calm down, Rambo. You'll see her in time, if you do what I say."

Agitated, Antonio moved back into the house. "I'm not doing anything until you let me speak to her."

Dorian muffled the phone. He heard shuffling then a clicking sound.

"Tony?"

The soft voice, laced with fear punched him right below the gut. "Chante, baby, you okay?"

"Yes. Devon and I are together. He's okay, but we . . ." The phone was snatched away.

Antonio willed his voice to stay calm.

"Pay attention," Dorian began. "Otherwise, I'll kill them both."

Chapter Twenty-five

Chante twisted her wrist and tried to regain circulation. She had no idea where she was or where she was going because the van had no windows.

She still had a hard time understanding what had happened. One minute she was climbing out the window sneaking to her car and the next thing she knew she had been gagged and stuffed in the back of a van with duct tape wrapped around her wrist. The only relief was her darling son sleeping soundly on the floor beside her, holding the puppy that was used to lure him away. She didn't know how he could sleep through all this, but she was thankful that he did.

While waiting for something to happen, she thought about Antonio. Had it only been hours ago that she was lying in his arms in the house that was soon to be her home as well? Closing her eyes, she hoped that he would find her. If not, she hoped that regardless of what happened he knew how much she loved him.

The van hit a bump and her eyes flew open. She needed to find a way to escape. To get away from Dorian as fast as she could, but with every second that passed that sent her further away from Antonio, she lost hope. Right now what was most important was that she protected her son from Dorian's madness.

She wrapped her arms around herself, afraid that the emotions she felt would overwhelm her. No way was she going to give in to the panic.

The van came to a stop. Shortly after the back door swung open, and Dorian yanked her out on to her feet.

"Wait!" she cried, dragging her feet. "What about Devon?"

"He'll be fine. Now come on," he ordered, yanking her by the arm.

He tightened his hold and dragged her alongside him with her hands strapped in front of her. As they moved down the driveway she recognized the three-story house as his parent's summer home. There was a FOR SALE sign in the front yard. She had forgotten that his parents had a house within walking distance to the boardwalk.

Dorian opened the door and dragged her to the back room his father had once used as his office. Once there he removed the tape from her wrist, but not before first showing her the gun he had in his pocket.

"One false move and I'll shoot you."

"How can you do this to me? I thought you'd changed?" she said in a croaking voice.

He fixed her with a hard stare as he replied, "I took all those anger management classes so I could be a better husband and now you tell me there is no us. How could you love someone other than me? You are my family."

She tried pleading with him. "Please, Dorian, understand that people change."

His cold voice was dripping with sarcasm. "Obviously you already have." He headed toward the door.

"Please, if you love me, you'll bring my son to me."

He turned sharply toward her. "*Our* son," he said between gritted teeth.

At this point she was willing to say anything to get her son back. She knew the worst thing she could do was to make him angry. She nodded in agreement. "Yes, our son."

"For some reason you have a hard time remembering that," he said tightly. "Well, I plan to take care of that little problem." Without another word, he swung around and left the room, turning the lock behind him.

She sprang to the door and banged on it with her fist. "Dorian, please bring me Devon! Please!"

All she got was silence. Twisting around, she quickly scanned the room. Nothing but a desk and a futon. There was also a small refrigerator in the corner. On the floor was worn coffee-brown carpet. No television. No phone. Both had been removed. There wasn't even a lamp or some other instrument she could have used as a weapon.

Chante moved over to a window with bars, preventing her escape. Even if she broke the glass, there was no one close enough to hear her.

She brushed tears from her eyes and gazed out the window. All she could see was the dock out back and a large, old fishing boat that Dorian and his father had spent many weekends on. It was the only memorable times of his childhood that her ex-husband had ever talked about.

"Mama!"

Hearing Devon's voice, her head snapped around to the door where Dorian came in holding Devon's hand. The puppy was trailing at his heels.

"Mama!" Devon dashed over to her and she embraced him. Tears flowing freely now.

"Are you okay?" she asked. Pulling back she stared into his sad little eyes.

His lower lip quivered as he looked from Dorian to her again. "That man says he's my daddy. Is that true?"

"Yeah Mom, is that true?" Dorian said, tauntingly.

She glared over at Dorian and bit her tongue, then her expression softened as she met Devon's waiting eyes. "Yes, he's your father."

"Well, isn't this sweet," Dorian sang merrily as he moved

toward the two of them with his arms out wide. "One big happy family. The way things should be."

Chante felt repulsed when he gathered them in a group hug and kissed her soundly on the lips. When she couldn't stand it a second longer, she pushed away from his hold.

Her reaction angered him. "Well, I wish I could stay and chat but I've got business to take care of. There are sandwiches and sodas in the refrigerator." When she tried to speak, he cut her off. "I'll be back soon with a big surprise." He then left and locked the door behind him.

The look of despair on Devon's face was almost her undoing. She knelt onto the floor and gathered him close to her.

"Mama, when can we go home?"

She reached up and stroked his hair soothingly. "Soon, sweetheart, soon."

Chante was grateful that the dog started licking Devon's hand. Tears sprung to her eyes—it was as if the puppy was trying to tell her son everything was going to be all right.

Devon moved from her embrace and crawled after the puppy, who was now under the futon. While he played, she let her mind wander to Antonio. She wondered if he was going to be foolish enough to come by himself or if he had called the police for help.

Antonio arrived on the boardwalk. Shops and restaurants were closing for the night. Waves rocked against the deserted beach. The crowd long gone. He strolled down the boardwalk on guard, waiting. He had spoken with Martin and told him the plan was for him to meet Dorian on the boardwalk near the Beach Inn to talk.

As he neared the amusement park, Antonio noticed movement to his right. However, before he could react, everything went black.

* * *

Chante had a bad feeling about being led down to the dock, but she tried to slow her tears and questions for Devon's sake. Holding his hand, she led him out toward the large fishing boat with Dorian behind them with his hand in his pocket, clutching the gun Devon knew nothing about.

"Mama, are we going for a ride on my daddy's boat?" Devon asked.

She gave him a strained smile and nodded.

"Oh, boy!" he exclaimed, then galloped the rest of the way.

As they neared the end of the dock, she noticed a heap at the other end of the boat.

Antonio!

Panic filled her lungs as she raced onto the boat and kneeled beside him. The sight of him lying on the deck of the boat unconscious and bleeding, twisted her heart.

"Antonio, can you hear me?"

Shaking him eventually caused him to stir. Chante blew out a breath of relief. "Tony, thank God you're alive."

As his view came into focus. He saw Chante sitting near the edge of the boat. Dorian was to the left clutching his crying son close to him, gun drawn.

"It's so nice of you to finally join us. Now we can get this party started."

Chante tried again to plead with him. "Dorian please, let us go!"

"Not until we find out who you love most. Him or the son you and I created?" He stepped back away from them with Devon shielding him. "Sweetheart, you get one choice and the other dies." He then started laughing uncontrollably, drowning out Devon's cries for his mommy.

"Why are you doing this?" she asked.

Dorian sobered then said, "Because I want my family back. If I can't have you then no one can." He waved his gun, signaling for her to move away from Antonio. She moved and stood to his right, while Antonio was to his left. "Come on.

You've got one minute to choose. Otherwise, I'll be forced to do it for you."

Before she realized what was happening, Devon slammed down on Dorian's foot and when he released him, he raced over to his mother. Without a second to lose, Antonio lunged at Dorian, sending him reeling back from the blow, and knocking the gun from his hand. As soon as he landed on his back, Antonio sent a closed fist to his nose.

As the two fought, Chante moved Devon out of the way then went searching for the gun.

Dorian swung at him but Antonio ducked and hit him again with quick speed. When he moved in, Dorian recovered and kicked him low, knocking him off guard. He then turned toward Chante, who was still looking for the gun. Before she realized it, Dorian grabbed Devon and dived into the chilly waters.

"No!" she shrieked.

Antonio dived into the water after them. Chante scanned the waves. Seeing nothing, she rose and moved to the edge of the boat. Unable to wait, she took a deep breath and jumped into the ocean. Within seconds she swam up to the surface and opened her eyes, ignoring the sting from the salty water. Treading frantically, she desperately searched for signs of the three. She scanned the rippling waves, kicking until she heard a splash behind her. She turned around, and headed toward the motion in the water, slicing the water with her arms. She prayed it was Devon and Antonio.

Antonio surfaced and directly in front of him, he was clutching a sputtering Devon.

"I've got him."

Chante swam harder. No matter how hard she kicked, she couldn't get to them fast enough.

"Mama!"

"I've got you, baby." She gathered Devon in her arms.

"Thank God you're both alive," she said her breathing ragged with emotion.

Cautiously, Antonio looked around for any sign of Dorian, and was relieved to see there was none. He helped the two of them back onto the dock then pulled himself up.

"Are you okay?"

Chante pulled back and looked directly in Antonio's eyes, the wind whipping around them. "I'm fine. How about you?"

"Relieved. I'm never letting either of you go again." He circled both of them in his arms.

Devon rested his cheek against Chante's chest. "Mama, can I take the puppy home?"

She started sobbing with laughter. "Sure baby anything you want."

All that mattered was that she had her family together again.

Antonio lowered his mouth to hers. The sound of the police sirens drawing near was the only reason they came up for air.

Hours later, Chante tucked Devon in bed with his pup curled beside him. Turning out his light, she took one final look, then moved into the living room. She had almost lost the two people she loved the most tonight. Closing her eyes, she had said a silent prayer. She had a lot to be thankful for. Within minutes, after climbing back onto the dock, Martin, Zearl, and Chenoa arrived with the Rehoboth Police Department. Shortly after, Dorian was caught trying to swim to the other side of the beach.

She moved into the living room where Antonio was waiting on the couch.

"Come here," he whispered hoarsely, holding his hand out to her.

She flopped down on his lap, and he held her close.

Leaning forward, he gazed down at her. "I love you."

She closed her eyes. After what she put him through, she

wouldn't blame him if he never wanted to see her again. "You still love me after all that madness?"

Antonio reached out and lifted her chin with his finger. "Baby, it's gonna take a hell of a lot more to make me stop loving you."

This man had always been honest with her and she couldn't say the same.

She gazed up at him, seeing his love for her in the depths of his eyes. "My fear of love and trust has put you through so much. Even after everything, I'm still afraid that one day you'll stop loving me," she said as tears burned her eyes.

"I know. I'm the man that proposed not once, not twice, but three times," he reminded.

She gave a much needed laugh. "I'm yours for as long as you want me."

Antonio pressed his lips to her forehead and said in a deep voice, "I want you."

"Really?"

"Really."

Then she felt herself being lifted into his strong arms. "Let me show you how much," he whispered against her lips as he carried her down the hall.

Epilogue

The first weekend in September, music and laughter wafted through the banquet of the Modern Maturity Center. Chandeliers shed light on the rehearsal dinner that Mr. and Mrs. Campbell were holding in Chante and Antonio's honor.

Antonio retrieved two glasses of champagne and went in search of his bride-to-be. He hadn't seen her for the last ten minutes. She had excused herself to catch up with two of her cousins.

He was still amazed at how large Chante's family was. The close-knit family was traveling to Delaware from all around the globe to share in their happiness. If this was only part of the family, he could only imagine how many more would be present on their wedding day.

As he moved through the crowd, he spotted Martin at a small table to the far left talking to Candace Price. Although Martin tried to deny it, it was apparent he was quite taken by the beautiful young woman. One man to another, he was certain Martin would realize what was happening soon enough.

After moving around the buffet table, he spotted Chante in a group with his sister and Chenoa. The women were doting over the newest member of the family—Anasia Brazil

Sinclair. Zearl stood behind his wife beaming with pride. She was indeed a beautiful baby.

For a moment Antonio feasted on the sight of his fiancée who looked downright sexy in a free-flowing blue gown. He watched as she raised her niece to her lips, then kissed her tiny cheek. Last week, he and Chante had discussed having a baby right away and she had agreed. The thought of her carrying his child made his blood flow down to his loins. Suddenly he was anxious to be alone with his fiancée so that they could begin practicing.

He moved over to the group and stood behind Chante. She glanced over her shoulder and gave him a heart-stopping smile before handing Anasia to her father.

After she removed one of the fluted glasses from his hand, he cupped her elbow. "Excuse me," he said. "But I need to steal this beautiful woman away for a few moments."

He led her over to a private spot near the door then wrapped an arm around her waist and pulled her against him. "We've been here long enough. I'm ready to go back to the house and make love to you."

Chante smiled and stroked his arm. "Sounds like a wonderful idea. However, since this is our party, I don't think that's a good idea."

He frowned. "I thought the guests of honor were always the first to leave?"

She chuckled. "That's at the wedding reception."

Antonio groaned. "Damn!"

"Sorry, Romeo. You're just gonna have to wait. It shouldn't be too much longer. Several guests have already said their good-byes. Pops and his wife Mildred have already left with Devon. I think the party will break up in another hour or two."

"How about you follow me into the coat closet. I want to show you something?" he asked, and Chante laughed. "What's so funny?"

"You! I'm not going into the closet with your nasty behind. Just be patient."

His lip brushed her ear. "I have no patience when it comes to you."

She kissed his lips. "Then we're gonna have to work on that."

Chenoa and her family approached. "We're leaving," she said. "It's way past Anasia's bedtime."

Zearl reached over and slapped a hand onto Antonio's shoulder. "Congratulations again, we're so happy for you both."

"Thanks, man."

"Tony, you did us a favor. We Campbells appreciate you taking our big sister off our hands."

"She's joking," Chante said, giving her sister a gentle poke with her forefinger. "The miracle was the day Zearl fell in love with this crazy girl."

Zearl slipped his arm around his wife's waist. "Yep, and I haven't regretted it one day."

Chenoa gave Chante a triumphant smile only seconds before the group dissolved in laughter. They said their good-byes and headed out to the parking lot. Antonio suddenly had the need to hold his fiancée in his arms and led her out onto the dance floor.

Within the next hour the party broke up. The only ones left were Mr. and Mrs. Campbell.

"Mom, Dad, thank you so much for the party."

"We're glad to have you as part of the family," Mrs. Campbell said to Antonio.

Antonio brushed a kiss across her cheek. "Thank you both again." He clasped Mr. Campbell on the shoulder.

"We're just thrilled that you love our daughter," Mr. Campbell said. He looked at his daughter's smiling face. "You make her very happy."

"I'm going to do everything in my power to keep her happy or die trying."

Her father draped an arm around his wife's waist and the two smiled knowingly at each other.

"We'll see you tomorrow," Chante said. She kissed her parents then allowed Antonio to lead her out to the car.

They pulled into her driveway and she glanced over at the SOLD sign posted at the center of her yard. As soon as she and Tony returned from a week in Aruba, Chante and Devon were joining Antonio in Chicago to start their new life.

They raced out of the car and within minutes were beneath the cool sheets.

"Tomorrow's the big day. Any last minute doubts?"

Chante looked over at her handsome fiancé. "Not on your life."

"Good." He pulled her into his arms and kissed her.

Chante returned the passionate kiss while her heart pounded with excitement. She knew she was the happiest bride-to-be on the planet. She loved him with all her heart.

Dear Readers,

Since the release of *Love Uncovered*, I have been bombarded with requests for the rest of the Campbell family. I hope you enjoyed reuniting with the Campbells—especially Chenoa, Dame, Martin, and Chante. The family will be returning again with another suspenseful twist.

Thanks again for the comments and keep them coming. Check out my Web site for up-to-date information at www.angiedaniels.com or you can always e-mail me at angie@angiedaniels.com.

Until we meet between the pages again,

Angie

GREAT BOOKS, GREAT SAVINGS!

When You Visit Our Website:
www.kensingtonbooks.com
You Can Save Money Off The Retail Price
Of Any Book You Purchase!

- **All Your Favorite Kensington Authors**
- **New Releases & Timeless Classics**
- **Overnight Shipping Available**
- **eBooks Available For Many Titles**
- **All Major Credit Cards Accepted**

Visit Us Today To Start Saving!
www.kensingtonbooks.com

All Orders Are Subject To Availability.
Shipping and Handling Charges Apply.
Offers and Prices Subject To Change Without Notice.